Tales *from 5000 Years* of Chinese History

Volume II

by Lin Handa & Cao Yuzhang

Better Link Press

This book is edited and designed by the Editorial Committee of *Cultural China* series

Managing Directors: Wang Youbu, Xu Naiqing

Editorial Director: Wu Ying

Editors: Zhou Kexi, Yang Xinci, Patrick Wallace, Jennifer Wilde

Assistant Editor: Yao Feng

Chinese Text by Lin Handa, Cao Yuzhang

Translation by Yawtsong Lee

Interior and Cover Design: Yuan Yinchang, Xia Wei

ISBN-13: 978-1-60220-114-9

Address any comments about *Tales from Five Thousand Years of Chinese History (II)* to:

Better Link Press

99 Park Ave

New York, NY 10016

USA

or

Shanghai Press and Publishing Development Company

F 7 Donghu Road, Shanghai, China (200031)

Email: comments_betterlinkpress@hotmail.com

Computer typeset by Yuan Yinchang Design Studio, Shanghai

Printed in China by Shanghai Donnelley Printing Co. Ltd.

1 2 3 4 5 6 7 8 9 10

CONTENTS

PREFACE 9

NORTHERN AND SOUTHERN DYNASTIES (420 AD–589 AD)

93. Zu Chongzhi the Great Inventor 11
94. Emperor Xiaowen of Wei Reforms Social Customs 15
95. The Last Emperor of Chen Presides over a Declining Dynasty 19

SUI DYNASTY (581 AD–618 AD)

96. Emperor Yang of Sui Tours Jiangdu 23

TANG DYNASTY (618 AD–907 AD)

97. Li Yuan Raises Arms in Taiyuan 28
98. Li Shimin Takes Control of Dongdu 32
99. Incident at Xuanwu Gate 37
100. Wei Zheng Dares to Speak Unwelcome Truths 41
101. Li Jing Attacks Yinshan by Night 45
102. Master Monk Xuanzang Brings Back Buddhist Texts from India 49
103. Princess Wencheng Goes to Tubo 54
104. Empress Wu Zetian 58
105. Di Renjie Commands the Loyalty of the Nation's Cream of the Crop 62

106. Li Linfu, a Tongue of Honey and a Heart of Cruelty 66
107. Li Bai Has a Low Opinion of the Rich and Mighty 70
108. The Rebellion of An Lushan 75
109. Mutiny at the Post House of Mawei 80
110. Li Bi Retires to His Hermitage 85
111. Li Guangbi Drubs Shi Siming 89
112. Du Fu, a Writer of Historical Poetry 94
113. Steel-willed Yan Zhenqing 98
114. The Sweet Dew Incident 101
115. War of the Factions 105
116. Huang Chao, the Sky-high Grand General 108
117. The Last Days of the Tang Empire 114

FIVE DYNASTIES AND TEN STATES
(907 AD–960 AD)

118. Opera Actors in Politics 117
119. Shi Jingtang, the Son Emperor 122
120. Emperor Shizong of Zhou Upbraids Feng Dao 126

SONG DYNASTY (960 AD–1279)

Northern Song Dynasty (960 AD–1127)

121. The Imperial Yellow Robe Is Now His 130

122. A Cup of Wine Relieves the Generals of Their Command 134
123. Li, the Last King, Loses His Kingdom 137
124. Zhao Pu Receives a Gift 141
125. Yang, the Invincible 144
126. Kou Zhun Holds off Liao Aggression 149
127. Di Qing Sees No Shame in His Low Birth 155
128. The New Deal of Fan Zhongyan 159
129. The No-nonsense, Impartial Bao Zheng 163
130. The Reforms of Wang Anshi 167
131. Sima Guang Writes *Zi Zhi Tong Jian* (*Historical Events Retold as a Mirror for Government*) 172
132. The Plants and Rocks Convoys 176
133. Fang La Rises in Rebellion 180
134. Aguda's Defiance at the Fish Feast 183
135. Li Gang Defends the Capital 187
136. Two Emperors Are Taken Prisoner 191

Southern Song Dynasty (1127–1279)

137. Zong Ze Thrice Cries, "Cross the River!" 195
138. Han Shizhong Blocks the Passage of the Jin Army 201
139. Yue Fei Routs Wuzhu's Army 205
140. The Traitor, Qin Hui 211

141. "A Plausible Case" 216
142. Genghis Khan Unifies the Mongols 220
143. Jia Sidao Sells the Country down the River 225
144. Wen Tianxiang Raises an Army 230
145. Zhang Shijie Defends Yashan to the Death 235

YUAN DYNASTY (1279–1368)

146. Ode to the Force of Virtue 239
147. Marco Polo, a Visitor from Europe 244
148. Dou E's Grievance Moves Heaven and Earth 248
149. A One-eyed Stone Figurine 252
150. A Monk Turned Grand Marshal 257
151. Battle at Lake Poyang 262

MING DYNASTY (1368–1644)

152. Liu Bowen Prays for Rain 267
153. The Hu Weiyong Affair 271
154. The Prince of Yan Marches into Nanjing 275
155. Sanbao the Eunuch Explores the "Western Oceans" 280
156. Yu Qian Defends Beijing 284
157. Hai Rui, Man of Integrity and Independence 289
158. Qi Jiguang Gets Rid of the *Wo Kou* *294*
159. Li Shizhen Scours Mountains for Medicinal Herbs 298

160. The Tutelage of Zhang Juzheng 302
161. Nurhaci Founds the Later Jin 306
162. Battle at Sarhu 309
163. Xu Guangqi Studies Western Sciences 313
164. Zuo Guangdou Goes to Jail 317
165. The Battle of Ningyuan 321
166. Hung Taiji Sows Disinformation 325
167. Li Zicheng, the Trailblazing King 329
168. Zhang Xianzhong's Stealth Attack on Xiangyang 334
169. Li Yan and the Red Lady 338

QING DYNASTY (1644–1911)

170. Wu Sangui Borrows Qing Troops 342
171. Shi Kefa's Valiant Defense of Yangzhou 347
172. Zheng Chenggong Recovers Taiwan 352
173. Li Dingguo Campaigns in Southwest China 356
174. Emperor Kangxi Subdues the Three Feudatories 360
175. Victory at Yaksa 365
176. Three Expeditions against Galdan 368
177. Literary Inquisition 372
178. Emperor Qianlong's Book Bans and Anthology Creation 376
179. Cao Xueqin Writes *A Dream of Red Mansions* *380*
180. He Shen, Corrupt Mandarin with an Insatiable Greed 384

PREFACE

TALES FROM FIVE Thousand Years of Chinese History is a collection of stories arranged in chronological order, covering a period from ancient times to the pre-Opium-War Qing dynasty.

The topics were selected by the educator and linguist, Lin Handa (1900–1972), who drew up the outline for the collection and contributed some chapters. Following Lin's death, Cao Yuzhang (1924–1996) took over his mantle and completed the work. This combined effort of two consecutive authors has enjoyed wide appeal by virtue of its historical accuracy, well-structured narrative, fluent writing and distinctive style.

The English edition of *Tales from Five Thousand Years of Chinese History* consists of two volumes. Volume Two starts from Northern and Southern dynasties (420–589) to the last years of the Qing dynasty (1616–1911). For the sake of brevity, the original Chinese work has been slightly abridged in this English edition.

NORTHERN AND SOUTHERN DYNASTIES (420 AD–589 AD)

93. Zu Chongzhi the Great Inventor

THE FOUNDING OF the Southern Song dynasty in 420 AD by Liu Yu (Emperor Wu) ended the 103-year rule of the Eastern Jin dynasty. With the consolidation of northern China under Emperor Taiwu of the Northern Wei dynasty nineteen years later, China was effectively divided into a north and a south. In the some 150 years that followed, southern China saw a succession of four dynasties: the Song, the Qi, the Liang and the Chen. In the north, the Northern Wei eventually split into the Eastern Wei and the Western Wei. These were later respectively supplanted by the Northern Qi and the Northern Zhou. This period is known to history as the Age of Southern and Northern dynasties.

After the accession of its third ruler, Emperor Xiaowu of Song, the Southern Song dynasty became increasingly corrupt and went into decline. This period, however, saw the rise of an outstanding scientist named Zu Chongzhi. His grandfather, Zu Chang, was in charge of Southern Song construction projects. Growing up in these circumstances, Zu Chongzhi had ready access to many books which he read avidly since childhood, causing him to acquire a reputation as an erudite youth. While mathematics was his favorite subject, he also delved into astronomy and various calendars, regularly tracking and recording in detail the movements of the Sun and other celestial bodies. His fame prompted Emperor Xiaowu of the Southern Song to send him to the Hualin Academy (a government institute) to conduct research. Though political office had no appeal for him, at the academy he was able to devote more of his time and energy to the study of mathematics and astronomy.

China had a long tradition, unbroken by dynastic changes, of appointing officials to study astronomy and devise calendars based on their observations and findings. By the time of the Southern Song, great strides had been made in the creation of calendars, but Zu Chongzhi found them still lacking in precision. After a long period of observation, he created a new calendar called the Daming Calendar (Daming being the era name of Emperor Xiaowu's reign). In this calendar, the length of time calculated for a solar year comes to within 50 seconds of modern calculations, and the length of time calculated for one lunar revolution around the Earth comes to within one second of modern calculations. The accuracy of his measurements was thus impressive.

In 462 AD, Zu Chongzhi petitioned Emperor Xiaowu to institute the new calendric system. At a meeting of ministers called by the emperor to discuss the proposal, Dai Faxing, a favorite of the emperor, came out against it, arguing that Zu Chongzhi's arbitrary rejection of the traditional calendar was heresy. Zu Chongzhi refuted Dai Faxing's argument by presenting his research data at the meeting.

Emboldened by his status as favorite of the emperor, Dai Faxing dismissed the calendar peremptorily, "The current calendar has been handed down through the ages. It should not be tampered with by posterity."

Unfazed and unintimidated, Zu Chongzhi said, his voice taking on a hard edge, "If you have any factual basis for your argument, I am eager to hear it. But spare me the bluff and bluster."

In an attempt to bolster Dai Faxing's position, Emperor Xiaowu invited people with knowledge of calendars to debate with Zu Chongzhi, but he successfully refuted every one of them. However, Emperor Xiaowu maintained his refusal to adopt the new calendar.

When the emperor died a short time later, the country was plunged into turmoil. In 479 AD, Xiao Daocheng, the Governor of Nanyanzhou Prefecture, overthrew the Southern Song dynasty and declared himself Emperor of the Qi dynasty, titling himself Emperor Gao.

The social unrest and political turmoil of his time did not prevent Zu Chongzhi from assiduously pursuing his scientific research, and he made even greater achievements in the field of mathematics, annotating the ancient mathematical treatise *Nine Chapters on Mathematics* and writing his *Method of Interpolation*. One of his most outstanding contributions was his accurate derivation of pi, the ratio of the circumference of a circle to its diameter. Long and hard research enabled him to become the earliest scientist in the world to calculate pi to seven decimal places, arriving at a value of pi that was between 3.1415926 and 3.1415927.

Zu Chongzhi was also a versatile inventor. Among his many inventions were a "south-pointing chariot," which had a bronze statuette that consistently pointing south no matter which way the chariot turned, a "thousand-*li* boat," which was tested on the Xinting River (southwest of modern-day Nanjing) and found to be able to travel a hundred *li* in one day, and a stone mill driven by water to grind grain. This invention created such a sensation at the court that Emperor Wu of the Qi dynasty personally attended a demonstration of the device.

Ten years after the death of Zu Chongzhi, the Daming Calendar was finally officially adopted. His son Zu Gengzhi and his grandson Zu Hao took up his mantle in devoting themselves to the study of mathematics and calendars. Legend says that when Zu Gengzhi studied, he was always so engrossed in his work that thunderclaps would not rouse him. He had a habit of mulling over research questions even when walking. On one such occasion, he crashed into a top bureaucrat, Xu Mian, as he walked because he had not seen him coming. Zu Gengzhi only came out of his trance-like state and returned a greeting when Xu Mian called out his name. However, Xu Mian did not rebuke him because he knew Zu Gengzhi's mind had been occupied by his studies.

94. Emperor Xiaowen of Wei Reforms Social Customs

FOLLOWING THE DEATH of Emperor Taiwu of the Northern Wei, the oppression of ordinary citizens by the Xianbei aristocracy and major business interests in the Northern Wei led to protracted civil unrest. Upon his accession in 490 AD, Emperor Xiaowen of the Northern Wei committed himself to reform.

Emperor Xiaowen established official pay scales for civil servants and began meting out harsh penalties to corrupt officials. He also instituted a system to distribute farmland fairly, allocating uncultivated plots to peasants for planting grain, with men receiving 40 acres each and women 20 acres each. The peasants were also allotted mulberry orchards for sericulture. In return for the award of land, the peasants paid rent to and performed services for the government. When a peasant died, all of the land allocated to him, with the exception of the mulberry orchards, returned to the government. Under this new system, the acreage under cultivation increased considerably, peasants were assured of a relatively steady income and greater security, and the coffers of the Northern Wei treasury swelled.

Emperor Xiaowen had great political savvy. He was convinced that the consolidation of the Northern Wei regime would not be assured unless it shed its old-fashioned ways and assimilated the culture of Central Plains. To achieve this radical shift, he decided to move his capital from Pingcheng (northeast of modern-day

Datong in Shanxi Province) to Luoyang, which had a more central location.

To preempt opposition from his top advisers to the move, he first brought up the idea of launching a massive attack against the Southern Qi. When he brought his proposal before his court, his top aides objected immediately to this proposal. In particular, Tuoba Cheng, the Prince of Rencheng, protested quite vociferously, angering Emperor Xiaowen. The emperor said, "The country is mine. Are you saying you can stop me from making war?"

Tuoba Cheng countered, "The country may be Your Majesty's, but as your adviser I cannot remain silent when I know the risks of the military action you are contemplating."

Emperor Xiaowen considered his statement, and then dismissed his court. Returning to his quarters, he summoned Tuoba Cheng for a private meeting, at which he said, "To be frank, I scolded you in public really just to deter the others. I believe Pingcheng is an ideal location for making war, but not fertile ground for political reform. To achieve my vision of reform, there is no alternative to moving the capital elsewhere. The real intent behind my proposal to make war on the Qi is to take the opportunity to move the whole court to the Central Plains. What do you think about my plan?"

Thus enlightened, Tuoba Cheng gave his immediate endorsement to the emperor's proposal.

In 493 AD, Emperor Xiaowen of the Northern Wei, at the command of 300,000 infantry and cavalrymen, set out from Pingcheng on a southward march. By the time they reached Luoyang, a month-long spell of incessant autumn rain had turned all the roads into muddy tracks, hampering their movements. Still, the armor-clad Emperor Xiaowen rode on out of the Louyang city gate and ordered the troops to continue their march.

Since his ministers had never really supported this expedition against the Qi, they now tried to use the heavy rains as an excuse to have the operation called off. Hearing their pleas, Emperor Xiaowen answered solemnly, "We would go down in history as laughingstocks if we came this far with such a large force and then had nothing to show for it. If you really don't want to go further south, then why don't we stay here and make this city our new capital? What do the ministers think?"

They merely looked at each other without speaking. The emperor pressed his question, "This is no time for delay. All those who are for the new capital, move to the left, and those against to the right!"

A nobleman said, "If Your Majesty agrees to scuttle this southern expedition, then we will also go along with the idea of the new capital." Although many of the ministers were not fans of the idea of moving the new capital to Louyang, the promised abandonment of the southern campaign made unwilling converts of them.

After Emperor Xiaowen and his court settled down in Luoyang, he dispatched Tuoba Cheng, the Prince of Rencheng, to Pingcheng to persuade the nobility of the benefits of the move to the new capital. Afterwards, the emperor himself went back to Pingcheng to discuss the matter with the assembled ministers and members of the aristocracy.

Many of the aristocracy in Pingcheng were against the move. However, the emperor was able to shoot down each of their excuses one by one. When the noblemen ran out of arguments, they invoked one final defense: "Moving the capital is no light matter. We should consult the oracle to find out if the move would be auspicious or not."

Emperor Xiaowen replied, "Divination is used to solve hard-to-decide cases. It is uncalled for in the present case because all the questions about moving the capital have been answered. We who have the charge of running the country should feel at home anywhere in our dominion. We should be ready to be here one day and in another place the next. Nothing is set in stone. Besides, in past eras others moved their capital. There's no reason why we cannot do the same."

The noblemen and ministers had no answer to the emperor's arguments, and so the decision to move the capital to Luoyang was finalized.

After the official move of the new capital to Luoyang, Emperor Xiaowen set out to take the reform of society's old ways and old-fashioned customs one step further.

At a discussion of statecraft, he asked his top aides, "Are you for business as usual, or for changing the old ways of doing things?"

Tuoba Xi, the Prince of Xianyang, replied, "We are certainly all for change."

Emperor Xiaowen answered, "In that case, I will announce reform measures. Since you have already given your pledge of support, you cannot go back on your word."

The emperor soon promulgated decrees that, among other things, made the Han language the official language of the country. This new requirement was waived for people above the age of 30 who might find it difficult to learn a new language. However, court officials under 30 had to speak the Han language. Anyone found in violation of this rule would be demoted or dismissed. The new regulations also required civilians and officials to wear traditional Han clothing. Xianbei natives were encouraged to intermarry into Han scholar-official families and adopt Han People surnames. The original name of the Northern Wei royal lineage was thenceforth changed to Yuan. Emperor Xiaowen himself adopted the Han People name of Yuan Hong.

The radical reforms of Emperor Xiaowen of the Northern Wei were instrumental in advancing its political and economic development, and in promoting the harmonious intermingling of the Xianbei and the Han peoples. However, the prosperity of the Northern Wei did not survive Emperor Xiaowen, and his death marked the beginning of its decline. Following the accession of Emperor Xiaoming, the Northern Wei was racked by internal strife. Real power fell into the hands of two generals, Gao Huan and Yuwen Tai.

In 534 AD, Emperor Xiaowu of the Northern Wei fled to Chang'an to seek the protection of Yuwen Tai. Meanwhile, Gao Huan installed another emperor in Luoyang with the title of Emperor Xiaojing of the Northern Wei. The Northern Wei thus split into two separate courts. The one with its capital at Chang'an is historically known as the Western Wei, and the one at Luoyang, the Eastern Wei.

95. The Last Emperor of Chen Presides over a Declining Dynasty

FOLLOWING THE RISE and fall of three dynasties—the Song, the Qi and the Liang—in southern China, in 557 AD Chen Baxian founded the Chen dynasty in Jiankang and acceded to the throne as Emperor Wu. By that time, the Eastern Wei and Western Wei in the north had been replaced respectively by the Northern Qi and the Northern Zhou. Gao Yang, son of Gao Huan of the Eastern Wei, established the Northern Qi; Yuwen Jue, son of Yuwen Tai of the Western Wei, established the Northern Zhou. The two kingdoms warred with each other continuously until Emperor Wu of the Northern Zhou quashed the Northern Qi and unified North China.

Emperor Wu of the Northern Zhou was a politically savvy and active ruler, but his successor, Emperor Xuan, was a debauched tyrant. Upon his death, power fell into the hands of his father-in-law Yang Jian. In 581 AD, Yang Jian founded the Sui dynasty and became Emperor Wen.

Political turmoil in north China provided a respite to the Chen, whose economy began to recover in the temporary peace. However, things were spoiled by its fifth emperor, the Last Emperor of Chen, a superlatively fatuous and dissipated ruler named Chen Shubao, who did not have the faintest idea about statecraft and spent most of his time carousing. At great expense, he built three magnificent pavilions to house his favorite concubines. His Prime Minister Jiang Zong, Imperial Secretary Kong Fan, and others were a corrupt lot of literati. The Last Emperor of Chen invited them to frequent feasts hosted for his favorite ladies in the palace. Those were all-night affairs where poems were composed and responded to over free-flowing wine. On occasion, these poems were set to popular tunes, and sung by the over 1,000 ladies-in-waiting selected for that purpose.

Needless to say, to finance his profligacy, the Last Emperor of Chen subjected his subjects to ruthless plunder, destroying the livelihood of many ordinary citizens, turning them out of hearth and home. Corpses of displaced people were a common sight.

A minister, Fu Zai, presented a petition to the emperor that said, "The present situation in the country has incurred the wrath of the Heavens, not just the common folk. The government is losing support even among its close allies. This kingdom in the southeast will be doomed if this situation does not change."

The emperor, infuriated by the petition, sent word to Fu Zai, "Will you recant? If you do, the emperor is ready to pardon you."

Fu Zai replied, "My mind is like my face. I could no more change my mind than I can change the way I look."

The Last Emperor of Chen had Fu Zai executed.

The emperor was able to enjoy his dissolute life for five years. Meanwhile, the increasingly powerful Sui in the north decided to destroy the Chen dynasty in the south.

Following a strategy suggested by his advisers, at the start of every harvest season in the south, Emperor Wen of Sui massed his troops along the border between the two kingdoms and threatened to invade the Chen. This invariably meant that Chen farmers were unable to harvest their crops. Then, when the Chen assembled its forces and got ready to resist the seemingly imminent attack, the Sui army held back. The scenario was repeated several years in a row, wreaking havoc on the agricultural production of the Chen, and sapping the fighting will of the Chen troops defending the border. The Sui army also sent out foraging parties from time to time to raid the granaries of the Chen troops, torching the grain held in storage, causing huge losses to the Chen.

In 588 AD, Emperor Wen of Sui commissioned the construction of a large fleet of battleships of varying sizes. He appointed his son

Yang Guang, the Prince of Jin, and Yang Su, his Prime Minister, as Marshals, and He Ruobi and Han Qinhu as Generals-in-Chief, to lead a 510,000-strong army across the Yangtze River in an 8-pronged attack against the Chen.

Emperor Wen of Sui personally read out an edict announcing punitive action against the Chen, enumerating a twenty-count indictment against the Last Emperor of Chen. He then had 300,000 copies of the edict made and widely distributed across Jiangnan. This edict aroused the citizens of the Chen, who already had a visceral hatred for their Emperor, causing their loyalty to Chen to increasingly waver.

The waterborne army under Yang Su's command set out from Yong'an and sailed down the Yangtze in thousands of great ships with yellow dragons as figureheads. The river was a sea of banners and flags: the suits of armor worn by the warriors glistened in the sun. The sight awed the defenders of the Chen so much that they lost all appetite for resistance.

The other Sui battle groups advanced unopposed to the banks of the river. He Ruobi led a northern group to Jingkou, and Han Qinhu led a group to Gushu. One urgent alert after another went out to Jiankang from the Chen troops assembled near the riverbanks. The emperor, his favorite concubines, and the literati who surrounded him received these reports in an inebriated state, and threw them unread under the sofas of the court. Nevertheless, the alerts kept coming, and at closer intervals. Finally, at the insistence of some ministers, the emperor agreed to call a meeting of his advisers to discuss the Sui invasion.

The Last Emperor of Chen said, "Our country is a blessed land in the southeast. In the past, we defeated three attacks by the Northern Qi and two by the Northern Zhou. The Sui army is courting the same fate by taking on the Chen. There's nothing to be afraid of."

Kong Fan, a favorite minister of his, echoed his view, "Your Majesty is right. We have the Yangtze serving as a natural barrier. The river is impassable, unless the Sui troops all grow wings. Our officers at the riverside must have exaggerated the dire nature of the situation in order to claim more credit for themselves."

In their half-hearted exchange of views, they took the Sui invasion lightly. After some more bantering, the participants reverted to carousing and drinking to music played by the ladies.

In the first lunar month of 589 AD, with He Ruobi's troops crossing the river at Jingkou and Han Qinhu's group crossing at Caishiji, the two Sui armies pressed closer to Jiankang. The impending battle finally brought the Last Emperor of Chen to some sobriety. There were over a 100,000 Chen troops in the capital, but none of his favorites, such as Jiang Zong and Kong Fan, knew how to command an army. The emperor wept in panic as the Sui army marched into the capital without encountering much resistance. All of the Chen troops either surrendered or were captured.

The Sui troops that entered the imperial palace could not find the Last Emperor of Chen at all. They captured a number of eunuchs, and learned that he had run to a rear palace and thrown himself down a well. Searching the rear palace, they found a well. However, on closer look they discovered it to be dry. They could make out human forms below, but when they called out to them they got no response.

The soldiers shouted menacingly, "If we don't hear a response we are going to drop a big rock into the well." They then hoisted a boulder over the well, ostensibly to drop it in. The Last Emperor, hidden in the darkness below, uttered a shrill cry of terror. At this, the soldiers threw down a rope to haul up the emperor and two favorite concubines.

The Chen dynasty, the last of the Southern dynasties, was thus extinguished. After more than 270 years of division, begun in 316 AD with the demise of the Western Jin, China was once again a unified country.

SUI DYNASTY (581 AD–618 AD)

96. Emperor Yang of Sui Tours Jiangdu

AFTER UNIFYING CHINA, Emperor Wen of Sui consolidated his rule by instituting civil service and military reforms, establishing national civil service examinations, promoting capable officials, and harshly penalizing corrupt ones. Through a series of shakeups and reforms, he was able to bring political stability and social and economic prosperity.

Shortly after his accession, Yang Guang, Emperor Yang of Sui, undertook two ambitious projects. He had a new capital built in Luoyang, henceforth known as Dongdu ("the Eastern Capital"), and he commissioned the construction of the Grand Canal, connecting North and South China. These projects had the purpose of reinforcing his political control over the country as a whole, facilitating the transport of materials and goods from southeast China to the north, and indulging his own pleasure-seeking habits.

In 605 AD, he put Yuwen Kai, Minister of Buildings and Construction, in charge of the construction of Dongdu. Yuwen

Kai, a capable engineering expert eager to cater to the emperor's luxurious tastes, built the new city on a lavish scale. All the high-grade timber and stone required for the palace were brought from south of the Yangtze and north of the Five Ridges. A thousand workers were needed to move one single column. For the building of the new Eastern Capital, work went on day and night, with 2,000,000 workers conscripted and deployed each month. A large West Garden a hundred miles around, boasting manmade lakes and mountains, gazebos and pavilions, and a myriad of rare plants and flowers, was built in the western outskirts of Luoyang for the pleasure of the emperor. This garden sported a novel feature: colorful silk flowers and leaves were tied to the leafless trees in winter in order to simulate an eternal spring.

In the same year the construction of Dongdu started, he had 1,000,000 workers conscripted from the Henan and Huaibei areas to dig a canal from the West Garden of Luoyang to Shanyang (modern-day Huai'an, Jiangsu Province) on the south bank of the Huai River. The canal was named the Tongji Canal. He had another 100,000 workers conscripted to dredge the canal known as the Han Ditch. This had been built by Fu Chai, Prince of Wu, during the Spring and Autumn Period, and connected Shanyang with Jiangdu (modern-day Yangzhou, Jiangsu Province). As a result of this project, river transport from Luoyang to southeast China was greatly facilitated.

In the five years that followed, Emperor Yang deployed conscripted labor on two other occasions to build canals, one which was called the Yongji Canal, from the north bank of the Yellow River in Luoyang to Zhuojun (modern-day Beijing); another canal called the Jiangnan River, which connected Jingkou (modern-day Zhenjiang, Jiangsu Province) across the river from Jiangdu, with Yuhang (modern-day Hangzhou, Zhejiang Province). After their completion, these four canals constituted the Grand Canal which connected South and North China. Boasting a total length of some 4,000 *li*, it is one of the great public works in Chinese history, and has played a positive role in China's economic and cultural development and in unifying the country. Needless to say, it came about at great cost of civilian labor and life.

Emperor Yang of Sui enjoyed traveling about the country for the pleasure of seeing new places and sights as well as for parading his imperial power among his subjects. No sooner had the canal from Dongdu to Jiangdu been completed than the emperor, accompanied by a 200,000-strong entourage, traveled to Jiangdu. Well in advance of this trip, the emperor had ordered 10,000 large ships to be built. These included two 4-storey-high ships emblazoned with dragons for the emperor and his wife, Empress Xiao. Each came complete an ornate palace on board and close to a hundred well-appointed chambers. The many thousands of other ships that followed the two lead vessels carried troops, weapons and tents. On the day of departure, the convoy of 10,000 ships extended down the canal for close to two hundred *li*.

It was a challenge to move such a large fleet on the canal, but those whose job was to attend to the pleasures of the emperor had had it all planned out. Along both banks of the canal, an imperial promenade bordered by shade-giving willows had been built, along which 80,000 civilian conscripts helped to pull the ships. Two detachments of cavalry escorted the brightly-painted convoy of ships on land, as multi-colored flags whipped in the wind. When night fell, the fleet was ablaze with torches and lamps and rang with drumbeats and music. It was an endless panorama of pageantry.

To ensure the gastronomic delight of his huge following, Emperor Yang ordered the populace along the way to provide so-called "food donations" to his troops. The commandery and county officials would force the people in their jurisdictions to prepare and deliver banquets to the fleet. Some localities donated a hundred tables, way beyond the digestive capacity of the emperor, his concubines, court ladies, eunuchs and ministers combined. Much of the unconsumed food was buried in hastily dug pits on the riverbank, while the local residents forced to make the donation were further impoverished by the levies.

Jiangdu was a bustling town at the time. Emperor Yang had a grand time there sightseeing and indulging in his favorite pastimes and pleasures. He also had a chance to show off his imperial power. A hundred thousand workers and a prodigious sum of money were devoted to the outfitting of his honor guard alone. After six months of general fuss, the emperor returned triumphantly to Dongdu.

This trip became the forerunner of the emperor's nearly annual inspection tours. For one such tour by land through North China, he conscripted civilian workers from a dozen commanderies in Hebei to carve out a road through the rocky Taihang Mountains. To ensure his safety, a 1,000,000 workers were conscripted for rush work on the Great Wall with a twenty-day deadline. After all these preparations, he embarked on his northern tour under the protection of 500,000 troops. There were no palatial buildings in the north at the time of the tour. However, Emperor Yang had the good fortune of having a resourceful engineer Yuwen Kai at his service. Yuwen Kai built a mobile palace for the emperor which could accommodate hundreds of palace staff. Moving nimbly on wheels, it could be easily put together when needed, and disassembled for transport when not in use. It is a pity that the remarkable invention was for the sole enjoyment of one man—Emperor Yang of Sui.

The construction of Dongdu, the Grand Canal, and the Great Wall, the annual grand tours of Emperor Yang, as well as relentless forced labor and increasingly onerous levies, were becoming an unbearable burden on the populace. However, Emperor Yang's hubris and profligacy only increased over the years. Then, in 611 AD, he launched a campaign against Korea to prove his military mettle. He departed Jiangdu on his dragon-emblazoned flag ship, and arrived via the Grand Canal at Zhuojun to personally direct the campaign. Ordering troops across the country to converge on Zhuojun, regardless of their distance from the destination, he commissioned the construction of three hundred battle ships in Donglai (modern-day Ye County, Shandong Province). The conscripted civilian laborers worked on the boats day and night without respite, under strict surveillance. As they worked waist-deep in the sea water, the long periods of immersion in the briny water caused their bodies to develop worm-infested sores below the waist. Many laborers succumbed to the harsh conditions and died at the worksite.

Emperor Yang then ordered the manufacture of 50,000 large transport vehicles in Henan, Huainan and Jiangnan. These were to be delivered to Gaoyang for the purpose of transporting the troops' armor and tents. Civilians and civilian boats south of the Yangtze and the Huai River were commandeered to transport food supplies from Liyang (southeast of modern-day Jun County, Henan Province) and the Luokoucang granaries to Zhuojun. Huge convoys of vehicles and large fleets of boats streamed day and night toward the north. Many of the hundreds of thousands of conscripted laborers transporting the supplies died of exhaustion or hunger along the way, their corpses strewing the fields. To make up for the excessive number of deaths among the laborers, oxen were press-ganged into pulling the carriages. As a result there was a shortage of oxen to work the fields. The subsequent poor harvests caused a steady deterioration of the life of common folks. Peasant uprisings became endemic.

Of the many insurgent forces, the strongest was the Wagang Army led by Zhai Rang and Li Mi. In a serious internal rift, Li Mi killed Zhai Rang. The Wagang Army went downhill as a result. As this internecine drama played out, an anti-Sui insurgency led by Li Yuan gained strength in the north.

TANG DYNASTY (618 AD–907 AD)

97. Li Yuan Raises Arms in Taiyuan

LI YUAN WAS BORN into the Sui aristocracy and inherited the title of the Duke of Tang. In 617 AD, Emperor Yang of Sui appointed him regent of Taiyuan with the charge of suppressing the peasant uprisings there. After a number of initial victories, Li Yuan became alarmed by the increasing number and strength of the rebellions.

Li Yuan had four sons. His second son, Li Shimin, was 18 at the time and was known for having bold ideas and insight. He had a natural ability to draw people of talent to him, and his generosity and gregarious nature gained him many friends. Convinced that the end of Sui rule was near, he quietly began making plans.

Liu Wenjing, the County Magistrate of Jinyang (modern-day Taiyuan, Shanxi Province), was much impressed by Li Shimin. In turn, Li Simin considered Liu Wenjing a bosom buddy. Liu Wenjing was also a blood relation of Li Mi. Later, when Li Mi joined the insurgency, Emperor Yang of Sui issued a warrant for the arrest of Li Mi's relations and friends. Consequently, Liu Wenjing was stripped of his official functions and jailed in Jinyang. Li Shimin, hearing the news, hastened to visit Liu Wenjing in jail.

Holding Liu's hands, Li Shimin said to him, "Big brother, I am not here to exchange greetings, but mainly to seek your advice."

Having previously guessed Li Shimin's intentions, Liu Wenjing replied, "The emperor is far away in Jiangdu. Li Mi is approaching Dongdu with his insurgent troops, and there are uprisings everywhere. This is a good time to make a bid for the throne. I can help you raise 100,000 men. With the several tens of thousands of troops your father already commands, we can capture Chang'an and make it a rallying point for the country. We will have the country in our pocket within six months."

Elated, Li Shimin answered, "You read my mind!"

Considering Liu Wenjing's words after returning home, Li Shimin became increasingly convinced of the logic of Liu's advice. However, it would be a challenge to convince his father. In that period the Khan of the Tujue (a Turkic tribe that was one of the northern ethnic groups in ancient China) north of Taiyuan was attacking the city of Mayi. The defending army deployed by Li Yuan had suffered a series of defeats at the hands of the Khan. This made Li Yuan nervous, as he feared the consequences once the bad news reached Emperor Yang.

Li Shimin took advantage of Li Yuan's quandary to urge him to raise up arms against the Sui court. Li Yuan was scared witless by the idea, replying "How can you say such treasonous things! If I report this, you will be arrested."

Unfazed, Li Shimin answered, "Go ahead and denounce me if you want to. I am not afraid to die."

Naturally, Li Yuan would do no such thing. However, he did warn him against repeating such remarks in the future.

The next day, Li Shimin again pitched the idea to Li Yuan, "Father, you've been charged by the emperor with putting down rebellion. But do you really think you can deal with the increasing number of insurgencies? Besides, given the suspicious temperament of the emperor, even your victories put you in greater peril. The suggestion I made yesterday remains the only way out."

After a long pause during which Li Yuan wavered indecisively, he finally heaved a heavy sigh and said, "I gave some thought to your idea last night, and could find no fault with its logic. I can't make up my mind. From now on I leave it to you to decide our fate. Either our family will fall and die, or we will take over the country."

Shortly afterwards, Li Yuan let Liu Wenjing out of the Jinyang jail. Liu Wenjing then helped Li Shimin raise an army, and Li Yuan summoned his two other sons, Li Jiancheng and Li Yuanji, who were fighting insurgencies in Hedong.

Two deputy regents of Taiyuan tried to stop Li Yuan and his sons, but they had them arrested and killed on trumped-up charges of collusion with the Tujue.

On Liu Wenjing's advice, Li Yuan sent an envoy carrying valuable gifts to the Khan of the Tujue. He sued for peace and invited him to join the rebellion against the Sui. Finding the proposal in his own interest, the Khan agreed to help.

With the Tujue appeased, Li Yuan started his rebellion in earnest. He gave himself the title of General-in-Chief, and appointed Li Jiancheng and Li Shimin as Left and Right Commanders-in-Chief of the armies. Liu Wenjing was named Adjutant. They called their army *yi shi* (those who rebel against evil rule), and marched with 30,000 men from Jinyang towards Chang'an. Along the way, they continued to pick up supporters. They also emulated the peasant rebels in opening up government granaries to the poor, an act that attracted still more adherents to their cause.

As the Tang army drew near Huoyi (modern-day Huo County, Shanxi Province), it was intercepted by the troops led by the Sui general Song Laosheng, who encamped in the city. The narrow roads in the Huoyi area had been made impassable by days of heavy rain, and food supplies dried up for the Tang army. Rumor was afoot among the soldiers that the Tujue was preparing a sneak attack against Jinyang. Li Yuan began to waver and considered pulling back to Jinyang.

Li Shimin said to Li Yuan, "This is the autumn harvest season, and there is plenty of food for the picking in the fields. We have nothing to fear from Song Laosheng, either. We are now trying to rally the nation in rebelling against the corrupt rule of the Sui. If we pull back before we even engage the enemy, people will lose heart. We will not be able to survive a retreat to Jinyang."

Li Jiancheng agreed with his brother, causing Li Yuan to change his mind and scuttle his plans for a retreat.

One August day, the sun made its first appearance after a long spell of rain. The Tang army arrived at the edge of Huoyi after a forced march along a hillside trail. Li Yuan sent his son Jiancheng with dozens of cavalrymen to challenge the defenders for a fight. Seeing just a small Tang contingent at the foot of the city walls, General Song Laosheng personally led a 30,000-strong force out of the city gate to engage it. At this point, Li Shimin charged down from the high ground of the south hills and decimated General Song's army. By the time General Song tried to retreat back into the city, Li Yuan's army had already gained control of it and had locked up the city gates. The cornered general was slain by the Tang troops.

After the capture of Huoyi, the Tang army continued its march westward, crossing the Yellow River with the help of the peasant army in the Guanzhong area. Li Yuan's daughter also raised a 10,000-strong contingent named the Ladies' Army in support of the Tang army's advance into Guanzhong.

Li Yuan unleashed his more than 200,000 troops on Chang'an, overwhelming the Sui defenders. After overrunning Chang'an, he announced a 12-point contract with the people to win their loyalty. It abrogated all draconian decrees of the Sui government, but kept Yang You, grandson of Emperor Yang of Sui, as the nominal emperor.

It was only in the summer of the following year (618 AD), when news arrived from Jiangdu that Emperor Yang had been killed, that Li Yuan deposed Yang You. He changed the dynasty name to Tang, and ascended the throne as Emperor Gaozu of Tang.

98. Li Shimin Takes Control of Dongdu

EVEN AS LI YUAN took control of Chang'an, insurgencies were sprouting and growing across the country. In addition to the Wagang Army, other major insurgent forces continued to fight the Sui army. These included one led by Dou Jiande in Hebei, and another led by Du Fuwei in the Jianghuai area. The cruel, dissolute despot Emperor Yang of Sui, sensing the approaching doom, fled to the safety of Jiangdu and wallowed in a life of drinking and merrymaking with his consorts.

Despite his studious attempt to insulate himself against bad news, he could not help saying with alarm to Empress Xiao, "I've heard about plots against my life. What the heck! Let's revel and drink to our heart's content!"

He once held a mirror and looked at his own image for a while before declaring, "What a handsome head! I wonder who's going to cut it off."

The fateful day feared by Emperor Yang finally came. A number of the officers in the palace guard, most of whom were natives of Guanzhong, planned to slip home because they saw they had no prospects with Emperor Yang. Taking advantage of the soldiers' homesickness, General Yuwen Huaji mutinied and entered the palace with a detachment of troops. They placed the emperor under house arrest.

Emperor Yang of Sui asked the officials keeping him under surveillance, "What crime have I ever committed?"

They replied, "You started wars and indulged in profligate living. You trusted evil-minded officials and turned a deaf ear to wise counsel. Because of you, men died in battle, women and children have lost their livelihood, and people became displaced. Do you still insist you are innocent?"

Emperor Yang answered, "It's true that I have let the people down. But I've done right by people like you. You've shared the good life. Who's behind this?"

The officials said, "There is not one person behind this. The entire nation hates you because you're a despot."

At this, Emperor Yang fell silent and untied the sash around his waist. He gave this to the officials, who used it to strangle him. Thus, the Sui dynasty, which had ruled China for 38 years, came to an end.

After the death of Emperor Yang of Sui, Luoyang, the eastern capital, remained in the hands of Yang Tong (grandson of Emperor Yang) and Wang Shichong, a minister of the Sui court. Wang Shichong set up Yang Tong as the emperor and continued fighting the insurgents in the name of the Sui dynasty.

The Wagang insurgent army had been active in the areas surrounding Dongdu, and Li Mi had defeated the Sui army in numerous battles there. However, in his arrogance Li Mi let a rift develop between himself and his commanders, and saw his strength dwindle in the wake of a battle with the troops marching north under Yuwen Huaji. Wang Shichong detected Li Mi's vulnerability, and attacked and routed his army. Li Mi was forced to take his remnant of troops to Chang'an to seek the protection of the Tang dynasty.

After chasing off Li Mi, Wang Shichong got up the nerve and deposed Yang Tong, declaring himself Emperor of a new Zheng dynasty.

In this period, the Tang army had neutralized several local separatist strongholds in the northwest, thus pacifying its backyard. In 620 AD, Emperor Gaozu of Tang sent Li Shimin at the head of a massive army to march on Dongdu. At the approach of Li Shimin's troops, many prefectural and county governments declared the support for him, and Dongdu was soon encircled by hostile forces. Li Shimin was not only good at waging war, but also wise in knowing how to get others on his side. He co-opted a number of the commanders of the Wagang Army and other separatist strongholds who had surrendered to him. Well-known historical figures such as Qin Shubao, Cheng Yaojin and Yuchi Jingde became members of his able staff.

On an inspection of the frontline with his 500 cavalrymen, Li Shimin was suddenly surrounded by 10,000 infantry and cavalrymen deployed by Wang Shichong, who had somehow found out his whereabouts. Wang's general, Shan Xiongxin, rode up to Li Shimin and thrust his lance at him. Yuchi Jingde, who was behind Li Shimin, galloped to his rescue and unhorsed Shan Xiongxin with a shout and a thrust of his lance. Li Shimin was able to break out of the encirclement with Yuchi Jingde's help and protection. The two then turned around with their cavalry and charged into the Zheng camp, overwhelming its troops, who dared not offer any serious resistance. With the waves of Tang reinforcements joining the battle, the Zheng army was routed.

From autumn to the spring of the following year, the Tang army kept tightening the noose around Dongdu by nonstop attacks day and night. Wang Shichong put up a stiff resistance inside the city walls and kept the Tang army under a constant barrage of rocks and arrows. As the days dragged on, the Tang troops began to feel exhausted. Proposals were made to Li Shimin to hold off the attacks temporarily so that the troops could return to Chang'an to regroup and recoup strength.

Li Shimin declared, "With the surrender of the surrounding prefectural governments, Luoyang has become an isolated city. Its capture is a matter of time. How can we stop in the middle of this?"

He then issued this order to his troops, "We will not pull back until we've captured Dongdu."

With his back to the wall, Wang Shichong had no alternative but to send a secret emissary to Dou Jiande of Hebei for help. Dou Jiande was the leader of a strong insurgent force in Hebei. Following Wang Shichong's accession as Emperor of Zheng, Dou Jiande had also proclaimed himself Emperor, giving his dynasty the name Xia and captured large swaths of Tang territory. After receiving the request for help from Wang Shichong, Dou Jiande sent 300,000 men over land and on water towards Dongdu to lift its siege. At the same time he sent a letter to Li Shimin via a messenger, demanding that he return to Guanzhong.

Many of the officers and men of the Tang army were cowed by the strength of the Xia army, and advocated a temporary retreat from Dongdu. Still others believed that Wang Shichong's troops were the main threat, and had as their only weakness a shortage of food. If Dou Jiande's force were allowed to join up with the Wang army and assure Dongdu of supplies from Hebei, there would be no prospect for a Tang victory. Thus, they believed it was absolutely necessary to cut off the southward advance of Dou Jiande's army.

This later view was accepted by Li Shimin. He left Li Yuanji in charge of the siege of Wang Shichong's force in Dongdu, and took 3,000 elite troops to reinforce the defence of Wulao Pass (also known as Hulao Pass, near modern-day Sishui in Xingyang, Henan Province). When Dou Jiande's army arrived at Wulao Pass, its advance was cut off by the Tang force. Repeated attempts by the Xia army to storm the pass failed, while a light cavalry detachment sent by Li Shimin via a back road successfully cut off its supply route. Dou Jiande believed that by virtue of his army's numerical advantage, he would be able to capture Wulao Pass. Against the advice of his lieutenants and his wife, he arrayed his force for an all-out attack.

As the Xia army marched foward amid drumbeats and battle cries, Li Shimin surveyed the fighting formation from his vantage point and observed, "Dou Jiande has never fought a formidable foe. His arrogance and underestimation of his enemy are evident by the way he fielded his troops. All we need to do is sit tight and wait till their soldiers are exhausted. Then we will go out and deal them a crushing blow."

The Xia troops had gone out in the morning, in full battle array, primed for a fight. However, no Tang troops came out to engage them in battle. At noon, the Xia soldiers, tired and hungry, either sat on the ground or went for a drink at the river's edge. Seeing the moment had come, Li Shimin ordered his troops to cross the Sishui River and storm Dou Jiande's command center.

Dou Jiande was in his tent in the middle of a meeting with his commanders when the Tang cavalry rushed into his camp. He immediately led his cavalry to repel the attack. The two sides engaged in a fierce fight amid flying dust and showers of arrows.

Taking the Xia army unawares, Li Shimin himself sneaked behind the Xia lines at the head of a small force, and raised the standards of the Tang dynasty. When the Xia troops looked over their shoulder and saw those flags, they thought the Tang army had taken control of the Xia headquarters. The demoralized troops scattered in all directions, and Dou Jiande, wounded in the confusion, was taken captive by Tang troops.

After the defeat of Dou Jiande, Li Shimin turned around to reinforce the seige of Dongdu. Wang Shichong still harbored hopes of breaking out of siege, but his commanders said, "Now that the king of Xia is defeated, we have no hope, even if we could break out of this encirclement." Realizing that fortune no longer smiled on him, Wang Shichong surrendered to the Tang force.

Shortly after being taken to Chang'an, Dou Jiande was killed. His lieutenant Liu Heita continued to fight the Tang army at the head of the Xia army in Hebei. It took the Tang army another three years before it finally succeeded in pacifying Hebei. By 623 AD, the Tang dynasty's campaign to unify China largely succeeded. However, internal tensions within the Tang imperial family intensified.

99. Incident at Xuanwu Gate

AFTER HIS ACCESSION to the throne, Emperor Gaozu of Tang made Li Jiancheng Crown Prince, Li Shimin the Prince of Qin, and Li Yuanji the Prince of Qi. Of the three sons, Li Shimin rightfully claimed most of the credit for his family's new success. The rebellion in Taiyuan was conceived by him, and he had achieved the bulk of their battlefield victories. Li Jiancheng had been made Crown Prince solely because he was the firstborn, even though his military achievements paled in comparison with Li Shimin's. Li Shimin not only possessed bravery and political savvy, but also the loyalty of a talented group of people. The household of the Prince of Qin boasted the "Eighteen Scholars," comprised of such literary lights as Fang Xuanling and Du Ruhui, as well as well-known generals, such as Yuchi Jingde, Qin Shubao and Cheng Yaojin. Crown Prince Li Jiancheng, knowing that his authority and prestige were dwarfed by Li Shimin's, out of jealousy formed an alliance with his brother Li Yuanji, the Prince of Qi, in order to marginalize Li Shimin's influence.

Jiancheng and Yuanji discovered Emperor Gaozu's preferences among his concubines, and did their best to ingratiate themselves with his favorites, showering them with gifts and flattery. Li Shimin did none of this. After he captured Dongdu, some of Gaozu's concubines had privately asked him for treasures and jewelry from the Sui palace and demanded patronage for their kinsmen. He rebuffed all such requests. As a result, these concubines often praised the Crown Prince and badmouthed the Prince of Qin in front of Emperor Gaozu. Influenced by the concubines' tirades,

Emperor Gaozu became estranged from Li Shimin. Meanwhile, Li Shimin continued to achieve success, only deepening Jiancheng and Yuanji's jealousy and hostility. Consequently, they vowed to eliminate him.

On one occasion, Jiancheng invited Li Shimin for a drink at the Eastern Palace (which was reserved for the Crown Prince). After a few drinks, Li Shimin began to feel stomach cramps. He returned home, and in extreme pain began vomiting blood. Knowing that Jiancheng had poisoned his wine, he immediately sent for a doctor, who gave him an antidote that helped him to recover.

Jiancheng and Yuanji were still intent on harming Li Shimin, but feared retaliation if they tried anything because Li Shimin was surrounded by many brave generals, so they decided to buy these men's allegiance. Jiancheng sent a secret emissary carrying a letter to General Yuchi Jingde, who was in the service of the Prince of Qin, expressing his eagerness to befriend him. The letter was accompanied by a cartful of gold and silver.

Yuchi Jingde said to the emissary, "I am a subordinate of the Prince of Qin. If I were the kind of man who would secretly consort with the Crown Prince and betray the trust of the Prince of Qin, I would be a lowdown scoundrel who allowed greed to compromise his integrity. Why would the Crown Prince want to have a person like that working for him?" At that point, he returned the cartful of gold and silver unopened to the sender.

Jiancheng was infuriated by Yuchi Jingde's rebuff. That night, Yuanji sent an assassin to Yuchi Jingde's home to kill him. Yuchi Jingde had expected as much and decided beforehand that he and his friends would not make it easy for Jiancheng. At nightfall, Yuchi Jingde left the front door open. When the assassin slipped into the garden and peeked in through the window, he saw Yuchi Jingde reclining on his bed with a lance by his side. The assassin had heard of Yuchi Jingde's fabled skills at martial arts, and became afraid that Yuchi Jingde was prepared for his visit. He slinked away without making a move.

This failed attempt did not deter them from trying another tack. During that time, the Tujue were making frequent incursions into Central Plains. Jiancheng proposed to Emperor Gaozu that

Yuanji replace Li Shimin as commander of the northern expedition against the Tujue, and that Generals Yuchi Jingde, Qin Shubao and Cheng Yaojin, and all the elite troops of the Prince of Qin, be put under the command of Yuanji. They figured that once these generals and troops were transferred to the front, the path would be clear for Li Shimin's liquidation.

This secret plot was reported to Li Shimin. Sensing the urgency of the situation, he immediately called in his brother-in-law Zhangsun Wuji and Yuchi Jingde for consultation. The two advised him to take preemptive action, but Li Shimin replied, "Killing one's siblings like this is not right. Let's wait till they make their move. Then we'll strike."

Yuchi Jingde and Zhangsun Wuji both became agitated at his response. They argued that if Li Shimin refused to take action, they did not wish to stay and wait to be slaughtered. Seeing the determination of his subordinates, Li Shimin made up his mind.

That very night Li Shimin requested an audience with Emperor Gaozu. There, he made a complaint about how the Crown Prince and Yuanji were plotting to have him killed. Emperor Gaozu promised to summon the three brothers first thing in the morning to personally cross-examine them. The next morning, Li Shimin had Zhangsun Wuji and Yuchi Jingde, with an elite detachment, set an ambush for Jiancheng and Yuanji near the Xuanwu Gate, north of the palace.

Soon Jiancheng and Yuanji were seen riding toward the Xuanwu Gate. As they approached the gate, they sensed an unusual tension in the air. Filled with foreboding they turned their horses around.

Li Shimin rode from the gate, calling out "Your Highness, don't leave!"

Yuanji turned around and drew his bow intending to kill Li Shimin, but his hands were so shaky that he could not get an arrow into it. Meanwhile, the sharp-eyed, agile Li Shimin got off a volley at Jiancheng, killing him. Yuchi Jingde then charged out with his seventy cavalrymen, and with a arrow shot Yuanji off his horse.

When the troops of the Eastern Palace and the Prince of Qi learned of the incident at the Xuanwu Gate, they poured out of their quarters and launched a fierce attack against the troops of the Prince of Qin. With Li Shimin directing his troops in battle, he sent Yuchi Jingde into the imperial palace.

Emperor Gaozu was still waiting in the palace for his three sons. Yuchi Jingde appeared before him, breathless with a lance in hand, and reported, "The Crown Prince and the Prince of Qi were going to stage a coup, but were killed by the Prince of Qin. The Prince was concerned that Your Majesty should not be injured, and sent me to protect Your Majesty."

Emperor Gaozu was at a loss as to what to do when he learned of the incident.

Chief Minister Xiao Yu and other court ministers said, "Jiancheng and Yuanji had never earned any credit, and had plotted against the Prince of Qin in their jealousy. It is a good thing that the Prince of Qin has eliminated them. All Your Majesty has to do is turn the reins of state over to the Prince of Qin and everything will be fine."

As any objection on the part of Emperor Gaozu at this late stage would have been pointless, he was left no choice but to heed the ministers' advice. He declared the guilt of Jiancheng and Yuanji, and ordered that all the troops of the deceased princes be put under the Prince of Qin's command. Two months later, Emperor Gaozu of Tang abdicated in favor of the Prince of Qin, and became the Retired Emperor. Li Shimin acceded to the throne as Emperor Taizong of Tang.

100. Wei Zheng Dares to Speak Unwelcome Truths

AFTER THE XUANWU Gate Incident, Li Shimin, the Prince of Qin, received a petition denouncing an official at the Eastern Palace named Wei Zheng. It said that he had been a part of Li Mi and Dou Jiande's insurgency, and that after the insurgency had failed he returned to Chang'an and offered his services to Crown Prince Li Jiancheng, and had even tried to persuade Jiancheng to kill the Prince of Qin.

The Prince of Qin immediately sent for Wei Zheng.

At the meeting, the stern-faced Prince of Qin asked Wei Zheng, "Why did you try to drive a wedge between me and my brothers?"

The ministers in attendance feared for Wei Zheng, thinking the Prince of Qin was going to settle old scores with him. However, Wei Zheng was unperturbed, answering with composure, "It's a pity the Crown Prince did not follow my advice. If he had, what happened today would not have happened."

Finding that Wei Zheng had been willing to speak honestly, and had bold ideas and insight, the Prince of Qin did not fault Wei Zheng, but on the contrary said to him amicably, "That is all in the past. Let's put it behind us."

After his accession to the throne, Emperor Taizong of Tang promoted Wei Zheng to Grand Master of Remonstrance. He also invited into the government a number of people who had worked for Jiancheng and Yuanji, to the indignation of officials of his household, who privately grumbled, "We've served His Majesty for all these years, but when it comes to awarding titles and making appointments to government jobs, the people at the Eastern Palace and the Prince of Qi household get all the goodies. What kind of logic is this?"

Fang Xuanling, the Prime Minister, reported the complaint to Emperor Taizong of Tang, who answered with a laugh, "The court makes appointments to ensure good government. It is only natural that recruitment should be based on merit rather than on connections. If a new recruit proves to be more capable than an incumbent, there is no reason to reject the new just to maintain the status quo."

With those remarks, he succeeded in silencing the critics.

In his emphasis on merit, Emperor Taizong of Tang demonstrated a readiness to put aside past enmity. He also encouraged his ministers to candidly air their views in his presence. At the urging of the emperor, the ministers became emboldened in offering advice. Wei Zheng was particularly forthright in presenting his well-thought-out views on affairs of state to the emperor, who placed great trust in him and summoned him for consultation on a regular basis.

On one occasion Emperor Taizong of Tang asked Wei Zheng, "Why are some monarchs wise and others fatuous and incompetent?"

Wei Zheng replied, "Wisdom comes to those who are willing to listen to diverse opinions. Ignorance results from wearing blinders." Citing the examples of Emperors Yao and Shun, Emperor Ershi of Qin, Emperor Wu of Liang and Emperor Yang of Sui, he said, "If a country's supreme ruler heeds the views of those he leads, he will be able to know what's happening in the country even if those in his immediate circle try to pull the wool over his eyes."

Emperor Taizong of Tang nodded energetically, signaling his approval, "Well said!"

After reading through the collection of writings by Emperor Yang of Sui, Emperor Taizong of Tang said one day to his ministers, "Emperor Yang of Sui was such a well-read monarch and knew all about the virtuous Emperors Yao and Shun and the evil King Jie of Xia and King Zhou of Shang. Why did he still rule so badly?"

Wei Zheng rejoined, "It is not enough for an emperor to be smart and well read. He has to be willing to listen with an open mind to the advice of his ministers. Emperor Yang of Sui, in his arrogance and conceit, talked the talk of Yao and Shun but walked the walk of Jie and Zhou. His increasing confusion eventually led to his self-destruction."

Emperor Taizong of Tang, deeply affected by these observations, answered with a sigh, "Past lessons are our teacher."

Emperor Taizong of Tang was gratified to see his rule consolidated. Finding the advice of his ministers to be of great help, he said to them, "Government is like treating an illness. Even after recovery, the patient needs convalescence and continued care and vigilance. There is peace now in the Central Plains and all our neighbors have voluntarily pledged their allegiance to us. This is unprecedented in the country's history. But I need to maintain vigilance lest the prosperity be short-lived. For this reason I want to hear more unvarnished advice from you."

Wei Zheng replied, "It is wonderful to know that Your Majesty could think energetically about future peril even while you preside over an unprecedented prosperity."

From then on Wei Zheng became even more of a prolific critic and dispenser of advice. Whenever he perceived any failure on the part of Emperor Taizong, he would state his objections to the emperor's face. Even when the emperor, soured by the criticism, assumed a sullen look, Wei Zheng would continue his screed, giving the emperor no face-saving way out of the situation.

During one such heated argument with Wei Zheng in the imperial audience hall, Emperor Taizong was on the point of losing his temper, but he checked himself for fear of tarnishing his good name for openness to advice and criticism. After the audience, he returned to his quarters full of spite. He said with unabated anger to his consort, Queen Zhangsun, "One of these days I am going to kill that country bumpkin!"

The Queen, struck by the rare fury in Emperor Taizong, asked, "Who does Your Majesty wish to kill?"

Emperor Taizong replied, "Who else? That Wei Zheng, who enjoys humbling me in front of everyone! I can't take it anymore."

Queen Zhangsun went into her boudoir without uttering a word, and then changed into the garb appropriate for an imperial audience. She bowed down before the emperor.

Emperor Taizong asked in puzzlement, "What are you doing?"

Queen Zhangsun replied, "I hear that only wise monarchs deserve upright counselors. The integrity of Wei Zheng is a fitting testimony to the wisdom of Your Majesty. That's why I must offer congratulations to Your Majesty."

These words acted like a bucket of cold water, dousing the flaming fury of Emperor Taizong. After this episode, instead of bearing Wei Zheng any grudge, the emperor praised him, "People like to fault Wei Zheng for his clumsiness and coarseness. But this in my view is what makes him so charming."

In 643 AD, the straight-talking Wei Zheng died of illness. Overcome with grief, Emperor Taizong said in tears, "One can see in a bronze mirror whether or not one is impeccably dressed. In the mirror of history, one can see the reasons for the rise and fall of a dynasty. A person can be a mirror that enables one to see where one has erred. With Wei Zheng's death, I've lost a valuable mirror."

The economic prosperity and civil peace in the early Tang period is historically known as "zhen guan zhi zhi" or the "Benign Reign of Zhen'guan" ("Zhen'guan" being the title of Taizong's reign). This golden age was made possible largely by Emperor Taizong's emphasis on meritocracy, his openness to candid advice from his counselors, his relatively enlightened policies, his reduction of compulsory service obligations of civilians, and his adoption of measures to stimulate production.

101. Li Jing Attacks Yinshan by Night

BY THE EARLY years of Emperor Taizong's reign, the war on the Central Plains had ended, but the western frontiers were far from quiet. The Eastern Tujue remained strong and posed a major threat to the Tang dynasty. From the time he had raised arms in Taiyuan, Emperor Gaozu of Tang had concentrated on overthrowing the Sui dynasty, and had had to stay on good terms with the Eastern Tujue by making concessions. However, this had not prevented the Eastern Tujue aristocracy from making constant incursions across the Tang border, harassing the populace on the frontier.

Barely twenty days after the accession of Emperor Taizong of Tang, Jieli Khan (also known as Illig Qaghan) of the Eastern Tujue led 100,000 men on a march to the banks of the Wei River, 40 *li* from Chang'an. Jieli believed that the newly installed Emperor Taizong might not have the nerve to put up much resistance. He sent an emissary to see Emperor Taizong in Chang'an with the warning that 1,000,000 Tujue warriors would arrive shortly.

A seasoned leader, Emperor Taizong dismissed Jieli's threat and jailed his emissary. He placed the Tang troops in Chang'an in battle array, then ride with six generals, including Fang Xuanling, to a bridge over the Wei River. There he demanded to have a dialogue with Jieli.

Jieli had been taken aback by the imprisonment of his emissary. Now, when he saw Emperor Taizong appear in person on the battlefield, and when he saw the impressive arrays of the Tang troops with their flags fluttering smartly in the wind, he became apprehensive. He and his commanders dismounted and made an obeisance to Emperor Taizong across the river.

Emperor Taizong said to Jieli, "We have signed a pact and have not stinted on gold and fineries for you through the years. Why have you invaded us in violation of our covenant?"

Jieli had no reply to this accusation, and agreed to a truce. Two days later, the two sides signed a pact on the bridge and Jieli withdrew his troops.

Chastened by the experience, Emperor Taizong intensified the training of his troops. He would arrange archery practice for hundreds of troops per day in front of the palace. He said to them, "It is not unusual for foreign foes to make incursions into our country. This is no cause for alarm. Rather, we must guard against complacency. Sometimes, there are apparent lulls on the frontier which make people forget what war is like and lose the ability to repel an invasion. From now on, I will be your archery instructor in times of peace, and your commander in times of war."

Encouraged by Emperor Taizong, the troops trained hard. Within a few years, they transformed themselves into an elite fighting force.

The following year, a heavy snow in north China caused both the death of a large number of livestock in Eastern Tujue, and a famine north of the Gobi Desert. Consequently, Jieli Khan's increasingly high taxes and his oppression of other tribes and ethnic groups were met with growing resistance. Jieli sent his cousin Tuli to put down the revolts, and Tuli was soundly defeated. When Tuli fled home, he was given a tongue-lashing and a severe beating by Jieli. The two had a falling-out and Tuli defected to the Tang court.

Seizing the opportunity, Emperor Taizong of Tang sent four generals, including Li Jing and Xu Shiji, at the head of 100,000 troops on a multi-pronged attack against the Tujue. Li Jing was the supreme commander of the campaign. A noted military strategist in the early Tang period, he was well-versed in the art of war. He had switched loyalty to the Tang during the waning years of the Sui dynasty, and had made significant contributions in the Tang's war of unification.

In 630 AD, Li Jing marched from Mayi at the head of a 3,000-strong elite cavalry force. The unit advanced day and night, approaching the Tujue bivouacs when Jieli least expected it. Jieli was caught off guard and lost control when the Tang force made its unexpected appearance. The commanders and troops were also thrown into a panic, saying "The Tang court must have mobilized all its troops for this attack. Why else would Li Jing dare to penetrate deep into enemy territory with such a small, unsupported force?"

This panic occurred even before the Tang forces had launched its attack. In addition, Li Jing had infiltrated a spy into the Tujue camp who persuaded a general close to Jieli to defect. Realizing the odds were heavily against him, Jieli slipped away.

On Li Jing's triumphant return to the capital after capturing Dingxiang, Emperor Taizong said with elation, "Li Ling of the Han dynasty led a 5,000-strong force against the Xiongnu, but was unfortunately captured by the enemy. With your 3,000-strong light cavalry brigade, you were able to penetrate behind enemy lines and take control of Dingxiang, projecting Tang military power throughout North China. This is an unprecedented accomplishment!"

After fleeing to north of the Yinshan Mountains, Jieli, fearing continued pursuit by Tang troops, sent an emissary to Chang'an to sue for peace, expressing a desire to seek an audience with the Tang Emperor. Emperor Taizong sent Tang Jian to Tujue on a conciliatory mission, while ordering Li Jing and his troops to keep close watch over Jieli's movements.

Li Jing's forces marched to Baidao (northwest of modern-day Huhhot, Inner Mongolia) to join up with Xu Shiji's force. The two huddled to find a way to deal with Jieli. Li Jing said, "Although Jieli suffered a defeat, he still commands a large force. If we let him slip through our fingers, it will be hard in the future to catch up with him. We should field a 10,000-strong elite force carrying a 20-day supply of food, and keep him in hot pursuit. We will definitely be able to capture him alive."

Xu Shiji endorsed this view and the two forces marched on toward the Yinshan Mountains.

Jieli's peace overtures were actually a delay tactic to buy more time and enable him to escape to the north of the Gobi in time for spring, when the grass would grow allowing his horses to be well-fed. When he saw the arrival of Tang Jian, he secretly gloated, thinking Emperor Taizong had played into his hand. He relaxed his vigilance as a result.

That evening the Tang troops led by Li Jing and Xu Shiji reached the Yinshan Mountains. The divisional subaltern, Su Dingfang, was ordered to take 200 light cavalrymen on a march through the foggy night. By the time the Tujue advance guards discovered the Tang troops, the latter were only seven *li* from Jieli's tent.

When Jieli learned of this attack by the Tang cavalry, he sent for Tang Jian. However, taking advantage of the light surveillance, Tang Jian had already returned to the Tang camp. Jieli immediately jumped on his winged steed and decamped. Li Jing rode after him in hot pursuit at the head of his troops. The leaderless Tujue troops were in disarray, and 10,000 of them were slain by the Tang troops. Large numbers of soldiers and livestock were taken captive.

After running away to escape capture, Jieli ended up hiding on a hill with a few of his closest bodyguards. However, he was eventually caught by his former subordinates and turned over to the Tang troops. He was then taken to Chang'an.

The once powerful Eastern Tujue was finally extinguished. Emperor Taizong spared the lives of the prisoners and established an area command on Eastern Tujue territory, headed by Tujue noblemen to administer Tujue affairs.

The victory enhanced Emperor Taizong's prestige among the ethnic groups of the northwest. That year leaders of the ethnic groups, including the Uygur, made a joint visit to Chang'an where they were received in audience by Emperor Taizong. They proclaimed Emperor Taizong their common leader, and honored him with the title of Heavenly Khan.

From then on, Chang'an received a steady stream of visitors from the Western Regions and many other Asian countries. In the same period China's eminent monk Xuanzang traveled to India through the Western Regions.

102. Master Monk Xuanzang Brings Back Buddhist Texts from India

XUANZANG WAS A monk at the Daci'en Temple of Chang'an. A native of Goushi, Henan Province, his secular name was Chen Hui. He became a monk at the age of thirteen, devoting himself to the study of Buddhism. He studied under many Buddhist masters and became an expert on Buddhist scriptures and classics, earning the honorific appellation of *sanzang fashi* (Master Monk Sanzang; *sanzang*, or triptaka in Sanskrit, is a term denoting the Buddhist scriptures). He found many errors in the translations of the scriptures and decided to travel to India, where there was a wealth of Buddhist literature.

In 629 AD (627 according to some), he started out from Chang'an and arrived in Liangzhou (modern-day Wuwei, Gansu Province). In that period, Tang citizens were forbidden from traveling abroad. Consequently, he was stopped by border guards at Liangzhou and told to go back to Chang'an. He managed to circumvent border checkpoints and made it to Guazhou (modern-day Anxi, Gansu Province) near Yumen Pass.

In Guazhou, Xuanzang learned that once outside Yumen Pass there were five fortresses at 100 *li* intervals. There was no water between the fortresses, and the only source of water was at the fortresses, which would be guarded by soldiers. In the meantime officials in Liangzhou had already found out he had slipped through border security, and had put out a warrant out for his arrest in Guazhou. If he were to pass by the fortresses he would almost certainly be caught by the soldiers.

Just when he was feeling helpless, he ran into a local resident by the name of Shi Pantuo, of the Hu ethnicity, who volunteered to act as his guide. Xuanzang was overjoyed. He sold some clothing in exchange for two horses, and set out with Shi Pantuo that same night and finally made it out of Yumen Pass. They slept in a grassy spot, getting ready to march westward.

Unexpectedly, after riding for a while Shi Pantuo balked at going any further with him, and even had a mind killing Xuanzang. Thus, Xuanzang sent him away.

From then on Xuanzang traveled alone, groping his way forward through the desert. After about eighty *li*, he came to the first fortress. Fearing detection by the guards, he hid in a sand pit during the day, and came out that night to sneak up and get some water. When he was getting ready to fill his leather flask, an arrow whizzed by, narrowly missing his knee. Knowing he had no hope of running away, he shouted in the direction of the fortress, "Don't shoot! I am a monk from Chang'an."

The soldiers stopped shooting and opened the gate to let Xuanzang in. By happy coincidence Wang Xiang, the subcommander of the fortress, was a Buddhist. After learning Xuanzang's background and plans, not only did he not make a fuss, but he had his flask filled with water, gave him some bread, and personally escorted him for several miles, giving him directions to the fourth fortress via a shortcut.

The subcommander of the fourth fortress was of the same clan as Wang Xiang. After learning that Xuanzang had been sent there by Wang Xiang, he offered warm hospitality. He warned him that the guards at the fifth fortress were mean, and that it was best to skip that fortress and get his water at the Wild Horse Springs instead. From there on out he would have to trek through eight hundred *li* of desert sand.

One hundred *li* from the fourth fortress Xuanzang got lost and could not find the Wild Horse Springs. When he raised his water flask for a drink of water, he accidentally dropped it and all the water was spilled onto the sand. It would be impossible to cross a desert without water, so Xuanzang made his way back toward the fourth fortress. However, he remembered after a few *li* his vow that he would not turn back before reaching his destination. How could he turn back now as soon as he encountered a difficulty? With that thought he turned his horse around and continued his westward journey.

In the vast, boundless desert, not a bird or beast was to be seen. Gusts of whirling wind sent up sand that filled the sky and fell back to the earth like a rain storm. Xuanzang traveled through the desert for five days without drinking a drop of water, his mouth parched with thirst and seemingly on fire. He finally succumbed and fainted. Late on the fifth night, a cool breeze resuscitated Xuanzang. He stood up and walked with his horse for several miles before encountering a grassy patch and a pond. With water and grass, both man and horse had a new lease on life. After two more days of travel, they finally left the desert. Passing Yiwu (modern-day Hami, Xinjiang) they reached Gaochang (east of modern-day Turfan, Xinjiang).

Qu Wentai, the king of Gaochang, was also a Buddhist. When he learned that Xuanzang was an eminent monk from the Tang Empire, he was filled with respect and asked him to give lectures on Buddhist scriptures. The king sincerely invited Xuanzang to stay in Gaochang but Xuanzang firmly declined. Unable to make him stay, Qu Wentai fixed him up with fresh supplies and provided an escort composed of 25 men and 30 horses. The king prepared letters to the kings of 24 kingdoms along the way, asking them to facilitate and protect Xuanzang's passage.

Xuanzang and his entourage struggled across snow-capped mountains and glaciers, through storms and avalanches before finally arriving in Suiye (near modern-day Tokmok in the north of Kyrgyzstan), where he was received by the Khan of Western Tujue. From that point on, it was smooth sailing through the kingdoms of the Western Regions to his destination, India.

India was the cradle of Buddhism and boasted many ancient sites important to Buddhism. Xuanzang traveled across India, undertaking pilgrimages to sacred sites and learning from eminent monks. Once when he was being ferried across the Ganges, he ran into a band of bandits. In their benighted adoration of some evil gods, they needed human sacrifices every fall. The bandits in the boat had their eyes on Xuanzang, and were going to kill him as sacrifice to their gods. No amount of explanation on Xuanzang's part did any good. Xuanzang closed his eyes and began to recite his mantras. By coincidence a strong wind sprang up at that precise moment, whipping up huge waves on the river, nearly causing the boat to capsize. The bandits, awestruck and filled with dread, knelt before him in contrition and Xuanzang was spared. The news of this episode soon spread and local people were led to believe that Xuanzang had the protection of some Buddhist charms.

There was a big, ancient temple called Nalanda Temple in Magadha, India, where Xuanzang studied for five years under Silabhadra, a prominent scholar, and familiarized himself with all the Buddhist texts there.

King Harshavardhana of Magadha was a devout Buddhist. When the fame of Xuanzang reached his ears, he invited him to give a series of lectures in his capital Kanyakubja (modern-day Kanauj, Uttar Pradesh). The conference was attended by the kings of eighteen kingdoms in India and more than three thousand monks, and included interactive dialogues and debates. During the eighteen days of the conference, Xuanzang inspired great admiration among the participants, who were won over to his views. Finally King Harshavardhana had Xuanzang's kasaya raised in veneration and pronounced the seminar successfully concluded.

When King Harshavardhana received Xuanzang, he mentioned having heard about a warrior king called the Prince of Qin. Xuanzang told him that the Prince of Qin was now the emperor of the Tang Empire.

Xuanzang's travels not only made a significant contribution to the development of Buddhism, but fostered cultural exchanges between the East and the West. In 645 AD, he brought more than six hundred Buddhist works back to Chang'an, a city he had not seen for more than a decade.

The heroic saga of Xuanzang's fearless, single-minded quest for Buddhist scriptures created quite a sensation among the citizens of Chang'an. Emperor Taizong, who was in Luoyang, had high praise for Xuanzang's feat and received him in his palace in Luoyang to hear a detailed report on his odyssey through the Western Regions.

After his return, Xuanzang settled down and devoted his life to the translation of the Buddhist scriptures he brought back from India. Together with his disciples he compiled *Records of the Western Regions of the Great Tang Dynasty*, which chronicled the geography, customs and mores of the one hundred and ten kingdoms he had visited and twenty-eight kingdoms he had heard about. It is an important book about history and geography.

The legendary nature of Xuanzang's quest spawned a slew of folk myths about the Tang monk, his quest for Buddhist scriptures and his numerous encounters with evil genies and monsters on the way, which were all fiction of course. During the Ming dynasty, the novelist Wu Cheng'en put artistic touches to the folk legends and created a wonderful novel, *Journey to the West*, which went on to become one of the classics of Chinese literature. The stories told in the book, however, are at best only remotely related to the reality of Xuanzang's adventures.

103. Princess Wencheng Goes to Tubo

AFTER QUASHING THE Eastern Tujue, Emperor Taizong of Tang sent Li Jing to defeat the Tuyuhun (an ethnic minority in ancient China that was active in what is now Qinghai Province) in the southwest, ensuring an unobstructed passage through the Western Regions and greatly facilitating exchanges between kingdoms in the west and the Tang Empire. Even the Tubo (a regime established by China's Tibetan minority in ancient China) in the far southwest sent its envoy to China.

In that period the tsenpo (title of the kings in Tubo) was Songtsan Gampo, a leader well-known for his literary as well as military talents. Since the age of thirteen, he had mastered martial skills such as horsemanship, archery and swordsmanship. He had also developed a strong interest in folk songs and a fine style in writing verse, and enjoyed great popularity among the people of Tubo. In the wake of his father's death, the aristocracy of Tubo started a mutiny which was soon quelled by Songtsan Gampo in a display of bravery and resourcefulness.

The young Songtsan Gampo was not content with living a high life like the rest of the aristocracy of Tubo. With a view to absorbing the Tang culture, he sent a mission to faraway Chang'an to seek friendly relations with the Tang Empire.

Having heard good things about Tubo, Emperor Taizong of Tang responded positively to the overtures and reciprocated the good will by sending emissaries to Tubo.

Two years later, Songtsan Gampo sent an envoy to Chang'an to request marriage with a Tang princess, but Emperor Taizong demurred. The Tubo envoy, fearing the chiding of Songtsan Gampo for his incompetence, told his king a lie upon his return to Tubo, "The Tang emperor was on the point of agreeing to marry his princess to Tubo, but the matter was put aside only because the Tuyuhun king also demanded her hand."

Relations between the Tubo and the Tuyuhun kingdoms had already been tense before Songtsan Gampo heard this report from his envoy to Chang'an. Now his resentment against the Tuyuhun rose to a new pitch. He immediately threw 200,000 troops against the Tuyuhun kingdom. The king of the Tuyuhun, driven by the strong offensive of the Tubo army, entrenched himself in the Huanhai area.

After defeating the Tuyuhun, Songtsan Gampo pressed his new military advantage by attacking Songzhou (modern-day Songpan, Sichuan Province) inside Tang territory and winning another major victory. Inflated by his military feats, Songtsan Gampo sent an envoy to the Tang court with the threat, "If I do not get to marry your princess, I am taking my troops into Chang'an."

The furious Emperor Taizong sent an army led by his general Hou Junji on a counterattack. The Tubo generals had never approved of their king's deliberate provocation of a war with the Tang Empire, and they clamored as one man for a pullback in the face of a massive response by the Tang army. Songtsan Gampo also realized that if he persisted in his foolhardy venture, he was doomed to certain defeat. He decided to sue for peace with the Tang. Emperor Taizong, whose intention to maintain friendly relations with Tubo had never changed, readily agreed to a peace accord.

In 640 AD, Songtsan Gampo again sent a seasoned envoy, Lu Dongzan (Blon-stong-btsan), at the head of a 100-member delegation carrying 5,000 taels of gold and many rare treasures to Chang'an to propose marriage. Blon-stong-btsan was received by Emperor Taizong, who was won over by the charming way Blon-stong-btsan conveyed his young king's wish to be on friendly terms with the Tang Empire. He selected a beautiful and gentle-mannered lady from among the younger generation of the royal family, gave her the title of Princess Wencheng, promising her hand to Songtsan Gampo.

Legend says the envoy Blon-stong-btsan was one of the smartest men in his time. He became a legend in a moving story later circulated among the inhabitants of the Qinghai-Tibet Plateau called "The Marriage Envoy Who Took on Five Challenges." The story is recapped here:

When Blon-stong-btsan arrived in Chang'an to request marriage on behalf of his king, there was a host of envoys from other kingdoms with the same object. Emperor Taizong devised a test of five challenges to be taken by these foreign marriage envoys. A royal marriage would be arranged with the country whose envoy correctly mastered all five challanges.

The first challenge was to pass a thin silk thread through a pearl's crooked hole, which had nine bends. Blon-stong-btsan tied the silk thread to the waist of an ant, which crawled through the pearl's nine-bend channel pulling the thread out the other end.

The second challenge was to tell which foals were the offspring of which mares in a group of a hundred foals and a hundred mares. Blon-stong-btsan separated the mares from the foals for one day, and denied fodder and water to the foals. The next day when the mares and the foals were reunited, the hungry foals ran to their respective mothers for milk. In this way, Blon-stong-btsan was able to match the foals to their mothers.

After clearing one hurdle after another, Blon-stong-btsan now faced the moment of truth. The last puzzle was to pick out Princess Wencheng from a bevy of 2,500 young beauties. With his sharp eyes, he was able to quickly identify the princess by her graceful manners.

Although these tales are unlikely to have been based on fact, they reflect the Tubo people's friendly intentions toward the Tang, and their praise for the envoy who accomplished his mission.

In 641 AD, the 24-year-old Princess Wencheng set out for Tubo under the escort of Li Daozong, the Prince of Jiangxia. The Tang court prepared a generous dowry, consisting of the customary gold, silver, jewelry, silk and satin, as well as goods that were unavailable in Tubo, such as grain, fruit, vegetable seeds, medicinal materials, and silkworm eggs. She also took along tomes of books on medicine, tree planting, engineering, astronomy and calendric systems.

As news of Princess Wencheng's marriage spread to Tubo, there was no shortage of horses, yaks, boats, food at the ready all the way from the Tang border through Tubo to ensure the comfort of the princess. Songtsan Gampo traveled all the way from Rasa (modern-day Lhasa) to Baihai (Lake Eling or Lake Zhaling in modern-day Qinghai) to meet her. They had a sumptuous wedding there.

After the wedding, Songtsan Gampo and Princess Wencheng traveled across snow-capped mountains and plateaus to arrive at Rasa. On the day of Princess Wencheng's arrival in town, the inhabitants of Rasa turned out en masse in a festive mood, dancing and singing in the streets to welcome her. Songtsan Gampo commissioned the construction of a Tang-style walled palace for the princess in Rasa.

In her forty years in Tubo, Princess Wencheng was instrumental in fostering friendship and exchanges between the Han and the Tibetan ethnic communities and in promoting Tibet's economic and cultural development. The statues of Songtsan Gampo and Princess Wencheng have been maintained to this day in the Jokhang Temple and the Potala Palace in Tibet for worshippers' veneration.

In 650 AD, Songtsan Gampo died. Emperor Taizong of Tang died of illness before him in 649 and was succeeded by his crown prince Li Zhi as Emperor Gaozong of Tang.

104. Empress Wu Zetian

EMPEROR TAIZONG WAS a shrewd and capable ruler, but his son, Emperor Gaozong, turned out to be an unremarkable, incompetent monarch. After his accession, he was ignorant of statecraft and depended on his uncle, Prime Minister Zhangsun Wuji, to make all the decisions for him. The situation changed with his naming Wu Zetian as his queen.

Wu Zetian had been an imperial concubine in Emperor Taizong's harem. She started waiting on Taizong when she was fourteen. In that period Taizong had in his imperial stable a famous horse called Lion, a strong, handsome but also foul-tempered and balky animal. Once, when taking his concubines to see the horse, Emperor Taizong jokingly said to them, "Who among you can tame this horse?"

In the awed silence, the fourteen year old Wu Zetian bravely stepped out of the group and said, "Yes, Your Majesty, I can!"

The surprised Taizong stared at her, asking how she proposed to do it. Wu Zetian replied, "Just let me have three things: an iron whip, an iron hammer and a dagger. If the horse acts up, I will whip it; if he still refuses to submit, I will hit his head with the hammer; if he continues to make mischief, I will cut off his head with the dagger."

Emperor Taizong had a hearty laugh at her bravura. Although he found Wu Zetian's idea on the childish side, he liked her spunky temperament.

After the death of Emperor Taizong, following established court protocol Wu Zetian was sent to a Buddhist nunnery, obviously against her wish.

Emperor Gaozong had already had his eye on Wu Zetian from his days as a Crown Prince. Two years after his accession, he released Wu Zetian from the nunnery and conferred the title of *Zhaoyi* on her. He intended to demote Empress Consort Wang and replace her with Wu Zetian, but ran into strong opposition from the older ministers, especially his uncle Zhangsun Wuji, who was adamantly against the idea.

Privately Wu Zetian lobbied a number of ministers to push for her to replace Empress Wang as the Empress Consort. Some of these argued in front of Emperor Gaozong, "This is Your Majesty's private affair and brooks no interference from others." This clinched his determination to demote Empress Wang and replace her with Wu Zetian.

After becoming Empress Consort, Wu Zetian showed her spunky, ruthless side to the world in punishing those opposed to her by demoting and banishing them. Even Zhangsun Wuji was forced to commit suicide.

Shortly afterwards, the incompetent Gaozong was further debilitated by an illness that left him in a constant state of bleary-eyed dizziness. Sometimes he had difficulty opening his eyes. Seeing that Wu Zetian was capable and literate, Emperor Gaozong decided to hand over to her the affairs of state.

With the reins of power in her hands, Wu Zetian became dismissive of Emperor Gaozong. Without her approval, Gaozong was unable to move anything on his agenda. The emperor resented the situation and consulted the Prime Minister, Shangguan Yi, about it. Opposed to Wu Zetian's grab of power, Shangguan Yi said, "Since Your Majesty resents the Empress Consort's highhandedness, why don't you demote her?"

The weak-willed Gaozong immediately agreed and ordered Shangguan Yi to draw up a decree.

Their conversation was overheard by a eunuch who happened to be a partisan of Wu Zetian's. He reported it to Wu. When Shangguan Yi handed the completed decree to Emperor Gaozong, Wu Zetian turned up and demanded in a stern voice, "What is this?"

Seeing Wu Zetian, Emperor Gaozong appeared to shrivel in size. Hiding the draft decree in his sleeve, he stammered out, "It was not my idea. Shangguan Yi talked me into it."

Wu Zetian had Shangguan Yi summarily executed.

From then on Wu Zetian became a fixture at the daily imperial audiences of Emperor Gaozong, watching the goings-on with an eagle eye. All matters, big or small, required a nod from her prior to a decision.

After Emperor Gaozong of Tang died in 683 AD, Wu Zetian set up her two sons as emperor in quick succession, but neither Li Xian (Emperor Zhongzong) nor Li Dan (Emperor Ruizong) made the grade in her eyes. Deposing Zhongzong and placing Ruizong under house arrest, she ruled as regent in her capacity as Empress Dowager. Her move met with opposition from some ministers and members of the royal household.

This also gave Xu Jingye, an official demoted by Wu Zetian, a pretext for starting a rebellion against Wu Zetian in Yangzhou. When Wu Zetian consulted the Prime Minister, Pei Yan, on this matter, he said, "The emperor has come of age. As long as he is prevented from governing, there is always an excuse to make trouble. The moment the Empress Dowager returns power to the emperor, Xu Jingye's rebellion will go away."

Believing that Pei Yan, like Xu Jingye, wished to force her to give up power, Wu Zetian, in a fit of anger, threw Pei Yan in jail and sent 300,000 troops on a punitive campaign against Xu Jingye. Greatly outnumbered and without external support, Xu Jingye was defeated after putting up a short-lived resistance.

Subsequently a revolt by two members of Tang royalty—Li Zhen, the Prince of Yue, and Li Chong, the Prince of Lanya—was also quashed by Wu Zetian.

After these two mutinies, the country regained peace, and no one dared challenge Wu Zetian again. With her rule firmly established, Wu Zetian was no longer content with governing as Empress Dowager.

Wu Zetian's ambition did not escape the keen eye of a perspicacious monk, who presented to her a Buddhist sutra that he himself had made up. The sutra claimed that Wu Zetian was in reality Maitreya reincarnated, and was sent down by Buddha to govern the Tang Empire on behalf of the emperor.

A few months later, an official called Fu Youyi got 900 people in the Guanzhong area to sign a petition asking the Empress Dowager to accede to the throne. Wu Zetian, while demurring, went ahead and gave Fu Youyi a promotion. This had the effect of encouraging more and more people to come out in favor of her accession to the throne. By some counts similar petitions were presented by more than 60,000 people, including civil and military leaders, members of the aristocracy, common folks near and far, and headmen of ethnic communities, as well as Buddhist and Daoist monks.

In September of 690 AD, Wu Zetian bowed to popular demand and gave herself the title of Emperor Shengshen, changing the dynasty name to Zhou. She became the only female emperor in China's history.

105. Di Renjie Commands the Loyalty of the Nation's Cream of the Crop

WHILE ON THE one hand, Wu Zetian ruthlessly stamped out all opposition to her power grab, on the other she was keen to use the best people she could find for her administration. She sent out talent scouts across the country, and whenever they found someone possessing needed talent, they would be invited to join the government. This occurred regardless of family background, experience or seniority. As a result, she was able to surround herself with a capable group of ministers, the most celebrated of them being her Prime Minister, Di Renjie.

As the Governor of Yuzhou, Di Renjie had distinguished himself and won public trust by fairly and strictly enforcing the law. Impressed by his abilities, Wu Zetian summoned him to the capital to be her Prime Minister.

Wu Zetian said to Di Renjie one day, "You've made a good name for yourself during your administration of Yuzhou, but there are some who badmouth you in front of me. Do you want to know who they are?"

Di Renjie replied, "If my critics happen to be right, then I should rectify my mistakes. It will be my good fortune if Your Majesty finds out I am not at fault after all. I have no interest in knowing who speak ill of me behind my back."

Di Renjie rose in Wu Zetian's esteem as a result of this display of magnanimity.

Lai Junchen, a nasty beaurucrat who wielded great influence, had Di Renjie thrown in jail on trumped-up charges of plotting a revolt. Trying to force a confession out of Di, Lai Junchen dangled this bait before him, "If you confess, you'll be spared the death sentence."

Di Renjie replied unconcernedly, "With the founding of the Zhou dynasty by the Empress Dowager, the country needs a fresh start in everything. It stands to reason that an official left over from the Tang dynasty like me should be eliminated. You'll have my confession."

Another official whispered to Di Renjie, "If you can name your co-conspirators, you'll be let off easy."

Di Renjie became angry at hearing this and said, "Heaven and earth be my witness! There is no way Di Renjie would stoop so low!" In a rage he rammed his head into a post in the jailhouse. His face became instantly covered with blood. The official got scared and did his best to calm him down.

Based on the coerced confession, Lai Junchen relaxed the security around Di Renjie. Taking advantage of a guard's momentary lapse of vigilance, Di tore a scrap of cloth from his quilt, wrote a complaint on it and sewed it into the lining of his winter tunic.

It was springtime, and so Di said to the warden, "It is getting warmer and I have no use for this warm clothing. Could you please send for my servant to take it home?"

The unsuspecting warden allowed Di's servant on his next visit to take the tunic home. Di's son found Di's complaint in the lining of the tunic, and sent it to Wu Zetian.

After reading the complaint, Wu Zetian ordered Di Renjie released from jail. Wu asked Di, "Since you profess innocence, why did you confess in the first place?"

Di Renjie replied, "If I had not confessed, they would have tortured me to death."

Wu Zetian commuted Di Renjie's death sentence, but took away his title as Premier, and demoted him to county magistrate away from the capital. It was only after Lai Junchen was killed that

Di Renjie was reinstated as Prime Minister.

Before Di Renjie had ever became Prime Minister, the General, Lou Shide, had often sung his praises in front of Wu Zetian. Unaware of this, Di Renjie thought of him as just another general.

On one occasion, Wu Zetian pointedly asked Di Renjie, "What do you think of Lou Shide?"

Di Renjie replied, "Lou Shide is fine as a dutiful general commanding a border garrison. As for any outstanding abilities and qualities, I must plead ignorance."

Wu Zetian went on, "Do you think Lou Shide is good at discerning talent?"

Di Renjie said, "I've worked with him, and have not heard seen this quality."

Wu Zetian said with a smile, "I discovered you because of Lou Shide's recommendations."

Di Renjie was deeply touched. He knew that he could in no way equal Lou Shide's generosity of spirit and kindness. From then on, Di became more active in seeking out people of talent and recommending them to Wu Zetian.

One day Wu Zetian said to Di Renjie, "I need a recommendation from you as to a capable man."

Di asked, "What kind of abilities is Your Majesty looking for?"

Wu Zetian replied, "I'm looking for someone capable of being a Prime Minister."

Di Renjie had long known of an official in the prefectural government of Jingzhou by the name of Zhang Jianzhi, who was an efficient administrator despite his advanced age. He knew he would be a good candidate for premiership. Upon his recommendation, Wu Zetian promoted Zhang Jianzhi to Deputy Governor of Luozhou (with its seat at Luoyang).

A few days later Wu Zetian again asked Di Renjie about his recommendations. Di said, "I already recommended Zhang Jianzhi but Your Majesty has not yet appointed him."

Wu Zetian said, "Haven't I already appointed him?"

Di Renjie said, "I have recommended a candidate for the position of Prime Minister, not as a Deputy Governor."

Wu Zetian soon promoted Zhang Jianzhi to Deputy Minister,

and eventually appointed him as Prime Minister.

Like Zhang Jianzhi, several dozen people were recommended by Di Renjie at different times, and all became prominent ministers of their time. These ministers had great admiration for Di Renjie and considered him their mentor. Some remarked to Di Renjie, "You've collected the cream of the crop of the country."

Di Renjie replied in humility, "I recommend people of talent in the interest of the country, not for my own profit."

Di Renjie lived to the ripe old age of 93. Wu Zetian venerated him as Guo Lao or "Elder of the Nation." His repeated requests to be allowed to retire to his home town were denied by Wu Zetian. After his death, Wu Zetian was often heard to say with a sigh, "Why has heaven taken away my Guo Lao so soon?"

In 705 AD, Wu Zetian became gravely ill. Taking advantage of her illness, Prime Minister Zhang Jianzhi and some other officials took over the imperial guard and restored Emperor Zhongzong of Tang to the throne. Soon afterwards, Wu Zetian died.

After his restoration, Emperor Zhongzong allowed power to fall into the hands of his consort, Queen Wei, who created chaos in the running of the state. Following the death of Zhongzong in 710 AD, Li Longji, a son of Emperor Ruizong, killed Queen Wei in a coup and restored Ruizong to the throne. Two years later Ruizong abdicated in favor of Li Longji, who became Emperor Xuanzong of Tang.

After his accession, Emperor Xuanzong of Tang devoted his energies to putting the country back on a path to peace and prosperity. He purged his court and turned the chaotic administration of the Zhongzong period around. Prosperity returned to the Tang Empire. In the first two decades of his rule, the Tang dynasty was once again a powerful empire with brimming coffers. It is said that the storehouses of its prefectural and county governments were piled high with grain and fabric, and the price of rice and cloth in Chang'an and Luoyang fell steadily. This is known historically as the "Benign Reign of Kaiyuan" (Kaiyuan being the title of Xuanzong's reign).

106. Li Linfu, a Tongue of Honey and a Heart of Cruelty

TWENTY YEARS INTO his peaceful reign, Emperor Xuanzong of Tang grew arrogant and complacent. Thinking he had no reason to worry while peace reigned in the empire, which was well administered by his Prime Minister and ably defended by the generals of the border garrisons, he began devoting less attention to affairs of state and pursuing a life of pleasure. Zhang Jiuling, his Prime Minister, was worried by this and raised frequent objections before the emperor. Although Zhang Jiuling had always enjoyed the respect and trust of Emperor Xuanzong, the emperor became increasingly impervious to his objections.

Li Linfu, an unschooled and uncultured minister, was incompetent in everything except in the art of flattery. He consorted with court eunuchs and imperial concubines in order to stay abreast of the goings-on in the palace. He was one of the first to know what Emperor Xuanzong had been saying or thinking. Therefore, when Emperor Xuanzong called him in for consultation, he was always able to quickly come up with ideas that bore an uncanny resemblance to Xuanzong's own thoughts. Emperor Xuanzong was soothed by these ready responses, and found Li Linfu to be capable and compliant. That was more than he could say for Zhang Jiuling!

Emperor Xuanzong of Tang consulted Zhang Jiuling about his intention to promote Li Linfu to Prime Minister. Knowing Li Linfu was a scoundrel, Zhang Jiuling made no bones of his objection,

"The position of Prime Minister is pivotal to the country's well-being and survival. If Your Majesty made Li Linfu Prime Minister, it would have disastrous consequences for the country."

When this conversation was reported to Li Linfu, he gnashed his teeth in hatred for Zhang Jiuling.

There was a general in Shuofang (with its seat in what is modern-day Lingwu, Ningxia) called Niu Xianke, who was an expert money manager despite his illiteracy. Emperor Xuanzong's proposal to promote Niu Xianke did not win Zhang Jiuling's support. Li Linfu said to Emperor Xuanzong, "Someone like Niu Xianke is the best candidate to the post of Prime Minister. Zhang Jiuling is bookish and doesn't see the big picture."

When Emperor Xuanzong summoned Zhang Jiuling on a subsequent occasion to once again discuss promoting Niu Xianke, Zhang still would not give his consent. Emperor Xuanzong lost his temper, chiding him in a stern voice, "Do you think you are the master of every decision?"

Emperor Xuanzong's increasing dislike of Zhang Jiuling, fueled by Li Linfu's constant calumnies, led to Zhang Jiuling being dismissed on a pretext, and replaced by Li Linfu as Prime Minister.

Once in the position of Prime Minister, Li Linfu set out to accomplish his first order of business, which was to insulate Emperor Xuanzong from the other ministers and counselors, who were now forbidden to give advice to the emperor. He called together the Remonstrance Officials and publicly declared to them, "The emperor is a wise ruler. All we need to do is comply with his wishes. There is no need for us to second-guess him. Look at the horses used in the imperial honor guard! They are fed food worthy of third-rank officials, but if any of them gives a neigh, it will be taken out of service without mercy."

A Remonstrance Official ignored Li Linfu's directive and presented a proposal before Emperor Xuanzong. The next day he received orders demoting him to county magistrate in a remote locality. Everyone knew this was Li Linfu's doing. From then on, no one dared to provide advice to the emperor.

Li Linfu was well aware of his bad reputation among the court officials. He did his best to push out any minister who outshined him. He did it quietly, always maintaining a smiling mask that belied his unrelenting back-stabbing.

One day, Emperor Xuanzong saw from a second-story window his Deputy Minister of War, Lu Xuan, ride past the building. He marveled at his military bearing. The next day when Li Linfu heard about the emperor's praise for Lu Xuan, he demoted him to Governor of Huazhou. Shortly after Lu Xuan took up his post in Huazhou, he was demoted a second time on the false pretext of poor health and unsuitability for the job.

Another official, Yan Tingzhi had been transferred to a remote prefecture as governor. Emperor Xuanzong asked Li Linfu one day, "Is Yan Tingzhi still around? He is a capable man and I can use a man like that."

Li Linfu replied, "Since Your Majesty misses him, I'll find out."

After the imperial audience, Li Linfu sent for Yan Tingzhi's younger brother and said to him, "I know your brother wishes very much to come back to the capital to see the emperor. I have an idea."

Yan Tingzhi's younger brother was grateful for Li Linfu's concern for his brother and was eager to know more. Li Linfu said, "Just ask your brother to write a memorial to the emperor, saying he is ill and wants to come to the capital for treatment."

After reading his younger brother's letter, Yan Tingzhi wrote a memorial to request leave to return to the capital for medical treatment. Li Linfu took the memorial to the emperor and said, "It's a pity. Yan Tingzhi is now gravely ill and can no longer handle important responsibilities."

Emperor Xuanzong gave a sigh and the matter was forgotten.

There was no shortage of people who had been conned like Yan Tingzhi. However, for all the clever subterfuges of Li Linfu, his intrigues and underhanded schemes were eventually found out. Li Linfu was described as someone who had "a tongue of honey and a heart of cruelty"—more to be feared than a dagger-thrust. This is the origin of the Chinese phrase *kou mi fu jian*, or "a mouthful of honey, bellyful of daggers."

In the nineteen years of Li Linfu's premiership, all upright ministers were marginalized and scoundrels good at flattery and in cultivating connections were promoted in large numbers. From this point on, the Tang government went into decline. The prosperity of the "Benign Reign of Kaiyuan" gave way to the "Tianbao Rebellion" (Tianbao being the title of the reign of Emperor Xuanzong of Tang in its later years).

107. Li Bai Has a Low Opinion of the Rich and Mighty

AT THE AGE of 61, Emperor Xuanzong of Tang became enamored of his young concubine Yang (called Yang Guifei. Guifei was the highest ranking imperial concubine), who was, according to legend, a rare beauty. She was clever and bright and musically gifted. She obtained royal appointments for two of her brothers from Emperor Xuanzong and the title of "Lady" for three of her sisters. Yang Zhao (who later changed his name to Yang Guozhong), a distant cousin of Yang Guifei, fell on hard times in what is now Sichuan. When he heard his young cousin had been made guifei, he traveled to Chang'an bringing gifts to see her. After Yang Guifei put in a few words of praise for him to Emperor Xuanzong, Yang Guozhong was made Adjutant of the Imperial Guard.

By that time, Emperor Xuanzong had already given the reins of state over to Li Linfu. Since Yang Guifei entered his harem, he spent more time than ever indulging in revelries in his inner palace, eventually neglecting even the duty of presiding over the daily imperial audiences. He did everything he could to satisfy Yang Guifei's every whim. Yang Guifei loved to eat fresh lychees, a fruit grown only in South China. How could they be delivered fresh to Chang'an, thousands of miles away in northwest China? To please Yang Guifei, Emperor Xuanzong ordered officials in what is today's Guangdong Province to rush the fruit by fast horses in uninterrupted relays to Chang'an. When the lychees were handed to Yang Guifei, they were still red and fragrant, without having lost any of their freshness.

At their daily carousing and drinking parties, Emperor Xuanzong and Yang Guifei would listen to tunes played and sung by court musicians. When they got tired of the same old tunes sung over and over again, Emperor Xuanzong looked about for new songs and lyrics.

An official called He Zhizhang mentioned to the emperor the arrival in Chang'an of the great poet Li Bai, who was a genius at writing both verse and prose. Having long heard of Li Bai's fame, Emperor Xuanzong directed He Zhizhang to summon Li Bai to the palace.

Li Bai, whose courtesy name was Taibai, was one of the most renowned poets of the Tang dynasty. He was born in Suiye and his father's family lived in Chengji of Longxi (east of modern-day Qin'an, Gansu). He was widely read when he was still a child and was a free spirit. Besides book knowledge, he also acquired skills in swordsmanship. In his twenties, Li Bai began traveling to broaden his horizons. His travels took him to big cities such as Chang'an, Luoyang, Jinling and Jiangdu, as well as to scenic spots like Lake Dongting, the Lushan Mountains and Guiji. Informed by his broad knowledge, experiences, and superior intellect, his writing scaled great heights.

Li Bai aspired to make a difference in politics. Haughty by nature, he was repulsed by the corrupt culture permeating the bureaucracy and hoped he would be given a chance by the imperial court to demonstrate his ability to clean up government. Thus he was thrilled when told the emperor wanted to see him.

At the imperial audience, Emperor Xuanzong found, after talking to Li Bai for a while, that he was indeed gifted. Delighted, he said to Li Bai, "You are a commoner, but even I have heard about you. That's because you possess real talent and erudition."

After the reception, Emperor Xuanzong kept Li Bai in the Hanlin Academy with the responsibility of drafting imperial edicts.

Li Bai had a weakness for wine. Once he started drinking, he could not stop until he was stone drunk. He could not kick the habit even after his appointment to the Hanlin Academy.

Whenever he got time off, he would gather his poet friends for a drink at a tavern in Chang'an.

Court musicians created a new tune one day at the behest of Emperor Xuanzong, but it needed lyrics. The emperor sent eunuchs to look for Li Bai, but failed to find him either at the Hanlin Academy or at his home. Someone told the eunuchs that Li Bai had gone out drinking.

After some searching in the streets of Chang'an, the eunuchs finally found him in a tavern, stone drunk and in deep slumber. When the eunuchs woke him and told him the emperor had summoned him, Li Bai rubbed his eyes and rose to his feet, asking what it was about. The eunuchs did not waste time explaining, but stuffed him into a sedan chair and hauled him to the palace.

Li Bai was carried into the inner palace. Raising his eyes, he saw Emperor Xuanzong in front of him. He tried to bow, but had no control over his own body. One of the eunuchs had to pour a bucket of cold water over his face to bring him out of his stupor. An admirer of his talent, Emperor Xuanzong did not chide him but told him to write the lyrics then and there.

The eunuchs quickly readied brush and ink, and spread a silk cloth on the low table before Li Bai. Soon after he sat down on the floor, Li Bai found the boots on his feet bothering him a lot. Seeing an elderly eunuch near him, he stretched out his legs and said to the eunuch, "Please take these boots off for me."

That eunuch was none other than the head eunuch, Gao Lishi, who was then in favor with the emperor. Emboldened by his status as a favorite, he had got accustomed to lording it over other officials. Now this minor bureaucrat at the Hanlin Academy had the nerve to order him to take off his boots for him! He nearly lost his head with rage but checked himself to keep from blowing up. After all, the emperor was waiting for Li Bai to finish the lyrics. Gao Lishi was not ready to take the consequences of spoiling the emperor's mood by offending Li Bai. Hiding his indignation and feigning unconcern he sighed and said with a smile, "What can you do with someone as drunk as that?" He then went down on his knees to take Li Bai's boots off.

Freed of his boots, and already turning away from Gao Lishi, Li

Bai picked up the brush and started to write in a "dragons-fly-and-phoenixes-dance" flourish. Shortly later, he handed three sets of lyrics in the style of *qingping* music to Emperor Xuanzong.

After reciting the lyrics a few times, the emperor found them to be elegantly written, with a lively rhythm. He loved the lyrics so much that he immediately asked the court musicians to perform the song.

Li Bai won the admiration of Emperor Xuanzong, but earned the eternal hatred of Gao Lishi, who had been compelled to take off his boots. One day, Yang Guifei took a stroll in the imperial garden with Gao Lishi in attendance, and in a happy mood started to sing a tune set to Li Bai's lyrics.

Gao Lishi reacted with feigned surprise, "Huh! This fellow Li Bai insulted the Guifei in these lyrics. Doesn't your ladyship realize it?"

Yang Guifei asked for an explanation. Gao Lishi fabricated some hearsay, embroidering it with the assertion that one sentence in Li Bai's verse pointedly compared Yang Guifei to Zhao Feiyan of the Han dynasty, a queen notorious for her loose morals. Falling for Gao Lishi's trickery, Yang Guifei took offense at Li Bai and began speaking ill of him in front of Emperor Xuanzong. Consequently, the emperor increasingly looked at Li Bai with an unfavorable eye.

Li Bai came to the realization that Emperor Xuanzong was surrounded by despicable characters like Li Linfu and Gao Lishi, who groveled before the powerful. By staying in the company of the emperor, he might at best provide some entertainment for the emperor, but he had lost any hope of making a difference in the political life of the country. The following spring, he presented his resignation to the emperor. As it perfectly suited Emperor Xuanzong, he readily agreed to the request. To show his appreciation for his talent, he sent Li Bai home with a "golden handshake."

After his departure from Chang'an, Li Bai returned to the carefree life of a poet, dividing his time between secluded periods of reading and travels. It was in this period that he produced many poems dedicated to the splendors of China's natural beauty.

On one of his trips he sailed from Baidi towards Jiangling

through the Three Gorges of the Yangtze River. Inspired by the landscape about him, he composed a poem:

Leaving Baidi, its walls clad
In the pink clouds of dawn,
I sailed three hundred miles
To Jiangling in barely a day;
The calls of the monkeys on the river banks
Still rang in my ears,
Even though my light bark was already
Ten thousand bluffs away.

Many of Li Bai's poems exhibit a boldness and freedom of spirit, rich imagination, and passion. They have become enduring masterpieces of Chinese literature. As Li Bai celebrated China's natural beauty in his poems, the corruption in the Tang government brought the country to disaster.

108. The Rebellion of An Lushan

DURING THE REIGN of Emperor Xuanzong of Tang, the need to beef up border defenses led to the establishment of ten *fanzhen* (military districts) in strategic border areas, each headed by a *jiedushi* (military commissioner). The powerful military commissioner had both the command of his troops and administrative and financial decision-making powers. According to the practice of the time, a military commissioner credited with outstanding achievements had a chance of being made Prime Minister.

After Li Linfu became all powerful, he not only did all he could to sideline other civil officials at the imperial court, but also kept a wary eye on the military commissioners defending China's borders. Wang Zhongsi was a military commissioner in charge of four districts. He had many military exploits to his credit, and had under him numerous valiant, battle-hardened generals of great renown, such as Geshu Han and Li Guangbi. Worried that the accomplishments and prestige of Wang Zhongsi might lead to his promotion as Prime Minister, Li Linfu had someone falsely accuse Wang Zhongsi of plotting to topple the emperor and replace him with the Crown Prince. This fabricated charge nearly cost Wang Zhongsi his life. It was only after Geshu Han forcefully vouched for Wang's innocence in front of Emperor Xuanzong that his life was spared, but the emperor still demoted him. Wang never recovered from the humility of being wrongly accused, and died after a short illness brought on by his indignation at being wronged.

In the border garrisons of that period there were some generals who were of Hu ethnicity. In the belief that these Hu generals were an uneducated lot and had no prospect of ever being elevated to the post of Prime Minister, Li Linfu began ardently advocating to Emperor Xuanzong that they be given important responsibilities. He argued that the Hu warriors were excellent combatants, and their loyalty was assured because they had no association with the court officials. Mutiny by his generals manning border defenses being one of his worst fears, Emperor Xuanzong heeded Li Linfu's advice and promoted some Hu generals to military commissioner.

Among these Hu military commissioners, one was looked on with particular favor by Emperor Xuanzong and Li Linfu. His name was An Lushan, the Military Commissioner of the Pinglu Military District (with its seat in what is now Chaoyang, Liaoning Province).

In his younger years, An Lushan was a general in the Pinglu garrison. However, he had suffered a defeat in a battle because he had disobeyed orders, and was sent by the commanding officer to Chang'an to await punishment. Zhang Jiuling, the Prime Minister at the time, sentenced An Lushan to death to enforce military discipline. However, Emperor Xuanzong, having heard of An Lushan's abilities, ordered his release.

Zhang Jiuling said to Emperor Xuanzong, "According to military law, An Lushan has to die because he has caused heavy casualties by disobeying his superior's orders. Besides, I've watched him carefully. He is not a good sort. I am afraid he will bring no end of grief if he is allowed to live."

Turning a deaf ear to Zhang Jiuling's exhortation, Emperor Xuanzong went ahead and pardoned An Lushan. Zhang Jiuling would later be fired. Meanwhile, through flattery and fawning, An Lushan rose rapidly through the ranks to become the Military Commissioner of the Pinglu District. In less than three years, he also became commander of the Fanyang District (with its seat in what is now Beijing).

After becoming Military Commissioner, An Lushan began collecting rare fowl and beasts, pearls and precious stones to be presented to Emperor Xuanzong in order to curry favor with him. Knowing that the emperor liked to hear news of military victories, he used underhanded ruses to lure chieftains and warriors of ethnic minorities in the Pinglu vicinity to feasts. At the feasts, he would drug the drinks so that he could easily have the soldiers killed and the heads of their leaders cut off. These heads would be presented to the imperial court as war trophies.

Emperor Xuanzong frequently summoned An Lushan to Chang'an. An Lushan seized these opportunities to please the emperor in his characteristic sly ways. He was portly and short. His pot belly and affectations of naiveté never failed to amuse Emperor Xuanzong.

On one occasion Emperor Xuanzong made fun of his bulging belly by saying, "What could be in such a big belly?"

An Lushan answered without thinking, "Nothing but a loyal heart."

An Lushan was thus able to reinforce in Emperor Xuanzong's mind the perception of his loyalty, and further ingratiate himself with the emperor. Emperor Xuanzong soon made An Lushan a Prince, and built in Chang'an a mansion for him that matched in sumptuousness the residences of members of the royal family. After An Lushan moved into his lordly mansion, every day Emperor Xuanzong sent over people for An Lushan to drink and feast with. With the emperor's encouragement, Yang Guifei adopted An Lushan as her son, and he got to enter and leave the palace at his pleasure like a member of the royal family.

Having won the trust of Emperor Xuanzong and Li Linfu by trickery, An Lushan soon received the command of the Hedong Military District (with its seat in what is now Taiyuan, Shanxi Province) in addition to his Fanyang and Pinglu commands, thus extending his control over most of the northern border. Secretly, he built up his troop strength, promoting valiant warriors such as Shi Siming and Cai Xide to general. For strategic planning and advice, he turned to Gao Shang and Yan Zhuang, who were of the Han ethnic group. He also assembled an elite force of 8,000 men. These men were selected from those soldiers of border tribes who had surrendered. He began to hoard grain and feed, and intensified military training, biding his time to stage a rebellion upon the death of Emperor Xuanzong.

When Li Linfu died of illness, Yang Guifei's relative Yang Guozhong succeeded him as Prime Minister on the strength of his blood ties with the imperial concubine. An Lushan had a low opinion of Yang Guozhong, because he was known as a hoodlum in his home town. At the same time, Yang Guozhong thought An Lushan was obnoxious. Tensions grew between the two men. Yang Guozhong had repeatedly warned Emperor Xuanzong that An Lushan was going to rebel sooner or later, but the warning was wasted, as An Lushan had gained the trust and favor of the emperor.

As time went on, however, signs of An Lushan's seditious intentions became more apparent. For example, he requested that the central government replace all 32 generals of the Han ethnic group in Fanyang, and grant him the discretion to appoint his own commanders. Then, when Emperor Xuanzong summoned An Lushan to Chang'an by handwritten edict, An Lushan would excuse himself on account of non-existent illnesses. Emperor Xuanzong began to have his doubts about An Lushan's loyalty, but neither the emperor nor Yang Guozhong could come up with a plan to forestall An Lushan's rebellion.

In October of 755 AD, An Lushan believed his meticulous preparations were complete, and he was ready to launch the long-planned rebellion. Taking advantage of the presence of an official who happened to be visiting from Chang'an, An Lushan fabricated an imperial edict supposedly issued by the emperor from Chang'an, and told his assembled troops, "I just received a top-secret order from the emperor instructing me to immediately march to the capital on a punitive action against Yang Guozhong."

His troops, caught by total surprise, looked at each other incredulously. However, no one dared to voice any doubt about an imperial edict.

The first thing the next morning, An Lushan marched his troops southward. The 150,000 infantry and cavalry troops advanced through the plains of Hebei to the beat of battle drums, setting off clouds of dust. The Central Plains had enjoyed a century of peace. Generations of people had not known what war was like, thus when the juggernaut of war rolled by, government officials either fled or submitted. The rebellious force of An Lushan continued its rapid advance towards the south, without meeting much of a resistance.

When news of the rebellion in Fanyang reached Chang'an, at first Emperor Xuanzong dismissed it as malicious rumor. However, as battle alerts kept pouring in, he began to panic and immediately called his ministers together for consultation. None of the ministers had ever had to face a crisis of such a magnitude, and all were petrified with fright. Yang Guozhong said gloatingly, "I told you An Lushan was going to rebel! But not to worry, Your Majesty! His troops will not go along with the rebellion. In ten days someone will present An Lushan's head on a platter to Your Majesty."

Emperor Xuanzong was somewhat reassured by this remark. They never dreamed that shortly thereafter rebellious troops would cross the Yellow River to take control of Luoyang.

109. Mutiny at the Post House of Mawei

TONGGUAN PASS WAS the gateway to the imperial capital Chang'an. It was a narrow pass through forbidding terrain, defended by Emperor Xuanzong's trusted General Geshu Han at the head of a large force. Cui Qianyou, a general in the rebellious army, tried to storm the pass for half a year without any success. Every night the defenders of the pass would kindle a fire on a beacon tower as signal that things were fine. This signal of reassurance would be relayed in like manner through a series of similar towers all the way to Chang'an, setting its inhabitants at ease.

While the rebellious troops were stalled at Tongguan Pass, the Tang court was riven by internal division. Geshu Han advocated a strictly defensive posture at Tongguan Pass, in preparation for an opportune moment for an offensive operation. At the same time, Guo Ziyi, the Military Commissioner of Shuofang, and Li Guangbi, the Military Commissioner of Hedong, wrote to the emperor from the front requesting permission to march their troops northward to attack Fanyang, An Lushan's home base, and warning against any sallies by the troops at Tongguan Pass to strike at the enemy force outside the pass.

Yang Guozhong, the Prime Minister, however, opposed this approach. Many people had said to Yang Guozhong, "Geshu Han now controls the bulk of the army. If he returns to Chang'an after defeating the rebellious force, your premiership will be in peril."

Knowing he was the least-popular Prime Minister ever, Yang Guozhong became increasingly alarmed. He argued to the emperor that the rebels outside Tongguan Pass were on their last legs, and if Geshu Han continued to hold off an attack, the opportunity of crushing the rebellion would be lost. The besotted Xuanzong bought this argument, and sent messenger after messenger to Tongguan ordering Geshu Han to launch an offensive.

Though well aware that such an action would have detrimental consequences, Geshu Han could not very well disobey the emperor's orders. Giving a shout, he led his troops out of the pass.

In the meantime, the troops of the rebel general Cui Qianyou had been well rested. This was the moment they had been waiting for. When the 200,000-strong Tang force led by Geshu Han sallied out of the pass, it ran into an ambush by elite troops placed near Lingbao (west of what is now Henan Province) by Cui Qianyou. The Tang troops were decimated. Out of the 200,000 combatants, only 80,000 survived.

Before Geshu Han had a chance to regroup, his lieutenants mutinied. Consequently, the victorious rebels captured Tongguan Pass and took Geshu Han prisoner.

With the loss of Tongguan to the enemy, there were no defensible natural barriers between it and Chang'an. Officials of local governments and troops all the way from Tongguan to Chang'an fled their posts in droves.

At first, messengers earlier sent by Geshu Han to Chang'an requesting reinforcements still arrived, but eventually these ceased. At night, the reassuring signal fires were not lit. Only then did Emperor Xuanzong finally realize the urgency and precariousness of the situation. In a panic, he sought advice from Yang Guozhong. Yang Guozhong called a meeting of the civil and military officials, but they were all frustrated, unable to come up with any good ideas to reverse the situation. Knowing that staying in Chang'an was no longer a viable option, Yang Guozhong advised Emperor Xuanzong to retreat to Shu territory.

That same evening, under the escort of General Chen Xuanli and the imperial guard, Emperor Xuanzong and Yang Guozhong, followed by Yang Guifei, and the children and grandchildren of the royal family, slipped out of the palace compound and fled Chang'an. They were preceded by eunuchs charged with making arrangements along the way for the proper reception of the imperial entourage by local officials.

Unexpectedly, when the entourage reached Xianyang, they found that both the advance team of eunuchs and the local county magistrates had all vanished into thin air! The entourage traveled for a long distance without anyone providing food to them. With some effort, the eunuchs in the entourage finally found some local residents and asked them for food. They produced a small quantity of coarse bread made from Chinese sorghum. It was something the high-living royalty had never before had to eat, but these hungry aristocrats wolfed it down anyways, handling the food with their hands, dispensing with chopsticks and bowls, as well as with ceremony.

As Emperor Xuanzong swallowed, with difficulty, a few morsels of the coarse bread, tears rolled down his cheeks. An old man squeezed through the crowd and approached the emperor's carriage. He said to the emperor, "An Lushan has been planning his rebellion for a long time. Many who denounced his sinister intentions to the government were killed in reprisal. Your Majesty is surrounded by ministers and counselors who do a good job of flattering and fawning on you, but insulate the emperor from what's been happening around the country. We ordinary people have known it would come to this one day, but the imperial court was so inaccessible it has been impossible to share our knowledge with Your Majesty. It is a pity that it has taken a catastrophe like this to enable us to present our views before Your Majesty."

Emperor Xuanzong replied dejectedly, "I have been such a fool. But it's already too late."

On the third day of the flight punctuated with pauses for rest, the entourage arrived at the post house at Mawei (west of modern-day Xingping County, Shaanxi Province). The troops escorting the imperial refugees were overwhelmed by hunger and exhaustion, and embittered by the thought that they had been forced to leave the comfort of Chang'an to wander the roads and endure no end of hardship. They blamed all the suffering on Yang Guozhong, and they intended to settle accounts with him.

Twenty or so Tubo emissaries encircled Yang Guozhong, who was in his saddle, demanding food from him. Before he had a chance to respond, the soldiers around him began to shout, "Yang Guozhong is starting a mutiny!" Then they unleashed their arrows.

Yang Guozhong panicked flight was intercepted by a few soldiers, who cut off his head.

After slaying Yang Guozhong, the soldiers, still in an agitated mood, surrounded the post house where Emperor Xuanzong had been lodged. The emperor demanded to know what the clamor outside his lodging was all about. The eunuchs in attendance told him that the soldiers had killed Yang Guozhong. The visibly shaken emperor, supporting himself with a cane, walked out of the post house to reassure the soldiers and asked them to return to their bivouac for rest.

The soldiers were not appeased and continued their clamor. Emperor Xuanzong sent Gao Lishi to fetch Chen Xuanli and asked him why the soldiers refused to disperse. Chen Xuanli replied, "They believe that since Yang Guozhong attempted to mutiny, her Ladyship Guifei can't be allowed to live."

Emperor Xuangzong was in a quandary. He did not have the heart to kill his favorite concubine. After a long pause for reflection, he lifted his head and said, "How could Lady Guifei, who was in her room, know about Yang Guozhong's mutiny?"

Well aware that the soldiers would be appeased only with thc death of Yang Guifei, Gao Lishi said, "Lady Guifei is innocent, but the troops have killed Yang Guozhong and their fear of reprisals would not be allayed if Lady Guifei were allowed to live. Your Majesty should weigh the matter carefully. After all, Your Majesty's safety depends on the loyalty of your troops."

To save his own neck, Emperor Xuanzong, steeling himself for the painful decision, told Gao Lishi to take Yang Guifei to an out-of-the-way spot. There, Gao Lishi strangled her. Informed of the execution of Yang Guifei, the troops retired to their bivouacs, finally feeling vindicated.

In the aftermath of the mutiny, Emperor Xuanzong, feeling flustered "like a bird who has just been missed by an arrow by a hair," scampered away to Chengdu. The Crown Prince, Li Heng, was asked by the local people of Mawei to stay and be their ruler. He collected stragglers and remnant troops on his way north from Mawei, and ascended the throne in Lingwu (southwest of modern-day Lingwu, Ningxia) with the title of Emperor Suzong of Tang.

110. Li Bi Retires to His Hermitage

WHEN EMPEROR SUZONG of Tang ascended the throne, he had fewer than thirty top civil and military officials to assist him. The provisional court was in a disorganized state. Some generals were less than ready to take orders from the emperor. To put down the rebellion, Emperor Suzong desperately needed the help of capable people.

He remembered from his days as Crown Prince a good friend named Li Bi. He sent for him in Yingyang (in what is modern-day Henan Province) to come to Lingwu.

Li Bi's home town was Chang'an. As a child, he was already known for his cleverness and his avid reading habits. Zhang Jiuling, the Prime Minister at the time, was much impressed by his poetry and called him a child prodigy. By the time Li Heng was made Crown Princc, Li Bi had already come of age and often presented his views on affairs of state to Emperor Xuanzong in written memos. Emperor Xuanzong enjoyed reading his memos, and summoned him with the intention of offering him a position in the government. Li Bi declined, pleading immaturity. Emperor Xuanzong then encouraged him to befriend the Crown Prince. Li Bi began to frequent the Eastern Palace, reserved for the Crown Prince. In turn, the Crown Prince enjoyed Li Bi's company and treated him as a mentor.

Li Bi, revolted by Yang Guozhong's abuse of power, wrote poems satirizing the Prime Minister, and as a consequence was banished from Chang'an by Yang. Disgusted by the political chaos, and not wishing to waste his life fretting about it, he went to

Yingyang to lead the life of a recluse.

When he received Emperor Suzong's invitation, he agreed to come to Lingwu because the Tang court was at a difficult juncture. When Emperor Suzong saw Li Bi, he was overjoyed as if he had just hit the jackpot. At the provisional court, protocol was dispensed with and the two were in each other's company most of the time, just as in their younger years. The emperor consulted Li Bi on everything, and heeded every piece of advice offered by him.

Emperor Suzong wanted him to be his Prime Minister, but Li Bi declined, saying "Your Majesty treats me like a bosom friend. This is a more honorable status than that of premiership. There is no need to give a title to me."

Realizing the firmness of Li Bi's refusal, Emperor Suzong did not insist. In Lingwu, Li Bi continued to wear the same cotton tunic he had worn when he as a rustic hermit.

On one occasion, when Li Bi rode with Emperor Suzong on an inspection of troops, thc soldiers pointed their fingers behind their backs and observed, "The one in the yellow robes is the emperor, and the one clad in a white, cotton tunic is a hermit who lived on a mountain."

After learning of the gossip among the soldiers, Emperor Suzong felt that Li Bi's tunic was too much of a distraction, and so insisted that he wear an official purple outfit. When Li Bi finally gave in, Emperor Suzong said with a laugh, "Now that you are in an official uniform, we must give you an official title." Producing an edict from his sleeve, he named him Army Aide of the Military Command.

When Li Bi continued to resist, Emperor Suzong said, "The country is in great difficulty, and I am sorry you are being forced into this. But once the rebellion is quashed, I'll let you do what you want."

At that time, Guo Ziyi had arrived in Lingwu. The Tang court had its hands full directing the war effort across the nation. Documents and messages poured in without interruption from all corners of the country day and night. Emperor Suzong ordered that all documents should go directly to Li Bi, and only those considered of utmost urgency would be opened by Emperor

Suzong in person. The Crown Prince, Li Chu, and Li Bi were made custodians of the keys to the palace doors. The heavy schedule gave Li Bi little time to eat and sleep properly.

Intent on returning to Chang'an, Emperor Suzong asked Li Bi, "How are we going to deal with an enemy as powerful as An Lushan?"

Li Bi replied, "Those who truly support him in his rebellion make up a minority. The rest have been forced into it. In my estimation, we can beat them within two years." He then went on to draw up a military plan for Emperor Suzong, which called for temporarily holding off any action to recover Chang'an, while Guo Ziyi and Li Guangbi would march their troops toward Hebei on a two-pronged attack on Fanyang, the home base of the rebel force. This would cause the rebel force to be split in two, giving an opening to government troops to converge on the rebel force from all sides and crush it.

The following spring, the rebel force suffered an internal rift when An Lushan was killed by his son, An Qingxu, who proclaimed himself Emperor. This would have been a good opportunity to deliver a coup de grace to the rebels. However, in his eagerness to return to Chang'an, Emperor Suzong deviated from Li Bi's plan and ordered Guo Ziyi to bring his troops back from Hedong and throw them against Chang'an. Guo Ziyi lost the initial battle. Eventually, he was able to capture Chang'an by putting together a force of 150,000 soldiers. He did this by incorporating elite troops borrowed from the Huihe (a northern minority in ancient China, also known as the Uyghur). He went on to recover Luoyang, forcing the rebel leader An Qingxu to flee to Hebei, and obtaining the surrender of Shi Siming.

After taking back Chang'an and Luoyang from the rebels, the jubilant Emperor Suzong had Li Bi escorted to Chang'an on a handsome steed.

Emperor Suzong's favorite concubine Zhang Liangdi and the eunuch Li Fuguo, however, had long been plotted together to eliminate Li Bi, who was too powerful for their comfort.

Li Chu, the Crown Prince, discovered Zhang Liangdi's plot against Li Bi and alerted him. Li Bi said, "That's all right. By an agreement with the emperor, I am free to retire to my hermitage once the capital is recaptured. And that settles it."

Since the Tang army had recovered both capitals, Li Bi considered his mission accomplished and made up his mind to leave the Tang court.

One evening Emperor Suzong invited Li Bi for a few drinks and asked him to sleep over. Li Bi seized the opportunity to say to Emperor Suzong, "I've repaid Your Majesty's trust. Please allow me to return to my carefree life."

Emperor Suzong replied, "I've shared so many years of prosperity and woe, and mostly woe, with you. Now that we can share more of the prosperity, why do you want to leave?"

Li Bi answered with candor, "I go back a long way with Your Majesty, too long. And Your Majesty has placed too much trust in me. It is precisely for that reason that I have to leave."

Emperor Suzong said, "Let's sleep on it."

Li Bi insisted, "You must give your consent tonight as we still sit together on the same couch, because I'll be deprived of a voice once I am hauled before a kangaroo court. If you refuse to let me go, you'll be pronouncing my death sentence."

Reluctant as he was to let Li Bi go, Emperor Suzong finally gave in to his insistent request.

Li Bi built a house up in the Hengshan Mountains (in Hunan Province) and resumed his life of seclusion.

With Li Bi gone, Emperor Suzong lost a counselor with integrity, and the power and influence of eunuchs such as Li Fuguo grew.

111. Li Guangbi Drubs Shi Siming

AFTER THE TANG government recaptured its two capitals, An Qingxu fled to Hebei and continued to put up a stiff resistance from a base made up of the sixty cities still under his control. Emperor Suzong decided to mount a massive operation to mop up An Qingxu's forces. The Tang expedition was joined by 600,000 troops commanded by nine military commissioners. Both Guo Ziyi and Li Guangbi had the stature and prestige to be the supreme commander of the nine armies, but the paranoid Emperor Suzong, wanting to curb the power of Guo and Li, deliberately left the position of supreme commander vacant. Instead, he appointed a eunuch, Yu Chaoen, who had no battle experience, as Inspector of the Armies, to whom all nine military commissioners must report.

When the Tang force attacked Yecheng, Shi Siming raced to An Qingxu's rescue. Before the 600,000 Tang troops had time to assume their battle formation for a showdown with the rebels, a strong gust blew across the battlefield, raising a storm of dust that obscured the daylight. Without a unified command, the nine armies of the Tang force dispersed in disarray like startled horses.

Yu Chaoen shifted the blame for the defeat to Guo Ziyi. Emperor Suzong believed Yu's version and stripped Guo of his position of Military Commissioner of Shuofang. His command was given to Li Guangbi.

A rift developed at this time inside the rebel force. Shi Siming killed An Qingxu in Yecheng, and then proclaimed himself Emperor of Greater Yan. He soon marched his troops toward Luoyang.

When Li Guangbi arrived in Luoyang, some local officials, frightened by the strong offensive launched by Shi Siming, advocated a pullback to Tongguan. Li Guangbi said to them, "The two sides are of equal strength. If we pull back now, the enemy will be emboldened. We could instead move our troops to Heyang (modern-day Meng County, Henan Province), from where we can opt for offense or defense."

Li Guangbi ordered the evacuation of all officials and residents from Luoyang, and moved his troops to Heyang. When Shi Siming entered the city of Luoyang, he found it devoid of people and food. Worried about possible surprise attacks by Li Guangbi, he left the city and entrenched his troops south of Heyang, in a face-off with the Tang force led by Li Guangbi.

Li Guangbi, a seasoned commander, knew that his troop strength was inferior to the enemy's and his only chance lay in trying to outsmart him. A frontal attack was out of the question. Having received intelligence that the 1,000 battle horses brought by Shi Siming from Hebei were led to the sandbars near the riverbank every day for watering and feeding, he arranged to have the mares in his army corralled in one place and the foals kept separately in the stables. When the battle steeds of the rebel force were brought to the sandbars, his troops let out their own mares, which commingled with the enemy horses. After a while the mares remembered their foals and started to neigh. As they ran back, the enemy horses followed them into the Tang camp.

The wholesale loss of his 1,000 battle steeds to the enemy infuriated Shi Siming. He immediately ordered several hundred battleships to launch an attack. The flotilla was preceded by boats set aflame with the purpose of burning down the Tang army's pontoons.

Li Guangbi got wind of this tactic. He responded by positioning hundreds of soldiers on the pontoons, wielding metal-tipped poles. When the flaming boats of the rebel force neared, the Tang soldiers staved off the attacking craft with the poles. Unable to advance further, the flaming boats burnt up and sank. The Tang troops then started to bombard the enemy battleships with huge stones, bloodying the rebel soldiers on board. Some ships sank, pulling their crews down to the bottom of the river. Some rebels struggled onto the riverbank and fled helter-skelter.

Repeated attacks by Shi Siming's generals on Heyang were foiled by Li Guangbi by his astute use of ruses.

In a determined push, Shi Siming threw a huge force against Heyang, with his general Zhou Zhi leading the attack on the North Gate of the city and himself commanding an elite contingent storming the South Gate. When Li Gaungbi and the rest of the brass surveyed the enemy movements from the embattlements on the North Gate, they were greeted by the sight of legions of enemy troops that extended to the horizon advancing towards them. The Tang generals did not say anything, but in their hearts they began to panic. Guessing what was on the generals' minds, Li Guangbi said to them calmly, "Don't be frightened by their numbers! You can see that they are a disorganized, undisciplined lot, and that they evidently have a high opinion of themselves. Don't worry! By noon we will crush them."

Li Guangbi ordered his troops deployed at various points to engage the enemy. No sooner had his valiant troops beat back the enemy troops' advance, however, than fresh enemy reinforcements took their place. By the time it was noon, no clear victor had emerged.

Li Guangbi called a meeting of his commanders and asked them, "In your assessment of the enemy deployments, where do you think their greatest fighting strength lies?"

His generals replied, "In the northwest and the southeast corners."

Nodding in agreement, Li Guangbi immediately deployed five hundred cavalrymen each under two generals to attack the northwest and the southwest flanks of the enemy formation.

He called the rest of his troops together and issued the strict order: "The troops will watch my flag before making a move. If I wave it slowly, it means you can fight as you see fit. If I agitate it vigorously, it will be the signal for a general attack. At that signal, you must advance toward the enemy resolutely. No turning back is allowed." Sticking a short sword in his boot he went on, "Combat is a life-and-death affair. I am a top official of the government and

I will not die by the hands of the enemy. If you fall on the front lines, I will kill myself here."

Inspired by Li Guangbi's pep talk, the troops forged ahead toward the enemy positions, more courageous than ever. After a while, his lieutenant Hao Tingyu was seen turning about and racing back. Li Guangbi immediately sent soldiers carrying his sword to intercepted and execute him on the spot.

When Hao Tingyu realized the soldiers were coming for his head by Li's orders, he yelled, "I came back because my horse was shot by an arrow. I am not retreating."

When the messengers came back to Li Guangbi to report what was said, Li quickly gave Hao Tingyu a fresh battle horse. Hao rode back into the battlefield to direct the combat.

Seeing the high morale of his troops, Li Guangbi agitated his signal flag vigorously for a general attack. At that signal, his troops lost no time in charging into the enemy lines, raising deafening battle cries. Unable to resist the strong offensive, the rebel force crumbled and took flight. More than 1,000 rebels were killed or taken prisoner, and another 1,000 were driven into the river and drowned. Zhou Zhi, the rebel general leading the attack on the North Gate, fled in the rout.

Shi Siming in the meantime continued his offensive against the South Gate. It was only when Li Guangbi herded toward the edge of the water the rebels taken captive in the battle at the North Gate that Shi Siming realized Zhou Zhi's troops had been routed. He immediately ordered a retreat and fled back to Luoyang.

In a stand-off that lasted two years, Li Guangbi repelled repeated offensives launched by Shi Siming. At Yu Chaoen's urging, Emperor Suzong of Tang ordered Li Guangbi to attack Luoyang, but Li Guangbi believed the enemy's military strength was still formidable and advised against a premature attack. As eunuch after eunuch was sent by the emperor to order him to march on Luoyang, Li Guangbi had no choice but to implement the order against great odds. He was defeated as expected, and was stripped of his title of Commander-in-Chief.

With a formidable foe taken out of action, Shi Siming made a push toward Chang'an in the wake of a string of victories. Luck had it that at this juncture a third major rift occurred inside the ranks of the rebels. Shi Siming was killed by his son Shi Chaoyi, and the rebel force badly fragmented. In 763 AD, Shi Chaoyi committed suicide after a major military defeat.

From the start of An Lushan's rebellion till the defeat of Shi Chaoyi, China's Central Plains saw eight years of civil war, historically known as the "An (Lushan)-Shi (Siming) Rebellion."

112. Du Fu, a Writer of Historical Poetry

THE AN SHI Rebellion was finally over. This was indeed cause for celebration for the populace, who craved order and stability after so many years of suffering the ravages of war. When news of the end of the rebellion reached the great poet Du Fu, who was a war refugee in Zizhou (modern-day Santai, Sichuan Province), he wept with irrepressible joy.

Du Fu's courtesy name is Zimei. Like Li Bai, he has a prominent place in the pantheon of Tang poetry. In Chinese literature they are often mentioned in tandem as "Li and Du." Du Fu's home town was Gong County, Henan, where he was born into a family of bureaucrats who had fallen on hard times. His keen interest in reading started at a very young age. He visited many parts of the country famed for the beauty of their mountains and rivers, leaving a rich legacy of beautifully written verse. In his thirties, he met Li Bai in Luoyang, who was 11 years his senior and had a very dissimilar temperament. However, they became good friends because of many shared interests and opinions.

He went to Chang'an to participate in the court-administered National Civil Service Examination during the time when the villainous Li Linfu was Prime Minister. Li Linfu had a visceral hatred for intellectuals, and was especially worried that students coming from humble origins would be inimical to his interests if they were allowed to comment on affairs of state at the court once they passed this examination. In collusion with the examiners, he falsely informed Emperor Xuanzong that none of the candidates had made the grade. As Emperor Xuanzong puzzled over this unusual result of the examination, he received a congratulatory memorial from Li Linfu, explaining that the result spoke volumes about the wisdom of the emperor, who had clearly invited into his government all the people of talent in the realm, leaving no more candidates of like caliber outside the government.

Intellectuals and scholars of the time regarded the court-administered Civil Service Examinations as a way to advance their career prospects. With his hopes thus frustrated, Du Fu was understandably upset. He lived in poverty in Chang'an, where he had a chance to witness the contrast between the extravagance and profligacy of the rich and powerful on the one hand, and the deprivation and want of the poor inadequately fed and clothed on the other. In indignation, he denounced this inequity through verse. In a memorable line, he once wrote: Behind vermilion gates, excess wine and meat turns rancid / As corpses of the frozen dead strew the streets.

Du Fu stayed in Chang'an for ten years. Shortly after Emperor Xuanzong offered him a commission, the An Shi Rebellion broke out, forcing the civilians in the area to take to the road. Du Fu and his family joined the exodus of refugees. After an odyssey filled with hardships, they came to a farming village, where they were finally able to settle down in a manner. It was in this period that he learned of the accession of Emperor Suzong in Lingwu. He decided to leave his family in the village and go to Lingwu to offer his services to Suzong, but ran into some rebels on the way and was taken to Chang'an.

Chang'an had by that time fallen to the rebels, who were burning and looting everywhere; palaces and civilian dwellings were engulfed in flames. Officials of the Tang court either surrendered or were taken to Luoyang by the rebels. Once in Chang'an, Du Fu was let go by the rebel chief, who did not believe he was a high official of the Tang.

The following year Du Fu managed to escape from Chang'an. Having heard that Emperor Suzong was then in Fengxiang (modern-day Fengxiang, Shaanxi Province), he set off to seek a meeting with the emperor there. Du Fu was so poor at the time that he could not afford a decent outfit, and had to wear a threadbare tunic and a pair of well-worn hemp sandals. As a token of appreciation for the hardships he faced in coming all the way to offer his services to the Tang court, Emperor Suzong of Tang made him *zuo shi yi*, a Remonstrance Official.

Emperor Suzong's token of appreciation was just that-a token, but Du Fu took it very seriously. Thus, when Prime Minister Fang Guan was dismissed by Emperor Suzong, Du Fu presented a petition to the emperor arguing against the dismissal, because in Du's opinion Fang Guan was a capable Prime Minister. By this act Du Fu managed to offend the emperor. Thanks to the intercession of friends before the emperor, he was spared severe punishment and received only the sanction of being fired and sent home.

After the recovery of Chang'an by the Tang army, Du Fu returned with many other officials to the capital. He was sent by Emperor Suzong to Huazhou (modern-day Hua County, Shaanxi Province) to fill a minor post in charge of sacrificial rites and school affairs. A disillusioned Du Fu arrived in Huazhou at a time when war was still raging with pockets of An and Shi rebels, despite the recovery of Chang'an and Luoyang by government troops. The civilians' lives were disrupted, and they faced the constant fear of being drafted to replenish the Tang troops.

Late one night, Du Fu sought lodging at a humble home in Shihao (a village southeast of modern-day Shan County, Henan Province) on his way to another place. His hosts were an elderly peasant couple. In the middle of the night as he tossed and turned in bed unable to fall asleep, he was startled by an urgent knocking. As Du Fu listened in his room without making a sound, he realized his elderly host had run away by jumping over their back fence while his elderly wife went to answer the door.

It turned out the midnight visitors were lackeys sent by the government to round up anybody deemed fit for military service. They yelled menacingly at the old peasant woman, "Where are the men in your household?"

The elderly woman answered in a teary voice, "My three sons have been drafted to fight in Yecheng. I received a letter two days ago from one of them that said his two brothers had died on the battlefield. I have with me only a daughter-in-law and a suckling grandson. What more do you want?"

The lackeys were not placated by the pleading of the elderly woman, who had no alternative but to follow them to a barracks, where she pressed into hard labor.

When Du Fu took to the road at daybreak, only the elderly peasant man was left in the house.

Deeply disturbed by this tragic episode he had witnessed, Du Fu wrote a poem with the title "A Lackey of Shihao." In his tenure in Huazhou, he wrote a total of six poems along this theme, known as the "San Li San Bie" ("Three Lackeys and Three Partings"). These poems are, "A Lackey of Shihao," "A Lackey of Tongguan," "A Lackey of Xin'an," "Parting of the Newly-weds," "Parting in One's Old Age," and "Parting of the Homeless." Du Fu's writings have often been referred to as historical poetry, because most of them deal with the stark human suffering during the An Shi Rebellion, and depict the decline of the Tang dynasty from its former glory.

Du Fu occupied his post for only a year before resigning. The Guanzhong area was soon hit by a serious drought and, no longer able to make ends meet, Du Fu took his family on the road again and sought the help of a friend in Chengdu. He lived there for nearly four years as a recluse, in a thatched hut he built on the bank of a stream in the western fringe of the city. When his friend died, he was again in dire straits. He and his family moved east to seek a better life. In 770 AD, ill and penniless, he died on a small boat on the Xiang River.

In memory of this great poet, his dwelling in Chengdu has been preserved for posterity. This is the famed Thatched Hut of Du Fu.

113. Steel-willed Yan Zhenqing

IN THE AFTERMATH of the An Shi Rebellion, the Tang Empire steadily declined from the height of its glory. The commissioners of the military districts carved out their own turf while the control of the central government weakened, splitting the country into semi-independent spheres of influence centered around the military districts. Following Li Chu, Emperor Daizong of Tang's (also known as Li Yu) death, his son Li Kuo succeeded him with the title of Emperor Dezong of Tang. When he tried to reverse the growth of the military districts' power that had been eroding the control of the central government, the military districts rose up in rebellion. Further, when Emperor Dezong sent punitive expeditions out against them, this only fueled the rebellion instead of quashing it.

By 782 AD, five separate military districts were in rebellion, with Li Xilie, military commissioner of Huaixi, posing the strongest challenge. Proclaiming himself National Commander-in-Chief, he launched an offensive into the interior of Tang territory.

The rebellion of the five military districts was a deep shock to the Tang court. When Emperor Dezong consulted Prime Minister Lu Qi on the matter, he reassured him, saying "Don't worry! All Your Majesty needs to do is send a respected minister to talk them out of it, and the rebellion will end peacefully."

Emperor Dezong asked him, "Who do you think is right for the job?"

Lu Qi recommended the Crown Prince's mentor and teacher, Yan Zhenqing, and Emperor Dezong gave his immediate approval.

Yan Zhenqing was at the time a revered minister enjoying great prestige. Before the An Shi Rebellion, he was governor of Pingyuan. After the An Shi Rebellion broke out, most of the counties in Hebei fell into the hands of the rebels. Because of Yan Zhenqing's stiff resistance, only Pingyuan was saved. When his cousin Yan Gaoqing raised up an army in Gaocheng to fight against the An Shi Rebellion, seventeen counties in Hebei rallied to the cause, and by popular demand Yan Zhenqing became leader of the alliance. Consequently, the alliance won major victories against the rebels, and Yan Zhenqing was made Duke of Lu Prefecture by Emperor Daizong of Tang. This is the origin of his other appellation, Yan the Duke of Lu.

Historically, Yan Zhenqing was also a famous calligrapher. His forceful and majestic style, reflecting his steel will, is revered as the Yan style.

As a staunchly moral and principled individual, Yan Zhenqing was often the target of smear campaigns by unscrupulous characters bent on marginalizing his influence. These schemers, however, had to maintain an appearance of deference to him because of his national stature. Prime Minister Lu Qi, a ruthless man, had always resented Yan's prestige and longed for an opportunity to do him harm. This new rebellion of the military districts was the opportunity he had been waiting for. Hoping to set him up for a fall, Lu Qi sent Yan Zhenqing, who was already in his seventies, on the mission to dissuade the mutineers. When other civil and military officials heard about Yan Zhenqing's assignment, many feared for his safety. However, Yan himself was unconcerned. Taking only a few aides, he set off for Huaixi.

The rebellious military commissioner of Huaixi, Li Xilie, decided to teach Yan Zhenqing a lesson. At their meeting, he packed the interior and exterior of the hall with a thousand followers, including soldiers and his adoptive sons. The moment Yan Zhenqing began his plea that they cease their rebellion, Li Xilie's men armed with swords surged forward and surrounded Yan Zhenqing, hurling insults and threatening to kill him. None of the blustering gestures had any effect on Yan Zhenqing. Fearless and composed, he stared at them derisively.

Li Xilie rose from his chair and made a show of protecting Yan Zhenqing from the threatening mob. Before leading Yan Zhenqing to the guesthouse, he ordered his adoptive sons to leave. His plan was to slowly soften Yan's stand.

A few days later, the leaders of all four other rebellious military districts sent emissaries urging Li Xilie to proclaim himself Emperor. Li Xilie invited Yan Zhenqing to the banquet he had prepared for these emissaries.

Seeing the presence of Yan Zhenqing at the banquet, the emissaries congratulated Li Xilie, saying "We have long been impressed by the prestige and stature of the Grand Mentor Yan. He has arrived at an opportune time. With the imminent accession of the Commander-in-Chief to the throne, he is the ideal candidate for Prime Minister."

Arching his eyebrows, Yan Zhenqing replied, denouncing the four emissaries, "Prime minister my foot! I am close to eighty; I am not afraid of death. What makes you think I would succumb to your enticements or buckle under your threats?"

Cowed by his indomitable aura, the four emissaries drew their necks in and fell silent.

Unable to budge Yan Zhenqing, Li Xilie arrested him up and had him placed under guard. The soldiers guarding him dug a big pit in the courtyard and declared their intention to bury him alive. The next day Yan Zhenqing said to Li Xilie, who came to visit him, "My fate has been decided. Why play games with me? Just chop off my head. It would be so much easier."

A year later, Li Xilie proclaimed himself Emperor of Chu; he again sent one of his generals to demand Yan's fealty. Soldiers prepared a pile of firewood in the courtyard where Yan was imprisoned, and doused it liberally with oil. They then threatened Yan, saying "If you still refuse to surrender, you will be burned alive."

Without a word, Yan Zhenqing rushed to throw himself into the fire, but was stopped in time by the rebels, who reported it to Li Xilie. Try as he might, Li Xilie was unable to make Yan Zhenqing submit, so he forced him to commit suicide. Eventually, Li Xilie himself was killed by his own lieutenants, following numerous setbacks on the battlefield.

114. The Sweet Dew Incident

IN 820 AD, Li Heng ascended the throne as Emperor Muzong of Tang. From Emperor Muzong onward, all Tang emperors were installed on the throne and sustained by powerful eunuchs. No one dared to ruffle the feathers of these kingmakers.

In the second year of the reign of Li Ang, Emperor Wenzong of Tang (son of Emperor Muzong), candidates who had passed the Imperial Civil Service Examinations at the provincial level flocked to the capital to take the next higher level of examination. One of these so-called *ju ren* (a candidate recommended by the provincial authorities) by the name of Liu Fen openly argued in his essay against the concentration of power in the eunuchs. He took the view that in order to assure the stability of the country, the political power now usurped by the eunuchs should be restored to the prime minister, and the control of the army should once again revert to the top generals.

The essay was passed around among the examiners, who heaped praise on it, considering it a rare exemplar of fine writing, distinguished by the elegance of its style and the cogency of its argument. However, when the time came for the final selections, none of them dared say anything for fear of antagonizing the eunuchs. They did not wish to run the risk of losing their positions if Liu Fen passed the examination.

Twenty-two other candidates who took the examination with Liu Fen passed the examination, while Liu Fen, who was widely regarded as an outstanding scholar, was rejected solely because of his candid critique of the abnormal political situation. Everyone felt sorry for him. The successful candidates said, "We feel so ashamed that we were chosen over Liu Fen."

Emperor Wenzong very much resented being manipulated by the eunuchs and was intent on eliminating them. During a bout of an illness, Emperor Wenzong cast around for a good doctor. It so happened that the chief eunuch, Wang Shoucheng, had in his service an official called Zheng Zhu, who possessed excellent medical knowledge and skills. Wang Shoucheng recommended Zheng Zhu to the emperor. He soon noticed steady improvement under Zheng's care. Pleased by the results of the treatment, Emperor Wenzong summoned Zheng Zhu for an audience. He found him articulate, intelligent and capable. He decided to promote Zheng Zhu to Censor-In-Chief.

A friend of Zheng Zhu's by the name of Li Xun, a petty official, was frustrated that his talent was not put to greater use. When he learned that Zheng Zhu's stars were rising at the imperial court, he called on him and plied him with presents. Since Zheng Zhu happened to be looking for an assistant, he asked Wang Shoucheng to recommend Li Xun to Emperor Wenzong. Li Xun was able to win the trust of the emperor, and eventually became Prime Minister.

After Li Xun and Zheng Zhu had gained Emperor Wenzong's trust, he confided in them his intention of eliminating the eunuchs. The three of them huddled together to figure out a way to reduce Wang Shoucheng's power. Li Xun and Zheng Zhu discerned that there were tensions between a eunuch called Qiu Shiliang and Wang Shoucheng, and so they urged Emperor Wenzong to make Qiu Shiliang Left Commandant of Inspired Strategy, giving him control of part of the imperial guard.

Subsequently, Li Xun took away Wang Shoucheng's control over the army, thus rendering him more vulnerable. Finally, Emperor Wenzong had Wang Shoucheng killed by giving him some wine which had been poisoned.

With Wang Shoucheng dead and gone, it was time to eliminate Qiu Shiliang. After making necessary preparations, Li Xun got in touch with General Han Yue of the imperial guard. Together they agreed on a course of action. One day in 835 AD, Han Yue reported at an imperial audience that sweet dew had descended the previous night on a pomegranate tree in the garden behind the quarters for the imperial guard.

According to superstitious beliefs prevalent in feudal China, the fall of sweet dew was an auspicious omen. Li Xun came forward, followed by all officials in attendance, to offer congratulations to Emperor Wenzong. He proposed that the emperor take a personal look at the sweet dew.

Emperor Wenzong ordered Prime Minister Li Xun to take a look first. After a perfunctory trip to the garden, Li Xun returned with the report, "I took a look and found that it is unlikely to be real sweet dew. Your Majesty should send someone else to make another inspection."

Emperor Wenzong then ordered Qiu Shiliang to take the other eunuchs with him to have another look. Qiu Shiliang asked Han Yue to accompany him. When the party approached the door, Han Yue became nervous and his face turned ashen. This struck Qiu Shiliang as unusual. "General Han, what's the matter with you?" he asked.

Just then a gust of wind lifted the curtain of the door, and Qiu Shiliang discovered armed soldiers lying in ambush behind it.

Startled, Qiu Shiliang took a quick step back and ran towards Emperor Wenzong. Li Xun immediately ordered the soldiers in hiding to go after the fleeing Qiu Shiliang, but by that time Qiu and the other eunuchs had seized Emperor Wenzong and whisked him away in a sedan chair.

When Li Xun caught up and grabbed the sedan chair, a eunuch stepped forward and hit him with his fist. In the meantime, Qiu Shiliang disappeared with the sedan chair into the inner palace.

His plot having failed, Li Xun put on a civilian outfit borrowed from a petty official and fled in disguise. Qiu Shiliang wasted no time in launching a large-scale dragnet to round up and kill officials in the plot. Li Xun was kept on the run, and finally cornered and killed. Zheng Zhu, who was marching his troops toward the capital from Fengxiang, turned back after hearing about what had transpired. However, when he did so, he was killed by the eunuch attached to his army as an army supervisor.

Thus the plot woven by Emperor Wenzong, Li Xun and Zheng Zhu to kill the eunuchs ended in a fiasco. It cost the lives of more than a thousand people found to have something to do with it. This historically is called the "Sweet Dew Incident."

In the wake of this incident, the eunuchs placed Emperor Wenzong under close surveillance, making life increasingly unbearable for him. He died five years later of an illness. Qiu Shiliang then installed Wenzong's brother Li Yan on the throne with the title of Emperor Wuzong of Tang.

115. War of the Factions

IN THE YEARS of the eunuchs' oligarchy, all officials who dared to challenge them were sidelined or persecuted. Those who clung to power on the eunuchs' coattails formed two factions, each trying to gain ascendancy over the other. They were embroiled in endless squabbles that lasted forty years. This period is known in Chinese history as the "War of the Factions."

The bickerings dated back to the time of Emperor Xianzong's reign. One year in that period, an examination was held in Chang'an to recruit talented people who were not afraid to speak their mind to the emperor. Two low-ranking officials who took the examination, Li Zongmin and Niu Sengru, leveled criticism in their essays against the government. The examiners found these two met the criteria of the examination and recommended them to Emperor Xianzong.

This matter came to the attention of Prime Minister Li Jifu, who had descended from a family of scholar-officials, and had always despised officials recruited through civil service examinations. The criticism leveled by Li Zongmin and Niu Sengru, both coming from humble origins, at the government he headed struck a raw nerve in him. He went before Emperor Xianzong with the story that these two had been recommended solely because they had close ties with the examiners. The emperor bought the story and demoted the examiners. Li Zongmin and Niu Sengru ended up without being given a post in the government.

After the death of Li Jifu, his son Li Deyu, aided by the prominence of his father, became a Hanlin scholar. Li Deyu never forgave Li Zongmin, who was at the time also serving in the government, for criticizing his father's ability to govern.

On the occasion of the Imperial Civil Service Examination in the early years of Emperor Muzong of Tang's reign, two high officials at the imperial court privately interceded for two acquaintances taking the exam, only to be rebuffed by the examiner, Qian Hui. A relative of Li Zongmin also taking part in the exam was accepted. The two ministers went before Emperor Muzong and accused Qian Hui of favoritism and fraud. When Emperor Muzong consulted the Hanlin scholar, Li Deyu corroborated the story. As a result, Qian Hui was demoted by Emperor Muzong and Li Zongmin was exiled from the capital because of his alleged involvement.

Li Zongmin intensely detested Li Deyu, who he believed was bent on sidelining him. Niu Sengru naturally sympathized with Li Zongmin. Two blocs eventually emerged, with Li Zongmin, Niu Sengru and some officials promoted through civil service exams forming one faction, and Li Deyu along with officials born into families of scholar-officials forming another faction. Covert and overt factional fighting was intense.

After the accession of Emperor Wenzong, Li Zongmin became Prime Minister with the help of eunuchs. Upon his recommendation, Emperor Wenzong also made Niu Sengru a prime minister. The two men now in power engineered the transfer of Li Deyu out of the capital, making him the military commissioner of faraway Xichuan (with its seat in modern-day Chengdu, Sichuan Province).

During that time, a Tubo general had surrendered near Xichuan. Li Deyu took advantage of this opportunity to recover the strategic district of Weizhou (with its seat in modern-day Li County, Sichuan Province). This should have been counted as an accomplishment by Li Deyu. However, Prime Minister Niu Sengru said to Emperor Wenzong, "The recovery of merely Weizhou means little if it comes at the cost of worsening relations with Tubo." He advised Emperor Wenzong to have Li Deyu return Weizhou to Tubo, to Li Deyu's great indignation.

Later, Emperor Wenzong heard another viewpoint, which argued that pulling out of Weizhou was a mistake, and attributed the action to Niu Sengru's desire to marginalize Le Deyu. In his compunction, Emperor Wenzong began to distance himself from Niu Sengru. Emperor Wenzong was a man without strong views, making him easily manipulated by the eunuchs. He would vacillate between Li Deyu and Niu Sengru. When one faction gained ascendancy, it would make life unbearable for the other faction. The two factions replaced each other in the seat of power as in a game of musical chairs. The government was in constant flux and chaos, and Emperor Wenzong was never able to conclude who was in the wrong and who was in the right. He often said lamentingly, "It was much easier to pacify Hebei than to try and eliminate factional politics."

In their pursuit of power and money, both factions curried favor with the eunuchs. When Li Deyu was military commissioner in Huainan, the eunuch who served as the army supervisor, Yang Qinyi, was summoned to the capital. It was widely speculated that once back in the capital he would be given full power. Li Deyu arranged a banquet in honor of Yang Qinyi and lavished gifts on him before his departure. After Yang Qinyi returned to the capital, he reciprocated by lavishing praise on Li Deyu before Emperor Wuzong.

After the full enthronement of Emperor Wuzong, Li Deyu himself became Prime Minister. He did all he could to marginalize Niu Sengru and Li Zongmin, exiling them to the far south. Basking in the trust of Emperor Wuzong, Li Deyu held the position of Prime Minister for a number of years, managing to antagonize many ministers at the imperial court with his heavy-handedness.

In 846 AD, Emperor Wuzong died of an illness, and the eunuchs installed his uncle Li Chen as Emperor, with the title of Emperor Xuanzong of Tang. He sidelined all the ministers who had served Emperor Wuzong. On the very first day of his accession, he removed Li Deyu as Prime Minister. A year later, Li Deyu was exiled to Yazhou (near modern-day Haikou, Qiongshan and Wenchang, Hainan Province). This marked the end of factional strife that had lasted forty years. However, the Tang Empire emerged from the chaos in worse shape than before.

116. Huang Chao, the Sky-high Grand General

DURING THE LATE Tang period, government was characterized by increasing confusion in the aftermath of the rebellion of the military districts, the eunuchs' seizure of power, and the factional fighting among officials of the imperial court. Even Emperor Xuanzong, a relatively astute monarch, was unable to reverse the decline. After his death, the emperors that followed —Li Cui (Emperor Yizong) and Li Xuan (Emperor Xizong)— passionately indulged in revelry and led profligate lives. The royal house, officials, and landlords intensified their exploitation of the peasants. Tax levies became increasingly unbearable. Frequent natural disasters helped to bankrupt the peasants and force them into mass migration. Some, fed up with perennial privation and misery, took the path of rebellion.

In the year of Emperor Yizong's accession, a peasant uprising led by Qiu Fu erupted in the east of Zhejiang. It grew from a force of 100 to 30,000 people, and fought for eight months, sending a tremor across Yuezhou (with its seat in modern-day Shaoxing, Zhejiang Province).

Eight years later, 800 soldiers stationed in Guilin (most of them peasants from Xuzhou) killed their superiors because they had repeatedly stalled their rotation home upon completion of their tour of duty. They made Pang Xun the leader of their uprising, and marched northward in the direction of their native land, picking up peasant supporters along the way. Their strength grew to 200,000 by the time they reached Xuzhou.

Both uprisings were put down by the government. However, a deepening, rebellious mood stalked the land, and each new uprising dwarfed previous ones in scale.

During the late Tang period, the salt tax was particularly onerous. After the profiteering salt merchants engaged in price gouging, the populace could no longer afford the seasoning and had to forgo its use in their food. Some impoverished peasants sold "illicit" salt to avoid paying the salt tax. Because of the high risks involved, they needed to band together. With time, they formed armies of salt smugglers, some of whose leaders would go on to head peasant uprisings.

In 874 AD, the year of Emperor Xizong's accession, Wang Xianzhi, a leader of the salt smugglers in Puzhou (with its seat in modern-day Fan County, Henan Province), gathered several thousand peasants and staged a rebellion from Changyuan (in modern-day Henan). Wang Xianzhi proclaimed himself the "Heaven-Sent Grand General of Equitable Distribution", and publicly indicted the immoral policy that had created such an inequitable distribution of wealth. The impoverished peasants quickly rallied to his cause. It soon garnered the support of the salt smuggler Huang Chao in Yuanju (north of modern-day Cao County, Shandong Province).

Huang Chao had gone to school and was an accomplished horseman and archer. He had gone to Chang'an on several occasions to take the Imperial Civil Service Examination, but had repeatedly failed, but through this had gained the opportunity to observe up close the corruption and decadence of the Tang government in Chang'an. He was filled with indignation at all the shadowy practices and shady dealings involved in politics. It is said that his "Ode to the Chrysanthemum" dated to that period. The chrysanthemum was a metaphor of his determination to topple the Tang dynasty:

Every autumn on the eighth of September,
I burst into bloom when all other flowers begin to wither;
Billows of my sky-high fragrance permeate Chang'an,

As the city is blanketed with a coat of golden armor.

After the insurgents led by Huang Chao and Wang Xianzhi joined forces, they marched across Shandong and Henan, taking control of many prefectures and counties. Their rebellion gathered momentum, sowing panic among the court officials. An order went out to all parts of the country to put down the insurgents, but the military districts, afraid to engage the insurgents, simply sat on their hands in a waiting game. There was not a thing the Tang government could do.

When the big stick failed, the Tang government dangled a carrot. After the insurgents captured Qizhou (modern-day Qichun, Hubei Province), the Tang court sent a eunuch to Qizhou with an offer to make Wang Xianzhi "Left Commandant of Inspired Strategy and Investigating Censor." The lure of a position in the government proved irresistible for Wang Xianzhi, who accepted the appointment.

Huang Chao was infuriated by this development. He took a group of insurgents with him to see Wang Xianzhi, saying to him, "We have sworn to fight together until we take control of the country. Now you want to become a government official. Where does that leave us?"

As Wang Xianzhi tried to stall, Huang Chao bloodied Wang's face with his fists while the other insurgents showered him with invectives. Conceding his mistake, Wang Xianzhi sent the eunuch away.

With this episode behind them, Huang Chao and Wang Xianzhi decided to pursue a two-pronged attack, with Wang marching west and Huang Chao heading east. Shortly after, the insurgents led by Wang were defeated by government forces at Huangmei (in modern-day Hubei), and was killed in combat.

Following Wang Xianzhi's defeat, the insurgents regrouped and made Huang Chao their king, giving him the title "Sky-high Grand General."

The government had the military advantage in the Central Plains, and mustered an overwhelming force near Luoyang waiting to hem in the insurgents once they launched their attack into

Henan. Detecting his foe's intentions, Huang Chao decided to march his troops south through areas with weaker concentrations of government troops. Thus, they were able to cross the Yangtze without much difficulty, and penetrate the eastern part of Zhejiang. The insurgents advanced, all but unopposed, taking Yuezhou and Quzhou (modern-day Qu County, Zhejiang) in quick succession. Blazing a seven-hundred-*li* long trail through the mountainous areas between Quzhou and Jianzhou (modern-day Jian'ou, Fujian Province), they went on a long march that took them to Guangzhou in a year's time.

The insurgents rested and regrouped in Guangzhou. However, the Lingnan region was hit by an epidemic, forcing Huang Chao to take his troops back north. The Tang government ordered Wang Duo, the Military Commissioner of Jingnan, and Gao Pian, the Military Commissioner of Huainan, to intercept him with massive forces along the way. However, all attempts to block Huang Chao were foiled by his insurgent army, which successfully crossed the Yangtze. Shaken by his defeat, Gao Pian pulled back into the safety of the walled city of Yangzhou, excusing himself from engaging the enemy on account of a stroke he had allegedly suffered.

Once across the Huai River, the insurgent army disseminated a declaration, addressed to government army commanders, which promised: "We are attacking the capital only to hold the emperor to account. We have no quarrel with the rest of the country. You will be wise to entrench yourselves in your respective areas of command and refrain from trying to blunt our offensive."

After reading the declaration, many government commanders decided not to risk their future for the Tang court, because of their fear of the insurgents and a desire to preserve their military strength. When this came to the knowledge of the court in Chang'an, Emperor Xizong broke down in tears before his ministers.

In 880 AD, the 600,000 troops of Huang Chao arrived at Tongguan, blanketing the fields and mountains as far as the eyes could see with the pure white banners of the insurgent army. The defending government troops had at first tried to put up a last-ditch fight, but when Huang Chao came in person to the front lines to the deafening acclaim and wild, earthshaking cheers of the insurgent troops that reverberated in the gorge, the government troops were so demoralized they burned their tents and scattered in flight, without offering the least resistance.

The loss of Tangguan Pass sent the Tang court into a panic. Emperor Xizong, accompanied by his concubines and the chief eunuch Tian Lingzi, fled to Chengdu. The court officials who were unable to run away in time came out en masse to offer their surrender.

That afternoon, Huang Chao entered the city of Chang'an on a gilt sedan chair under the escort of his generals and troops. The residents of the city came out in force to greet him along the streets. Shang Rang, a top general of the insurgent army, took that occasion to announce to the gathered crowds, "Prince Huang has risen up in arms in the interest of the people. He will not abuse you like the Li clique (meaning the Tang royalty). You can now live and go about your business."

The troops then volunteered to distribute their war spoils to the crowds.

A few days later, Huang Chao ascended to the throne in Daming Palace, founding a new dynasty called Da Qi. The insurgents' seven-year war was finally crowned with success.

However, Huang Chao's insurgent army had a problem: In their long years of warring across the country, they had left no troops behind to hold their conquests. When the hundreds of thousands of insurgent soldiers entered Chang'an, they were an island in an ocean of areas controlled by the government. It did not take long before the Tang court was able to assemble a huge force. It besieged Chang'an, which soon suffered a serious shortage of food.

Zhu Wen, a general dispatched by Huang Chao to defend Tongzhou (modern-day Dali, Shaanxi Province), chose this most difficult moment for the insurgents to switch his allegiance to the Tang court, making himself a despised turncoat.

The Tang government summoned Li Keyong, Military Commissioner of Yanmen and a Shatuo Turk (a northwestern minority in ancient China) nobleman, to attack Chang'an with his 40,000 cavalrymen. The 150,000-strong insurgent army was routed and forced out of Chang'an.

When Huang Chao withdrew his insurgents to Henan, he was attacked from all sides by the troops of Zhu Wen and Li Keyong. In 884 AD, Huang Chao's assault on Chenzhou (modern-day Huaiyang, Henan Province) was beat back. With government troops hot on his tail, Huang Chao retreated to the Wolves and Tigers Valley of Mount Tai, where he fought in a last stand to his death.

117. The Last Days of the Tang Empire

FOLLOWING THE FAILED Huang Chao rebellion, Emperor Xizong returned to Chang'an. The Tang central government by this time had become an empty shell, existing in name only, while the power of the military districts had expanded while the central government was in the process of suppressing the rebellion. These military districts fought each other to establish their respective spheres of influence, becoming separatist regimes of varying sizes. Li Keyong, Military Commissioner of Hedong, and Zhu Wen, Military Commissioner of Xuanwu (with its seat in modern-day Kaifeng, Henan Province), were among the most powerful of them.

Zhu Wen came from humble origins. He had been a loafer since he was a child, and among the three brothers in the family, he was the meanest and wiliest. After joining the insurgent army of Huang Chao, he won his trust. However, he had chosen a moment of great peril for the insurgents to switch loyalty to the Tang court, crossing over with his troops and rendering them a great service. The Tang Emperor not only rewarded him with a prominent position in the government and high pay, but also conferred the name "Quanzhong" (total loyalty) on him, and sent him after the insurgents.

At the time Huang Chao had pulled back to Henan, he still had a strong fighting force. In Huang Chao's attack on Bianzhou, Zhu Wen asked Li Keyong for help. When Li Keyong returned to Bianzhou after defeating the insurgents, Zhu Wen prepared a sumptuous feast for him. In the meantime, Zhu Wen ordered his troops to surround the building in which the now stone-drunk Li Keyong was staying in an attempt to kill him. Li Keyong got out of the trap with the help of his bodyguards. This was the beginning of a running feud between Li Keyong and Zhu Wen that pitted two separatist regimes against each other in constant warfare. In this feud, Zhu Wen was able to expand his influence, while Li Keyong could only hold on to his original power base in Hedong.

After Emperor Xizong died of an illness, his younger brother Emperor Zhaozong (Li Ye) tried to challenge the power of the eunuchs with the help of his ministers. However, all of his attempts failed. The eunuchs eventually placed Emperor Zhaozong under house arrest, and installed another emperor.

This represented a great opportunity for the ambitious Zhu Wen, who sent a trusted aide to Chang'an for a confidential discussion to hatch a secret plan with Prime Minister Cui Yin. Emboldened by the backing of Zhu Wen, Cui Yin dispatched troops to kill the chief eunuch, Liu Jishu, and restore Emperor Zhaozong to his throne.

As Emperor Zhaozong and Cui Yin prepared to slaughter of all eunuchs, some of them sought the protection with Li Maozhen, the Military Commissioner of Fengxiang. They took Emperor Zhaozong with them as a hostage.

At Cui Yin's request, Zhu Wen marched his troops to Fengxiang and demanded that Li Maozhen hand over Emperor Zhaozong. Zhu Wen's troops laid siege to the city, cutting off its food supply, and handing Li Maozhen a series of defeats. The situation was compounded by a snow storm. Untold numbers of soldiers and civilians starved or froze to death. Li Maozhen had no alternative but to surrender.

After capturing Fengxiang, Zhu Wen grabbed Emperor Zhaozong and brought him back to Chang'an. From then on, the reins of power passed from the eunuchs to Zhu Wen, and life became even more miserable for Emperor Zhaozong.

Now having full rein, Zhu Wen had all the eunuchs slaughtered.

He then forced Emperor Zhaozong to move the capital to Luoyang. Before setting off from Chang'an, Zhu Wen had all the city's palaces, government buildings, and civilian dwellings dismantled and the salvaged materials transported to Luoyang. The officials and residents of Chang'an were compelled to move with them to Luoyang. The people of Chang'an took to the road with their elderly and the very young in tow, under the prodding of the soldiers, denouncing in tears the traitor Zhu Wen for the havoc and misery he wrought on the country and the people.

When Emperor Zhaozong arrived in Luoyang, he secretly planned to summon the heads of the military districts for help, but before the plan could materialize Zhu Wen had killed the emperor, installing a 13-year-old puppet as Emperor with the title of Emperor Zhaoxuan.

With the eunuchs eliminated and the emperor killed, there were still a large number of ministers to deal with. Zhu Wen's advisers said to him, "These people will be a serious hindrance to your ambitious plans. You should get rid of all of them."

One of his advisers called Li Zhen, nicknamed Owl, had an added reason to hate the ministers: he had failed the Civil Service Examination. He said to Zhu Wen, "These people fancy themselves superior to the rest of us and take great pride in belonging to the 'clear and pure stream'. They deserve to be thrown into the turbid waters of the Yellow River." Heeding his advice, Zhu Wen rounded up thirty ministers one late night, had them killed and thrown into the Yellow River.

In 907 AD, Zhu Wen deposed Emperor Zhaoxuan and proclaimed himself Emperor. He gave his new dynasty the name, Liang, and set up his new capital at Bian (modern-day Kaifeng, Henan Province). The traitor Zhu Wen thus became Emperor Taizu of Liang. The Tang dynasty was thus extinguished after ruling China for nearly three hundred years.

FIVE DYNASTIES AND TEN STATES (907 AD–960 AD)

118. Opera Actors in Politics

IN THE FIVE decades following the founding of the Liang dynasty by Zhu Wen, five short-lived dynasties succeeded one another in China's Central Plains. They are called the Liang, Tang, Jin, Han and Zhou (known to history as the Later Liang, the Later Tang, the Later Jin, the Later Han and the Later Zhou, to distinguish them from previous dynasties of the same names), and are known collectively as the Five Dynasties. During the Five Dynasties Period, there were nine separatist regimes (the Former Shu, Wu, Min, Wuyue, Chu, the Southern Han, Nanping, the Later Shu and the Southern Tang) at different times in the south and Bashu area, headed variously by self-described emperors or kings. With the Northern Han in the north, these were collectively called the Ten Kingdoms. The Five Dynasties Period is therefore also called the Five Dynasties and Ten Kingdoms Period.

When Zhu Wen founded the Liang dynasty, there were two other major separatist regimes in the north of China. One was headed by Liu Rengong of Youzhou, and the other Li Keyong of Hedong (Prince of Jin). During the same period, the Khitans in the north were also growing stronger, and their leader Yelü Abaoji (Yelü is the last family) established a kingdom after uniting the various Khitan tribes. In 907 AD, Abaoji at the head of a 300,000-strong army captured Yunzhou (with its seat in modern-day Datong, Shanxi Province). Li Keyong contacted Abaoji with a view to using the Khitan force to defeat Zhu Wen. The two met in Yunzhou and swore brotherhood with each other. They also agreed on a timeframe for an attack on the Liang. However, when Abaoji realized the growing strength of Zhu Wen, he changed his mind and sent an emissary to Zhu Wen to forge an alliance with him instead.

Li Keyong was furious when he learned of the betrayal. The following spring, he fell ill from all the aggravation and exhaustion. His back was covered with festering sores. Sensing he would not recover, he called his son Li Cunxu to his bedside and made him listen attentively, "Zhu Wen is our enemy. You don't need me to tell you that. Liu Rengong owes his good fortunes to my recommendation, but he is a chameleon with shifting loyalties and has eventually cast in his lot with Zhu Wen. The Khitans swore brotherhood to me, but then tore up our pact and turned against us from one day to the next. I cannot go in peace unless I know I will be avenged."

He handed three arrows fetched by his attendant to Li Cunxu with the instruction, "I am leaving these with you. Remember the three enemies of our family and be sure to avenge our honor."

On his knees by the bed, in tears Li Cunxu took the arrows from his father and pledged he would never forget his instructions, whereupon Li Keyong closed his eyes and gave up the ghost.

After the death of Li Keyong, Li Cunxu succeeded his father as Prince of Jin. By tightening up military training and discipline, he was able to mold the slack Shatuo soldiers into a formidable fighting force. As a token of his determination to destroy his enemies, Li Cunxu kept the three arrows left by his father in a place of honor in the family ancestral shrine. Before he set off on any military campaign, he would have those arrows brought to him so that he could wrap them in silk and take them with him into battle. The arrows would be returned to the ancestral shrine afterwards. In several major battles with the Liang army, Li Cunxu's force roundly defeated the half a million troops led by Zhu Wen, causing them to flee in all directions in disarray. Humiliated and infuriated, Zhu Wen fell ill and died shortly after. Soon, Li Cunxu took control of Youzhou, taking Liu Rengong and his son Liu Shouguang alive and transporting them back to Taiyuan.

In 916 AD, Yelü Abaoji proclaimed himself Emperor. Five years later, he marched his troops south. Li Cunxu personally led his troops into battle with the Khitan army, routing it and driving Abaoji back north.

After the death of Zhu Wen, his son Emperor Mo of Liang continued the war with Li Cunxu for another ten years. In 923 AD, Li Cunxu toppled the Liang dynasty and unified north China. He proclaimed himself Emperor and changed the dynasty name to Tang, with Luoyang as its capital. He became Emperor Zhuangzong of the Later Tang.

Having avenged his father, and believing his enemies had been eliminated and China's Central Plains had regained peace and stability, Emperor Zhuangzong of the Later Tang became complacent and began to pamper himself with the many pleasures of life. He had enjoyed watching and acting in opera performances since a child, since the Prince of Jin had a resident opera troupe in his residential compound to perform for his family. Emperor Zhuangzong had developed a closeness with the opera actors in the troupe when he was a child. His love affair with the opera was temporarily eclipsed by his fierce campaigns on the battlefields of Hebei. However, once enthroned he picked up his old love again, spending an inordinate amount of time with the actors and donning costumes to perform in operatic plays, neglecting the running of state. He gave himself the stage name of "Li Tianxia" (meaning "Li governing the country").

When he twice called out "Li Tianxia" in a performance on the stage, an opera actor rushed up and slapped his face. Emperor Zhuangzong was baffled by the gesture. Other performers were equally startled. They grabbed the slapper, demanding an explanation. The giggling slapper said, "I slapped you because you committed a serious fault. There could only be one person who governs the realm and you called out 'Li Tianxia' twice. How could the emperor rule the realm with another person?" Emperor Zhuangzong realized it was a playful joke, and bore no grudge for being slapped.

The emperor liked these opera performers so much that he allowed them the freedom to move about in the palace. They monkeyed around with the emperor, and assumed grand airs with government officials. The officials mistreated by these actors deeply resented it, but none of them dared to stand up to them. Some officials, desiring the actors to put in a good word for them in front of the emperor, even tried to ingratiate themselves with the actors by plying them with gifts. One of the actors called Jing Jin enjoyed spying for the emperor and informing him of what was happening. Woe to anyone who incurred his displeasure, because the emperor could be counted on to hear some pretty nasty things about him from Jing Jin. The sight of Jing Jin would make many an official quake in his shoes.

When Emperor Zhuangzong planned to appoint two opera performers as prefects, some tried to dissuade him from it by arguing, "After the founding of the new dynasty, many of the generals who had fought with Your Majesty in countless battles have not yet received any title or reward. There would be grumblings if opera actors were to be invited into the government."

Completely ignoring all such advice, Emperor Zhuangzong went ahead and made the appointments, to the great indignation of some officers in the army. Within a few short years, trouble broke out inside the government of the Later Tang. General Guo Chongtao was killed and another general Li Siyuan (foster son of Li Keyong) nearly became a victim of court infighting.

With the support of his troops and generals, Li Siyuan decided to challenge Emperor Zhuangzong. He attacked the capital Bianjing with his troops with the aim of proclaiming himself emperor.

Having learned of this attack while he was in Luoyang, Emperor Zhuangzong set off for Bianjing, but soon learned Li Siyuan had entered the capital Bianjing. Realizing he was now completely isolated, the dejected Emperor said to the officers in his entourage, "This time I am really done for!"

Emperor Zhuangzong turned back towards Luoyang, from where he intended to continue resisting the attack of Li Siyuan. Guo Congqian, the commander of the Imperial Armies, an opera actor and an adoptive nephew of General Guo Chongtao, had borne a deep grudge against the court since the death of General Guo. He seized this opportunity to stage a mutiny of the Imperial Army. They entered the palace, taking Emperor Zhuangzong by surprise. He did not have time to put up a fight, and died after being hit by a stray arrow.

Li Siyuan replaced Emperor Zhuangzong as Emperor Mingzong of Later Tang.

119. Shi Jingtang, the Son Emperor

DURING HIS REIGN, Emperor Mingzong of Later Tang had two great generals: one was his son Li Congke; the other was his son-in-law Shi Jingtang, the Military Commissioner of Hedong. Both were valiant, skilled fighters, but neither of them was ready to concede ground to the other. After the accession of Li Congke (the last Emperor of Tang) of the Later Tang dynasty, the feud between the two finally came out into the open.

Li Congke sent tens of thousands of troops against the city of Jinyang, where Shi Jingtang was stationed. As Shi Jingtang's resistance faltered and Jinyang was in imminent danger of falling, his adviser Sang Weihan had the idea of appealing to the Khitans for help. At that time Yelü Deguang had succeeded his father Yelü Abaoji, who had died, as leader of the Khitan kingdom. Sang Weihan drafted a letter on Shi Jingtang's behalf, appealing to Yelü Deguang for help and expressing Shi's readiness to be adopted as a son by the leader of the Khitans. Shi Jingtang further promised that after the Tang army was repelled, he would cede sixteen prefectures north of the Yanmen Pass to the Khitans. These prefectures included Youzhou and Yunzhou, in the north of modern-day Shanxi and Hebei.

However, his plan to subordinate himself to the Khitans did not sit well with his generals. His lieutenant Liu Zhiyuan said, "One could argue in favor of appealing to the Khitan chief for help and swearing loyalty to him, but being adopted as a son is a bit too much. Additionally, it is reasonable to promise them gold, silver and jewelry, but you shouldn't cede territory to them."

Intent on preserving his own power to the expense of his country, Shi Jingtang turned a deaf ear to Liu Zhiyuan's argument. He promptly sent Sang Weihan to offer Yelü Deguang these concessions, selling out his country in the process.

Yelü Deguang had always aspired to expand southward, so he was overjoyed at the incredibly favorable concessions offered by Shi Jingtang. He immediately sent 50,000 of his best cavalrymen to relieve the siege of Jinyang. With Shi Jingtang's troops sallying out of the city walls in coordinated attack, they hemmed in from two sides and routed the Tang forces.

When Yelü Deguang himself later arrived in Jinyang, Shi Jingtang came out of the city gate to greet him, obsequiously calling Yelü Deguang "Father," despite being ten years older than Yelü Deguang. He humbly asked how the Khitan troops could have ever beaten the Tang army in so short a time, allowing the highly flattered Yelü Deguang to give a glowing account of the prowess of his army. Shi Jingtang appeared duly impressed and expressed his admiration for the Khitans, pleasing Yelü Deguang with his compliments.

After a period of observation, Yelü Deguang finally concluded that Shi Jingtang had indeed cast in his lot with him. He said to Shi, "I haven't traveled three thousand *li* to rescue you in vain. I believe you have the bearing and aura to be ruler of the Central Plains. I'll make you Emperor."

In false modesty, Shi Jingtang at first declined this offer, but at the urging of his close associates soon accepted it with pleasure. Shortly afterwards, the leader of the Khitans formally proclaimed Shi Jingtang Emperor. Upon his accession Shi Jingtang immediately ceded the sixteen prefectures to the Khitans, as promised.

With the support of the Khitans, Shi Jingtang marched south to attack Luoyang. Having suffered repeated defeats at the hands of the Khitans, Li Congke, the last Emperor of the Late Tang dynasty, had lost his will to fight. He spent his days waiting for the end to come, drinking and sobbing. As Shi Jingtang's troops approached Luoyang, the last Emperor torched his palace, and threw his entire family and then himself into the flames in a collective suicide.

After Shi Jingtang captured Luoyang and overthrew the Later Tang dynasty, he formally became the emperor of China's Central Plains. He named his new dynasty, Jin, and established his capital at Bian, giving himself the title of Emperor Gaozu of the Later Jin. In gratitude to Yelü Deguang, the leader of the Khitans, Shi Jingtang wrote a memorial to the Khitan leader, calling him "Father Emperor" and himself "Son Emperor." In addition to an annual tribute to the Khitan court of 300,000 bolts of silk fabrics, on festive occasions Shi Jingtang regularly sent envoys bearing gifts to the Khitan king, his mother, members of the aristocracy and top officials. Whenever any of the Khitan bigwigs was less than satisfied, they would immediately send Shi Jingtang messengers to take him to task, and Shi would unfailingly give abject and reverent apologies. Envoys of the Jin would frequently suffer indignities and insults from the insolent Khitan officials who received them. These humiliating experiences would be recounted back in the capital Bian. The entire Jin court felt the pain of humiliation, except Shi Jingtang, who remained unconcerned and unaffected.

After seven years of being propped up by the Khitans as the "Son Emperor," Shi Jingtang fell ill and died. His nephew Shi Chonggui succeeded him as Emperor Chudi of Later Jin. When Emperor Chudi presented memorials to the king of the Khitans, he called himself "Grandson," but gave no indication that he was their subject. For that reason, Yelü Deguang became offended, and sent troops against the Later Jin.

The troops and people of the Later Jin united in their struggle against the invaders, twice repelling the Khitans as they invaded the Central Plains. However, with the help of traitors in the Jin court, the Khitan troops were finally able to march into Bianjing. They took Emperor Chudi prisoner, and transported him to the Khitan Kingdom. This marked the end of the Later Jin dynasty.

In 947 AD, Yelü Deguang entered Bianjing and proclaimed himself Emperor of Da Liao. That same year, the Khitans had changed their dynasty name to Liao. The residents of the capital Bianjing fled when the Liao army invaded the city. This sparked Yelü Deguang to climb up to the top of the city gate and announce through an interpreter, "Folks, you have nothing to fear from me. I am a human like you. I had not originally intended to come here, but was invited in by Han people. I will make sure you have a better life."

His deeds, however, did not match his words. He gave the Liao troops a free hand to loot and exact goods everywhere in the name of provisioning their horses. This kind of so-called "foraging for hay and grain" had the effect of turning the farmland around Bianjing and Luoyang into hundreds of miles of deserted, uncultivated waste land. He ordered Jin officials to extort money from public servants and civilians alike, in the name of "rewarding the soldiers for their service to the country". Fed up with the killings and looting by the Liao troops, the people of Central Plains began to organize insurgencies against the Liao. Their scale ranged from a few thousand men to tens of thousands. They attacked prefectures and counties and killed officials appointed by the Liao. The insurgency in the east was particularly strong, and took control of three prefectures.

Yelü Deguang became frightened, saying to his attendants, "I didn't expect the people of Central Plains to be such a tough group of people." After some time, he summoned the high officials of the Late Jin dynasty and announced to them, "It's getting too warm for me here. I am going to Up Country (the kingdom of the Liao) to visit my mother."

Thus, the Liao army was forced to withdraw from Central Plains. However, the sixteen prefectures ceded by Shi Jingtang remained under the control of Khitan nobility, and would become the base for their future assault on the Central Plains.

120. Emperor Shizong of Zhou Upbraids Feng Dao

UPON THE WITHDRAWAL of Liao troops from Bianjing, Liu Zhiyuan, a top general of the Later Jin dynasty, proclaimed himself Emperor and led a massive army southward. His highly disciplined army won the support of the people of the Central Plains. Liao generals fled in haste before the advancing Liu troops. It did not take Liu Zhiyuan long to recover Luoyang and Bianjing. In June of that year, Liu Zhiyuan made Bianjing his capital and changed the dynasty name to Han. He became Emperor Gaozu of the Later Han dynasty.

He died after only ten months of reign. Following the succession of his son Liu Chengyou as Emperor Yindi of the Later Han, internal rifts soon appeared. Feeling threatened by the power of his generals, Emperor Yindi secretly sent assassins after General Guo Wei in Yedu. When the plot was discovered, Guo Wei staged a coup. In 950 AD, Guo Wei overthrew the Later Han and was acclaimed Emperor by his troops.

The next year Guo Wei ascended the throne in Bianjing as Emperor Taizu of the Later Zhou dynasty. His humble origins made Emperor Taizu a ruler responsive to the concerns of the common people. His literacy made him sensitive to the need to bring talent into the government and to institute political reforms. Under his rule, China gradually emerged from the chaos of the Five Dynasties Period.

At the founding of the Later Zhou, Liu Chong, a younger

brother of Liu Zhiyuan, refused to submit to its rule and took control of Taiyuan, establishing a separatist regime known to history as the Northern Han (one of the ten Kingdoms). In order to become a credible force against the Later Zhou, Liu Chong swore fealty to the Liao, calling its ruler "Uncle Emperor" and himself "Nephew Emperor." His several offensives against the Zhou, supported by Liao troops, were beat back by Emperor Taizu of the Later Zhou.

In 954 AD, the sonless Emperor Taizu died. His wife, Empress Chai had a nephew called Chai Rong, who was bright, capable, and had acquired an impressive array of martial skills. Emperor Taizu had always treated him like a son. Upon Emperor Taizu's death, Chai Rong became Emperor Shizong of the Later Zhou.

With Emperor Shizong freshly installed as Emperor, Liu Chong, King of the Northern Han, believed that the uncertain political situation in the Zhou offered an opportunity for him to gain control of the Central Plains. He assembled a force of 30,000 men, supplemented by 10,000 cavalrymen sent by the king of the Liao at his request, and marched on Luzhou (with its seat in modern-day Changzhi, Shanxi Province).

When news of the offensive reached Bianjing, Emperor Shizong of Zhou called an urgent meeting of his ministers. He proposed to personally lead an army to repel the attack, but his advisers said, "Your Majesty has just ascended the throne and has yet to secure the loyalty of the country. It wouldn't be prudent at this juncture for Your Majesty to undertake a campaign away from the capital. It is much wiser to delegate the task to a general."

Emperor Shizong insisted, "Liu Chong is taking advantage of the recent death of the emperor, my young age, and my fresh ascension to the throne to try to take control of the Central Plains. He is personally leading the offensive, so I have no choice but to face him in person."

Seeing the firm resolve of their sovereign, the ministers fell silent. However, the Grand Preceptor Feng Dao continued to speak out against it. Feng Dao had been Prime Minister during the time of Emperor Mingzong of the Later Tang. Through four successive dynasties he had always managed to adapt to new circumstances and ingratiate himself with every new master. When the Liao troops captured Bianjing, he went of his own accord to make obeisance before the Liao king. Some of the rulers of new dynasties found it to their benefit to keep him in their service. He consequently alternated between important positions such as Prime Minister, Grand Preceptor, or Grand Mentor. On this occasion, the young age and relative inexperience of Emperor Shizong prompted Feng Dao to assume the air of a veteran politician as he argued against the military action contemplated by the monarch.

Emperor Shizong said to Feng Dao, "Emperor Taizong of Tang personally led his troops in gaining control of the country. How can I hide behind my troops for my personal safety?"

Feng Dao retorted with a snort, "Does Your Majesty think you are comparable to Emperor Taizong of Tang?"

Aware of Feng Dao's disdain for him, Emperor Shizong said with vehemence, "With our overwhelming force, crushing Liu Chong is as easy as quashing an egg under the weight of a mountain."

Feng Dao rejoined, "Only I wonder if Your Majesty has the weight of a mountain."

Emperor Shizong was infuriated by the rejoinder and, giving a violent flick of his sleeve, left the imperial audience hall in a huff. The other officials eventually rallied to the emperor's side, and Emperor Shizong made the final decision to lead the expedition.

This incident left a bitter taste in the mouth of Emperor Shizong, so he soon sent Feng Dao away by putting him in charge of the building and maintenance of the tomb of Emperor Taizu of the Later Zhou. Feng Dao never got over this rebuff by the emperor, dying an unhappy man.

When Emperor Shizong's army approached Gaoping (in modern-day Shanxi Province), it ran into Northern Han forces. The two armies then arrayed themselves for battle. Liu Chong of the Northern Han was buoyed by a sense of superiority when he saw that the Zhou army was outnumbered. He said with disdain, "If I had known, I wouldn't have requested help from the Khitans. This time I am not only going to defeat the Zhou army, I am going to show the Khitans what I am capable of accomplishing."

Under the strong offensive of the Northern Han army, the right flank of the Zhou army folded. Its cavalry was beaten back, while many of its infantrymen surrendered. At this critical juncture, Emperor Shizong rode into battle amid showers of arrows. His two generals, Zhao Kuangyin and Zhang Yongde, each led 2,000 imperial guardsmen into the enemy lines. The sight of their self-assured Emperor calmly directing the battle galvanized the Zhou soldiers. They felt their strength and spirit multiplied a hundred fold as they charged headlong into the enemy lines. In the end, the Northern Han army suffered a dramatic defeat.

The Liao troops had stayed in the background. When they witnessed the collapse of the Northern Han army, they quietly pulled back. In one defeat after another, Liu Chong of the Northern Han retreated with the Zhou army in hot pursuit and no reinforcements in sight. He was finally left with only 100 cavalrymen who escorted him on an abject flight back to Jinyang.

In the aftermath of the battle of Gaoping, the emperor Shizong's prestige soared. After his return to Bianjing, he embarked on reforming the military, alleviating taxes, and actively preparing to unify China. Two years later, he led an expedition against the Southern Tang (one of the Ten Kingdoms) and captured fourteen prefectures north of the Yangtze. In a subsequent northern expedition on land and by water, he recovered large tracts of territory in North China. Unfortunately he fell ill just as he was on the point of fulfilling his ambition to unify China.

In 959 AD, six years into his reign, Emperor Shizong of Later Zhou died and was succeeded by his seven-year-old son, Chai Shixun, as Emperor Gongdi of the Later Zhou dynasty.

SONG DYNASTY (960 AD–1279)

NORTHERN SONG DYNASTY (960 AD–1127)

121. The Imperial Yellow Robe Is Now His

WHEN EMPEROR GONG of the Later Zhou dynasty ascended to throne, he was too young to govern, so his chief ministers Fan Zhi and Wang Pu acted as regents. As Later Zhou had been racked by political uncertainties, rumors began circulating among the anxiety-ridden residents of the imperial capital that Zhao Kuangyin was on the point of grabbing the throne.

A trusted military commander of Emperor Shizong of the Later Zhou dynasty, Zhao Kuangyin had achieved an impressive string of battlefield successes as he followed Emperor Shizong in his campaigns across China. The emperor placed so much trust in Zhao that he appointed him a commander of the Imperial Army in charge of defending the emperor and the capital, with the title of Palace Inspector-General. The Imperial Army was the best-trained and most well equipped military unit in the Later Zhou dynasty.

Upon the death of Emperor Shizong, the control of the armed forces fell into the hands of Zhao Kuangyin. The history of the Five Dynasties Period was replete with instances in which military commanders took over the throne. Speculation about Zhao's intention to seize power was therefore not at all surprising.

In 960 AD, at a grand audience in the Zhou court during the Spring Festival, a messenger brought an urgent war alert to the capital from the frontiers. An allied force of the Northern Han dynasty and the Liao dynasty had launched an attack on the Zhou borders. Amid the general panic at the court, Fan Zhi and Wang Pu made the decision to dispatch Zhao Kuangyin to repel the attack.

When he received this order, Zhao immediately set about appointing his commanders and mustering his forces, and within two days he led his massive army out of Bianjing, the capital. He took along his brother Zhao Kuangyi and his trusted adviser Zhao Pu.

Arriving that evening at the Chenqiao post house about ten miles out from the capital, Zhao Kuangyin ordered his troops to set up camp for the night. The soldiers fell asleep before their heads hit the pillow. In the meantime, some commanders gathered in private consultation. Some said, "The emperor is so young he won't be able to remember or recognize our contribution in the future even if we risk our lives to fight the battles for him now. It would be so much more worth our while to acclaim Inspector-General Zhao as Emperor!" The idea won general approval among all those present at the discussion, and a representative conveyed it to Zhao Kuangyi and Zhao Pu.

Before the representative had a chance to finish his presentation, the other commanders had rushed in with their swords drawn and clamored in unison, "We've decided. We must have the Inspector-General as our Emperor!"

Keeping their joy in check, Zhao Kuangyi and Zhao Pu admonished them to calm their troops and see that the situation did not get out of hand. At the same time, they dispatched a messenger to inform General Shi Shouxin and General Wang Shenqi, who had stayed behind to defend the capital.

As word quickly spread through the camp, the troops, now aroused from their sleep, thronged enthusiastically to the post house where Zhao Kuangyin was staying and waited outside until daybreak.

Zhao Kuangyin, after drinking himself to sleep, was awakened by the din of voices coming from the outside. He opened the door and heard a loud appeal: "We want the Inspector-General to be Emperor!"

Before Zhao Kuangyin could utter a word, several soldiers had scrambled in and draped a yellow robe on him. The troops fell on their knees and kowtowed before him amid a general clamor of "Long live the emperor!" They put Zhao Kuangyin on a horse, not without some pushing and dragging, to lead the troops back to the capital.

Once in his saddle on the horse, Zhao Kuangyin finally had a chance to make himself heard, "Since you've made me Emperor, will you be able to follow my orders?"

The troops answered as a man, "We are certainly at Your Majesty's orders."

Therefore, Zhao Kuangyin issued the order that his troops were to ensure the safety of the Empress Dowager and the young Emperor of the Later Zhou dynasty upon their entrance into the capital, forbidding them to do any harm to the court officials or to raid the state treasury or storehouses. Those carrying out these orders would be rewarded and those breaching them would be severely punished. Since Zhao Kuangyin was supreme commander of the Imperial Army and enjoyed the support of his generals, there was no question of anyone not following his orders to the letter. The troops marched toward the capital in a disciplined, orderly fashion.

With inside support provided by Shi Shouxin and Wang Shenqi, taking the capital Bianjing was easy for Zhao's army.

When Fan Zhi and Wang Pu were brought before Zhao Kuangyin, he said to them with feigned embarrassment, "I know I owe a deep debt of gratitude to Emperor Shizong. But what could I do when the troops wouldn't take my no for an answer?"

Fan Zhi and Wang Pu did not know how to reply. A general barked, "We owe allegiance to none other than the Inspector-General, and we want him to be our Emperor as of today!"

Frightened, Fan Zhi and Wang Pu went down on their knees to pay homage to Zhao Kuangyin.

With the abdication of Emperor Gong of the Later Zhou dynasty, Zhao Kuangyin became Emperor of a new dynasty called the Song, and chose Dongjing (modern-day Kaifeng, Henan Province) as his capital. This became known to history as the Northern Song dynasty. Zhao Kuangyin assumed the title of Emperor Taizu of the Northern Song dynasty. The Five Dynasties Period characterized by five decades of war and conflict thus ended.

With Zhao Kuangyin in the throne, his mother was now the Empress Dowager. When the ministers extended congratulations to her, the Empress Dowager looked worried, her brow knitted tightly.

After the departure of the ministers, her attendants asked the Empress Dowager, "Why are you unhappy on the occasion of your son's enthronement?"

The Empress Dowager said, "I understand that it's tough to be an emperor. The emperor earns respect only when it governs the country well. If his rule leads to chaos, the emperor is stuck and can no longer return to civilian life even if he wants to."

The Empress Dowager's worry was not unfounded. China was divided at the time of Zhao Kuangyin's accession. Some military commissioners who controlled parts of the Central Plains during the Later Zhou dynasty begrudged Zhao's accession to the throne. There were also independent governments on the outer fringes of China.

122. A Cup of Wine Relieves the Generals of Their Command

BARELY SIX MONTHS into the reign of Emperor Taizu of the Northern Song dynasty, two military commissioners rebelled. Emperor Taizu personally led his army to quash the rebellion, which was put down after much effort.

This experience deeply unsettled Emperor Taizu, who privately asked Zhao Pu, "Why have five dynasties already risen and fallen in the short space of time between the end of the Tang dynasty and now, all plagued by endless strife that took a huge toll on civilian lives?"

Zhao Pu replied, "The reason is quite plain. The anarchy in the country has its origin in the uncontrolled growth of the military governors' power. Once the control of the military is centralized in the hands of the court, the country will be at peace."

Emperor Taizu nodded in approval.

On another occasion, Zhao Pu said to Emperor Taizu, "Shi Shouxin and Wang Shenqi, the two generals of the Imperial Army, wield too much power over the army. It's a good idea to transfer them out of the Imperial Army."

The emperor reassured him, "Don't worry. These two are old friends of mine and will not challenge me."

Zhao Pu replied, "I'm not worried about the possibility of their rebelling against you. They lack leadership qualities; if trouble brews in their ranks, they will be overwhelmed."

Emperor Taizu tapped his temple and said, "Thanks for the

timely warning!"

A few days later Emperor Taizu hosted a banquet in his palace, to which he invited senior generals, including Shi Shouxin and Wang Shenqi.

After a few rounds of wine, Emperor Taizu ordered the eunuchs in attendance to withdraw. Raising his cup, he proposed a toast and invited the guests to drink up, saying, "Without your help I wouldn't be here today. But does any one of you realize that the emperor has his share of problems. A military commissioner would have it easier than the emperor. To be candid with you, I haven't had a good night's sleep for the past year."

Shi Shouxin and the others were surprised to hear this from the emperor and asked for clarification.

Emperor Taizu said, "Isn't it obvious? The throne is a much coveted prize."

Shi Shouxin and the others got the drift and went down on their knees in fear, saying, "Why does Your Majesty say this? Now that stability has been re-established in the country, who would have the temerity to waver in his allegiance to Your Majesty?"

Shaking his head, Emperor Taizu said, "I have full trust in you. However, if some among your troops should be tempted by wealth and power and put a yellow robe on you, would you be able to resist?"

Shi Shouxin and the others now clearly sensed danger; they kept knocking their heads on the floor and said in a teary voice, "Unsophisticated military men that we are, the thought never entered our mind. Will Your Majesty point a way out for us?"

Emperor Taizu said, "I think it would be in your interest to hand your control over the army to the court and take up a sinecure someplace away from the capital. You will be able to buy some land and some houses, which could be bequeathed to your offspring, and live out the rest of your life in happiness and without care. You and I will be like family, with no more reason for any mutual mistrust. Isn't that better for all of us?"

Shi Shouxin and the others replied in unison, "Your Majesty has seen to every detail with our interest in his heart!"

The guests went home after the banquet. The next morning

each one of them submitted a memorial asking permission to resign their office because of age and illness. Emperor Taizu immediately granted their request and took back their power over the military. They were subsequently sent away with large sums of money to take up office as regional military commissioners.

This incident is known to Chinese history as "a cup of wine that relieves the generals of their command."

On a later occasion when some military commissioners came to the capital for an imperial audience, Emperor Taizu invited them to a banquet in the imperial garden. He said to them, "You are all veteran ministers of the government and busy in your military districts. I am really sorry to ask you to undertake such a strenuous trip."

A smart military commissioner came up with a quick answer, "I haven't made any major contribution that would justify my staying in office. I request Your Majesty's permission to retire to my home town."

Another, less tactful military commissioner began talking about his achievements, which caused Emperor Taizu to comment with a frown, "There's no need to rehash this old stuff."

The next day Emperor Taizu relieved all these military commissioners of their command.

After taking back the power of the regional military commanders, Emperor Taizu reorganized the military, with the best men selected from armies away from the capital recruited to constitute the Imperial Army, which was put under the direct control of the emperor. Top local officials were now appointed by the central government. With the implementation of these measures, the Northern Song dynasty finally began to see a measure of stability.

123. Li, the Last King, Loses His Kingdom

WITH HIS HOUSE in order, the ambitious Emperor Taizu was now poised to unify the country by military force. Of the Ten Kingdoms of the Five Dynasties Period, the Northern Han in the north, and the Southern Tang, Wuyue, the Later Shu, the Southern Han and Nanping in the south were left. Which one should he take on first in his quest to unify China? Should he start by attacking the Northern Han, or tackle the south first? Emperor Taizu reflected on these matters for days without coming to a conclusion.

One freezing night, Zhao Pu was keeping himself warm by a stove when he heard someone knocking on his door. He wondered who could be visiting in such a snowstorm. He opened the door and took a close look at the unexpected visitor in a cape standing in the snow. He recognized, to his great surprise, Emperor Taizu.

Zhao Pu quickly ushered Emperor Taizu into the house, stoked the fire and started boiling a pot of meat. He told his wife to bring wine to the table.

Zhao Pu asked, "Why has Your Majesty come out in such a blizzard?"

Emperor Taizu said, "I couldn't sleep with all these things on my mind, so I thought I might as well come to you for advice."

After hearing Emperor Taizu out, Zhao Pu paused for reflection before saying, "If we take the Northern Han first, we will face threat from the Liao. It would be better to pacify the south before turning around to attack the Northern Han, which is so tiny that sooner or later it will submit to Your Majesty."

Emperor Taizu was pleased with the advice, "That's the conclusion I've come to, as well."

Once Emperor Taizu and Zhao Pu undertook the pacification of the south, it would be another ten years before Nanping, the Later Shu and the Southern Han were conquered, leaving only the two separatist regimes, the Southern Tang and Wuyue.

The Southern Tang was the largest of the Ten Kingdoms. It was economically prosperous because it was blessed with fertile land and was spared the ravages of war suffered by the Central Plains. Unfortunately, in their collective political ineptitude, a succession of kings of this once wealthy kingdom managed to put it on a path of decline.

The last of these kings, Li Yu, known to Chinese history as Li, the Last King of the Southern Tang, was a renowned poet, exceptionally accomplished in the arts of verse, music, calligraphy and painting, but dismally ignorant of the art of governance. Following the founding of the Northern Song dynasty, Li Yu paid huge annual tributes to it in gold, silver and other treasures in the hope of preserving his status. After three smaller neighboring states were conquered by Emperor Taizu of the Northern Song dynasty, he became apprehensive and lost no time in sending an emissary with a letter to Emperor Taizu, declaring his willingness to rename his kingdom "Southern Tang" and to change his title to "King of Jiangnan." This tiny concession proved insufficient to alter the determination of Emperor Taizu to unify China.

In September of 974 AD, Emperor Taizu sent his generals Cao Bin and Pan Mei at the command of 100,000 troops to attack the Southern Tang by land and by water. Cao Bin's waterborne force sailed out of Jingnan eastward on the Yangtze River and soon reached Caishiji (modern-day Ma'anshan, Anhui Province) after taking control of Chizhou (modern-day Guichi, Anhui Province). Pan Mei's infantry found its advance barred by the wide river after it reached the north bank of the Yangtze.

A suggestion was made to the Song troops to build a pontoon bridge made of bamboo rafts and big boats across the river so that the infantrymen could safely and quickly cross over. Pan Mei immediately acted on the suggestion and started building the pontoons.

When this information reached Jinling (modern-day Nanjing, Jiangsu Province), the capital of the Southern Tang dynasty, the king was drinking with his ministers. Li, the Last King asked his ministers for advice. They replied, "Never since ancient time have we heard of such a thing as crossing a river on pontoons. It will never work!"

The Last King said with a peal of laughter, "I knew these were a bunch of kids dabbling in adult stuff."

Three day later, the Song troops finished the pontoons, and Pan Mei's infantry crossed the Yangtze as if marching on land. The commanders of the Southern Tang forces either were defeated or surrendered. The 100,000-strong Song army was soon at the gates of the city of Jinling.

As this happened, Li, the Last King, was chanting mantras and discussing scriptures with Buddhist and Daoist monks in his palace, oblivious of what was going on. On one of his routine inspections on the battlements, he was surprised by the sight of a sea of Song flags and standards outside the city walls. He rushed back to his palace and dispatched his minister Xu Xuan to Dongjing to sue for peace.

Xu Xuan said to Emperor Taizu, "Li Yu has submitted to Your Majesty like a dutiful son. Why does Your Majesty still want to attack him?"

Emperor Taizu turned the question back, "Tell me then. Why should father and son live in separate households?"

Xu Xuan had no answer to that question and returned to Jinling to report to Li, the Last King. Another month elapsed and the noose around the city tightened another notch. Li, the Last King, sent Xu Xuan on another mission to Dongjing.

Xu Xuan implored Emperor Taizu not to attack Jinling, but the emperor began to lose his patience. With his hand on his sword, he said angrily to Xu Xuan, "Save your breath! I'm not saying Li Yu has committed any offense. But what I want now is a unified country, and to achieve it I cannot allow someone else to snore at my bedside."

Recognizing the futility of any further entreaties, Xu Xuan returned to Jinling. After hearing his report, Li, the Last King, knew the peace overture was doomed. He immediately called in the 150,000 troops stationed in Shangjiang to come to his rescue. These Tang troops were attacked on two flanks by the Song army at Wankou. When the Tang army tried to set fire to the Song camp, the wind turned and the Tang troops were themselves engulfed in flames and perished in large numbers.

Cao Bin sent a messenger into the city to urge Li, the Last King, to surrender as soon as possible to avoid loss of life and property. When Li, the Last King, tried to stall, Cao Bin gave the order to attack.

The following day the city fell. Cao Bin's troops entered the city in a disciplined and orderly fashion. Li, the Last King, had asked for a pile of kindling to be prepared in his palace for the purpose of self-immolation, but his nerves failed him at the last moment, and he walked out of his palace with his court to surrender to Cao Bin.

Li, the Last King, was taken to Dongjing, where he was treated well by Emperor Taizu. However, he never got over the fact that he had fallen from the power and glory of a monarch to the status of a person under house arrest whose kingdom was no more. He passed his days in tears. An expert poet, he composed a number of poems suffused with a deep wistfulness. One of his most popular lines is, "Pray tell how much melancholy weighs on thee? It's like so much water in spring rushing east to the sea!"

124. Zhao Pu Receives a Gift

FROM THE TIME of Emperor Taizu's seizure of power through the pacification of the south, Zhao Pu's advice was largely responsible for the successes enjoyed by Emperor Taizu of the Northern Song dynasty. Emperor Taizu, who regularly consulted him on matters big and small, appointed Zhao Pu Chief Minister.

Zhao Pu started his career as a minor official. His erudition fell far short of that of most other, much more cultured high officials. Following his appointment as Chief Minister, Emperor Taizu urged him to get into the habit of reading. Zhao Pu would get a book out of his book chest when he came home from work, close the door of his study and start reading aloud. The next day he would dispose of weighty matters of state in an effective and decisive manner. His family eventually found out that the only books in that chest were the *Analects of Confucius*. A popular legend began to circulate that by reading through only half of the *Analects of Confucius*, Zhao Pu was already able to run thc government as well as he did.

Because of Emperor Taizu's trust in him, Zhao Pu was unafraid to hold to his convictions in front of the emperor. On one occasion, Zhao Pu recommended someone to Emperor Taizu as a good choice for an office. For two days, Emperor Taizu withheld his consent. On the third day, when Zhao Pu again presented a memorial at the daily audience to urge the emperor to endorse his recommendation, Emperor Taizu took umbrage. He shredded the memorial and threw the pieces on the floor.

Zhao Pu got down on all fours to pick up the pieces in an unhurried fashion and stuffed them into his sleeve. After returning home from the audience, he glued the pieces back together and handed the salvaged memorial to the emperor a few days later at an imperial audience. Zhao Pu's insistence finally persuaded Emperor Taizu to accept his recommendation.

On another occasion, Zhao Pu's recommendation to promote an official was rejected by Emperor Taizu. Again, Zhao Pu insisted. Emperor Taizu said, "My answer is no. What are you going to do about it?"

Zhao Pu replied, "Promoting talented people is in the state's interest. How can Your Majesty decide such weighty matters on a whim?"

His face blanching in anger, Emperor Taizu flicked his sleeves and walked off in a huff towards his inner palace. Zhao Pu followed him closely and refused to budge from the door to the inner palace after Emperor Taizu disappeared behind it.

The guard went in to report to the emperor that the Chief Minister was refusing to leave. By this time, the emperor's anger had subsided. He sent a eunuch to inform Zhao Pu that he had agreed to his recommendation and that he could go home.

In his ten years as Chief Minister, Zhao Pu accumulated enormous power. In time, people began to cultivate connections with him, often with gifts.

Emperor Taizu was a frequent unannounced visitor at Zhao Pu's home. One day, Qian Chu, the king of Wuyue, sent a messenger with a letter to Zho Pu, bearing a gift of ten jars of "fruits of the sea." Zhao Pu placed the ten jars in the main hall and was on the point of opening the envelope containing the letter when Emperor Taizu arrived.

Emperor Taizu sat down in the hall and asked about the ten jars. Zhao Pu replied, "Some fruits of the sea sent by the king of Wuyue."

Emperor Taizu said with a laugh, "Fruits of the sea from Wuyue! They must be of superior quality. Let's look inside."

When Zhao Pu had his servants open the jars. All present were mesmerized. The jars contained not any products of the sea, but bars of gold.

Emperor Taizu, who had long taken a dim view of officials accepting bribes and abusing their power, was appalled by what he saw and his face darkened.

Breaking out a sweat and in great consternation, Zhao Pu begged for forgiveness, "Your humble servant has not had time to read the letter and had no knowledge of the content of the jars. I beg Your Majesty's forgiveness."

Emperor Taizu said in an icy tone, "Accept the gift by all means! They must think it is scholarly officials like you who call the shots in government."

The incident planted seeds of misgivings in Emperor Taizu's mind about Zhao Pu. Zhao Pu's reputation suffered another blow when he was denounced by an official for allegedly selling timber in violation of the law. There was an official ban on private transportation and trafficking of the heavy timber logged in the Qin and Long regions (in modern-day Shaanxi and Gansu). Zhao Pu had transported timber from there to build a house for himself. Some of his subordinates took advantage of the opportunity to smuggle heavy timber in Zhao Pu's name to Dongjing where they sold it for profit. Zhao Pu was thus unwittingly implicated in the infraction. Emperor Taizu was incensed and decided to punish Zhao Pu. In spite of the intercession of other ministers with the emperor on Zhao Pu's behalf, he was in the end stripped of his position of Chief Minister.

125. Yang, the Invincible

IT TOOK EMPEROR Taizu thirteen years to quash the five kingdoms in the south. Thereafter, he undertook the campaign to capture Taiyuan, the capital of the Northern Han dynasty. With the help of Liao troops, the Northern Han defeated the Northern Song army. Emperor Taizu died of illness shortly after, and his younger brother Zhao Kuangyi succeeded him as Emperor Taizong of the Northern Song dynasty.

Determined to carry through the unification of China, Emperor Taizong personally led four armies in 979 AD to lay siege to Taiyuan, the capital city of the Northern Han dynasty. Once again, Liao troops came to the Northern Han's rescue. However, a force sent by Emperor Taizong cut them off. Taiyuan, now tightly encircled by the Song troops and cut off from reinforcements, began to run out of food and fodder. Liu Jiyuan, the king of the Northern Han, saw no way out but to surrender. His veteran general Yang Ye also transferred fealty to the Northern Song dynasty. Having long heard about the military talent of Yang Ye, Emperor Taizong entrusted him with important responsibilities and conferred the title of Chief General on him.

After quashing the Northern Han dynasty, Emperor Taizong decided to press his new military advantage by attacking the Liao dynasty to recover lost territory in the north. In the face of the strong offensive of the Song troops, a succession of Liao commanders defending several regions in the north surrendered. The Song army had advanced all the way to Youzhou (modern-day Beijing), when the Liao dynasty sent its top general Yelü Xiuge into battle to save the day.

The two armies joined battle by the Gaoliang River (west of modern-day Beijing), where the Song army was routed. Emperor Taizong fled back to his capital on a donkey-drawn cart.

From then on, the Liao kept up its attacks against Song borders. Gravely concerned, Emperor Taizong appointed Yang Ye as Governor of Daizhou and charged him with defending Yanmen Pass.

In 980 AD, 100,000 Liao troops were sent to breach Yanmen Pass, which was at the time defended by Yang Ye with only a few thousand men. Realizing he was seriously outnumbered, the veteran general knew he could not win in a direct confrontation with the enemy force. Leaving the bulk of his troops in Daizhou, he led a few hundred cavalrymen through back roads, outflanking the enemy and getting behind the attackers.

The Liao army forged southwards, its spirits buoyed by the absence of any resistance, when all of a sudden battle cries erupted behind the troops as a cloud of dust rose up. Soon a cavalry detachment pounced on them like tigers tearing into a flock of sheep, hacking their men to death right and left. Caught totally off guard and confused about the size of the enemy attack force, the Liao troops were thrown into a panic and fled north in disarray. Yang Ye led his men in pursuit, killing large numbers of Liao troops, including a nobleman of the Liao court, and capturing a Liao general.

The victory at Yanmen Pass spread Yang Ye's reputation everywhere. Whenever the Liao troops saw standards with the character Yang on them, they would be afraid to engage the enemy. Yang Ye acquired the nickname "Yang the Invincible."

His military successes also made Yang Ye a target of jealous bile from commanders of border garrisons. Some submitted memorials to Emperor Taizong making damaging accusations against Yang Ye. Emperor Taizong, however, considered Yang Ye an indispensable aide. Not only did he ignore those attempts to malign Yang Ye, but forwarded those slanderous memorials in sealed envelopes to Yang Ye, who was naturally deeply touched by this trust the emperor showed toward him.

A few years later, Yelü Longxu, who was only twelve, succeeded Yelü Xian, Emperor Jingzong of the Liao dynasty, on his death. He took the title of Emperor Shengzong of the Liao dynasty. Empress Dowager Xiao, Longxu's mother, ruled as regent. This prompted the commanding general of a border garrison to write a memorial to Emperor Taizong of the Northern Song dynasty, urging him to take advantage of the political transition in the Liao court to recover the lost territory of the Sixteen Regions, including Yanzhou and Yunzhou. Emperor Taizong took his advice, and in 986 AD launched a northern expedition with three armies led respectively by Cao Bin, Tian Chongjin and Pan Mei, with Yang Ye as Pan Mei's second-in-command.

The three armies scored early victories as they advanced along their respective routes, with Pan Mei and Yang Ye recovering four regions as soon as their army marched out of Yanmen Pass. However, the main force led by Cao Bin was later routed by the Liao troops because it had penetrated too deeply into enemy territory without ensuring sufficient support. Emperor Taizong immediately ordered all the troops to pull back.

Upon receiving the order, Pan Mei and Yang Ye withdrew their troops as well as the civilians of the four liberated regions under their protection to the safety of the village of Langya. At that time, the Liao army had taken control of Huanzhou (east of modern-day Shuo County, Shanxi Province) and possessed an overwhelming numerical superiority. Yang Ye proposed a tactic of feigning an attack to hold down the main force of the Liao army, while positioning an elite contingent to provide cover for the retreating troops and civilians.

Wang Shen, the Army Supervisor, challenged this tactic, arguing, "We have an elite force of tens of thousands of troops. Why should we be afraid of them? In my view we should just march in formation on the high road leading from Yanmen, flaunting our standards and beating our drums to strike terror into the hearts of the enemy troops."

Yang Ye objected, "Your tactic is doomed to failure because we are now seriously outnumbered."

Wang Shen countered derisively, "Isn't General Yang the fabled invincible one? What could be the real reason behind this sudden battle-shyness, I wonder?"

This had the effect of infuriating Yang Ye, who declared, "I'm not afraid of death. But I do believe our soldiers shouldn't be allowed to die in vain when we face such unfavorable odds. If you insist on engaging the enemy even under these circumstances, I will lead the first attack."

General Pan Mei also took Wang Shen's side. Yang Ye had no choice but to ride into action. Before riding into battle, he said in tears to Pan Mei, "I have no doubt that this is a lost battle. I had planned to wait for the right moment to deal a heavy blow to the enemy in fulfillment of my patriotic duty. But now I am compelled to die before I could fulfill that duty because I have to deflect the criticism that I am running from the enemy."

Pointing at Chenjiayu Valley (south of modern-day Shuo County, Shanxi Province) in the distance, he said to Pan Mei, "I hope you can place some infantrymen and archers in ambush on the two sides of the valley. When I am forced back to that location, you can attack from the two sides in my support. That way we might have a chance to turn the tide and snatch victory from the jaws of defeat."

As he had predicted, the Liao army ambushed Yang Ye's troops not long after they marched out of their camp. Yang Ye's heroic combat was useless against the tidal waves of Liao troops that kept surging ahead. Although putting up a valiant fight despite the odds, Yang Ye and his troops found themselves overwhelmed and Yang Ye drew the Liao troops towards Chenjiayu Valley as planned.

They reached Chenjiayu Valley at sunset to find the place deserted. The valley was eerily quiet and there was no sign of any Northern Song troops. Where was the main force under Pan Mei's command? It turned out Pan Mei's force did come to the Valley, and had been waiting for news from Yang Ye. After one day, when no news came, Wang Shen believed that the Liao force must have retreated. Worried that Yang Ye would claim credit ahead of him, he urged Pan Mei to withdraw the ambushers and pull out of the Valley. When they finally learned of Yang Ye's defeat, they fled by a back road.

When he found that the expected support was not there at the designated location, Yang Ye was frustrated beyond words. There was nothing to do but to lead his troops back into battle against the pursuing enemy. Soon Yang Ye had only about a hundred men left. Soldier after valiant soldier fell before the increasing numbers of Liao troops. Yang Ye shouted in tears to the soldiers, "You have parents and family. I don't want you to die with me here. I want you to make a break for it. One day you will be able to tell the government what really happened."

The soldiers were moved to tears by these words and by Yang Ye's determination to make a heroic last stand. Not one of them had the heart to leave him. All perished in battle, including Yang Ye's son Yang Yanyu and his lieutenant Wang Gui. Wounded in a dozen places on his body and covered in blood, Yang Ye never stopped fighting. Charging back and forth, he slew hundreds. When his steed, shot by an arrow, fell and threw him off, the Liao troops surrounded him, taking him captive.

After Yang Ye was captured, the Liao general urged him to surrender. He looked up with a sigh, saying, "I had wanted to perform my patriotic duty by defeating the enemy but I ended up losing all my men because of the actions of wrongheaded officials. I cannot live with this disgrace." He refused food and drink in Liao captivity, and died three days later.

When news of Yang Ye's death reached Dongjing, the entire court mourned the loss. Emperor Taizong was naturally heartbroken over the loss of a valiant, competent general. He demoted Pan Mei, relieved Wang Shen of his commission, and ordered an inquiry into his misconduct.

Yang Ye's descendents turned out to be his worthy successors. His son Yang Yanzhao and his grandson Yang Wenguang performed brilliantly in defending the Northern Song dynasty's borders against foreign aggression. Their heroic feats became a folk legend, and provided material for the popular stories about the "Yang Family of Generals" widely circulated and passed down through the ages in China.

126. Kou Zhun Holds off Liao Aggression

TAKING ADVANTAGE OF the pervasive incompetence at the Northern Song court, the Liao dynasty staged repeated border incursions into Song territory. Soon after the accession of Zhao Heng, son of Emperor Taizong, as Emperor Zhenzong of the Northern Song dynasty, the name Kou Zhun was submitted to the new Emperor as a highly recommended candidate for the post of Chief Minister by virtue of his loyalty to the government and his ability to solve difficult situations.

Emperor Zhenzong observed, "I've heard that Kou Zhun is a willful person who thinks he can do no wrong. How does one deal with that side of his personality?"

The high official who recommended Kou Zhun replied, "It is precisely someone like Kou Zhun who will prove equal to the challenge of warding off the Liao's designs on the Central Plains."

During previous stints of service to Emperor Taizong, including in his stint as Deputy Chief Minister, Kou Zhun had become famous for courageously speaking unwelcome truths to the emperor. On one such occasion, Kou Zhun managed to anger Emperor Taizong with his report and comments. When the emperor could no longer stand listening to Kou Zhun and rose to his feet to go back to his inner palace, Kou Zhun stopped him by seizing his gown and insisted that Emperor Taizong should hear him out. Emperor Taizong had no choice but to stay. He was heard later to heap praise on Kou Zhun, saying, "Emperor Taizong of Tang had an excellent adviser in Wei Zheng. I have my Kou Zhun."

However, Kou Zhun's uprightness also got him in trouble with some of the powerful and resulted in him being ostracized from the court as a regional governor. In the face of a clear danger at the borders, Emperor Zhenzong found himself compelled to accept his minister's recommendation and call Kou Zhun back to the capital.

In 1004 AD, Empress Dowager Xiao and Emperor Shengzong of the Liao dynasty led a 200,000-strong army southward. As its vanguard reached Chanzhou (modern-day Puyang, Henan Province), the Northern Song court was swamped by reports of the imminent danger faced by its regional commanders. Kou Zhun urged Emperor Zhenzong to personally lead the army to repel the attack, while Deputy Chief Minister Wang Qinruo and another minister, Chen Yaosou, were privately counseling the emperor to flee the capital. Wang Qinruo, who was from the south, believed that the capital should be moved to Jinling; Chen Yaosou, on the other hand, being from Shu country, advised Emperor Zhenzong to seek safety in Chengdu.

Torn between these alternatives, Emperor Zhenzong finally called in the new Chief Minister Kou Zhun for advice, "Some suggest that I move the capital to Jinling; others urge me to move to Chengdu. What do you think?"

Seeing Wang Qinruo and Chen Yaosou flanking the emperor, Kou Zhun immediately understood what was going on. He demanded in a stern voice, "Who are the wise guys who came up with these cute ideas? They should have their heads chopped off!" He maintained that if Emperor Zhenzong personally led the army into battle, the army would be highly motivated and could beat back the Liao invaders. He argued also that if the court deserted Dongjing and fled south, it would so demoralize the people that the enemy would be able to exploit the uncertainties and instability to topple the government. Kou Zhun's words bolstered Emperor Zhenzong's resolve. He decided to lead the army into battle with Kou Zhun as co-commander.

When the Northern Song army reached Weicheng (southeast of modern-day Hua County, Henan Province), some accompanying ministers, having learned of the strength of the massive Liao force moving southward, chose a time when Kou Zhun was absent to once again lobby Emperor Zhenzong for a temporary withdrawal to dodge the brunt of the invading army. Already weak in his resolve, Emperor Zhenzong began to be swayed by the urgings of these ministers. He again summoned Kou Zhun for advice.

He said to Kou Zhun, "Everyone says it's wiser to go south. What do you think?"

Kou Zhun replied in a sober tone, "Those who propose moving south are ignorant cowards. At this moment when the enemy presses closer and the people feel insecure, we can only move forward. We cannot afford the luxury of retreating one inch. If we move forward, the morale of the armies in the various garrisons of Hebei will soar. If we were to take a few steps backward, the entire army would disintegrate, with the enemy in hot pursuit. When that happened, Your Majesty would be prevented from reaching Jinling."

Emperor Zhenzong could offer no rebuttal to the cogent analysis of Kou Zhun. He fell silent, but deep down he remained conflicted, unable to make up his mind.

When Kou Zhun walked out of the imperial tent, he ran into Gao Qiong, the Palace Commander-in-Chief. Kou Zhun asked Gao Qiong, "How do you propose to repay the government for what it has done for you?"

Gao Qiong replied, "I am ready to die for the country."

Kou Zhun then took Gao Qiong back into the imperial tent and repeated his advice to the emperor, adding, "If Your Majesty still has doubts about my advice, would he please ask Gao Qiong for his view?"

Gao Qiong echoed Kou Zhun's view, saying, "The Chief Minister is right. The officers and men in the Imperial Army all have their families in Dongjing and will find it hard to support moving the capital to the south. If Your Majesty makes up your mind to lead the expedition to Chanzhou, we are determined to fight to the last man. We have no doubt that we will prevail against the Liao army."

Before Emperor Zhenzong had time to utter a word, Kou Zhun

added urgently, "It's now or never. Will Your Majesty order your army to set out now?"

At the urging of Kou Zhun, Gao Qiong and the troop commanders, Emperor Zhenzong finally made up his mind to advance toward Chanzhou.

By that time, the Liao army had closed in on Chanzhou from three sides. The Northern Song in the meantime had placed archers at strategic locations. When the head general of the Liao army, Xiao Talin, went on a reconnaissance mission accompanied by a few cavalrymen, the party walked into an ambush of Song archers, who killed Xiao Talin in a hail of arrows.

The loss of the head commander of the Liao army brought the Empress Dowager Xiao both grief and fear. The fact that Emperor Zhenzong of the Song dynasty was personally directing the campaign made her realize that the Northern Song dynasty would be difficult to defeat. She was now disposed to talk peace.

The city of Chanzhou straddled the Yellow River. Under the escort of Kou Zhun, Gao Qiong and other top officials, Emperor Zhenzong crossed the river to the northern part of Chanzhou. In the meantime, the other forces of the Song army had converged on Chanzhou. When the troops saw the emperor's large standard bearing the insignia of the yellow dragon, they broke out in thunderous cheers, their morale immeasurably raised.

Empress Dowager Xiao of Liao sent an emissary to the Song camp to negotiate a peace accord which would require concessions of territory by the Song dynasty. The peace overture found an eager listener in Emperor Zhenzong, who said to Kou Zhun, "Concessions of territory are out of the question, but if the Liao can settle for some money and goods, I don't see any objection."

Kou Zhu, who was opposed to peace parleys, said, "If they want peace, they must give back our territory in the Yanzhou and Yunzhou regions. Why should we give them any money or goods?"

However, Emperor Zhenzong, eager for peace, overrode Kou Zhun's objections and sent his emissary Cao Liyong to the Liao camp to negotiate the terms of the peace accord. Before sending him off, Emperor Zhenzong instructed Cao Liyong, "If they insist on indemnification, you have the authority to agree to annual reparations of 1,000,000 taels."

Kou Zhun was pained by this offer but did not want to offer a contrary view in the emperor's presence. He followed Cao Liyong out of the imperial tent. Grabbing Cao's hand, he said to him, "The reparation must not exceed 300,000. Otherwise I will demand your head when you return."

In fear of Kou Zhun, Cao Liyong drove a hard bargain at the Liao camp and succeeded in fixing the annual reparation at 300,000 taels of silver and silk.

When Cao Liyong returned to camp, Emperor Zhenzong was having his meal and was unable to immediately receive a report from him. However, eager to find out about the final terms of the accord, he sent a low-ranking eunuch to ask Cao Liyong how much reparation was agreed. Cao Liyong insisted on personally reporting to the emperor because he considered the information a state secret. As the eunuch pressed for a rough figure, Cao Liyong could no longer stall and held up three fingers.

When the eunuch reported back to the emperor, the latter, believing the reparation to be 3,000,000, cried in alarm, "So much!?" However, upon reflection he comforted himself with the thought, "So what! At least we got a major problem out of the way."

His meal over, Emperor Zhenzong summoned Cao Liyong for a full report. When Cao Liyong told him the reparation was 300,000 taels of silver and silk, Emperor Zhenzong nearly leaped with joy and heaped praise on Cao Liyong for his negotiating skills.

In accordance with the formal accord signed by the two sides, the Northern Song dynasty was to give the Liao 200,000 bolts of silk and 100,000 taels of silver every year. This large sum added to the burden of the people of the Northern Song for years to come. This accord is known to Chinese history as the "Treaty of Chanyuan" (Chanyuan is another name for Chanzhou).

Kou Zhun's insistence on fighting the Liao invaders averted greater losses. Emperor Zhenzong gave due credit to Kou Zhun, for whom he continued to have great respect. However, Wang Qinruo, a proponent for fleeing to the south, said to Emperor Zhenzong that Kou Zhun had used the emperor as a wager in his risky gamble on winning the war by getting the emperor to personally lead the expedition. He characterized the incident as a serious affront to the state. In addition, Emperor Zhenzong could not recall what happened at Chanzhou without some jitters. The rancor that began to build up in his heart against Kou Zhun finally led to the dismissal of the loyal Kou Zhun as chief minister.

127. Di Qing Sees No Shame in His Low Birth

BY MAKING CONCESSIONS for peaceful coexistence, Emperor Zhenzong of the Northern Song dynasty managed to appease the Liao. However, as the Northern Song dynasty was busy dealing with the Liao threat, the Dangxiang (also known as the Tangut) in the northwest was emboldened to make frequent attacks on the Song borders.

In 1038 AD, Yuan Hao, the chieftain of the Dangxiang tribe, formally proclaimed himself Emperor of the new dynasty of Great Xia, with its capital at Xingqing (modern-day Yinchuan, Ningxia). Because of its location northwest of the Northern Song dynasty, it is also known as the Western Xia dynasty.

Emperor Renzong of the Song dynasty sent his ministers Han Qi and Fan Zhongyan to Shaanxi to direct the campaign against the Western Xia. When Han Qi and Fan Zhongyan arrived in Shaanxi, someone recommended a young officer in the local army by the name of Di Qing, who was said to be a brave and skillful warrior and to possess the leadership qualities of a commanding general. Fan Zhongyan, who was looking for military leaders, was very much interested, so he asked his subordinates for more details about Di Qing. It turned out Di Qing had been a private in the Imperial Army in the capital. Because of the martial skills he had acquired since a child, his expert horsemanship and mastery of archery as well as bravery and physical strength, he was later promoted to become a low-ranking officer.

Following Yuan Hao's self-proclamation as Emperor of the Western Xia, Emperor Renzong of the Northern Song dynasty dispatched troops of the Imperial Army to the frontiers to garrison the borders. Di Qing was sent to Bao'an (modern-day Zhidan, Shaanxi Province).

When an army of the Western Xia attacked Bao'an, the Song troops defending the city, which had previously suffered numerous defeats in clashes with the Xia, were afraid to engage the enemy. As the commanding general, Lu Shouqin, was fretting about his troops' battle shyness, Di Qing volunteered to lead the vanguard to battle the army of the Western Xia. Relieved that Di Qing was willing to lead the vanguard into action, Lu Shouqin put a contingent at Di Qing's disposal.

Before every battle, Di Qing would change his costume. He would let down his long hair and put a bronze mask over his face, leaving two holes through which his eyes glared. Then he would ride into the enemy formation with a lance and start spearing the enemy combatants. In all their skirmishes into Song territory, the soldiers of the Western Xia had never encountered so formidable a foe, whose battle regalia struck terror into their hearts. With Di Qing and Song troops charging fearlessly into their midst, the Xia army was soon thrown into disarray and crumbled in defeat. Pressing their advantage, Di Qing and his troops pursued the enemy force until total victory was in hand.

When news of the victory reached the court, the elated Emperor Renzong of the Song dynasty promoted Lu Shouqin to a higher position and elevated Di Qing's military rank by four steps. Emperor Renzong had wanted to summon Di Qing to the capital for an audience but the plan was called off when Di Qing was sent to repel an attack by the Western Xia against Weizhou. A portrait of Di Qing was commissioned and later sent to the court.

For several years, the Western Xia continued to harass the Song borders, disturbing the peace of the border communities. In his twenty-five battles, Di Qing was wounded by arrows eight times, but never once lost a battle. The troops of the Western Xia were so awed by his name that they dreaded engaging him in battle.

After hearing the recommendation of his officers, Fan Zhongyan summoned Di Qing. When Fan asked Di what books he had read, Di Qing the soldier, who was not fully literate, was hard put to give an answer. Fan Zhongyan had this advice for him, "You are now a general. For a general it is no longer enough to be courageous in battle. You need to have a good knowledge of history and current events." He went on to give Di Qing a list of books to read.

Di Qing was grateful to Fan Zhongyan for his concern and encouragement, and made a point of reading assiduously whenever he had free time in his campaigns. In a few years, he had familiarized himself with all the books on military doctrine and the art of warfare written by famous generals since the Qin and Han dynasties. As his war achievements grew, he rose quickly through the ranks and his fame spread. He was later transferred back to the capital as Deputy Commander-in-Chief of the cavalry.

In order to prevent soldiers from deserting, the Northern Song dynasty resorted to an inhumane practice of tattooing or branding the soldiers' faces with identifying marks. Di Qing had had his face tattooed when he was a private. When he became a prominent general years later, he still had the black tattooed characters on his face.

In an audience with Emperor Renzong, the emperor told Di Qing that it was unseemly for a general to have these tattooed characters on his face, and that he should apply some special medication to remove them when he went home.

Di Qing replied, "I am grateful to Your Majesty for promoting me to where I am solely on the basis of my war achievements, without regard to my humble origin. I would rather keep these markings as an incentive to the soldiers to aspire for greater achievements."

Di Qing's perceptive analysis inspired greater admiration from Emperor Renzong.

On the strength of his numerous victories in military campaigns, he was eventually elevated to the post of Military Affairs Commissioner in charge of all national military affairs. It was unheard-of in Song history for someone to rise from the rank of private to that of Military Affairs Commissioner. Some ministers with a dim view of Di Qing's humble origins tried to dissuade Emperor Renzong from elevating Di Qing to such a high position, but Emperor Renzong, who was in that period in desperate need of military talent, dismissed such advice.

There were people who found Di Qing's stature as Military Affairs Commissioner grossly at variance with his lowly beginnings. A self-described descendant of Di Renjie, the famous Chief Minister of the Tang dynasty, presented a portrait of Di Renjie to Di Qing with this advice, "You must be a descendant of Lord Di. Why don't you adopt him as your ancestor?"

Di Qing smiled and answered modestly, "I am a person of low birth. It is by accident that I've risen to such prominence. There's no way I can claim such a distinguished personality as Lord Di as my ancestor."

128. The New Deal of Fan Zhongyan

FAN ZHONGYAN'S STRICT discipline over the army and measures he took to reduce the fiscal burden on frontier communities helped to solidify the Northern Song's border defenses. On the other hand, the Western Xia failed to reap any tangible benefits from years of war with the Northern Song. In 1043 AD Yuan Hao, the king of the Western Xia, was finally ready to submit to the Northern Song dynasty and sign a peace treaty. In exchange, the Northern Song dynasty promised him annual gifts of silver, silk and tea. Because of the accord, the Northern Song was able to enjoy a period of peace and stability along its northwestern borders.

Military strategy was not the only area where Fan Zhongyan's talent shone; he was also an outstanding statesman and man of letters in the Northern Song dynasty. A native of Wu County, Suzhou, his father died when he was still a child. He followed his mother to the household of a Mr. Zhu, whom she married to escape destitute poverty. Fan Zhongyan grew up amid great hardship. When he boarded at a temple in order to devote himself to his studies, he could not afford to have three meals a day and had to sustain himself on daily rations of thin gruel. However, none of this shook his determination to improve himself by studying and reading. When he read into the wee hours and could not even keep his eyes open out of sheer fatigue, he would douse his face with cold water to remain awake so that he could continue his. After five or six years of assiduous study, he became an erudite scholar.

When he was a Remonstrance Official (in charge of keeping watch over documents flowing to and from the throne and remonstrating with the ruler about conduct or policies that he considered improper), Fan Zhongyan denounced Lü Yijian, the Chief Minister, to Emperor Renzong for his nepotism and abuse of power. By stepping on the toes of such a powerful figure, he was courting trouble. Lü Yijian counterattacked by falsely accusing Fan Zhongyan of surrounding himself with a clique and driving a wedge between the emperor and the Chief Minister. Swayed by Lü Yijian's slander, Emperor Renzong banished Fan Zhongyan to a district in the south. He was transferred to Shaanxi only when the war with the Western Xia erupted.

Fan Zhongyan's brilliant performance in the war with the Western Xia convinced Emperor Renzong of his leadership qualities. This was a time when corruption in the government and the enormous war and reparations expenditure were depleting the coffers of the state treasury to a critical point. To deal with this pressing problem, Emperor Renzong summoned Fan Zhongyan from Shaanxi to the capital and named him Deputy Chief Minister.

When Fan Zhongyan returned to the capital, Emperor Renzong lost no time in calling him in for an audience to hear his proposals for good governance. Fan Zhongyan was fully aware that it was impossible to remedy all the ills that plagued the central government in one go, and that it had to be accomplished gradually. Nevertheless, at the urging of Emperor Renzong, he laid out a draft ten-point plan for reform, which included the following:

1. Periodic evaluation of government officials and promotion/demotion based on performance and merit, or lack thereof;

2. Strict restrictions placed on the obtaining of government jobs by children of high officials on their father's coattails;

3. Reform of the system of court-administered civil service examinations;

4. Careful vetting and recruitment of candidates for the top positions in local governments.

Other points related to the promotion of silk production and agriculture, reduction of mandatory labor required of citizens, enhanced military preparedness, and the tightening of the rule of law.

In his zeal for reform, Emperor Renzong immediately gave his approval for the implementation of the ten-point reform plan across the Empire. This plan is known to Chinese history as the "Qingli Reform" (Qingli is an era name of Emperor Renzong).

To implement the proposed reforms, Fan Zhongyan got together with other ministers, including Han Qi and Fu Bi, to review the candidates for the position of circuit supervisor in the various *lu* (circuits: administrative divisions in the Song period). One day when Fan Zhongyan was examining a list of circuit supervisors, he noticed the inclusion of someone known to be a corrupt official. He crossed out his name, signaling his removal from office.

Seeing this from a seat nearby, Fu Bi could not help commenting, "Mr. Fan, that stroke of the brush would bring tears to a whole household."

Fan Zhongyan gave this sobering answer, "Without bringing tears to that household, we would bring tears to the people of an entire circuit."

This reply immediately made Fu Bi see the light and admire even more the perspicacity and insight of Fan Zhongyan.

The introduction of the new reform measures had the effect of opening a Pandora's box. Members of the royal family and nobility, high officials and corrupt bureaucrats joined in a chorus of protest and started spreading rumors in an attempt to demonize the reforms. Ministers who had always harbored a grudge against Fan Zhongyan bombarded the emperor with daily allegations about Fan Zhongyan's clique-building activities and abuse of power.

As opposition to the reforms grew, Emperor Renzong began to waver in his resolve. Feeling the heat, Fan Zhongyan found his continued stay in the capital untenable and volunteered to go back to his garrison duty at the Shaanxi frontiers. Emperor Renzong was very happy to grant his wish and get rid of a controversial minister.

With the departure of Fan Zhongyan, Emperor Renzong abolished all the reforms.

Fan Zhongyan's reform proposals brought him immense personal grief, but he did not fret about it. A year after his ouster he was solicited for a commemorative article by his old friend Teng Zongliang, who was a government official in Yuezhou (with its seat in modern-day Yueyang, Hunan Province) on the occasion of the completion of the restoration of Yueyang Pavilion, a famous local landmark. In his article of dedication for Yueyang Pavilion, he wrote that a person with a grand political vision should in his heart and mind be prepared to "be proactive in foreseeing and feeling the concerns of society, and put the happiness and the interests of society before one's own." This has become a much-quoted motto through the ages. The dedication essay helped put Yueyang Pavilion on the national map.

129. The No-nonsense, Impartial Bao Zheng

IN THE AFTERMATH of the abolition of Fan Zhongyan's reforms, corruption in the central government became more pervasive, notably in the capital Kaifeng, where graft and bribery were rampant in the top echelons of government. Members of the royal family and nobility showed no regard for the law in their wanton pursuit of ill-gotten gains. This lawlessness began to change with the arrival of Bao Zheng, the new Governor of Kaifeng.

Bao Zheng was originally from Hefei, and had served a stint as the County Magistrate of Tianchang County (in Anhui Province). In his tenure as County Magistrate, he came across a case in which a peasant had put his ox in the cowshed overnight, and then woke up the next morning to find the ox lying in a pool of blood with its tongue cut out. The angry and pained peasant went to the county government office to file a complaint and ask Bao Zheng to find the perpetrator.

With no leads or suspects, the case appeared to be difficult to solve. After some reflection, Bao Zheng told the plaintiff, "Go home quietly and butcher the ox."

The peasant did not have the heart to kill his ox. Besides, butchering oxen used for tilling was prohibited by law for private individuals. On the one hand, an ox with its tongue cut out would not survive for more than a few days. On the other hand, now that he had the sanction of the county magistrate to butcher the ox, he should not need to fear the sanction of law.

He went home and butchered the ox. The next day someone filed a complaint with the county government accusing the peasant of illegally butchering an ox.

After hearing the complaint, Bao Zheng's face darkened. He thundered, "You have the nerve to denounce illegal butchering of an ox when it was you who cut out the tongue of that ox in the first place."

The plaintiff, stunned by what he heard, sank to his knees and repeatedly knocking his head on the floor admitted his guilt.

It turned out the person who cut out the ox's tongue had had a feud with the animal's owner. He had been driven by his grudge to cut out the ox's tongue and to denounce the peasant for illegal butchering.

By solving the case, Bao Zheng became widely known for his ability as a judge.

He reduced taxes and solved cases involving wrongful convictions everywhere he went as Chief Magistrate. In his tenure as a Remonstrance Official in the capital, he also proved a source of good advice. In an attempt to clean up Kaifeng, Emperor Renzong appointed Bao Zheng as its Governor.

Kaifeng was where royalty, nobility and the powerful congregated. Whoever became its governor in the past would cultivate the powerful elite and accept bribes from them. Bao Zheng was determined to change all that and deal a heavy blow to the culture of corruption.

It was a common practice in the Northern Song dynasty for a plaintiff to need someone to prepare a written complaint for him, which a petty official in the bureaucracy would then pass on to the governor. Some officials would seize this opportunity to extort money. Bao Zheng put an end to the practice; now an ordinary citizen with a complaint could simply go to the county building and beat the drum placed in front of the building, and the door would open allowing him to go directly before the presiding judge. This eliminated the possibility of petty officials demanding bribes or committing other shenanigans.

One year, devastating floods struck Kaifeng, and the Huimin

River could not channel away the floodwater. An investigation revealed that eunuchs and high officials had appropriated parts of the riverbed for their private use, upon which they had built gardens and pavilions, clogging the river. Bao Zheng ordered the owners to immediately dismantle all private structures on the riverbed. One high official balked at the order and refused to dismantle his structures. When officials sent by the Kaifeng government arrived to press for dismantlement, the high official countered with all kinds of specious arguments and produced a deed to prove his ownership of the land. Upon scrutiny, Bao Zheng found the deed to have been forged by the high official. Bao Zheng was furious and ordered him to immediately dismantle his garden, threatening to denounce the forgery in a memorial to the emperor. Realizing that it was not in his interest to have the matter escalate and be reported to the emperor, who might order an inquiry, the official gave in and dismantled the garden. The high officials and powerful figures who used to engage in shady behavior now drew back in fear of the no-nonsense style of law enforcement of Bao Zheng.

When a certain high official wanted to cultivate a relationship with Bao Zheng by offering him a gift, others told him to save his money because Bao Zheng was known for his incorruptibility. The official was told the following story: Bao Zheng once served in the government of Duanzhou (modern-day Zhaoqing, Guangdong Province), which was famous for its ink stones. The imperial court demanded that Duanzhou officials fulfill an annual quota of Duanzhou ink stones as a tribute. This annual quota was an opportunity for Duanzhou officials to line their pockets by plundering the community. They saved some ink stones for themselves to grease the palm of high officials. The number of ink stones that went into their private possession was many times the required number for the annual tribute. When Bao Zheng took up his post in Duanzhou he would collect only the number of ink stones required for the tribute to the imperial court, and not one more. He completed his term in Duanzhou without ever demanding one ink stone for himself.

The high official understood now that he would not get

anywhere with his bribery scheme, so he gave up. The incorruptible Bao Zheng became a household name among residents of Kaifeng, who circulated this ditty, "Don't expect to strike a bargain with either Yanluo (the God of the Netherworld) or with Lord Bao Zheng."

Bao Zheng applied the same stringent standards to his friends and relatives. He would rebuff all attempts by relatives to ride on his coattails. In time, his friends and relatives would understand the kind of person he was and would no longer dare to seek his help with their private affairs.

Emperor Renzong showed his appreciation for Bao Zheng by making him Deputy Military Affairs Commissioner. Even after reaching such heights in officialdom, he continued to lead a simple, frugal life, not much different from that of an ordinary citizen. Upon his death five years later, he left a will which stated, "if any of my descendants is convicted of corruption while serving in the government, he will not be allowed to return to the ancestral home, and will not be allowed to be buried in the Bao family cemetery."

Bao Zheng won praise for his honesty and incorruptibility when he was alive; he became a model of honesty in government service after his death. His honorary titles include "Bao Gong" (Lord Bao), "Bao Daizhi" (daizhi is an edict attendant, assigned to take notes on imperial pronouncements) and "Bao Longtu" (Longtu was the Dragon Diagram Hall, where he was academician). Folk stories about impartial Bao Gong's no-nonsense crusades against malfeasant officials abound, and some have been adapted into opera pieces and novels. While these stories involve more fiction than fact, they reflect society's admiration and longing for honest and clean government.

130. The Reforms of Wang Anshi

IN HIS THIRTY years in the throne, Emperor Renzong invited upright men such as Fan Zhongyan and Bao Zheng into the government to serve as his ministers. However, his commitment to reform was weak and the country went on a decline. Since he had no son, a member of the royal family succeeded him upon his death, as Emperor Yingzong of the Northern Song dynasty. Yingzong died of illness after only four years, and was succeeded by Crown Prince Zhao Xu, as Emperor Shenzong of the Northern Song dynasty.

Emperor Shenzong ascended the throne when he was only twenty. He turned out to be a young ruler who wanted to make a difference. He very much wanted to lift the country out of the sorry mess it was in by instituting reform, but he was surrounded by the old guard left by Emperor Renzong. Even people like Fu Bi, who used to support reform, had lost their enthusiasm. To change the status quo, Emperor Shenzong believed he needed a strong advocate of reform to help him.

Emperor Shenzong often heard some very good ideas from an official called Han Wei. However, when Emperor Shenzong praised his insights, Han Wei said, "These are actually ideas I borrowed from my friend Wang Anshi." Thus Wang Anshi favorably impressed Emperor Shenzong even before the two ever met. In his quest for a strong ally in his reform effort, he naturally thought of Wang Anshi. He had Wang Anshi transferred to the capital from Jiangning, where he was a local official.

Wang Anshi was a renowned man of letters and statesman in

the Northern Song dynasty. He was originally from Linchuan, Fuzhou (west of modern-day Fuzhou, Jiangxi Province). As a young man, he greatly impressed Ouyang Xiu with his essays. Because of his success in the court-administered civil service exam at the age of 20, he served as magistrate of local government in several locations. When he was county magistrate at Yin County (modern-day Yin County, Zhejiang Province), a natural disaster hit, causing great hardship to the local people. Wang Anshi brought some semblance of normalcy back to the community by undertaking waterworks projects and improving transport and communications. Whenever there was a temporary food shortage between harvests, he would open up the state granaries to loan grain to the poor, who would repay the loan with interest after the autumn harvest at officially fixed rates. This helped improve the peasants' lives because they no longer had to borrow from large landowners and wealthy gentry at usurious rates.

Because of his performance as the magistrate of various local governments over a period of twenty years, Wang Anshi rose to national prominence. He was subsequently summoned by emperor Renzong to the capital to deal with fiscal matters. Once in the capital, he presented a 10,000-word memorial to the emperor outlining his proposals for fiscal reform. Emperor Renzong, who had just abolished the reforms of Fan Zhongyan, found any mention of reform distasteful and put Wang Anshi's reform proposal to one side. Realizing that the central government did not have the requisite commitment to reform, and finding it hard to get along with some ministers, Wang Anshi resigned and went home, purportedly to attend his mother's funeral.

When he received another invitation to serve, this time by Emperor Shenzong, who was recruiting talent in earnest, he gladly accepted the invitation and set out for the capital.

On his arrival, he was invited to a private audience with Emperor Shenzong. The Emperir cut to the chase and asked him, "Where do you think I should start in order to restore good government?"

Wang Anshi replied with self-assurance, "The first order of business is to reform the old system and build a new legal order."

Emperor Shenzong instructed him to prepare a detailed presentation of his reform ideas. That evening Wang Anshi drew up a report elaborating his proposals. He submitted it the next day to the emperor. Wang Anshi's ideas resonated with Emperor Shenzong and reinforced the latter's trust in him. In 1069 AD, Wang Anshi was promoted to Deputy Chief Minister. In that period there were four chief ministers in the central government, but these were slowed down by frail health, advanced years, or a violent allergy to any mention of reform. Wang Anshi knew that nothing significant could be accomplished with these officials in power. With Emperor Shenzong's approval, he recruited a team of young officials and established a new agency tasked with the preparation of new laws. With the power to institute reform firmly secured, Wang Anshi had a free hand now in implementing his reforms in earnest.

The main elements of Wang Anshi's reform agenda were:

1. A seedling law, which was a government microfinance scheme to tide farmers over between harvests, piloted in Yin County and now to be applied across the country.

2. An agricultural land and waterworks law that offered incentives to local governments for waterworks and farmland reclamation projects undertaken by them.

3. A law of exemption from mandatory labor and services, which abolished the old system of requiring citizens to perform mandatory labor and services for the government. The government would now hire workers to perform these services, and levy service exemption fees from citizens that varied on a wealth scale. Government officials and landowners, who used to enjoy exemption from public services, would now be required to pay these fees. This law was designed to increase government revenue and reduce the burden of conscripted labor on farmers.

4. A farmland tax equalization law, designed to prevent large landowners from taking more land and falsifying information about land holdings and agricultural households. Under the new law, the government would conduct land surveys to ascertain holdings and levy land taxes based on the amount of holdings and their fertility.

5. The law of *bao* and *jia*, under which the government organized peasant households. Ten households constituted a *bao*; fifty households a greater *bao*; and ten greater *bao*s made a *du bao*. A household that had two or more adult males must contribute one as a reserve soldier of the bao, who was required to receive military training in peacetime and report for active duty in wartime.

Wang Anshi's reforms contributed to the consolidation of the rule of the Northern Song dynasty and increased government revenue. At the same time, they conflicted with the interests of large landowners, and consequently ran into strong resistance by many high officials and ministers.

Emperor Shenzong summoned Wang Anshi to see him one day and asked him, "People are grumbling about my disregard for the risks of destabilization, my disdain for public opinion and my disobedience to ancestral conventions. What should I do?"

Unperturbed, Wang Anshi replied, "By taking government as seriously as Your Majesty does, Your Majesty is preventing instability in the country. By consulting your advisers, Your Majesty is heeding public opinion. Besides, not all public opinion is right. As long as we are doing the right thing, we shouldn't be bothered by people's grumbling. As for conventions laid down by ancestors, they are not set in stone."

Despite all the attempts by Wang Anshi to assuage Emperor Shenzong's worries, the latter lacked the strength of character evident in Wang Anshi, and began to waver in the face of mounting opposition.

A devastating drought in Hebei in 1074 AD, following ten rainless months, caused a massive exodus of hungry peasants struggling to survive. An official saw an opportunity and presented a painting entitled "Refugees" to the emperor, on whose mind the famine weighed heavily. The official blamed the disaster on the reforms of Wang Anshi and called for his removal from office.

After viewing the painting, Emperor heaved deep sighs and slept badly. His grandmother, Empress Dowager Cao, and his mother, Empress Dowager Gao, went before him in tears to complain that the country had been plunged into this mess by

Wang Anshi. They pressed for the abolition of the reforms.

Realizing the insurmountable hurdles faced by his reforms, Wang Anshi submitted his resignation in disgust. Emperor Shenzong found it prudent to send Wang Anshi to Jiangning, sheltered from the political uproar brewing in the capital Dongjing.

The next year Emperor Shenzong summoned Wang Anshi back to the capital to be the Chief Minister. A few months later, a comet was seen streaking across the sky. This is a common enough phenomenon but was considered a bad omen at the time. In a panic Emperor Shenzong solicited the views of his ministers on the running of the government. Conservative ministers jumped at the chance to renew their attack on the reforms. Despite Wang Anshi's best efforts to defend the reforms and to dissuade Emperor Shenzong from a superstitious interpretation of the comet, Emperor Shenzong remained undecided.

Unable to have his vision implemented, Wang Anshi once again resigned from his post as Chief Minister in the spring of 1076 AD, three years into his tenure, and returned to Jiangning.

131. Sima Guang Writes *Zi Zhi Tong Jian* (*Historical Events Retold as a Mirror for Government*)

AFTER WANG ANSHI'S resignation, Emperor Shenzong maintained the reforms for nearly ten more years. In 1085 AD, he died of illness. He was succeeded by his ten-year-old son, Crown Prince Zhao Xu, who became Emperor Zhezong. Because of his young age, his grandmother Empress Dowager Gao ruled as his regent. A longtime opponent of reform, she invited Sima Guang, one of the fiercest foes of reform, to serve as the Chief Minister soon after she took over the reins of state.

Sima Guang, originally from Xia County of Shaanzhou (modern-day Xia County, Shanxi Province) was one of the most prominent ministers in the period. His fame began to spread at a very young age. At seven he was already an avid reader. In sweltering heat or freezing cold, he would keep on reading, sometimes forgetting to eat or drink. His zeal for books was matched by a nimble mind. One day he was playing with other kids in the backyard, where a big vat filled with water sat. A boy who climbed on the rim of the vat fell into the water and was on the point of drowning. Other kids cried in fright and ran to seek help from adults. Sima Guang calmly picked up a big rock and hurled it at the vat, cracking it with a "pong." As water emptied out of the broken vat, the drowning kid was saved.

The resourcefulness shown by him in this accident catapulted the young Sima Guang into instant fame. The deed was depicted in paintings widely circulated in Dongjing and Luoyang.

During the reign of Emperor Shenzong, Sima Guang was an Academician at the Hanlin Academy. He and Wang Anshi had been close friends, but the reform-minded Wang Anshi and the more conservative Sima Guang eventually parted ways. Every reform measure proposed by Wang Anshi as Chief Minister was invariably opposed by Sima Guang. Sima Guang even petitioned Emperor Shenzong for the repeal of the Seedling Law. He once wrote a letter as an old friend to Wang Anshi, faulting him for usurping the role of other officials, rocking the boat, amassing wealth and refusing to heed advice.

In his reply to the letter, Wang Anshi refuted Sima Guang point by point. He wrote, "Since I have been pushing reform at the orders of the emperor, you cannot accuse me of usurping others. I am doing all this in the interest of the country. I am not rocking the boat, as you alleged. I am getting the financial house of the country in order and not amassing any personal wealth as you charged. Challenging wrong ideas does not mean I do not heed advice."

Sima Guang steamed when he read the reply. However, he could not do anything because Wang Anshi had the backing of the emperor. He finally decided to resign from his post in the central government and leave the capital for Luoyang, where he announced he was giving up politics to devote his life to writing.

Sima Guang was a serious history buff. He believed that the ruling elite must be thoroughly versed in history, drawing lessons from the rise and fall of past dynasties. He believed that emperors simply lacked the time to read the plethora of historical accounts that had accumulated from ancient times to the Five Dynasties Period, so early in his career he started to compile a history spanning the time between the Warring States period and the Five Dynasties Period. During Emperor Yingzong's reign, he presented a partial draft to the central government. Emperor Yingzong greatly appreciated the work because he believed it would help consolidate his dynastic rule.

After the accession of Emperor Shenzong, Sima Guang

presented another installment of his work to the emperor. While not a subscriber to Sima Guang's political philosophy, Emperor Shenzong provided enthusiastic support to his writing project. He gave the 2,400 books he had collected since a young man to Sima Guang, and expressed the wish to see an excellent product from this endeavor. Emperor Shenzong even thought up a name for the work *Zi Zhi Tong Jian* (*Historical Events Retold as a Mirror for Government*).

After leaving his government post, it took Sima Guang nineteen years of hard work in Luoyang to finally complete the *Zi Zhi Tong Jian*. He often worked late into the night, and the undertaking took a heavy toll on his health. By the completion of the book, he was very weak. His vision was blurred and most of his teeth were loose.

The book itself presents a panoramic history in chronological order, spanning the 1,362 years between 403 BC of the Warring States Period and 959 AD of the Five Dynasties Period. To write this epic work, Sima Guang and his assistants collected and sorted through large amounts of data and material. Besides official government histories, they consulted more than 300 historical works of a less official nature. By the time of the book's completion, the manuscripts filled two entire rooms. Because of the wealth of material it was based on, its superb editing, rigorous textual research and the economy and vibrancy of its prose, it has become one of the most valuable works in the history of Chinese literature. It provides a wealth of information for students of history.

While he was writing his book, some conservative officials never forgot this man known for his fierce opposition to the reforms of Wang Anshi. Despite his professed abandonment of politics, many still considered him the "true Chief Minister." Even ordinary citizens knew there was a Lord Sima in Luoyang.

When the regent, Empress Dowager Gao, invited Sima Guang back to the central government, he was already a frail, sickly old man. However, even in this frail state, he had retained vigorous opposition to Wang Anshi's reforms. The first order of business for the new chief minister was to abolish them. To those who had concerns about the unseemly haste in abolishing the reforms so soon after the death of Emperor Shenzong, he replied angrily, "Good laws made by the late Emperor should naturally not be tampered with, but this stuff cooked up by Wang Anshi is a bane to society. Why can't we change it? Besides, Empress Dowager Gao is Emperor Shenzong's mother. What's to prevent a mother from changing her son's decisions?"

Overriding the opposition of many officials, he dumped all the reforms and laws instituted by Wang Anshi in 1086 AD. Wang Anshi was angered and saddened by the turn of events and soon died a heartbroken man. In September of the same year, the increasingly ill Sima Guang also died.

132. The Plants and Rocks Convoys

AFTER EIGHT YEARS as regent, Empress Dowager Gao died and Emperor Zhezong took over the reins of state. The young Emperor had never agreed to his grandmother's empowerment of the conservatives. Once he got power, he brought the reformists back into government. However, the latter-day reformists lacked Wang Anshi's true devotion and were forever embroiled in factional squabbles, and opportunists stirred up trouble in the name of reform. When Emperor Zhezong was succeeded at his death by his younger brother Zhao Ji, as Emperor Huizong of the Northern Song dynasty, the government was in worse shape than ever.

Emperor Huizong had a reputation of being a dissolute pleasure-seeker, uninterested and uninitiated in the art of governance. A trusted eunuch Tong Guan pandered to his propensities and scoured the country for artistic treasures, works of calligraphy and paintings for his viewing pleasure. One of Tong Guan's treasure-hunting trips took him to the Suzhou area, where he met an official called Cai Jing, who wanted to ingratiate himself with Tong Guan in order to improve his poor career prospects. He attended on Tong Guan, making him a gift of decorative screens and fans bearing his own calligraphy and paintings. To repay Cai Jing, Tong Guan immediately sent these on to Emperor Huizong in Dongjing, with a message that he had found a rare talent.

When Cai Jing was transferred to Dongjing, he got influential officials to lobby for him. An official said to Emperor Huizong, "Implementing reforms is a formidable task and none of the ministers in government can be depended on to make a success of it. If Your Majesty really desires to take up the mantle of Emperor Shenzong and finish his unfinished business, then Cai Jing is your only hope." The official drew up a chart for the perusal of Emperor Huizong, which listed all the conservative ministers on the right and the reformists on the left. All the incumbent ministers were put in the right column and only two names figured in the left, Cai Jing being one of them. Delighted by Cai Jing's reformist credentials, Emperor Huizong immediately decided to make him Chief Minister.

Soon after taking office, in the name of reform Cai Jing proceeded to brand many honest, upright officials members of scheming cliques, regardless of their conservative or reformist inclination. Under his machinations, Emperor Huizong approved the erection of a marker in front of Duanli Gate bearing the names of members of the so-called Yuanyou Clique. This was a group of about 120 former and incumbent officials, including luminaries such as Sima Guang, Wen Yanbo, Su Shi and Su Zhe, who were alleged to have formed a clique during the Yuanyou Era of the reign of Emperor Zhezong. Those no longer alive were stripped of their former official titles, while those still alive were all demoted and sent into exile. After the ouster of large numbers of officials with integrity, Cai Jing and his ilk prospered in government. The reforms of Wang Anshi were distorted and adulterated by Cai Jing beyond recognition. While the original intent of the service exemption law was to reduce the burden on civilians, the exemption fees, which were constantly raised by Cai Jing and his partisans, became a tool of extortion.

Driven by a superstitious belief in Daoism, Emperor Huizong and Cai Jing embarked on the construction of large numbers of Daoist temples. A Daoist priest called Lin Lingsu told a story before Emperor Huizong, claiming that there were nine levels in the firmament, the highest of which was called God's Sphere, where King Yuqing, eldest son of the Supreme God, held court. According to him, Emperor Huizong was the supreme god's eldest son incarnate on Earth. There were eight hundred celestial officials in God's Sphere, and Cai Jing and Tong Guan were among these celestial officials incarnate on Earth. Emperor Huizong, flattered by this nonsense, invited droves of Daoists to the palace to give lectures. The Daoist gave Emperor Huizong the title Guru Daoist Emperor, which ostensibly made him its leader.

Emperor Huizong of the Northern Song dynasty wallowed in decadence and indulged in pleasure seeking. Tong Guan commissioned thousands of craftsmen in Suzhou and Hangzhou to produce embroidery and handicrafts made of ivory, horn and rattan, for the sole pleasure of the emperor. All the raw materials were of course taken from civilians without little or no compensation. As time went by, Emperor Huizong began to tire of these trinkets and sought the novelty of rare plants and rocks. Pandering to the emperor's whims, Cai Jing and Tong Guan put a worthless man named Zhu Mian in charge of an agency called the Tributes Bureau, which existed for the express purpose of finding such rare flowers and rocks for the emperor. Whenever the bailiffs in his employ got wind of any plant or rock of some novelty or rare beauty, they would bring soldiers with them to the owner's home and slap a yellow ribbon on the object to designate it as a tribute to the emperor. Until it reached the emperor, the owner had to take good care of it, for objects suffering damage would cause the owner to be fined or even jailed for gross contempt. If a plant were too big or difficult to move, soldiers could dismantle a house or break down a wall to facilitate the removal of the plant. The bailiffs and the soldiers often used the occasion to extort money from the owners, some of whom were thus bankrupted and sometimes forced to sell their children.

Zhu Mian had these plants and rocks transported on ship after ship to Dongjing. When there were not enough ships, he would commandeer ships transporting grain or other cargo and dump their cargo to make room for the plants and rocks. The use of such a large number of ships naturally involved the conscription of civilian labor on a huge scale. The ships shuttled back and forth on the rivers, while conscripted laborers worked day and night for the transport of the plants and rocks. These were the so-called "Plants and Rocks Convoys."

When the first convoy of plants and rocks arrived in Dongjing, it pleased Emperor Huizong so much that he gave a raise and a promotion to Zhu Mian. Zhu Mian's political fortunes rose with ever more runs of the Plants and Rocks convoys, and those in the corridors of power scrambled to get into the good graces of Zhu Mian. As a testimony to the immense power wielded by Zhu Mian, his Tributes Bureau, which operated in Suzhou and Hangzhou, was given the nickname of "Court in Miniature in Southeast China" by his contemporaries.

133. Fang La Rises in Rebellion

THE PLANTS AND Rocks Convoys were ruinous for the people in southeast China. Those who lived in areas that were abundant in sources of the rare plants and rocks bore the brunt of the exploitation. One such place was Qingxi, Muzhou (modern-day Chun'an County, Zhejiang Province), whose richly diverse plants, rocks, bamboo and trees made it a target of frequent raiding parties sent by Zhu Mian's Tributes Bureau. A resident of the county by the name of Fang La, who eked out a subsistence selling the products of his lacquer trees, hated being victimized by the bailiffs' extortion and plunder. When he saw the misery suffered by the other peasants of his county because of the Plants and Rocks Convoys, he decided to organize them in a rebellion.

One day in 1120 AD, several hundred angry, aggrieved peasants assembled in Fang La's garden and heard him give a passionate speech. He told the crowd heatedly, "The country is like a family. When the young in a family labor all year round to bring some food to the table and clothing for the backs of its members, only to see the fruit of their labor squandered by their elders, and receive lashes from these elders at their whim, would you consider it normal and justified?"

The crowd roared, "Not justified!"

Fang La went on to say, "Not content with squandering the family's resources, these elders ingratiate themselves with enemies of the family with gifts. Is it justified?"

The crowd answered with anger in their voice, "No! It's

unconscionable!"

With tears in his eyes, Fang La said, "With government levies and conscripted labor already weighing so heavily on the people, those bureaucrats want to extort still more money out of us. Any lacquer or paper produced by the sweat of our brow has gone to line their pockets. For our yearlong toil, all we get in return is hunger and cold for our families. What do you think we should do?"

The crowd gave a thunderous answer, "Give us your order and we will follow you!"

Having obtained the support of the peasants, Fang La raised a rebellion with "Death to Zhu Mian" as their battle cry. Fang La assumed personal command of the insurgent army, giving himself the title of Shenggong. His troops donned turbans of various colors for identification purposes. The angry insurgents killed government officials and burned down their houses. The residents in the Qingxi vicinity, all victims of the exactions of the bureaucracy, rallied to the rebels and in less than ten days a rebel army of tens of thousands of men had been formed.

The troops sent by the local government to put down the rebellion were soundly beaten, and two Song generals were killed in the action. Pressing their victory, the rebels pushed into the county seat of Qingxi and sent its magistrate on the run. Dozens of counties were taken by the insurgents in quick succession before they reached Hangzhou.

As news of the rebellion reached Dongjing, Emperor Huizong was scared senseless. He immediately sent Tong Guan at the head of 150,000 government troops to the southeast to quell the rebellion.

When Tong Guan arrived in Suzhou, he realized the magnitude of the popular anger at the Plants and Rocks Convoys and immediately issued an edict in the emperor's name accepting blame, abolished the Tributes Bureau, and firing Zhu Mian.

The people of southeast China felt vindicated and somewhat placated by the cancellation of the convoys and the removal of Zhu Mian, little suspecting that Tong Guan was in that same moment actively deploying troops for the suppression of the insurgency.

In the face of the attack by a concentrated force organized by Tong Guan, Fang La's army was forced back to Qingxi, where he entrenched his troops in Bangyuan Caverns deep in a valley and settled down for a long resistance. The government troops, which were unfamiliar with the mountainous terrain, could not launch an immediate attack. Nevertheless, with the help of a traitor in the insurgents' ranks who guided the government troops to Bangyuan Caverns, Fang La was caught completely off guard and captured. He was taken to Dongjing, where he was killed.

Although the rebellion led by Fang La ended in failure, it was a heavy blow to the Northern Song dynasty. In the same period a large scale uprising had also erupted in the north, which began with some thirty-six men in Hebei led by Song Jiang, fighting a mobile war between Qingzhou, Qizhou and Puzhou (all in modern-day Shandong Province). They struck terror in the hearts of government troops, who often fled before their attack.

An uprising by fishermen also broke out at Liangshan Lake in Shandong. It is said that the insurgents of Song Jiang had been to Liangshan Lake. Two stories widely circulated since that time, "The Bunch of Good Men in Liangshan Lake" and the "Story of the One Hundred Eight Commanders," were based on the deeds of these rebels. During the period spanning the last years of the Yuan dynasty and the early years of the Ming dynasty, the novelist Shi Nai'an expanded the assorted legends surrounding the rebellions of the peasants of Liangshan Lake into an epic novel entitled *Heroes of the Water Margin*. This immortalized in artistic form the many heroes of Liangshan Lake, including but not limited to Lin Chong, Lu Zhishen and Wu Song, and become one of the masterpieces of Chinese literature.

134. Aguda's Defiance at the Fish Feast

SHORTLY AFTER TONG Guan's suppression of Fang La's rebellion, an emissary of the Jin dynasty was dispatched to Dongjing to urge the Northern Song dynasty to attack Yanjing as part of a two-flanked campaign against the Liao dynasty.

The Liao dynasty had been weakened by a succession of civil disturbances and rebellions by other ethnic groups. The Jurchens (called the Nüzhen in Chinese, and later known as the Manchus) grew in strength. In their long years under the yoke of the Liao aristocracy, the oppressed Jurchen had developed a strong anti-Liao sentiment.

In the spring of 1112 AD, Yelü Yanxi, Emperor Tianzuo of the Liao dynasty, went on a tour to Chunzhou (in modern-day Jilin Province), where he enjoyed himself fishing on the Huntong River (the modern-day Songhua River), and convoked the chieftains of all Jurchen tribes to pay homage to him.

As a local custom, every spring the first catch on the river had to be sacrificed to their ancestors in a big feast, so Emperor Tianzuo of the Liao dynasty invited the chieftains to a fish feast in Chunzhou. After a few rounds of wine, a slightly drunk Emperor Tianzuo ordered the chieftains to dance for him. Afraid to disobey this intensely resented order, the chieftains left their seats one after another to perform some Jurchen folk dances.

When it was the turn of one young man, he remained rooted

where he sat, fixing a cold glare on Emperor Tianzuo. He was Aguda, the son of Wuyashu, chieftain of the Wanyan tribe of the Jurchen.

Upset by Aguda's public defiance, Emperor Tianzuo insisted that he perform a dance. Some chieftains also urged him to comply for fear that his continued balking would anger the emperor. However, Aguda was not to be budged, putting Emperor Tianzuo in an awkward position.

The fish feast ended on a sour note. Although he refrained from exploding at the banquet, Emperor Tianzuo said to his minister Xiao Fengxian after the feast, "The arrogant defiance of Aguda is intolerable. Let's kill him before he turns into a future threat."

Believing that Aguda had committed no egregious offense and killing him would antagonize the other chieftains, Xiao Fengxian said, "He is an uncouth, ill-mannered person. It's not worth Your Majesty's while to lose sleep over him. Even if he harbors some ambition, a chieftain of a small tribe like him will never amount to much."

Finding Xiao Fengxian's analysis to make sense, Emperor Tianzuo of Liao put the incident behind him.

Aguda's refusal to dance certainly was not out of any lack of dancing skill. Rather, he was strong-willed, and had long resented the Liao aristocracy's oppression of the Jurchens. As he saw the decay and decline of the Liao dynasty, he made up his mind to strike.

When Wuyashu, his father, died shortly thereafter, Aguda succeeded him as chieftain of the Wanyan tribe. He built fortifications, upgraded weapons and put his soldiers through rigorous training. In preparation for war with the Liao dynasty, he embarked on a systematic integration of the various Jurchen tribes.

When Emperor Tianzuo of the Liao dynasty learned of Aguda's war preparations, he sent an emissary to challenge Aguda, and deployed several armies from Hebei to the northeast as a deterrent.

Aguda said to his officers, "The Liao will soon make the move. We need to strike first." He put together a cavalry of 2,500 men and led it in an attack against the Liao. The Liao general was caught by surprise and fled in defeat. When Emperor Tianzuo received news of the attack, he immediately sent a massive army to quash it. His troops were soundly beaten by Aguda's cavalry, which swelled to 10,000 as it pursued the crumbling Liao troops.

In 1115 AD, Aguda proclaimed himself Emperor in Huining (south of modern-day Acheng, Heilongjiang Province) with the dynasty name of the Great Jin. He gave himself the title of Emperor Taizu of Jin dynasty.

After his accession, Emperor Taizu of the Jin dynasty launched an attack against Huanglong (modern-day Nong'an County, Jilin Province), a strategic town in the northeast of Liao territory. The 200,000-strong infantry sent by Emperor Tianzuo of the Liao dynasty to defend its northeast was routed by the Jin army, abandoning all their weapons and farming implements. When Emperor Tianzuo made peace overtures, Emperor Taizu refused, insisting instead on Emperor Tianzuo's surrender.

Angered by this humiliation, Emperor Tianzuo led a 700,000-strong army on a march to Huanglong.

As Emperor Taizu was in the midst of building earthworks and digging trenches in preparation for battle, Emperor Tianzuo suddenly retreated because an internal dispute had erupted within the Liao government. Emperor Taizu ordered his army to keep the retreating enemy in hot pursuit, and the Liao army of hundreds of thousands crumbled in short order. Emperor Tianzuo fled to safety after riding hundreds of miles, day and night.

By that time the Liao had seen its fighting force largely neutralized. The people in the north, restive under the yoke of the Liao aristocracy, now rose up in revolt.

A suggestion was made to Emperor Huizong of the Northern Song dynasty that the imminent collapse of the Liao dynasty offered an opportunity to recover lost territory in the Yanzhou and Yunzhou regions. Emperor Huizon sent an envoy across the sea from Shandong to meet with Emperor Taizu of the Jin dynasty to convey his readiness to join the Jin in a two-pronged attack against the Liao. The two sides agreed that after the quashing of the Liao dynasty, the Northern Song would get back the sixteen regions of Yanzhou and Yunzhou ceded to the Liao in the Later Jin period, and the Jin dynasty would get the same annual gifts of silk and silver the Liao dynasty used to receive from the Northern Song dynasty. This is known to Chinese history as the "Pact on the Sea".

In its southward drive, the Jin army captured four Liao cities, leaving Yanjing to be captured by the Song army, as stipulated in the agreement.

Fresh after his suppression of the insurgency of Fang La, Tong Guan led a 150,000-strong army northward to attack Yanjing. He fully expected the taking of Yanjing to be easy because the main force of the Liao had been defeated by the Jin army. When the weakened Liao army turned out to be still very much superior to the Song army, he was unprepared. Tong Guan lost two battles in a row, but still had not taken back Yanjing. Worse, he suffered heavy casualties and lost all the weapons, grain and feed he had been able to accumulate through the years.

In an attempt to avoid blame, Tong Guan sent a secret emissary to the Jin general asking the Jin army to capture Yanjing for him. Once the Jin army took Yanjing, it refused to hand it over to the Northern Song. It was only after Tong Guan promised the Jin a million strings of copper coins a year from the tax revenue of Yanjing that Yanjing was given back to him.

This episode opened the eyes of the Jin dynasty to the corrupt culture pervading the Song government. In 1125 AD, Wanyan Sheng, Emperor Taizong of the Jin dynasty, younger brother of Emperor Taizu, sent his troops after Emperor Tianzuo, killing him and destroying the Liao dynasty. Soon he directed his attack southward against the Northern Song dynasty.

135. Li Gang Defends the Capital

AFTER CONQUERING THE Liao dynasty, Emperor Taizong of the Jin dynasty launched a two-pronged attack again the Northern Song dynasty on the pretext that it had harbored a fugitive Liao general. Zonghan led the attack against Taiyuan from the west, while Zongwang attacked Yanjing from the east. The two armies were to subsequently converge on Dongjing.

The court of the Northern Song dynasty was swamped by a steady stream of bad news and urgent appeals for reinforcement from the front. Emperor Taizong sent a delegation to Dongjing to pressure the Northern Song dynasty to cede territory and submit to the Jin dynasty. As the entire court of civil officials and military officers was petrified with fear, one man, Li Gang, Deputy Chamberlain for Ceremonies (in charge of rites and sacrifices), came out strongly for resisting the aggressor.

The Jin army attacking Yanjing from the east took the city, and Guo Yaoshi, the Song general defending it, surrendered. Making Guo Yaoshi his guide, the Jin commander Zongwang took the Jin army south, directly threatening Dongjing.

In the face of the critical turn of events, the angry and flustered Emperor Huizong grabbed the hand of a minister and lamented, "I never thought the Jin would do this to me." Before he had time to finish what he was going to say, he choked on his words and fainted, falling in his couch. The ministers scrambled to prop him up, finally resuscitating him with the help of the imperial physician who administered medicine to him. Asking his attendants for brush and paper, he wrote an edict announcing his abdication in favor of the Crown Prince. Shortly afterwards, he fled Dongjing under the guard of 20,000 troops loyal to him to the safety of Bozhou (modern-day Bo County, Anhui Province).

Crown Prince Zhao Huan ascended the throne as Emperor Qinzong of the Northern Song dynasty. Emperor Qinzong promoted Li Gang to Director of the Ministry of War and issued an edict announcing he was personally leading an expedition against the Jin army. While he went through the motions and put up a brave face, Emperor Qinzong was not much better than his father, and was at a loss as to what to do.

As the Song army suffered one defeat after another and the threat to Dongjing became more palpable, Chief Ministers Bai Shizhong and Li Bangyan urged Emperor Qinzong to flee the capital. The emperor began to waver.

When this situation came to Li Gang's knowledge, he immediately went to see Emperor Qinzong and said to him, "The Super-Emperor (meaning Emperor Huizong) abdicated in Your Majesty's favor in the expectation that Your Majesty would defend the dynastic capital. How can Your Majesty think of leaving?"

Before Emperor Qinzong could reply, the Chief Minister Bai Shizhong answered, "There is no way the capital can be defended against such overwhelming enemy forces."

Li Gang challenged the assessment, "There is no other city as impregnable as the capital. Besides, the capital is the center of the state, with the highest concentration of its civil and military elite. If the emperor personally leads the fight, there's no reason the capital can't be defended successfully."

An attending eunuch grumbled that Dongjing was not strong enough to resist the attack of the Jin army. Emperor Qinzong told Li Gang to tour the city walls to assess their solidity. After making an inspection, Li Gang reported, "The city gates are tall and solid. The moats are not deep enough, but we can manage with elite troops and archers." He went on to lay out tactics for defense, and asked Emperor Qinzong to rally the people and the military around him to resolutely defend the capital until the arrival of reinforcements, when a counterattack could be launched.

Still not totally convinced, Emperor Qinzong asked, "Who can be entrusted with the defense of the city?"

Li Gang glanced around at the ministers before replying, "The government has awarded high salaries and positions to high officials so that they can pay it back at times of crisis like this. Bai Shizhong and Li Bangyan, being Chief Ministers, should have the chief responsibility of defending the capital."

As he spoke, Bai Shizhong and Li Bangyan kept rolling their eyes in despair. Bai Shizhong finally lost his patience and protested loudly, "Li Gang! It's easy for you to say. Do you know how to fight?"

Li Gang said with composure, "If Your Majesty trusts me and orders me to lead the defense, I am ready to repay my country with my life."

Emperor Qinzong was moved by Li Gang's determination and decided to have him oversee the defense of the capital.

As soon as Li Gang turned his back, Bai Shizhong and a group of eunuchs again privately lobbied Emperor Qinzong to flee the capital. Early the next morning, on his way to an imperial audience Li Gang saw the imperial guards flanking the palace and carriages with imperial trappings waiting for Emperor Qinzong.

Li Gang was furious. He said in a stern voice to the imperial army officers and soldiers, "Are you ready to defend the capital or are you running away?"

The troops replied in unison, "We are ready to defend the capital!"

Li Gang then took the imperial army officers with him into the palace and said to Emperor Qinzong, "The officers and men of the imperial army are reluctant to leave Dongjing because they have their family here. If they are compelled to go, some of them might try to desert later. When that happens, who's going to protect Your Majesty against the enemy troops?" Realizing that running away also involved risks, Emperor Qinzong thought the better of it.

Li Gang immediately went outside with the announcement, "The emperor has decided to stay and defend the capital. Anyone who mentions running away again will be beheaded." A loud cheer went up from the soldiers.

After he succeeded in making up Emperor Qinzong's mind, Li

Gang plunged into active preparations for war, deploying troops around the city and erecting defenses. He also dispatched an elite force out of the city to protect the granaries against surprise attack.

Three days later, the Jin army led by Zongwang came to the foot of the city walls. Readying dozens of boats filled with flammable materials upriver, they planned to storm Xuanze Gate with flaming boats sailing downstream. Li Gang recruited a squad of 2,000 fearless men to defend the gate. When the flaming boats unleashed by the Jin army came close, these soldiers used grappling hooks to immobilize the boats and keep them from coming too close to the walls. Li Gang had his soldiers on the embattlements hurled large rocks at the flaming boats. Pelted by the raining rocks, the flaming boats sank, sending the Jin sailors into the river.

Realizing the impossibility of a quick capture of the impregnable capital, Zongwang sent an emissary to inform the Northern Song dynasty of his readiness for peace talks. This was what Emperor Qinzong and Li Bangyan and company had been longing for, and they immediately dispatched a delegation to the Jin camp to negotiate the terms of the peace accord.

Zongwang stonewalled by setting forth harsh conditions while intensifying his attacks against the city. Li Gang directed the battles on the battlements. When the Jin troops tried to scale the walls with ladders, he ordered his archers to unleash a shower of arrows, sending Jin soldiers tumbling off the ladders. Then a few hundred braves sent by Li Gang slid down ropes to destroy the ladders of the Jin army and killed dozens of Jin generals and officers. Countless numbers of Jin soldiers were either killed or drowned in the river.

136. Two Emperors Are Taken Prisoner

TEN DAYS LATER, Song reinforcements arrived from various places, totaling 200,000 men. This galvanized the morale of the Dongjing defenders and forced the withdrawal of the Jin army led by Zongwang.

After the withdrawal of the Jin army, Emperor Qinzong and many of his ministers believed they could now live in peace. They brought Emperor Huizong back to Dongjing. Li Gang constantly reminded Emperor Qinzong of the need to increase military preparedness against future Jin attacks, but his proposals were invariably opposed by defeatist ministers. Emperor Qinzong also faulted Li Gang for his nagging.

However, while Zongwang had withdrawn his eastern army, the western army led by Zonghan had persisted, and had even intensified its attack against Taiyuan. An army sent to relieve Taiyuan led by General Chong Shizhong was encircled and defeated by the Jin army before reaching its destination, and Chong Shizhong died in battle. At the same time, the defeatist ministers found Li Gang's presence in the capital inconvenient to them, so they lobbied Emperor Qinzong to send Li Gang to Hebei to prosecute the war there. Some honest and upright ministers expressed the view that this was not the time to send Li Gang away but Emperor Qinzong insisted.

Li Gang knew he was being pushed out, but he was happy to fight the Jin dynasty on the frontline. He was given 12,000 men by Emperor Qinzong. However, when he requested silver, silk and money to pay his men, the government approved one fifth of the requested amount. Then when Li Gang asked for time to prepare his force, Emperor Qinzong prodded him to set out at once, before his force had been properly prepared.

When Li Gang reached Heyang, he stopped there to recruit more men and to have his soldiers prepare their weapons. However, the central government ordered him to disband his new recruits and to rush toward Taiyuan. Li Gang tried to put together a three-pronged attack but the local commanders only recognized the authority of the central government and totally ignored Li Gang's orders. The three contingents were routed for lack of an integrated command.

Although he was the nominal Commander-in-Chief, Li Gang had no authority to go with the title. When he offered his resignation, the defeatists lambasted him for being hawkish and yet incurring heavy casualties on the battlefield. Emperor Qinzong fired him and sent him in exile to the south of China.

Li Gang was the most feared nemesis of the Jin Emperor and his court. With Li Gang out of the Song government they now had a clear field. Emperor Taizong lost no time in ordering Zonghan and Zongwang to attack Dongjing.

By that time, Taiyuan had been under siege for eight months by the western army of Zonghan. Wang Bing, the commander of the Taiyuan defenses, led its inhabitants and the military in a fierce resistance. All artifices used by the Jin army to storm the city had been beaten back by Wang Bing. As the siege dragged on, the city ran out of food and the troops killed cattle, horses and mules to assuage their hunger. When all the cattle and horses were eaten, the soldiers boiled the leather used on their bows for food. The civilians fed on wild grass and grain husks. However, no one contemplated surrender. Taiyuan was finally taken by force. After leading his hungry soldiers in a hopeless house-to-house fight, Wang Bing jumped to his death into the Fenshui River.

After the fall of Taiyuan, the two Jin armies resumed their southward march towards Dongjing. When the Song generals stationed away from the capital came of their own accord to the rescue of the imperiled capital, Emperor Qinzong and his defeatist ministers sent the reinforcements back to where they came from, as they were eager to offer a land-for-peace deal.

At this time there were still 120,000 Song infantrymen and 10,000 cavalrymen defending Song territory along the south bank of the Yellow River. When Zonghan's western army reached the north bank of the river, he did not want to take the risk of a forced crossing. After dark, the Jin troops beat their war drums through the night, creating a sense of imminent attack. The Song defenders on the south bank were led by the drum rolls to believe the Jin army was on the point of crossing the river, and all 130,000 of them fled in haste. Zonghan was thus able to take his army across the Yellow River without a fight.

In the meantime, Zongwang's eastern army had also taken Daming (in Hebei Province) and crossed the river in its southward march. As the two Jin armies got closer to Dongjing, Emperor Qinzong of the Northern Song dynasty was scared senseless. His ears assailed by his defeatist ministers' constant assertion that the only way out was to sue for peace, he finally gave in and sent his younger brother Zhao Gou, the Prince of Kang, to plead for peace with Zongwang.

When Zhao Gou passed through Cizhou (modern-day Ci County, Hebei Province), its governor Zong Ze said to him, "The Jin is playing a trick by inviting Your Highness for peace talks. What's the sense of suing for peace when its troops are within striking distance of the capital?"

The inhabitants of Cizhou grabbed the reins of Zhao Gou's horse, refusing to let him go to the Jin camp. Zhao Gou was also afraid of being detained by the Jin dynasty as a hostage, and decided to stay in Xiangzhou (modern-day Anyang, Henan Province).

The two Jin armies soon arrived outside the city walls of Dongjing and launched a brutal attack. The city was now defended by a paltry force of about 30,000 troops of the Imperial Army, half of which had already deserted. Army commanders from other garrisons had been ordered away by imperial edict, and now stayed away. Emperor Qinzong wanted to call Li Gang back into service but it was already too late.

As Emperor Qinzong despaired, a charlatan in the capital called Guo Jing claimed to possess magic powers by which he could assemble 7,779 "divine soldiers" to capture the Jin generals alive and beat back the Jin attack. Some desperate ministers clutched at the life-saving straw that Guo Jing presented them, and told him to go ahead and put together a ragtag force of local hooligans as "divine soldiers". The brigade of "divine soldiers" led by Guo Jing crumbled as soon as it met the attacking Jin troops and Dongjing was taken.

Emperor Qinzong realized the day of reckoning had come. He had a good cry before being escorted by his ministers to the Jin camp bearing an offer of surrender. Zonghan ordered Emperor Qinzong to cede all territory east and north of the Yellow River to the Jin dynasty, and to pay tribute consisting of 10,000,000 ingots of gold, 20,000,000 ingots of silver and 10,000,000 bolts of silk and other fabric to the Jin court. Only when Emperor Qinzong agreed to all these demands did the Jin general allow him to go back to Dongjing.

Back in the city, Emperor Qinzong requisitioned large amounts of gold and silver from the inhabitants to be transported to the Jin camp. The Jin general, finding the process too slow for his pleasure, soon ordered Emperor Qinzong back into custody in the Jin camp to wait for the fulfillment of the quotas of gold and silver. Emperor Qinzong assigned twenty-four officials to help the Jin troops thoroughly search the homes of royal family members, noblemen, officials and Buddhist and Daoist monks. After twenty days of rummaging, large amounts of gold, silver and other treasures were taken, along with rare antiques and valuable cultural relics. The map archives of the country's regions and provinces were also ransacked.

In April 1127 AD, Zonghan, Zongwang and the Jin armies under their command, loaded with loot, returned north with Emperor Huizong, Emperor Qinzong and two to three thousand Song officials and nobility in custody. The Northern Song dynasty founded by Zhao Kuangyin was thus extinguished after 167 years of reign.

SOUTHERN SONG DYNASTY
(1127–1279)

137. Zong Ze Thrice Cries, "Cross the River!"

FOLLOWING THE DOWNFALL of the Northern Song dynasty, Zhao Gou, Prince of Kang, who had opted to stay in Xiangzhou, fled to Nanjing (modern-day Shangqiu, Henan Province). In May 1127 AD, Zhao Gou ascended the throne in Nanjing as Emperor Gaozong of the Song dynasty. This rump regime of the Northern Song dynasty later moved its capital to Lin'an (modern-day Hangzhou, Zhejiang Province), and is known to Chinese history as the Southern Song dynasty.

After his accession to the throne, Emperor Gaozong of the Southern Song dynasty was forced by public opinion to call Li Gang back to the central government to serve as Chief Minister, but his ears were monopolized by two trusted aides Huang Qianshan and Wang Boyan.

Li Gang had many ideas about resisting the Jin. He said to Emperor Gaozong, "To take back Dongjing, Your Majesty needs the service of Zong Ze."

Zong Ze was a general committed to the resistance against the Jin. Before the Northern Song dynasty had been toppled, Emperor Qinzong had appointed him as his envoy to negotiate a peace accord with the Jin dynasty. Zong Ze said, "I am not counting on coming out of this mission alive. If the Jin agrees to withdraw its invading armies, then all's fine. If not, I will put my foot down and not yield an inch. I'd rather lose my head than bring humiliation and shame on my country."

When Emperor Qinzong learned of Zong Ze's tough talk, he considered him a possible liability rather than an asset to the peace talks. He revoked his commission as a peace envoy and sent him to Cizhou as a local government administrator.

Then during the second Jin campaign against Dongjing, Zong Ze at the command of his forces scored thirteen consecutive victories against the Jin troops. To take advantage of this favorable situation, he wrote to Zhao Gou, who was then the Prince of Kang, urging him to summon commanders of various garrisons to converge on Dongjing. He also wrote to three generals asking them to come to the rescue of the capital in a coordinated action. These generals not only refused to commit their troops, but also derided Zong Ze's idea as hare-brained. Zong Ze had no choice but to continue the fight without any help. In one action, his troops were encircled by the Jin army, which was ten times larger than his was. Zong Ze said to his troops, "Today we die if we advance and we die if we retreat. So let's fight, and then maybe we have a chance to come out alive." Inspired and encouraged by their commander's determination, the troops fought with ten times their usual mettle and succeeded in beating back the Jin army.

Emperor Gaozong of the Southern Song dynasty, who had long been aware of the valor of Zong Ze, accepted the recommendation of Li Gang and appointed him Governor of Kaifeng.

By that time, the Jin troops had pulled out of Kaifeng, but after the ravages of two major battles, all its city walls had been reduced to rubble. The military had to be barracked in civilian neighborhoods. The city's proximity to the Yellow River also meant that the activities of the Jin army on the north bank of the river had a demoralizing and destabilizing effect on the psyche of the inhabitants of Kaifeng.

Zong Ze, who enjoyed great authority among both civilians and the military, immediately issued an order when he took up his post in Kaifeng, "Anyone robbing civilian homes will be severely dealt with according to military law." When robberies did occur after the order was issued, Zong Ze executed the perpetrators, and order was gradually re-established.

Fed up with the looting, burning and killing perpetrated by the Jin troops against them, inhabitants of Hebei organized uprisings to battle the Jin army. Li Gang was a strong advocate for organizing a new coalition against the Jin by relying on these insurgent forces as allies. When he arrived in Kaifeng, Zong Ze actively pursued alliances with the insurgencies. When the insurgents in various parts of Hebei heard of the heroic deeds of Zong Ze, they voluntarily submitted to his command.

An insurgent leader in Hedong by the name of Wang Shan made plans to attack Kaifeng with his 700,000 troops. When Zong Ze learned of his intentions, he rode alone to meet with Wang Shan. He said with tears in his eyes to Wang Shan, "Our country is now in mortal danger. If good men like you can get together in a united fight against the Jin, we will no longer have to worry about being invaded by its army again."

Moved to tears, Wang Shan said, "I am at your order."

Other movements of resistance led by Yang Jin, Wang Zaixing, Li Gui and Wang Dalang commanded troops whose strength varied from tens of thousands to hundreds of thousands. Zong Ze sent delegations to lobby all of them for an alliance against the Jin army. This ensured a strong peripheral defense around Kaifeng, reassuring its inhabitants. As a result, the granaries were replenished, and prices stabilized to pre-war levels.

However, as Zong Ze got ready to launch a northern expedition to recover the lost territory of the Central Plains, Emperor Gaozong and his trusted advisers Huang Qianshan and Wang Boyan planned to flee further south from Nanjing, which they considered too insecure. Because Li Gang was opposed to this retreat, Emperor Gaozong removed him from office.

Zong Ze, frustrated and anxious, crossed the Yellow River

to lobby the leaders of the resistance movements in person for a united front against the Jin army. He commissioned the construction of twenty-four fortresses around Kaifeng, and a string of back-to-back military garrisons along the Yellow River, called "the Necklace of Stockades". The defensive capability of the Song army grew steadily with the support of the militias in various parts east and north of the Yellow River.

Zong Ze fired off memorial after memorial urging Emperor Gaozong to return to Kaifeng to lead the fight against the Jin army. However, these memorials invariably were intercepted by the treacherous Huang Qianshan and company, who derided Zong Ze as a lunatic. Soon Emperor Gaozong of Song fled from Nanjing to Yangzhou.

Shortly after, the Jin army, as predicted, launched another massive attack. Emperor Taizong of the Jin dynasty made his general Wuzhu commander of the campaign against Kaifeng. When Wuzhu approached Kaifeng with his army, Zong Ze deployed a few thousand elite troops to outflank the enemy and cut off its route of retreat. Wuzhu's army was routed when it came under the simultaneous attack from the front and an ambush in the rear by elite Song troops.

In another battle, the Jin general Zonghan led a force against Luoyang. The army sent by Zong Ze under the command of his lieutenants Guo Zhenmin and Li Jingliang was defeated by Zonghan. Guo Zhenmin surrendered to the Jin army, while Li Jingliang ran away to avoid punishment.

When Li Jingliang was caught and brought back by soldiers sent after him, Zong Ze took him to task, "Losing a battle can be forgiven. But your flight is insubordination." He ordered Li Jingliang beheaded.

Zonghan sent a Jin general, accompanied by Guo Zhenmin, who had surrendered to the Jin army, to Kaifeng to urge Zong Ze to submit. Zong Ze received them in the great hall of the governor's office. He said to Guo Zhenmin, "If you had died fighting, you would now be a patriotic martyr. But you chose surrender. How dare you show your face here?" He ordered his guards to behead Guo Zhenmin.

After the order was carried out, Zong Ze turned toward the Jin general with a disdainful laugh, "I have defended this city until now, and I've prepared myself for a fight to the death. You are a military man. You ought to be ashamed of yourself for trying to lure me with false promises because you don't have the ability to beat me on the battlefield."

The Jin general's face blanched with fear as Zong Ze barked an order. The Jin general was taken out by Zong Ze's guards and executed.

Zong Ze's execution of three men in a row attested to his determination to resist Jin aggression and greatly boosted the morale of the Song troops. By his strict discipline and nimble prosecution of the war, he scored numerous victories against the Jin army and as a result his fame spread. The Jin troops' fear of Zong Ze was mixed with admiration. They referred to him as "Grandpa Zong."

By relying on the resistance movements in Hebei, Zong Ze was able to increase his troop strength and replenish granaries. He was confident that he had the capability to take back the Central Plains. He fired off a succession of more than twenty memorials, urging Emperor Gaozong to return to Kaifeng. All those memorials were intercepted by Huang Qianshan and his ilk.

By this time Zong Ze was in his seventies. All the frustration and stress triggered a rash of festering sores on his back that finally brought him down. When his condition worsened, some of his lieutenants visited him. He opened his eyes and said to them in an emotional tone, "I've come down with these sores because I am frustrated by my inability to avenge my country. If I can be sure that you will continue to fight the enemy, I will be able to die without any regret."

These words brought tears into the generals' eyes. When they left, they could hear Zong Ze recite a line of verse by the famous Tang poet Du Fu, "The general dies before the battle is won, his breastplate covered with hero's tears!" Then mustering all the strength left in him, he shouted, "Cross the river! Cross the river! Cross the river!" before closing his eyes forever.

Zong Ze's death was deeply mourned by all the inhabitants and military men of Kaifeng.

After the death of Zong Ze, the Song government appointed Du Chong as defender of Dongjing. Du Chong was an incompetent and ruthless man. He undid all of Zong Ze's defensive deployments and works, and as a result the Jin army was soon able to retake all of the Central Plains.

138. Han Shizhong Blocks the Passage of the Jin Army

AS THE JIN army drove southward all the way to the seashores in Mingzhou, it ran into constant attacks by militias organized by resistance movements along the way. Remembering that large numbers of Song troops were still deployed along the Yangtze, the Jin general Wuzhu decided against tarrying for too long and pulled his troops back to the north after a fair amount of looting.

In March 1130 AD, Wuzhu arrived with his homebound troops near Zhenjiang, and was intercepted by the Song army under the command of General Han Shizhong. A strong advocate for resistance against Jin aggression, General Han Shizhong was angered by the atrocities of the invading Jin army, and was eager to deal a heavy blow to the Jin troops withdrawing to the north.

When Wuzhu's troops arrived at the river's edge, they were barred passage to the other bank by Han Shizhong, Wuzhu sent a messenger to the Song camp with a letter challenging them to a battle. Han Shizhong took the challenge and agreed with Wuzhu on the timing. The odds were heavily stacked against Han Shizhong, who was facing off against 100,000 Jin troops with his paltry 8,000. He was fully aware that the key to winning a battle with such a serious numerical disadvantage was troop morale. He discussed the matter with his wife Liang Hongyu, who was also a shrewd military officer well versed in the art of war. She subscribed to her husband's plan and volunteered for the battle.

Han Shizhong then called together his officers and said to them, "The most strategic spot in the surrounding terrain is the Dragon King Temple on Mount Jinshan (northwest of modern-day Zhenjiang). It is almost certain that the Jin army will send a scouting party to size up the area." He sent a lieutenant with 200 soldiers to prepare an ambush near the temple.

As predicted by Han Shizhong, a day later five Jin officers rode up Mount Jinshan on a reconnaissance mission to gather intelligence about Song deployments. When the Jin party approached, the Song ambushers in the temple charged out beating their war drums. The five Jin officers, realizing they had walked into a trap, quickly turned their horses around and galloped away. The pursuing Song troops captured two of the Jin officers, while the other three kept prodding their horses to run faster, their upper torsos leaning flat against the back of their mounts. A Jin general in a red battle tunic with a jade-studded belt around his waist fell off his horse during the desperate flight, but managed to jump back on and get away. After interrogating the captured Jin soldiers, the Song troops found out the general in the red tunic was none other than the Commander-in-Chief Wuzhu.

On the day of the decisive battle, the two opposing armies faced off each other by the river. A bloody battle followed. Han Shizhong donned his armor and rode into action while his wife Liang Hongyu, also in battle gear, beat war drums on a man-o-war on the river. Galvanized by the sight of the Commander-in-Chief's wife taking part in the war effort, the Song troops charged with redoubled valor into the enemy formation. The Jin army, while superior in numbers, was short on discipline. Further weakened by the fatigue of long marches, it could not withstand the strong offensive of the elite force under Han Shizhong's command. The Jin army suffered heavy casualties, and Wuzhu's son-in-law, Prince Longhu (Dragon and Tiger) was captured.

Wuzhu sent another messenger to the Song camp with the proposal to return all the loot they had taken from Jiangnan to the Song army as long as they were allowed to cross the river. The proposal was rejected by Han Shizhong. Wuzhu offered a treasured purebred horse to Han Shizhong, but it was rejected too.

Unable to cross the river, Wuzhu transported his troops by boat back to Huangtiandang (northwest of modern-day Nanjing, Jiangsu Province). It turned out Huangtiandang was a dead-end port with no outlet. When the convoy was stuck in this awkward situation, someone made a suggestion, "There used to be a canal here that led directly to Jiankang. It is now made impassible by silt. If the soldiers could dredge the canal, we will be able to shake off the pursuing Song army."

Wuzhu immediately ordered his troops to start dredging. With plenty of labor, the Jin army working through the night was able to open up some twenty miles of the canal for navigation. Wuzhu led his troops in a dash for Jiankang on the newly dredged canal, but they were driven back to Huangtiandang by the troops of the Song general Yue Fei before they could reach their destination.

The Jin army was encircled by the Song troops in Huangtiandang for forty-eight miserable days. In the meantime, the Jin troops stationed north of the river had sent reinforcements to relieve the siege. Wuzhu planned to cross the river by using smaller boats, but Han Shizhong was prepared. He loaded his ships with plenty of grappling hooks attached to iron chains. When the Jin troops started crossing the river in the smaller craft, the Song soldiers on the big ships would throw out the chains to hook the small boats and then with a forceful tug capsize the small boats, sending the Jin troops together with the boats to the bottom of the river.

Overwhelmed by anxiety, Wuzhu asked Han Shizhong for a dialogue on the battlefield, imploring him to allow the crossing. Han Shizhong said, "That's not a problem, provided you return all the territory you've taken from us."

Wuzhu returned to camp to consult his officers on ways to deal with the Song army. He said with dejection, "The Song troops are as good with their boats as we are with our horses. How can we hope to cross the river when their ships sail at such great speed?"

Someone said, "In a crisis like this, we should probably try to offer a reward for good ideas. That may help to find a way out."

When the reward was posted, a Song traitor came forward with the advice, "The sea-going ships of the Song army are wind-propelled. If you pick a windless day to cross the river, the big ships will be helpless in trying to stop you." He also suggested the use of fire attacks against the Song army.

A few days later the wind died down on the river and the sun was out. The Jin troops sneaked into small boats to cross the river in batches. When Han Shizhong attempted to stop them with his big ships, these proved too slow without the aid of the wind to catch up with the smaller, nimbler boats. The situation was made worse by the flaming arrows shot by the Jin soldiers. The sails on the Song ships caught fire and the ships were engulfed in flames, forcing the sailors to jump into the river. Han Shizhong had to abandon the burning ships and withdraw to Zhenjiang in smaller craft.

Wuzhu finally broke through the blockade of Han Shizhong and brought his troops back to Jiankang. After another round of looting, he got ready to return to the north. When his army reached Jing'an (northwest of modern-day Jiangning, Jiangsu Province), it was attacked and routed by the army commanded by Yue Fei. The Jin troops fled in disarray. Yue Fei drove away the Jin troops and recovered Jiankang.

139. Yue Fei Routs Wuzhu's Army

YUE FEI, WHO had recovered Jiankang, is considered a national hero in Chinese history. He was born to a poor family in Tangyin, Xiangzhou (in Henan Province) in the year the Yellow River breached its banks, flooding his hometown. He was an avid reader since a child, with a special love for books about the art of war. Endowed with great physical strength, in his teens he was able to wield a huge bow weighing three hundred *jin*. Later he studied under Zhou Tong, who was a venerable man famed for his excellent martial skills. Soon Yue Fei became an expert archer with deadly precision in shooting at moving targets.

He later joined the military. At the time the Jin army invaded the south, he was a low-ranking officer in Dongjing. One day, when he was training a hundred cavalrymen by the Yellow River, a large contingent of Jin troops surged into view. Yue Fei said calmly to his evidently scared soldiers, "The enemy may outnumber us, but they have no idea how many we are. We can defeat them before they realize our disadvantage." That said, he led the charge into the enemy formation and killed a Jin general. His soldiers, inspired by Yue Fei's example, followed him into battle and decimated the Jin contingent.

The incident cemented Yue Fei's fame as a courageous leader. A few years later, he served as a commander under Zong Ze. Zong Ze greatly valued his service and told him, "Your physical courage and insight are comparable to the best qualities of famous generals in history. But to ensure military success in the long run, courage in battle is not enough." He handed to Yue Fei a diagram of military formations passed down from ancient times, "Study this carefully."

Thanking Zong Ze, Yue Fei said, "It is military convention to follow these diagrams of battle formations in battle. But a commander still needs to use his judgment in adapting them to changing conditions on the battlefield."

Zong Ze nodded his approval, finding the young general's perception admirable.

Like Zong Ze, Yue Fei considered the fight against the Jin dynasty his mission in life. When Emperor Gaozong of the Southern Song dynasty ascended the throne, Yue Fei immediately submitted a memorial urging the emperor to lead a northern expedition in order to boost troop morale and recover the lost territory of the Central Plains. He also denounced the defeatist views of Huang Qianshan and Wang Boyan.

Emperor Gaozong disregarded the memorial and, finding it objectionable that a general relatively low in the pecking order did not know better than to mind his own business, stripped Yue Fei of his military commission.

After Zong Ze's death, Yue Fei served under Du Chong, the designated defender of Dongjing. In the face of a massive Jin offensive, Du Chong fled to Jiankang. Then when General Wuzhu attacked Jiankang, the shameless Du Chong surrendered. As troops led by other commanders under Du Chong disbanded, Yue Fei continued to engage the enemy with his army in the Jiankang area. As Wuzhu withdrew his army northward, Yue Fei had an opportunity, with the support of Han Shizhong, to rout the enemy force.

With the Jin army pulled back to the north, Emperor Gaozong returned to Lin'an from Wenzhou. In the meantime, the Jin dynasty had groomed a certain Liu Yu as a puppet emperor of the so-called Great Qi dynasty to be an accomplice of the Jin in its incursions into Song territory. Yue Fei led his army to many victories in beating back invasions by the Jin-Qi coalition force. At the age of 32, he was elevated to regional military commissioner, his status equaling that of renowned generals of the time, such as Han Shizhong, Liu Guangshi and Zhang Jun.

It was in that period that he composed the famous poem,

popular until this day, entitled *To the Tune of Man Jiang Hong* (A River of Red), which gave expression to his patriotic fervor and determination to defeat Jin aggression. The poem starts with,

My hair bristles with anger
As I look out by the rail
At a world freshened by recent rain
Raising my eyes, I roar at the sky
The passion that agitates my breast
After a career spanning thirty years
Of success and fame now turned to dust and
Eight thousand *li* on the road gone with the wind
Wait not until your young head turns all white
Leaving a lifetime of useless regret

In his unwavering passion for the recovery of lost territory in the Central Plains, Yue Fei set high ethical standards for himself. Emperor Gaozong built a house for him but Yue Fei declined the gift, saying, "As long as the enemy has not been defeated, I will have no time for a home." Asked when peace and stability would come, Yue Fei replied, "When civil officials are no longer venal and when military officers are unafraid to die, peace will have a chance to break out."

Yue Fei was a stickler for rigorous military training in peacetime. When his troops were recuperating, he would still put them through training as if in wartime by taking the lead in running up hills in armor and hopping over trenches. In a training exercise, his son Yue Yun fell off his horse when it tripped as they rushed up a hill. Yue Fei severely punished Yue Yun for the incident. When other soldiers saw the Commander-in-Chief apply the same rigorous discipline to his son, they trained even more conscientiously.

Discipline was strict in General Yue's Army. When he discovered that a soldier had used some civilian's rope to bind kindling wood, he dealt with that soldier severely. His troops slept along the road in open air when they stopped for the night at a village. Even when village inhabitants invited them to go inside their houses, no soldier would do so. A slogan of General Yue's Army was, "I'd rather freeze to death than take down a house for kindling wood. I'd rather starve to death than loot."

Yue Fei's strict discipline was accompanied by caring. When soldiers fell ill, he often personally prepared their medicine. When his lieutenants departed for battle, he would ask his wife to comfort their families. When troops died in battle, he would make sure their children received proper care. All material and monetary rewards he received from the government would be distributed to his troops. None was kept for himself or his family.

Because of the rigorous training and Yue Fei's caring attitude, his army was always highly motivated and valorous in battle. Before every military action, Yue Fei would call his commanders together to discuss the battle plans. This ensured that his army never lost a battle. General Yue's Army inspired terror among Jin commanders and soldiers, who reached the conclusion that, "It is easier to move a mountain than to win a battle against General Yue's Army."

With military commanders of the caliber of Yue Fei, Han Shizhong and many others, and the support of the militias of the resistance movements across the country, the Southern Song dynasty had the possibility of repelling the invading Jin army. Nevertheless, Emperor Gaozong was bent on seeking peace with the Jin even on humiliating terms, despite opposition by Yue Fei and others. In 1139 AD, he agreed to submit to the Jin dynasty. The Southern Song dynasty was to pay them an annual tribute of 250,000 taels of silver and 250,000 bolts of silk. In return, the Jin dynasty agreed to reward the Southern Song dynasty with territory in Shaanxi and Henan, territory which the Jin dynasty had taken from the Southern Song dynasty to begin with.

In October 1140 AD, the Jin dynasty tore up the accord and launched a massive campaign. Its best troops under the command of Wuzhu attacked the Southern Song dynasty on four fronts. Within barely a month, the Jin army retook all the territory returned to the Southern Song dynasty pursuant to the peace accord. With the Southern Song dynasty facing imminent collapse, Emperor Gaozong finally saw no alternative but to issue an edict calling on all Song troops to fight back.

After receiving the order to fight, Yue Fei immediately ordered his lieutenants Wang Gui, Niu Gao and Yang Zaixing to lead their troops into action. In the meantime, he sent a delegation to Hebei to get in touch with Liang Xing, the leader of a resistance movement, asking him to move his militias to the rear of the enemy army east and north of the river. Yue Fei directed the war effort from Yancheng.

A few days later, troops under his command won victories on various fronts, regaining control of Yingchang (east of modern-day Xuchang, Henan Province), Chenzhou (modern-day Huaiyang, Henan Province) and Zhengzhou in separate battles. When the supreme commander of the Jin invasion force Wuzhu learned in Dongjing of the action of Yue Fei, he was dismayed and immediately called his commanders together to agree on a response. The consensus of the meeting was that it would be easy to deal with other generals of the Southern Song dynasty, but General Yue's Army was a formidable foe. However, since they had come this far, there was no alternative but to concentrate all they had on a battle with General Yue's Army. Soon Wuzhu, King Longhu and King Gaitian led their troops on a massive attack against Yancheng.

When Wuzhu's army arrived near Yancheng, the two sides formed battle arrays. Yue Fei sent his son Yue Yun with an elite cavalry brigade to spearhead the action. He said to Yue Yun, "You must win this battle. Otherwise I will have your head chopped off when you return."

Yue Yun gave a quick acknowledgment, and bravely led the charge into enemy lines. The rest of the Song troops, who inflicted heavy casualties on the Jin army, followed Yue Yun's vanguard.

After losing one round, Wuzhu resorted to his specially trained cavalry units called "Iron Towers," each of which consisted of three heavily armored horsemen linked together. These were concentrated in the center. Two cavalry detachments using the *guai zi ma* device (several horses tied together) attacked the flanks.

Yue Fei soon discovered the weakness of the *guai zi ma*, and ordered his troops to go into battle carrying axes. When the Jin *guai zi ma* troops came at them, they would stoop low and hack at the horses' hoofs. The stumble of one horse would drag down the other horses with it, sending the riders to the ground. Yue Fei's troops would then set on the fallen Jin soldiers. The Iron Towers and *guai zi ma* devices failed miserably.

Wuzhu cried disconsolately at the news, saying, "I've always won my battles on the strength of the *guai zi ma*. Now all is lost." However, he refused to concede defeat. A few days later he led one 120,000 troops against the Song army. When Yue Fei's lieutenant Yang Zaixing inspected the frontline at the head of 300 cavalrymen, he saw the advancing Jin army and immediately engaged it, killing 2,000 enemy soldiers. He was shot dead by an arrow. Another Song general, Zhang Xian, joined the fray and succeeded in dispersing the Jin troops and sending Wuzhu fleeing.

After his defeat at Yancheng, Wuzhu made Yingchang the target of his next attack. Yue Fei had foreseen this development and sent Yue Yun with troops to relieve Yingchang. The Jin army proved no match for the 800 bravely charging cavalrymen under Yue Yun's command. With Song infantry and militias attacking its flanks, the Jin army was again routed.

The militias in the Taihang Mountains led by Liang Xing and other militias along the Yellow River were also joining the fight. They fought the Jin troops under the banner of General Yue's Army, cutting off the Jin army's supply routes. They generally gave the Jin troops a hard time.

Propelled by an unbroken winning streak, General Yue's Army marched to the town of Zhuxian, within some twenty kilometers of Dongjing.

The militias in Hebei were elated by the news that General Yue's Army had reached Zhuxian. They crossed the Yellow River to join forces with it. Local inhabitants brought food on oxcarts to General Yue's troops, greeting the soldiers with incense burners. Tears of excitement filled their eyes.

Buoyed by the victories and unable to contain his joy, Yue Fei cheered his troops on, "Let's keep up the good fight! When we enter Huanglong of the Jin dynasty, we will drink a big toast to our victory."

140. The Traitor, Qin Hui

FOLLOWING A MAJOR victory at Zhuxian, Yue Fei's army now approached Dongjing. Realizing he could no longer hold Dongjing, Wuzhu decided to cross the Yellow River, withdrawing his army to the north. When he was on the point of leaving Dongjing with his troops, a young scholar stopped his mount and said, "My prince! You don't need to leave. Shaobao Yue will withdraw his troops soon. I can assure you Dongjing is safe." ("Shaobao" was Yue Fei's official title; It meant "Junior Guardian.")

Wuzhu asked in disbelief, "Yue Fei was able to defeat my 100,000 with his 500 cavalrymen, and the inhabitants here pray for his attack against the city. How can Dongjing be safe?"

The young scholar said, "When there are power-hungry, scheming ministers in the central government, the generals will be prevented from claiming credit on the battlefield. In my view Shaobao Yue won't even be able to save his own neck, much less be given a chance to show his mettle and claim credit."

Struck by the cogency of the analysis, Wuzhu immediately turned his horse around and led his troops back to Dongjing.

One of the scheming ministers that young scholar had in mind was Chief Minister Qin Hui of the Southern Song dynasty. Qin Hui had been a minister in the Northern Song period. When Emperor Huizong and Emperor Qinzong were taken to the north as prisoners by the Jin army, Qin Hui and his wife followed them in captivity to the capital of the Jin dynasty. Qin Hui groveled before Emperor Taizong of the Jin dynasty and succeeded in impressing him with his ability to serve. He got himself appointed to a position in the military staff of the Jin General Talan.

At that time, the Jin dynasty witnessed with alarm the steady growth of anti-Jin forces in the Southern Song dynasty. Staunchly hawkish generals such as Yue Fei and Han Shizhong posed a particular challenge. It was decided that Qin Hui would be sent back to the south as a mole in the Song government. In 1130 AD, Qin Hui and his wife were slipped back into Southern Song territory when the Jin General Talan attacked Chuzhou (modern-day Huai'an, Jiangsu Province).

Qin Hui went to the traveling imperial palace of Emperor Gaozong in Yuezhou for an audience, during which he gave a vivid, though fictional, account of how he had killed enemy guards in Chuzhou and escaped on a boat he commandeered. Many ministers were very skeptical about the veracity of the account. Chuzhou was a long way from there; why was Qin Hui not intercepted by the Jin army as he escaped through Jin-controlled territory? Besides, even if he could have sneaked through lax enemy defenses, the escape must have been a hurried affair. How could he have had the leisure to bring his wife along?

However, Chief Minister Fan Zongyin, an old friend of Qin Hui's, vouched for him in front of Emperor Gaozong, praising Qin Hui's reliability and competence. Emperor Gaozong, who had been obsessed with the idea of reconciliation with the Jin dynasty, immediately sent for Qin Hui, in the belief that this man fresh from the Jin court must have an insider's insights into Jin affairs.

In their first meeting, Qin Hui immediately spoke to Emperor Gaozong of peace and reconciliation with the Jin dynasty. He had even come prepared with a peace offer he had drafted in the name of the Song government.

After meeting with Qin Hui, Emperor Gaozong found his views quite palatable. He said to his ministers, "Qin Hui's loyalty is unimpeachable. I was so excited about having him in the government that I couldn't sleep last night." Emperor Gaozong immediately made him Imperial Secretary of the Ministry of Rites. Three months later, he was promoted to Deputy Chief Minister. In another six month, Qin Hui became Chief Minister, concurrently holding the title of Military Affairs Commissioner, which gave him control over all civil and military matters.

Once in the post of Chief Minister, Qin Hui began working for reconciliation with the Jin dynasty, intending to sell out his country's interests. Eventually, he was demoted from the post of Chief Minister because of the intense opposition of many ministers to his approach. However, the fatuous Emperor Gaozong never ceased to take Qin Hui into his confidence, and reappointed him Chief Minister a few years later. Abusing his power and position, Qin Hui made common cause with the Jin dynasty and did his best to undercut the generals committed to the anti-Jin cause. He was greatly alarmed by the successive victories achieved by Yue Fei against the Jin army, and the prospect of his imminent drive into the Jin capital. He feared that once the Jin, his "backstage boss," collapsed, his position would become untenable in the Southern Song dynasty. Under his prodding, Emperor Gaozong ordered Yue Fei to withdraw his forces from the front.

Yue Fei found the order incomprehensible. In a memorial to Emperor Gaozong, he said, "The Jin army is demoralized, and our highly motivated troops are on the cusp of winning the war. We must not let slip this opportunity." He asked the emperor to rescind the withdrawal order and allow him to continue the campaign.

After reading the memorial by Yue Fei, Qin Hui took the cynical step of ordering the withdrawal of the troops of generals Zhang Jun and Liu Guangshi from the front in Huaibei. He then told Emperor Gaozong that Yue Fei's army was now an isolated, orphan army in the Central Plains, and therefore should no longer stay there in such an exposed position. He urged Emperor Gaozong to order an immediate withdrawal by Yue Fei.

Yue Fei was waiting expectantly for Emperor Gaozong's edict that would authorize him to continue his march toward the Jin capital, but what he received was a gold-colored tablet bearing the urgent order for him to withdraw his troops. When Yue Fei was still recovering from the shock of the first gold tablet, the second gold tablet arrived on a fast horse, and a third, then a fourth and so forth until he received a total of twelve. Yue Fei gave up any hope of seeing Emperor Gaozong change his mind; he said with anger and tears streaming down his cheeks, "I never would have imagined that my ten years of effort would come to naught overnight."

News of Yue Fei's withdrawal from Zhuxian shocked the inhabitants, who poured into the streets. Some stopped Yue Fei's horse and said with tears in their eyes, "The Jin army knows we welcomed the government troops with incense burners and cartfuls of food. When you leave, we are certain to be killed."

Yue Fei also shed tears of sadness. He asked his soldiers to show the crowd Emperor Gaozong's edict and said, "The central government issued this top-priority order. I couldn't stay here in defiance of the order."

Realizing they were unable to make Yue Fei stay, the inhabitants broke into loud sobs and the soldiers also cried with their hands covering their faces. The air reverberated with the sound of weeping in the town of Zhuxian.

Yue Fei could not bear leaving immediately, and announced that the withdrawal would be pushed back by five days, so that those inhabitants so disposed could leave with the troops. Five days later, the withdrawing troops were followed by large numbers of local people on the journey south. Later Yue Fei would request the central government to resettle these people in the south in areas where labor was in demand for land reclamation.

When Wuzhu received reports that General Yue's Army was gone for good, he immediately resumed his southern campaign. The many regions and counties in Henan recovered by Yue Fei once again fell into Jin hands.

Qin Hui and Emperor Gaozong had made up their mind to reconcile with the Jin dynasty. Not wishing to be hamstrung by the likes of Yue Fei and Han Shizhong, they summoned these generals back to the capital and made Han Shizhon Military Affairs Commissioner and Yue Fei Deputy Military Affairs Commissioner. It was a promotion in name, but was in fact designed to strip them of their control over the army.

After Yue Fei was stripped of his control over the army, Qin Hui sent a delegation to the Jin dynasty to sue for peace. In November 1141 AD, the Jin government sent a delegation to Lin'an to negotiate terms of the peace accord. The final accord included the following provisions: the Song-Jin boundary would be demarcated along the Huai River in the east and Dasan Pass (southwest of modern-day Baoji, Shaanxi Province) in the west; the Southern Song in submission to the Jin would pay an annual tribute of 250,000 taels of silver and 250,000 bolts of silk. This peace agreement is known to Chinese history as the "Treaty of Shaoxing" (Shaoxing was an era name of Emperor Gaozong). It was in fact an agreement of humiliation and surrender by the Southern Song dynasty.

141. "A Plausible Case"

AFTER THE SIGNING of the "Treaty of Shaoxing," Wuzhu sent an emissary bearing a confidential letter to Qin Hui, which read, "You keep assuring us of your desire for peace. But as long as Yue Fei lives, we will not feel reassured. A way must be found to get rid of him."

After receiving this secret missive from his master, Qin Hui set to work to engineer Yue Fei's downfall.

Investigating Censor Moqi Xie fired the first salvo. At the instigation of his political ally, Qin Hui, he wrote a memorial which denounced Yue Fei for his arrogance. He invented out of whole cloth the story that Yue Fei refused to send his army to relieve defenders of Huaixi when they were under Jin attack, and that he once left the battlefield without authorization. This was followed by successive salvos fired by other partisans of Qin Hui's cause.

Yue Fei knew that Qin Hui was out to get him, so he volunteered to resign from his post of Deputy Military Affairs Commissioner. Emperor Gaozong readily approved his resignation.

The matter did not end there. One of the top generals, Zhang Jun, once Yue Fei's superior, became jealous of Yue Fei for his feats on the battlefield. Aware of Zhang Jun's resentment of Yue Fei's successes, Qin Hui in collusion with Zhang Jun incited subalterns Wang Gui and Wang Jun in the Yue Army to falsely accuse another subaltern Zhang Xian of intending to take control of Xiangyang in order to mount a mutiny to help Yue Fei wrest back his control over the army. They also falsely accused Yue Yun (son of Yue Fei) of writing to Zhang Xian to make secret plans for the mutiny.

Based on the false testimony of the traitors Wang Gui and Wang Jun, Qin Hui arrested Zhang Xian and put him in the jail of the Court of Judicial Review, where he was tortured. However, Zhang Xian adamantly refused to confess to the fabricated crime. Soon after, Qin Hui requested Emperor Gaozong to order the arrest of Yue Fei and Yue Yun and put them on trial before the Court of Judicial Review.

When Qin Hui's people arrived to arrest him, Yue Fei said with a smile, "Heaven and Earth be my witness! I will be vindicated and cleared."

When Yue Fei and Yue Yun were taken to the Court of Judicial Review, they found a bloodied, almost unrecognizable Zhang Xian covered with bruises and injuries sustained during his torture. The sight filled Yue Fei with sadness and anger.

The trial judge was Moqi Xie. He placed the false testimony of Wang Gui and Wang Jun before Yue Fei and asked in a stern voice, "Hasn't the government been good to you? Why are you planning a mutiny?"

Yue Fei replied, "I have done nothing against the government. You are in charge of law and justice. You must not use trumped-up charges to frame officials loyal to the government and country."

Other officials present also echoed Moqi Xie, insisting that Yue Fei had seditious intentions. Yue Fei understood the futility of arguing with these partisans of Qin Hui's clique. He said with a deep sigh, "I've fallen into the hands of a bunch of traitorous thugs. There's no point in trying to prove to you my loyalty and patriotism."

Qin Hui had assigned Vice Censor-in-Chief He Zhu to try Yue Fei. When he began questioning Yue Fei, Yue Fei pulled up his shirt without uttering a word and showed He Zhu his bare back. What greeted He Zhu's eyes were the four deeply tattooed characters, *jing zhong bao guo* ("Dedicated to the service of the country"). He Zhu was so shaken that he could not go on with the inquiry. He remanded Yue Fei to his cell. After reviewing some more material related to the case, he could find no evidence to support the allegation of Yue Fei's seditious intent. He truthfully reported his conclusion to Qin Hui.

Sensing He Zhu's sympathy for Yue Fei, Qin Hui took him off the case and instructed Moqi Xie to continue fabricating charges against Yue Fei. Moqi Xie insisted that Yue Yun had written to Zhang Xian to make plans for a mutiny. Unable to provide any material evidence, they alleged Zhang Xian had destroyed the letters.

Moqi Xie put the three defendants through more torture, but Yue Fei would not give them the satisfaction of a confession. One day, when Moqi Xie tried to force Yue Fei to compose a confession, Yue Fei wrote down these eight characters: *tian ri zhao zhao, tian ri zhao zhao* ("Heaven be my witness, heaven be my witness").

After dragging on for two months, the trial still had not produced any conclusion. Everyone in government knew Yue Fei had been framed. However, some who had the courage to petition the emperor to clear Yue Fei's name themselves became victims of Qin Hui's reprisals.

The venerated general Han Shizhong went to see Qin Hui, and demanded evidence of Yue Fei's alleged plans for a mutiny. Qin Hui said in an arrogant and cavalier manner, "Although there is no evidence of Yue Yun's writing to Zhang Xian, one can make a plausible case of it."

Han Shizhong said angrily, "How can your plausible case convince the country?"

Han Shizhong's repeated efforts proved fruitless and he resigned as Military Affairs Commissioner.

One day after work, Qin Hui was drinking with his wife Wang by a window. Wang noticed him fiddling with an orange, absent-mindedly gouging the peel with his fingernail. Wang, who was even more ruthless than Qin Hui, understood that Qin Hui was still of two minds about whether to kill Yue Fei immediately. Wang said with a sinister snort, "You indecisive coot! It's easier to tie a tiger down than to set it free."

Wang's warning helped make up Qin Hui's mind. He immediately wrote a note which was secretly delivered to the prison. In a night in January 1142 AD, the patriotic national hero

Yue Fei was murdered. He was only 39. Yue Yun and Zhang Xian suffered the same fate that night.

After Yue Fei's murder, a prison warden in Lin'an named Kui Shun secretly buried his remains. Yue Fei's name was cleared only after the death of Emperor Gaozong, and his remains were moved to Qixia Peak for proper burial. A Yue Fei Temple was added later east of his tomb. A statue of Yue Fei clad in battle gear now sits in the great hall of the Yue Temple. Above the statue hangs an awe-inspiring board inscribed with the four characters, *huan wo shan he* ("Give back my country") in Yue Fei's handwriting. Opposite the tomb are four cast-iron kneeling figures with their hands tied behind their backs. They are the despised and hated traitors Qin Hui, his wife Wang, Moqi Xie and Zhang Jun. This arrangement is designed to reflect popular admiration for a national hero and revulsion for traitors.

142. Genghis Khan Unifies the Mongols

IN 1206 AD, the chiefs of the Mongol tribes held a kuriltai ("Great Assembly") by the Onon River, at which Timujin was hailed as the Great Khan, with the title of Genghis Khan. Timujin's father Yisugei was a chieftain of the Mongol Borjigin clan. He grew up under the ruthless rule of the Jin dynasty over the Mongol people. Life was made more unbearable by the constant feuds between different Mongol clans. One of Timujin's ancestors was killed by a Jin emperor.

When Timujin was nine, his father Yisugei took him to a friend's home to cement arrangements for his betrothal. Yisugei left Timujin at the friend's home and set out for home by himself. After traveling for a while he was famished and was looking for something to eat when he saw a group of Tartars having a feast on the steppe. He dismounted and walked into the reveling crowd and joined in the feast, as was the local custom.

There was a feud between the Tartars and the Borjigin clan, but Yisugei did not give it too much thought at the time. He was however recognized by the Tartars, and someone poisoned his food. On his way home after leaving the feast, he had an excruciating pain in his abdomen. He realized he must have been poisoned at the feast, but it was already too late. He died soon after he reached home.

In the aftermath of Yisugei's death, the headless Borjigin clan disbanded. Yisugei's followers, including members of the Taiyichi clan that had sworn fealty to him, defected to other clans, taking with them Yisugei's slaves and cattle, thus further impoverishing Timujin's family.

Fearing that Timujin would try to take revenge on them when he grew up, the chief of the Taiyichi clan sent a party after Timujin with the aim of killing him. Timujin was alerted and went into hiding in a forest.

He laid low in the forest for nine days, without food or drink. When he was forced by hunger to walk out of the forest, the Taiyichi pursuers immediately captured him. He was paraded past the tented homes of the clan in a pillory. One day, the Taiyichi chief and his tribesmen gathered for a feast by the Onon River. They left a lone, inexperienced guard to watch over Timujin. Timujin waited until the guard became distracted, and then knocked him unconscious with his pillory, escaping.

Timujin, his mother and his siblings once again took to the hills, where they sustained themselves by snaring rodents. Life became harsher than ever for them.

The young Timujin was determined to take over the mantle of his father. He was able through his tireless effort to locate and regroup blood relations and members of the clan who had dispersed. His power grew in the wake of numerous victories in his battles against other tribes.

Timujin had a friend Jamuka, who was the chief of another tribe. They had frequent daytime feasts in the shade of trees, and slept in the same bed at night, close as brothers. However, Jamuka was not amused when some of his followers went over to the increasingly powerful Timujin to offer their fealty. A confrontation of the two sides occurred when Timujin's people killed Jamuka's younger brother when he was trying to rustle Timujin's cattle. Jamuka put together a force of 30,000 men from the thirteen sub clans under his control to attack Timujin.

Rising to the challenge, Timujin deployed thirteen contingents totaling 30,000 men to engage the Jamuka forces. The two sides fought a fierce battle on the steppes by the Onon River. Timujin lost the battle, and Jamuka killed large numbers of prisoners of war. This had the effect of disaffecting his own followers, who defected to Timujin in droves. Ironically, defeat made Timujin stronger.

Timujin had never forgotten about Mieguzhen, the chief of the Tartars, who killed his father. Mieguzhen incurred the displeasure of the Jin dynasty. Wanyan Xiang, the Jin Chief Minister, formed an alliance with Timujin against the Tartars. Timujin grabbed this long-awaited opportunity to take his revenge on the Tartars. The joint forces of the Jin and Timujin routed the Tartar army, and large numbers of Tartar clansmen, cattle and large amounts of supplies were captured by the coalition. As a reward for his contribution in the campaign, the Jin government conferred on Timujin the title of Commander of the Vanguard.

In subsequent battles, Timujin conquered several tribes on the Mongolian plateau, and finally achieved the unification of the Mongol people. He was hailed as Great Khan by the chiefs of the Mongol tribes and is known to world history as Genghis Khan.

After his enthronement, Genghis Khan established a military and administrative system and a Mongolian writing system that contributed to building his khanate into a strong empire. In the meantime, the Jin empire continued to treat the Mongols as vassals, demanding tribute from Genghis Khan. Genghis Khan vowed to change this humiliating state of affairs.

When Wanyan Yongji, the Crown Prince, succeeded Emperor Zhangzong of the Jin dynasty at his death, he sent an emissary to Mongolia bearing an edict. When the messenger bade Genghis Khan to receive the edict on his knees, Genghis Khan asked him who the new Emperor was. When he was told that Wanyan Yongji had just ascended the throne, Genghis Khan spat scornfully and said, "I thought the master of the Central Plains must be of celestial caliber. I'm surprised a mediocre, incompetent man like him could qualify for the throne." With that, he mounted his horse and rode off, leaving the Jin emissary behind.

Genghis Khan broke with the Jin after that incident.

In 1211 AD, Genghis Khan mounted a massive campaign against the Jin dynasty. He went up a mountain and prayed to his god, "A Jin emperor killed one of my forefathers. Let me have my revenge!" Soon afterwards, he picked 3,000 of his best cavalrymen and led them south. These 3,000 men routed the 300,000 Jin troops led by General Hu Shaohu. Two years later, the Mongols breached the defenses of Juyong Pass and laid siege to Zhongjing (modern-day Beijing). The troops led by Genghis Khan and his four sons proved invincible as they waged war across the vast plains north of the Yellow River.

At this time, the Jin government was divided by internal strife, and Emperor Wanyan Yongji was killed in the upheaval. Emperor Xuanzong, who succeeded him, saw no alternative but to sue for peace with Genghis Khan. Genghis Khan withdrew his forces only after receiving large amounts of gold and silk, as well as a Jin princess in marriage.

After defeating the Jin dynasty, Genghis Khan's army became more powerful. In 1219 AD, when a Mongol caravan dispatched by Genghis Khan passed Khorasm (east of the Caspian Sea and west of the Aral Sea) on its journey west, its members were massacred by the soldiers stationed in the city. Genghis Khan responded by personally leading 200,000 Mongol troops to attack Khorazm. He then pressed on westward and took control of areas in what is modern-day Central Asia. His vanguard advanced all the way to eastern Europe and northern Persia before he decided to turn back with his troops.

When Genghis Khan went on his western campaign, he requested support from the Western Xia, but they not only refused to contribute any troops to help him, but also entered an alliance with the Jin dynasty. On his return from the western campaign, he set out to quash the Western Xia. In the final stages of the siege against the Xia capital, he fell seriously ill. Knowing he was not going to survive the illness, he said to his commanders, "When we attack the Jin, we need to pass through Song territory. The Song is certain to grant us passage because of the long-standing enmity between them."

After his death, Genghis Khan was succeeded by his son ügedei Khan. As instructed by Genghis Khan on his deathbed, ügedei Khan negotiated passage through Song territory and encircled the Jin capital of Kaifeng. In 1233 AD, the Mongols breached the defenses of Kaifeng, forcing Emperor Aizong to flee to Caizhou (modern-day Ru'nan, Henan Province). With Southern Song's support, the Mongols laid siege to Caizhou.

Emperor Aizong sent an emissary to Emperor Lizong of the Southern Song dynasty to sue for peace. He said through the envoy, "If the Jin is conquered now, the next target will be the Song. An alliance between us will be in the interest of our two countries."

This peace overture was snubbed by Emperor Lizong. Emperor Aizong of the Jin dynasty committed suicide out of despair. In 1234 AD, the Jin dynasty was extinguished under the joint attack of the Mongols and the Song army.

143. Jia Sidao Sells the Country down the River

AFTER THE JIN dynasty was destroyed by the Mongol-Song coalition forces, the Southern Song dynasty wanted to push on and recover lost territory in the Henan area. That gave ügedei Khan a pretext to mount a campaign against the Southern Song dynasty for breaching their agreement. The Mongols and the Southern Song dynasty were at war ever since.

After ügedei Khan's nephew Mongke Khan ascended the throne, he sent his younger brother Kublai Khan and his general Uriyangqadai on a campaign against Yunnan, gaining control of southwest China. In 1258 AD, Mongke's army attacked the Southern Song dynasty on three fronts. He himself led the main force to attack Hezhou (modern-day Hechuan, Sichuan Province); Kublai attacked Ezhou (modern-day Wuchang, Hubei Province); Uriyangqadai led an army north from Yunnan to attack Tanzhou (modern-day Changsha, Hunan Province). The three armies would then converge and advance on Lin'an.

When Mongke's army attacked Hezhou, it ran into fierce resistance by the local Song commander Wang Jian and the inhabitants, who heroically defended Diaoyu situated to the east of Hezhou. The Mongols were unable to take Diaoyu after five months of siege and attacks. In one of the offensives against the city, Mongke was seriously injured by a rock fired from a catapult. He died shortly after returning to camp.

Kublai received news of Mongke's death as he was on the point of crossing the river to advance on Ezhou. Some urged him to go back north to claim the throne, but Kublai replied, "I have been ordered to attack the Song. I can't very well return empty-handed."

After surveying the landscape along the river, Kublai put together a suicide squad of a few hundred men as a vanguard unit to cross the Yangtze. The Song troops were surprised by the appearance of the vanguard and their defenses crumbled. The Mongols were now able to move the bulk of their troops across the river and surround Ezhou.

The Southern Song court in Lin'an was shaken by the bad news pouring in. Emperor Lizong ordered Song troops in other locations to race to the rescue of Ezhou, and sent Jia Sidao, newly appointed as Chief Minister and Military Affairs Commissioner, to Hanyang to oversee the war.

The newly appointed Chief Minister Jia Sidao was an uneducated loafer who got into the government only because his sister was a favorite concubine in Emperor Lizong's harem. He was often seen drinking and reveling on West Lake in the company of female singers, totally neglecting his official duties. One evening, Emperor Lizong saw bright lights on the West Lake as he looked out from a high point in his palace. He remarked to the ministers in attendance, "It must be this young fellow Sidao having a good time."

Well aware that Jia Sidao was in Emperor Lizong's good graces, the ministers quipped, "He may be young and fun-loving, but he sure possesses great abilities."

Ordered by Emperor Lizong to oversee the war on the front in Hanyang, Jia Sidao went despite his fears. Once, when he was told that a Mongol detachment was not far away, he started shaking and asked pleadingly, "What's to be done? What's to be done?" In the end, the Mongols left after doing some looting, causing Jia Sidao to breathe a sigh in relief.

As Kublai intensified his offensives, Jia Sidao found the situation getting desperate. Without informing the central government, he sent a secret envoy he could trust to the Mongols to sue for peace, declaring that as long as the Mongols withdrew their forces, the Song government would be ready to submit to the Mongols and pay tribute in silver and silk. With his attack in full swing, Kublai rejected the ceasefire offer. At this time, Kublai received a confidential letter from his wife in the north, which said that some Mongol aristocrats were grooming his younger brother, Arik Boke, to be the next great Khan. In his rush to return to contend for the throne, Kublai agreed to Jia Sidao's offer and signed a secret pact with him. Jia Sidao promised to cede territory north of the river to the Mongols, and to pay an annual tribute of 200,000 taels of silver and 200,000 bolts of silk. Kublai hurriedly left with his troops after securing this promise.

Back in Lin'an, Jia Sidao did a good job of concealing the fact that he had made an unauthorized pact with the Mongols. With some Mongol prisoners of war in his custody, he bragged about the brilliant victories of the Song army, which not only drove away the Mongol troops attacking Ezhou, but mopped up all remnant pockets of resistance along the Yangtze.

Convinced by the whopping lies of Jia Sidao that he had made an outstanding contribution to the war effort, Emperor Lizong issued an edict praising him for his courage and his excellent performance as commander. Immediately, he promoted him and gave him a raise.

After returning to the north, with the support of a majority of the Mongol noblemen Kublai became the Great Khan. Remembering the pact he signed with Jia Sidao in Ezhou, he sent his emissary Hao Jing to the Southern Song dynasty to demand the implementation of the terms of the agreement.

When Hao Jing arrived in Zhenzhou (modern-day Yizheng, Jiangsu Province), he sent his deputy with a letter to Jia Sidao. Upon learning that Hao Jing was coming to Lin'an, Jia Sidao sent his people to Zhenzhou to lock up Hao Jing, for fear that his web of lies would now unravel. Kublai Khan was furious at the perfidy of Jia Sidao, but he was in a power struggle with his younger brother Arik Boke, and had to devote all his energies to dealing with him. The problem with the Southern Song dynasty was put on the back burners.

By weaving a web of deceit, Jia Sidao was able to cling to his post of Chief Minister for more than a decade. After the death of Emperor Lizong, Crown Prince Zhao Qi succeeded him as Emperor Duzong. Emperor Duzong appointed Jia Sidao as Grand Preceptor, and conferred on him the title of Duke of Wei. Jia Sidao was now at the zenith of his career. He pretended that he desired to retire. At the same time, he had his supporters put out rumors about an imminent attack by the Mongols. This caused the newly enthroned Emperor Duzong to beg him to stay in government. His political fortunes kept rising as a result. Emperor Duzong had a sumptuous villa built for Jia's exclusive use in the Geling Hills overlooking West Lake, where Jia Sidao indulged in a life of pleasure. Officials had to travel there to consult him and seek instructions on affairs of state.

After defeating Arik Boke and restoring the stability of his government, Kublai proclaimed himself Emperor in 1271 AD, giving the new dynasty the name Yuan, and himself the title of Emperor Shizu.

On the pretext of the Southern Song dynasty's non-compliance with the peace treaty, Emperor Shizu sent his generals Liu Zheng and Ashu on a campaign against Xiangyang, defeating the Song army in battle after battle. The siege of Xiangyang lasted for five years. Jia Sidao kept Emperor Duzong in the dark about the situation on the Xiangyang front. When an official submitted a memorial informing the emperor of the critical situation, it was intercepted by Jia Sidao, who immediately had the official fired.

One day Jia Sidao was asked by Emperor Duzong during the daily audience, "I've heard that Xiangyang has been in a siege by the Mongols for several years now. What should be done?"

Jia Sidao said with feigned surprise, "The Mongols have been beaten back by us years ago. Where did Your Majesty get that kind of news?"

Emperor Duzong said, "I just heard it from a maid-in-waiting."

After the audience was over, Jia Sidao found out the identity of the maid who leaked out the news, and had her killed on some trumped-up charge. From then on Emperor Duzong would never again hear any news about Mongol attacks.

The situation in Xiangyang was getting increasingly untenable under the offensives of the Mongols. However, Jia Sidao insulated himself from the crisis in his villa on Geling Hills. Once, a trusted aide found him on his haunches watching crickets fight in the company of maids. The official tapped on Jia Sidao's shoulder and asked, "Is this an important affair of state?" Engrossed in the game Jia Sidao took no notice of the remark.

When Xiangyang finally fell to the Mongols, the event sent shock waves through the Southern Song government. No longer able to keep the lid on the situation, Jia Sidao blamed the whole thing on the commanders leading the defense of Xiangyang, and fired them.

Witnessing the corruption and rotten state of the Southern Song government, Emperor Shizu of Yuan decided to press his military advantage and overthrow it. He sent his Chief Minister Boyan with 200,000 troops to attack Ezhou from the west and Yangzhou from the east.

By this time, Emperor Duzong had died, and Jia Sidao set up the four-year-old Zhao Xian as Emperor. After taking Ezhou, Boyan's army moved east along the river to attack Lin'an. Jia Sidao led 70,000 Song troops to defend Wuhu, while at the same time sending envoys to the Yuan camp to sue for peace. Boyan snubbed the peace overtures and ordered the Yuan army to launch attacks along both banks of the Yangtze. The Song resistance crumbled on all fronts and Jia Sidao fled back to Yangzhou. The Southern Song dynasty's fate was now sealed.

144. Wen Tianxiang Raises an Army

THE YUAN ARMY continued its triumphant march and was getting closer and closer to Lin'an. Four-year-old Zhao Xian was the nominal Emperor. After consulting the ministers, his grandmother, Empress Dowager Xie, rushed out an edict calling on the military commanders of various regions to come to the rescue of the government. The edict elicited little response except from Wen Tianxiang, the governor of Ganzhou, and Zhang Shijie, the general defending Chengzhou (modern-day Zhongxiang, Hubei Province), who immediately mobilized their troops.

Wen Tianxiang, a well-known national hero in Chinese history, was born in Luling of Jizhou (modern-day Ji'an, Jiangxi Province). Since a child, he enjoyed reading biographies of patriotic statesmen and heroes who gave their lives for the country, and was determined to emulate their example. When at the age of twenty he took the court-administered civil service exam in Lin'an, he so impressed the presiding examiners with his essay on ways to pull the country out of its current crisis that he won top honors.

Soon after entering public service at the level of the central government, Wen Tianxiang discovered that Jia Sidao and many powerful eunuchs had a cynical disregard for the well being of the country and the people. At the time of a Mongol campaign against the Southern Song dynasty, Dong Songchen, a eunuch, urged Emperor Lizong of Song to flee Lin'an. Wen Tianxiang immediately wrote a memorial calling for the execution of Dong Songchen to prevent public panic. This advice caused him to be stripped of his office. He eventually returned to Lin'an in a post writing speeches drafting edicts for the emperor, but he managed to step on the toes of Jia Sidao and was forced into retirement at the age of 37. It was not until the Southern Song dynasty was in imminent danger of foundering that he was sent to Jiangxi as governor of Ganzhou.

Shortly after receiving the edict calling him back into service, Wen Tianxiang recruited 30,000 men with the intention of racing to Lin'an. Some advised against the idea, "The Yuan army has penetrated deep into Song territory against crumbling resistance. If you try to stop them with your hastily formed unit, you will be sending a flock of sheep into the jaws of tigers. Why do you want to do something that's doomed to fail?"

Wen Tianxiang replied calmly, "I am aware of that. But I am pained to think that after years in the pay of the government, not one officer or soldier is now willing to come to the aid of the government at a time of crisis. I am fully aware of my limitations, but I'm ready to die for my country. I hope that by doing so I will inspire and mobilize my patriotic countrymen. The country has a chance of being saved only when there is a general mobilization of the masses."

Overcoming all hurdles, Wen Tianxiang finally brought his army to Lin'an. Chen Yizhong, the Chief Minister, sent him to Pingjiang (modern-day Suzhou, Jiangsu Province) to oversee the defenses there. At this time, the Yuan army commanded by Boyan had already crossed the Yangtze and was marching on Lin'an on three fronts. The Yuan troops that had left Jiankang and had by now marched passed Pingjiang, threatening Dusong Pass (modern-day Yuhang, Zhejiang Province). Chen Yizhong ordered Wen Tianxiang to pull his troops back to defend the Pass. However, Wen Tianxiang had barely left Pingjiang when Dusong Pass fell to the Yuan troops. Then by the time he turned around to return to Pingjiang, Pingjiang had also fallen.

Wen Tianxiang returned to Lin'an, where he had a discussion with General Zhang Shijie from Chengzhou. Together they urged the central government to concentrate its forces in a decisive battle with the Yuan army. However, the spineless Chen Yizhong would hear none of it.

By this time, Boyan's army had come to Mount Gaoting (northeast of modern-day Hangzhou), within fifteen kilometers of Lin'an. The spineless ministers, including Liu Mengyan, the Chief Minister, had all deserted the court. In a panic, Empress Dowager Xie and Chen Yizhong hastened to send an official to Boyan with the imperial seal and an offer to surrender. Boyan insisted on negotiating with the Song Chief Minister in person, but Chen Yizhong fled south for fear that once in the Yuan camp he would be detained. Inimical to the idea of surrendering, General Zhang Shijie set out to sea with his troops.

Empress Dowager Xie was left no choice but to announce the replacement of Chen Yizhong by Wen Tianxiang as Chief Minister, and to send him to negotiate the surrender with Boyan. Wen Tianxiang agreed to go to the Yuan camp, but had his own agenda. When he took his co-ministers Wu Jian and Jia Yuqing to meet with Boyan, he mentioned not a word about peace but reproachfully asked Boyan, "Do you have good will toward my country or are you bent on extinguishing the Song?"

Boyan said, "My Emperor is very clear about this. We are not out to extinguish the Song."

Wen Tianxiang said, "In that case, please immediately pull back your troops to Pingjiang or Jiaxing. If you insist on wiping the Song off the map, the people in the south and the Song army will fight you to the bitter end, and you will reap the bitter fruit."

Boyan's face darkened. He said in a threatening tone, "If you don't submit immediately, you'll suffer."

Wen Tianxiang riposted indignantly, "As Chief Minister of the Song dynasty, I am fully prepared to die for my country in this time of crisis. I am not afraid of going through a mountain of swords or a sea of flames."

Boyan's bluster was deflated by the booming voice and sharp words of Wen Tianxiang. The Yuan commanders present in the meeting were visibly disconcerted.

After the meeting Boyan gave orders to send the other envoys back to Lin'an to consult Empress Dowager Xie while keeping Wen Tianxiang in the Yuan camp. Realizing the sinister intent behind this arrangement, Wen Tianxiang protested to Boyan. Boyan said, feigning unconcern, "Don't be so upset. We need you here to negotiate the peace treaty."

Wu Jian and Jia Yuqing returned to Lin'an to brief Empress Dowager Xie on Wen Tianxiang's refusal to surrender. Eager to surrender, Empress Dowager Xie appointed Jia Yuqing to replace Wen Tianxiang as Chief Minister, and to carry the surrender offer to the Yuan camp. After receiving the surrender offer, Boyan invited Wen Tianxiang to his tent. and told him the Song court had sent another envoy with a surrender offer. Wen Tianxiang gave Jia Yuqing a severe chiding, but the surrender was a foregone conclusion.

In 1276 AD, Boyan took control of Lin'an with his army. Empress Dowager Xie and Zhao Xian went out of the palace to formally surrender to the Yuan. Zhao Xian departed for Dadu (modern-day Beijing) as a prisoner, as did Wen Tianxiang. Escape was constantly on his mind as the convoy made its way toward Dadu. When the convoy arrived near Zhenjiang, he and a few followers broke free from the Yuan camp in a moment of lax surveillance, and fled to Zhenzhou on a small boat.

Miao Zaicheng, the commander defending Zhenzhou, was delighted by Wen Tianxiang's arrival and opened the city gate to welcome his party. When Miao Zaicheng learned from Wen Tianxiang that Lin'an had fallen, he expressed his readiness to join Wen Tianxiang in regrouping the forces east and west of the Huai River to repel the Yuan invaders.

Wen Tianxiang was excited by this development, but in the meantime Li Tingzhi, the Song general defending Yangzhou, was led by rumor to believe Wen Tianxiang had surrendered to the Yuan and was a spy sent by the Yuan army to Zhenzhou. He ordered Miao Zaicheng to execute Wen Tianxiang. Miao Zaicheng did not believe the damaging story about Wen Tianxiang. However, on the other hand he could not very well disobey the orders of his superior Li Tingzhi. He lured Wen Tianxiang out of Zhenzhou, and asked him to leave as soon as possible after showing him the order from Yangzhou.

Wen Tianxiang had no alternative but to take his followers with him to Yangzhou overnight. The party reached one of the gates of Yangzhou before daybreak the next day and waited for the gate to open. Wen Tianxiang learned from the conversation among other people waiting for the gate to open that a reward was offered in Yangzhou for his arrest. This meant Yangzhou was out of the question for them.

Wen Tianxiang's party of twelve changed their names and assumed disguises to escape detection and arrest. They traveled east on relatively deserted roads in an attempt to get to the sea and find a boat to take them south. They ran into a Yuan cavalry detachment on their journey and hid behind an earthwork. Traveling by day and resting by night through many difficult circumstances, Wen Tianxiang's party finally were able to obtain help from some peasants, and get on a boat that took them to Wenzhou. There, he learned that Zhang Shijie and Chen Yizhong had set up a new emperor in Fuzhou, so he decided to go there.

145. Zhang Shijie Defends Yashan to the Death

HOW DID ZHANG Shijie and Chen Yizhong end up in Fuzhou? After the capture of Lin'an by the Yuan army, and the removal of the child-emperor Zhao Xian as prisoner to Dadu, his two brothers, the 9-year-old Zhao Shi and the 6-year-old Zhao Bing were escorted by royal family members and the minister Lu Xiufu to the safety of Fuzhou. Lu Xiufu then sent for Zhang Shijie and Chen Yizhong. After consultation among the three ministers, it was decided to set up Zhao Shi as the new Emperor to continue the resistance against the Yuan in the name of the Southern Song dynasty.

After learning of this development, Wen Tianxiang saw a ray of hope for the restoration of the Southern Song dynasty. He immediately went to Fuzhou, where he became Military Affairs Commissioner in the new government. He proposed to Chen Yizhong the idea of recovering territory in the Jiangsu and Zhejiang area by attacking the Yuan army from the sea, but Chen disagreed with the idea, deeming it too risky.

Wen Tianxiang had to find another way. He established an area command in Nanjianzhou (modern-day Nanping, Fujian Province), where he started recruiting in preparation for a campaign to recover lost territory. The next year, Wen Tianxiang marched his troops into Jiangxi and, with the allied militias, won a string of victories against the Yuan army, taking back Huichang and numerous other county seats.

At that time, a Yuan army had marched south to attack Fuzhou, defeating the Song troops in battle after battle. Chen Yizhong gave up hope on restoring the Southern Song dynasty and fled by the sea. Zhang Shijie and Lu Xiufu, with Zhao Shi in their protection, boarded an ocean-going ship to Guangdong. The ship nearly capsized in a sudden cyclone, and the young Zhao Shi, traumatized by the experience, fell ill and soon died.

Still at sea, Zhang Shijie and Lu Xiufu set up Zhao Bing as the emperor, and took their naval fleet to Yashan (south of modern-day Xinhui, Guangdong Province).

Zhang Hongfan, a Yuan general, said to Emperor Shizu of Yuan in a briefing, "If the rump Song court in the south is not quickly quashed, it might attract a larger following among the Song people." Emperor Shizu of Yuan sent an elite force of 20,000, with Zhang Hongfan as commander and Li Heng as deputy, south by both land and sea.

Zhang Hongfan first sent a force to attack Chaozhou, which was defended by Wen Tianxiang. Outnumbered, Wen Tianxiang was compelled to retreat to a mountain in Haifeng, where he was surprised by the Yuan army and taken prisoner.

When Yuan soldiers took Wen Tianxiang to the tent of Zhang Hongfan, Zhang Hongfan handled him with kid gloves and feigned solicitude. He ordered Wen Tianxiang untied and let him stay with him in his tent. At the same time, he ordered his naval troops to sail toward Yashan.

When the Yuan troops reached Yashan, Zhang Hongfan sent an emissary to Zhang Shijie urging him to surrender. Zhang Shijie said, "I know that by surrendering to the Yuan army, I can not only be spared my life but will be richly rewarded. But I'd rather die than betray my country."

Zhang Hongfan knew of Zhang Shijie's admiration for Wen Tianxiang, so he tired to persuade Wen Tianxiang to write Zhang Shijie urging him to surrender. Wen Tianxiang said with a snort, "I already deeply regret not being able to help my motherland. Do you expect me to encourage others to betray it?"

Zhang Hongfan had ink and brush brought in and forced him to write a letter. Taking the brush, Wen Tianxiang wrote the following line without pausing to think.

Man is mortal to be sure, a pure heart would longer endure!

This line was part of a poem previously written by Wen Tianxiang when he was traveling on the Lingding Sea.

When a soldier brought the sheet of paper with the line of verse to Zhang Hongfan, he could only smile wryly. Realizing he was not going to get the defending general to surrender, he resumed his strong offensive.

Yashan was strategically situated in a bay in South China, with a mountain overlooking the sea. Zhang Shijie placed more than 1,000 boats next to each other in a straight line, tied together with ropes and surrounded by defensive superstructures. He was digging in for a battle to the death with the Yuan army. The Yuan troops launched a fire attack by sending toward the Song troops small boats loaded with dry straw doused with kerosene and set aflame. The wind was unfavorable to the Song army. Zhang Shijie had been prepared for this: by daubing his ships with a thick coat of wet mud and equipping them with long wooden poles, he was able to keep the fireboats at bay.

His fire attack having failed, Zhang Hongfan started a blockade with a flotilla, cutting off Zhang Shijie's communication with the shore. The Song troops were reduced to eating rations of dry food and drinking from the sea. The briny, bitter seawater caused vomiting among the soldiers. In the meantime, Zhang Hongfan intensified his offensive. The Song troops fought back valiantly, resulting in a stalemate.

At this time, the deputy commander of the Yuan army, Li Heng, led his troops from Guangzhou to join forces with Zhang Hongfan in Yashan. With reinforcements, Zhang Hongfan renewed his offensive. He attacked the Song army on four fronts, surrounding it. At low tide, the Yuan army attacked from the north; at high tide, it attacked with the incoming tide from the south.

The Song troops were reeling from the two-pronged attacks when they heard music coming from Zhang Hongfan's ship. The Song troops, believing the Yuan general was hosting a banquet, seized the opportunity to get some rest. However, the music turned out to be a signal for an all-out offensive. At the sound of the music Zhang Hongfan's ship led the charge and arrows rained on the Song ships. By unleashing a barrage of arrows, the Yuan troops succeeded in seizing seven Song battleships. All Yuan units were pitched into the fierce offensive. From morning until evening, the sea at Yashan was a scene of billowing waves and ear-splitting battle cries.

Zhang Shijie was directing the battle when he caught sight of a Song ship lowering its flag and ceasing its fighting. As one Song ship after another did the same, Zhang Shijie realized the battle was over. He immediately deployed his best troops to the center, and sent a small boat to fetch Zhao Bing in preparation for an attempt to run the blockade.

Lu Xiufu protected Zhao Bing's ship. Unsure about the true intentions of the people coming to transfer Zhao Bing to a small boat, and worried that the young Emperor might fall into the hands of the Yuan army, Lu Xiufu refused the demand of the envoy. He said over his shoulder to Zhao Bing, "There's no hope now for our country. Your Majesty has no alternative but to die for the country." With that, he jumped with Zhao Bing on his back into the sea, and both were swallowed by the crashing waves.

Zhang Shijie had to leave without Zhao Bing. He led his fleet of battleships under cover of night to the Hailing Mountain, successfully getting through the blockade. When he counted his ships again, only a dozen were left out of 1,000. A cyclone then approached. His followers urged him to seek shelter on the shore, but Zhang Shijie adamantly refused, and a tall wave capsized his ship. The Song general, who had vowed to fight to the death, drowned.

In February 1279 AD, the Yuan dynasty unified China, and the Southern Song dynasty was extinguished.

YUAN DYNASTY
(1279–1368)

146. Ode to the Force of Virtue

AFTER TAKING CONTROL of Yashan, Zhang Hongfan summoned the Yuan commanders to a victory feast, where Wen Tianxiang was also an invited guest. Zhang Hongfan said to Wen Tianxiang at the banquet, "Now that the Song dynasty has been extinguished, you can say you've done your patriotic best as Chief Minister. If you change your mind and submit to the Yuan Emperor, you can continue to be Chief Minister."

Wen Tianxiang said, with tears in his eyes, "Now that my country is no more, I feel guilt-laden for not having been able to prevent its destruction. Even my death won't begin to redeem my guilt. How can I prolong my existence in ignominy?"

Unable to persuade Wen Tianxiang to surrender, Zhang Hongfan ordered him taken to Dadu. Six months later, Wen Tianxiang arrived in Dadu, where the Yuan court ordered that he be accommodated in the best guesthouse and given the best wine and food. A few days later, the Yuan Chief Minister Boluo sent Liu Mengyan, a Song official who had defected, to try to talk

Wen Tianxiang into surrendering. Wen Tianxiang, who had long detested and despised this traitor, was infuriated by his attempt to wangle an agreement to surrender out of him. Before Liu Mengyan opened his mouth, Wen Tianxiang gave him such a chiding that the humbled Liu Mengyan left in shame.

Unsuccessful in its attempts to make Wen Tianxiang surrender, the Yuan government transferred him to the Warden's Office, where he became a prison inmate in handcuffs and leg irons. A month later, Boluo had Wen Tianxiang brought to the Bureau of Military Affairs, where he personally conducted a trial.

Wen Tianxiang, flanked by guards, arrived in the hall of the Bureau of Military Affairs, where a glaring, mean-looking Boluo was already installed in his seat. Wen Tianxinag walked up with his back ramrod straight and his head held high, not deigning to cast a glance at the presiding judge. The soldiers yelled at him to kneel, but Wen Tianxiang refused.

Boluo was infuriated by this irreverence, and ordered the soldiers to make him kneel. By dragging and pushing, the soldiers pushed Wen Tianxiang to the ground.

Boluo said, "Now what do you have to say?"

Wen Tianxiang said calmly, "Countries rise and fall. Government officials are executed. This is in the nature of things. I am an official of a defeated country. All I want is to be killed as quickly as possible."

Not wanting the interrogation to bog down in confrontation, Boluo tried to inject a light note into the proceedings, "Tell me how many emperors there are from Pan Gu until now."

Wen Tianxiang said with a snort, "They fill seventeen tomes of historical chronicles, too many to count. Besides, I am not here to take an examination, and I am in no mood to engage in small talk with you."

Hurt by the brush-off, Boluo confronted Wen Tianxiang out of spite, "Why did you desert Lin'an? Why did you go along with the enthronement of Zhao Shi and Zhao Bing?" After rebutting him point by point, Wen Tianxiang concluded spiritedly, "Since I am in your hands, I'm prepared to die. There's no need to waste words."

Boluo was furious. He ordered Wen Tianxiang remanded to the

Bureau of Military Affairs, with the intention of having him killed. However, Emperor Shizu of Yuan did not give his consent, for fear that killing Wen Tianxiang would prove unpopular.

Wen Tianxiang was incarcerated in a dark, damp dungeon with a low ceiling and cramped space. When it rained, the cell would get flooded. In summer, the dampness rising up from the earthen floor made the air close and uncomfortably warm. The warden's stove and stale grain stored next door gave out smoke and a moldy smell, and the air was made more unbearable by the odor from the latrine and the stink of dead rats.

The harsh conditions of his cell made him physically weaker, but were powerless against his mental fortitude. He firmly believed that his love of the people and the country was a virtuous force that would enable him to endure any harsh conditions.

In his cell, he wrote the legendary *Zheng Qi Ge* ("Ode to the Force of Virtue"), a poem that is popular even today. In the poem, he cited examples from history of justice-upholding and death-defying heroes, who represented in his view the force of virtue. The main idea of the poem is as follows:

A force of virtue permeates Heaven and Earth.
It is embodied in all physical forms:
The rivers and mountains on Earth,
The sun and stars in Heaven.
In man, it manifests itself as a boundless spirit
So vast it fills the universe ...
True strength of character is revealed
Only in times of crisis and peril.
They are remembered by history.

In the third year of Wen Tianxiang's incarceration, a peasant uprising broke out in Zhongshan of Hebei. The rebel leader claimed to be a descendant of the royal Song family. He put together an army of several thousand men, and called for a march toward Dadu to rescue Chief Minister Wen Tianxiang. This development frightened the Yuan government. It now feared dire consequences if Wen Tianxiang was kept alive. However, Emperor

Shizu of Yuan had not given up the idea of turning Wen Tianxiang, and decided to give it a try himself. Wen Tianxiang was taken from his cell to the palace.

When he was brought before Emperor Shizu of Yuan, Wen Tianxiang refused to kneel, but only made a bow with his hands folded. Emperor Shizong asked him what he had to say. Wen Tianxiang replied, "As Chief Minister of the Song, I gave my best advice to my government. But the traitorous acts of some ministers prevented me from making a difference. I have been unable to recover lost territory, and have fallen into humiliating captivity. I will not die with peace of mind." He gritted his teeth and kept beating on his chest as he said this.

Emperor Shizu said affably and in a cajoling tone, "I can fully understand your loyalty and patriotism. But given the new reality, if you can change your mind and join the Yuan government, I will keep you on as Chief Minister. What do you think?"

Wen Tianxiang replied in a passionate voice, "I am Chief Minister of the Song government. There is no way I am going to serve two governments. Only by dying now would I feel comfortable in the company of the patriots and heroes who died before me."

Emperor Shizu said, "If you don't want to be Chief Minister, would you agree to be Military Affairs Commissioner?"

Wen Tianxiang answered directly, "All I want now is to die. I have no more to say."

Emperor Shizu knew then that he would never get Wen Tianxiang to surrender. He ordered Wen taken away. The next day, Wen Tianxiang was executed.

It was a day of a howling north wind and an overcast sky. Ten thousand inhabitants of the city flocked spontaneously to the heavily guarded Chaishi execution ground in the capital when they learned that Wen Tianxiang was going to his death that day. The crowd, several deep around the perimeter, saw a calm Wen Tianxiang arrive at the execution ground in handcuffs and leg irons. He asked the civilians closest to him which way was south. The people pointed it out to Wen Tianxiang, who made several bows in that direction. Sitting down with a straight back, he said to the official supervising the execution, "I'm ready."

In January 1283 AD, this national hero of China finally went to his death at the age of 47, embodying the boundless spirit of the force of virtue.

147. Marco Polo, a Visitor from Europe

DURING THE REIGN of Emperor Shizu of Yuan, the vast Mongol khanate founded by Genghis Khan was split into four divisions, with the Yuan Emperor nominally still the Great Khan ruling all four khanates. In that period, China was the most powerful and richest nation in the world, a strong magnet attracting many legations, merchants and travelers who flocked there to visit the land of fabled riches. One of the most famous of them is Marco Polo.

Marco Polo's father Niccolò and uncle Maffeo were merchants from Venice. The two Polo brothers made frequent business trips abroad. After the founding of the Mongol Khanate, they traveled to the Kipchak Khanate with a load of treasures they intended to sell. When war broke out there, they moved to Bukhara, a city in Central Asia, and settled down there.

An envoy sent by Kublai happened to see these two European merchants as he passed through Bukhara. His curiosity piqued, he said to them, "My Great Khan has never seen a European. If you agree to come with me to see my Great Khan, you will make a fortune. Besides, no one else can provide the kind of security that we can give you on your journey to China."

The Polo brothers were travel enthusiasts. When they heard that the Great Khan of China could receive them, they immediately grabbed the chance. The two men followed the envoy to Shangdu (northwest of modern-day Duolun County, the

Autonomous Region of Inner Mongolia). Kublai, as predicted, was happy to see the Europeans. He warmly received them in his traveling palace and asked many questions.

The Polo brothers did not intend to stay in China. Kublai, after hearing about Europe from them, asked them to return to Europe with a letter from Kublai to the Pope, asking him to send missionaries to China. The two men took leave of Kublai and left China. They traveled for more than three years before they arrived back in Venice. By that time Niccolò's wife had died of illness, leaving a son Marco Polo, who was a young man of 15.

After hearing the accounts of his father and his uncle about the riches of China, Marco Polo was captivated and begged his father to take him to China. Niccolò also felt uncomfortable about leaving his son behind with no one to take care of him, so he decided to take him along.

After an audience with the pope, Niccolò set out with Marco Polo for China. It was another three years on the road before they arrived in China, in 1275 AD. When Kublai, who had by that time become Emperor, heard about the arrival of the Polos, he sent a welcoming party to meet them when they were still a long way from Shangdu.

The Polo brothers took Marco Polo with them to the audience with Emperor Shizu of Yuan. The latter was surprised at the sight of a young man accompanying them and asked who he was. Niccolò replied, "My son at your service."

The handsome Marco Polo impressed Emperor Shizu. He said with enthusiasm, "Welcome, welcome!"

That evening Emperor Shizu invited them to a welcoming banquet in his palace. They were later asked to serve in the government.

Marco Polo was a smart young man, and was able to quickly pick up Mongolian and Han Chinese. Impressed by his rapid progress, Emperor Shizu soon sent Marco Polo to Yunnan on official business. Emperor Shizu was intrigued by different customs and ways of life in various parts of his dominion. In the past, officials sent on inspection tours to various parts of China would often be unable to answer Emperor Shizu's questions about local customs and culture. Marco Polo in contrast would pay close attention to local culture and make detailed reports to Emperor Shizu on his return from the missions. Emperor Shizu was full of praise for Marco Polo's abilities, and frequently entrusted important missions to him.

In his seventeen years in China, Emperor Shizu sent Marco Polo on inspection tours to many locations in China and as diplomatic envoy abroad. He went to several countries in Southeast Asia as a diplomat. He stayed for three years in Yangzhou, where he is said to have been appointed Supervisor-in-Chief.

As time went on, the three Europeans became homesick and repeatedly petitioned Emperor Shizu to be allowed to go home. However, because of Marco Polo's importance to him, Emperor Shizu was reluctant to let them go. It so happened that a concubine of the Khan of the Il Khanate had died, and he sent an envoy to Dadu to find a bride. Emperor Shizu selected a young lady called Kuokuozhen from the royal family as concubine for the Il Khan. The envoy from the Il Khan felt that travel by land was too arduous, and, knowing the Polo brothers' experience in sea travel, requested Emperor Shizu to ask the Polos to escort the concubine to the Il Khanate by sea. Emperor Shizu had no reason to refuse.

In 1292 AD, the Polos left China with the Il Khan envoy, and sailed across the Indian Ocean, escorting Kuokuozhen safely to the Il Khanate. They continued on, and after another three years of travel, finally arrived back in Venice.

By that time, they had been absent from Venice for twenty years. The local people thought they had died abroad because they had not heard from or about them for all those long years. Now that they came back in oriental outfits and reportedly brought loads of pearls and other precious stones from China, excitement rippled through the city. Marco Polo was given the nickname of Marco Millioni, or Marco of the Million.

Shortly afterwards, a conflict arose between Venice and the city-state of Genoa, and naval battles were fought between their fleets on the Mediterranean. Marco Polo obtained a battleship at his own expense and joined the Venetian fleet, with himself at the wheel of the ship. When Venice lost the battle, Marco Polo was captured and put in a jail in Genoa. The Genoans flocked to the prison to ask the famous world traveler to talk about the Orient and China.

A fellow inmate in the Genoan cell, by the name of Rustician, wrote down the oral accounts of Marco Polo, which were collected in the famous *Travels of Marco Polo*. In the book, Marco Polo gave detailed descriptions of famous Chinese cities like Dadu, Yangzhou, Suzhou and Hangzhou, and glowing accounts of the prosperity and civilization of China. Its publication stoked the fascination of Europe with Chinese civilization. With Marco Polo's fame growing, the Genoans freed him to go back to his country.

An era of increased exchanges and contacts between the Chinese, the Europeans and the Arabs was ushered in. The Arabs' knowledge of astronomy, mathematics and medicine began to spread to China. Three Chinese inventions—the compass, the printing press and gunpowder—were imported into Europe during this period (another of China's inventions, paper, having already spread to Europe at an earlier time).

148. *Dou E's Grievance* Moves Heaven and Earth

EMPEROR SHIZU OF Yuan introduced numerous incentives to promote production, contributing to an increased prosperity in the early years of his reign. However, the economic boom exclusively benefited the aristocratic class, landowners and officials. To meet the Mongol aristocrats' need for an extravagant lifestyle and to support the military, Emperor Shizu recruited ministers specializing in finance to help him fill his coffers by plundering the people. These ministers ganged up with local officials in illegal schemes of bribery and profiteering.

The Yuan government pursued an ethnic policy that divided its subjects into four classes. The first class consisted of the Mongols; the second, called the Semuren, consisted of people from the Western Regions and the Western Xia; the third, called the Han, consisted of the Han Chinese, the Kitans and the Jurchens, who had lived under the Jin rule; and, the fourth, called the Nanren (southern people), consisted of the ethnic communities who had lived under the rule of the Southern Song. Each of the four classes possessed a distinct political status and was treated accordingly, with the Han and the Nanren heavily discriminated against. In this system of oppression and ethnic discrimination, the working people lived a miserable life. Corruption was endemic and injustices were rampant.

Emperor Shizu of Yuan was succeeded by his grandson Temür as Emperor Chengzong of the Yuan dynasty. During the reign of

Emperor Chengzong, corruption and injustices became even more unwieldy. In one investigation, 18,000 officials were ferreted out as having been implicated in graft, and 5,000 cases injustice were discovered.

A theatrical genre called *zaju* (a form of poetic drama set to music) became popular in Dadu. Intellectuals disaffected with the benighted policies of the government resorted to the vehicle of *zaju* to lampoon official corruption, ineptitude and social inequity.

One such intellectual in Dadu called Guan Hanqin displayed an affinity for music and theater at a very young age. He mastered the *xiao* (a bamboo flute) and the zither, as well as singing and dancing. Although he had been an official doctor at the Imperial Clinic in the capital, his heart was not in medicine. Instead, he had a passion for playwriting. In those days, actors had a low social standing, but Guan Hanqin frequented their circles. Sometimes he would perform a role in one of their theatrical numbers. Because of his expertise in both music and theater, his creations were often possessed of an unusual charm and interest.

Theater-going was popular among both the aristocracy and the ordinary people in Dadu. Guan Hanqin's plays were not purely fare to amuse the aristocrats, but were often vehicles for putting across the common people's message. The miseries of the people that he witnessed or heard about were incorporated into his plays. One of his signature works was *Dou E's Grievance Moves the Gods* (also known as *Dou E's Grievance*).

The main protagonist in *Dou E's Grievance* is an impoverished woman called Dou E from Chuzhou. Her mother died when she was a child. Her father, Dou Tianzhang, sold her to an Auntie Cai as child bride for a sum of money so that he could travel to the capital to take part in the Civil Service exam. Less than two years after her marriage into the Cai family, her husband died of illness leaving her to live alone with the widowed Auntie Cai, who was also poor.

A hooligan in Chuzhou called Donkey Zhang, and his father, Oldman Zhang, emboldened by the fact that Dou E and Auntie Cai had no one to protect them, refused to leave the women's house unless Auntie Cai agreed to marry Oldman Zhang. After the timid Auntie Cai gave her reluctant consent, Donkey Zhang tried to coerce Dou E into marrying him, but she flatly refused and scolded him.

Donkey Zhang remembered the slight. A few days later, Auntie Cai fell ill and asked Dou E to make some mutton tripe soup for her. Donkey Zhang slipped some poison into the soup in order to kill Auntie Cai, and force Dou E to marry him. When Auntie Cai took the soup from Dou E and was about to drink it, she suddenly felt nauseous and handed the bowl of soup to Oldman Zhang, who drank it instead. Oldman Zhang fell down and died.

Donkey Zhang, whose poison killed his own father, now blamed the murder on Dou E, and denounced her to the Chuzhou government.

Tao Wu, the governor of Chuzhou, was a corrupt official. Having had his palm greased by Donkey Zhang, he had Dou E arrested and brought before him. He tried to force a confession out of her. Despite being severely tortured, Dou E still refused to admit to administering the poison.

Tao Wu found out that Dou E was a dutiful daughter-in-law. He had Auntie Cai beaten in front of Dou E, who then felt compelled to confess to a murder she did not commit, because she could not stand the sight of her elderly mother-in-law being tortured.

The corrupt Tao Wu sentenced Dou E to death, after torturing a confession out of her. As she was led to the execution ground, Dou E, despairing of having her false conviction overturned, railed at Heaven and Earth, "Earth! Shame on you because you can't tell good and evil! Heaven! Shame on you because you can't tell right from wrong!"

Moments before her execution, she made three wishes: first, that her head would be cleanly chopped off with one strike of the sword, and all her blood would spill on the white flag for the dead; second, that a heavy snow would cover up her body; third, that Chuzhou would suffer drought three years in a row. Her wishes moved Heaven and Earth and the moment after her execution a heavy snow started falling from a darkened sky, even though it was the hot month of June. Three years of drought then inflicted Chuzhou. Dou E's father, Dou Tianzhang, became a high official in the capital and Dou E's wrongful conviction was overturned. The real killer Donkey Zhang was sentenced to death, and the corrupt governor Tao Wu got his just deserts.

The play was fiction, and snow in June is a product of the playwright's imagination. However, the play gave expression to the strong desire of the people under feudal rule for justice and retribution. That is the explanation for the enduring popularity of this play, and Guan Hanqin's well-deserved reputation as one of the most acclaimed playwrights in Chinese history.

149. A One-eyed Stone Figurine

AFTER THE REIGN of Emperor Chengzong, nine more emperors passed through the Yuan throne. Infighting and internal strife intensified in the court, and political corruption deepened, bringing unbearable hardship to the population. Toghan-Temür, the last Yuan Emperor, with the title of Emperor Shundi of Yuan, was a dissolute, ruthless ruler, under whose reign the state coffers were depleted and prices soared. Many peasants, unable to eke out a living and driven to despair, rose up in revolt.

A teacher in Hebei was secretly using a cult called the White Lotus Society to organize an anti-Yuan peasant movement. The government discovered his activities, and sent him away to Yongnian (northeast of modern-day Handan, Hebei Province) to do forced labor for the military. His grandson, Han Shantong, then took up leadership of the cult, and began recruiting impoverished peasants and holding meetings in worship of Buddha. Han Shantong said to the peasants, "Buddha is going to send Maitreya Bodhisattva down to this anarchic world to rescue the masses." This prediction soon spread to the Henan and Jianghuai areas, where the people began waiting expectantly for the advent of Maitreya Bodhisattva.

At this time, the Yellow River breached the dike at Baimao. Heavy rains lasting for more than twenty days triggered devastating floods, causing widespread destruction to people on both sides of the river. A proposal was made to the central government to repair the breach while at the same time digging another channel in Huanglinggang (southwest of modern-day Cao

County, Shandong Province) to divert the river water. In 1351 AD, the Yuan government conscripted 150,000 civilians in Bianliang (modern-day Kaifeng, Henan Province) and Daming. They organized them into thirteen forced-labor detachments, and sent them with 20,000 soldiers to Huanglinggang to dig a new river channel.

As the digging project got underway, the civilian laborers were forced to toil day and night in the heavy rain, while the officials overseeing the project liberally helped themselves with the government funds earmarked for the work. As a result, not enough was spent on feeding the laborers, who often went hungry. Discontent swelled.

Han Shantong saw an opportunity to mobilize the masses. He sent a few hundred sect followers to join the forced-labor detachments. Upon arrival, they started spreading a ditty: "A one-eyed stone figurine heralds a revolt on the Yellow River."

The channel diggers did not really understand the ditty, but the mention of a "revolt" gave them a sense of imminent liberation and a vision of better days to come. When the digging progressed to Huanglinggang, a few laborers suddenly hit a stone figurine. Others flocked to look, and were flabbergasted at the sight of a stone man with only one eye. This curious fact immediately spread among the hundreds of thousands of laborers, who thought the ditty's prophecy had now been fulfilled. It naturally meant the day of revolt had come. Of course, the stone figurine had been secretly placed there by Han Shantong.

The masses were now stirred up. Liu Futong, a friend of Han Shantong's, said to him, "The people are nostalgic for the Song dynasty because they are fed up with the iron-handed rule of the Yuan dynasty. If we use the battle cry of restoring the Song dynasty, we will get a larger following."

Han Shantong liked this idea and announced publicly, "Han Shantong's original surname is not Han but Zhao. He is actually an eighth generation descendant of Emperor Huizong of Song. Liu Futong is a descendant of the Southern Song general Liu Guangshi." These invented details convinced the credulous laborers.

On an auspicious day selected by Han Shantong and Liu Futong, a public gathering was organized to witness the killing of a white horse and a black ox, which were offered to the gods above and below. The crowd acclaimed Han Shantong as their leader, with the title of King Ming. A date was set for launching a revolt in Yingshang, Yingzhou (modern-day Fuyang and Yingshang, Anhui Province), with red turbans as the insurgents' identifying mark. As the gathering proceeded to swear a blood oath of allegiance, government troops arrived and arrested Han Shantong, who was taken to the county government building and executed. His wife succeeded in evading the government troops, and went into hiding in Wu'an (in Hebei Province) with their son Han Lin'er.

After breaking through the encircling government troops, Liu Futong mustered the peasants who had agreed to participate in the revolt and took control of some positions around Yingzhou. When news of their action reached the laborers on the Huanglinggang project, these workers killed their supervisors and joined up with Liu Futong. Because of the red turbans of the insurgents, they were dubbed the "Red Army" by the people, and are known to Chinese history as the Red Turban Army. Within ten days, the Red Turban Army had grown to more than 100,000 men.

The Yuan government was alarmed at the rapid growth of Liu Futong's force, and immediately deployed the A-Su Army, comprised of 6,000 Semuren and a number of Han units, to quash the Red Turban rebellion. In the past, the A-Su Army was an elite force, but it was now a pale shadow of its former self, with its commanders wallowing in drink and revelry and the soldiers indulging in rampant looting. When the A-Su Army met the Red Turbans, its supreme commander turned his horse around and fled before fighting even started, shouting, "A bu! A bu!" ("Run, run!") His soldiers followed his example and scattered in all directions.

A month later, Liu Futong's Red Turbans succeeded in capturing several towns in a row. The peasants in the Jianghuai area, long under the influence of the White Lotus Society, joined Liu Futong's rebellion. Xu Shouhui of Qishui (modern-day Xishui, Hubei Province) and Guo Zixing of Haozhou (modern-day Fengyang, Anhui Province), for example, rebelled under the Red Turban flag.

At the same time, there were other rebels who did not use the Red Turban flag, such as Zhang Shicheng in north Jiangsu.

In 1354 AD, Emperor Shundi of Yuan ordered Chief Minister Tuotuo to muster a 1,000,000-strong army comprised of forces under the command of princes, troops from the provinces and from the Western Regions. They were to attack the insurgents led by Zhang Shicheng, who had taken control of Gaoyou. The Yuan army imposed a watertight siege around Gaoyou. At this critical juncture, an internal conflict broke out in the Yuan central government, with Emperor Shundi stripping Tuotuo of his position. The Yuan army, without its Commander-in-Chief, soon went into disarray and collapsed.

After the Yuan army disintegrated, insurgents led by Liu Futong in the north pressed on and routed the Yuan troops. In February of the next year, Liu Futong brought Han Shantong's son, Han Lin'er, to Bozhou (modern-day Bo County, Anhui Province) and proclaimed him Emperor of the Song dynasty. Han Lin'er was given the title King Ming, Junior.

After founding the new regime, Han Lin'er and Liu Futong embarked on a northern expedition. A western army led by Li Wu and Cui De was to campaign in Shaanxi, Gansu, Ningxia and Sichuan. An eastern army led by Mao Gui was to advance toward the Yuan capital of Dadu through Shandong and Hebei. While a central army led by Guan Xiansheng and Potou Pan would campaign from Shanxi to Liaodong, and support the eastern army in its attack against Dadu.

The three armies of the northern expedition made good headway, with Mao Gui's eastern army approaching Dadu. After taking control of Bianliang, Liu Futong brought Han Lin'er, King Ming, Jr., to Bianliang, which was now designated as the capital of their regime. The growing strength of the Red Turban Army alarmed the Yuan government, and they mustered armed bands of landowners to suppress the rebellion. The three armies of the northern expedition suffered battle losses, and Bianliang was retaken by the Yuan troops. By offering a high position in the Yuan government and generous material incentives, the Yuan court was able to buy off Zhang Shicheng. After escorting King Ming, Jr. to the safety of Anfeng (modern-day Shou County, Anhui Province), Liu Futong's force came under attack by Zhang Shicheng. In 1363 AD, Liu Futong died in battle and the insurgency of the north faltered after twelve years of fighting.

150. A Monk Turned Grand Marshal

AS THE RED Turbans of Liu Futong were fighting in the north, Red Turbans led by Guo Zixing grew in strength in Haozhou. Guo Zixing was a wealthy man in Dingyuan (in Anhui Province) who was a frequent target of extortion by local officials because of his humble origin. He joined the White Lotus Society out of indignation. He befriended Robin Hood types, wining and dining them at great expense and biding his time for a chance to avenge all the wrongs he had suffered by killing the corrupt officials.

In 1352 AD, the year after Liu Futong started the rebellion, Guo Zixing saw his chance and, under cover of night, he and four friends led a few thousand young men on a raid into the city of Haozhou, killing the governor and taking control of the local government. They announced the beginning of their rebellion, with Guo Zixing and his four friends as grand marshals.

The Yuan government sent General Cherig Bukha to lay siege to Haozhou. Cherig Bukha was afraid of the Red Turbans, so instead of launching an offensive he camped at a safe distance from the city. He had his soldiers capture some civilians outside the city, and reported these civilians as prisoners of war in order to receive credit and rewards from the government. The inhabitants outside city limits could not bear the exactions of the Yuan troops, and fled into the city to seek the protection of Guo Zixing. This influx of refugees swelled Guo's ranks.

One evening as the Red Turbans of Haozhou were on a patrol near the city gate, a young monk came toward them and expressed the wish to join the Red Turban Army. Suspecting that he was Yuan spy on a reconnaissance mission, the soldiers guarding the gate bound him up and reported the incident.

After hearing the report, Guo Zixing decided to give the monk the benefit of the doubt and rode to the gate to take a personal look. He found the monk tied up and in rags, but nevertheless possessing a strong build, thick eyebrows and big eyes. Guo Zixing liked what he saw, and immediately ordered his soldiers to untie the monk and bring him to the office of the Grand Marshal.

The young monk who wanted to offer his service to Guo Zixing was Zhu Yuanzhang. His father was a struggling peasant in Zhongli, Haozhou (east of modern-day Fengyang, Anhui Province). When Zhu Yuanzhang was 17, a serious drought and a plague of locusts struck the Huaibei area. This was followed by an epidemic, which killed his father, his mother and his eldest brother. Zhu Yuanzhang and his second elder brother survived, but did not have money to buy the coffins. Only with the help of some sympathetic neighbors were they able to bury their parents.

Now orphaned, Zhu Yuanzhang had a hard time feeding himself. At neighbors' suggestion he became a junior monk at the nearby Huangjue Temple so that he could at least have something to eat. This is how Zhu Yuanzhang became a monk. The junior monks in the temple were actually menial servants. Zhu Yuanzhang waited on his master and on the other students who were his seniors, rising early and going to bed late, performing chores such as sweeping the temple grounds, putting up incense sticks, ringing the bell and cooking meals.

However, getting fed at the temple was not easy, because the temple depended on rent paid to it in the form of rice. During this time of natural disasters, the temple was not receiving its rent. After only fifty days at the temple, Zhu Yuanzhang realized that they were running out of food. His master and fellow students had all gone out to beg for alms. Zhu Yuanzhang himself was sent out of the temple with an alms bowl and a small wooden fish drum to beg alms in the Huaixi area. Three years later, with the effects of the natural disasters easing a bit, he returned to the Huangjue Temple.

A year later, the Red Turban Army started its rebellion. News of Liu Futong's capture of Yingzhou, Sesame Li taking Xuzhou, and so forth, filtered into the temple and reached Zhu Yuanzhang's ears. At year's end, he heard that the Red Turbans had taken Haozhou. Zhu Yuanzhang had also heard some time ago about the coming of Maitreya Bodhisattva to bring salvation to the masses. The news about the spreading rebellion of the Red Turbans and the defeat of Yuan troops in battle after battle reinforced his sense that the salvation of the poor and the downtrodden was near. He decided to leave the Huangjue Temple to offer his service to Guo Zixing in Haozhou.

In his conversation with Zhu Yuanzhang, Guo Zixing was impressed by his articulateness. Immediately, he had him take off his cassock and change into a military uniform. Guo Zixing made him a close bodyguard.

Zhu Yuanzhang had an opportunity to show his talents in the Red Turban Army. He was courageous and astute in battle, and Guo Zixing placed great trust in him, always consulting him before a battle. Zhu Yuanzhang's stature grew among the Red Turbans.

A friend of Guo Zixing's, by the name of Ma, died of illness the year Guo started the rebellion. Ma had entrusted his only daughter to the care of Guo Zixing on his deathbed. The girl was brought home by Guo and given to his wife to take care of as if she were their biological daughter. Guo Zixing had been looking for a suitable husband for her. Recognizing Zhu Yuanzhang's abilities, he discussed with his wife the idea of marrying Ma's daughter to Zhu Yuanzhang. His wife approved of the idea, too. When the junior monk of the Huangjue Temple became the son-in-law of Grand Marshal Guo, he acquired a special status. The Red Turbans took to calling him "Master Zhu."

There were five Grand Marshals, including Guo Zixing, in the Red Turban Army in Haozhou. The five marshals were equal in rank, and therefore no one had authority over any of the other marshals. Unlike Guo Zixing, the other four marshals had carried over habits and styles acquired in their swashbuckling days, and had no respect for discipline. Guo Zixing was increasingly annoyed by them, and they by him. Tensions between them grew with the passage of time, and the other four ganged up to sideline Guo Zixing. Once they nearly killed Guo, but he was saved when Zhu Yuanzhang came to his rescue after learning of the plot.

Finding some commanders in the rebel army narrow-minded and petty, Zhu Yuanzhang felt he would not accomplish anything under them. He returned to his hometown to recruit for his own army. Xu Da and Tang He, friends from his youth, came to offer their service after hearing that Zhu Yuanzhang had become a commander in the Red Turban Army. In less than ten days, he was able to assemble a force of 700. In subsequent attacks against Yuan troops, he was able to pick up many defectors.

Having gathered a fighting force, Zhu Yuanzhang put it through intensive training and instilled rigorous discipline in the soldiers and officers, creating an army to be reckoned with.

An intellectual in Dingyuan called Li Shanchang, who was an expert in tactics and strategy, also came to Zhu Yuanzhang. Well aware of his knowledge, Zhu Yuanzhang kept him on as an adviser. Once, Zhu Yuanzhang asked Li Shanchang, "War is raging across the country. When will we have peace?"

Li Shanchang replied, "The same chaos plagued the waning years of the Qin dynasty. Emperor Gaozu of Han, a civilian, was able to unify the country in only five years because of his physical strength, his ability to tap talent, and his wisdom in avoiding needless killing. Now that the Yuan dynasty is in such political chaos and anarchy reigns, why don't you emulate Emperor Gaozu of Han?"

From that moment on, Zhu Yuanzhang set out to be another Emperor Gaozu of Han.

At the head of the army trained by him, Zhu Yuanzhang captured Chuzhou and Hezhou in quick succession. In the year Han Lin'er, King Ming, Jr., became Emperor in Bozhou, Guo Zixing died of illness. King Ming, Jr. made Guo Tianxu, Guo Zixing's son, Grand Marshal and Zhu Yuanzhang Deputy Grand Marshal.

With Guo Tianxu lacking experience in commanding an army, and with Zhu Yuanzhang commanding the loyalty of most officers and men of the Red Turban Army, Zhu Yuanzhang, the nominal Deputy Marshal, wielded real authority. Shortly afterwards, Guo Tianxu was killed by traitors in an attack against Jiqing (modern-day Nanjing, Jiangsu Province), and Zhu Yuanzhang became Grand Marshal.

With the military under his control, Zhu Yuanzhang routed the naval force of the Yuan dynasty and led his massive army across the river to attack Jiqing, where its half a million inhabitants and defenders surrendered. After entering the city, Zhu Yuanzhang issued an order to reassure the inhabitants, and changed the name of the city to Yingtian. From then on Zhu Yuanzhang would expand his influence to Jiang'nan with Yingtian as his base.

151. Battle at Lake Poyang

THE FIRST FORMIDABLE enemy encountered by Zhu Yuanzhang in his southward expansion was Chen Youliang, who was a commander in the insurgency led by Xu Shouhui. After murdering Xu, his former superior, Chen proclaimed himself king of a regime he called "Han." Owing to its vast area and abundant supply of combatants, Chen's separatist regime, which straddled Jiangxi, Hunan and Hubei, soon became a power to be reckoned with. In 1360 Chen Youliang sailed his powerful naval force down the Yangtze from Caishi in a bold bid to attack Yingtian in the east and gobble up the territory under Zhu Yuanzhang's control.

Zhu Yuanzhang called an urgent meeting of his commanders to discuss their response. One party believed they should surrender before being overrun by the overwhelming force of Chen Youliang; others argued for retreating to Mount Zhongshan, in modern-day Nanjing, where they would entrench themselves; still others advocated engaging the enemy in a decisive battle and only beating a retreat when defeated. In the heated discussion, only the recently recruited adviser, Liu Ji, remained conspicuously silent.

The discussion left Zhu Yuanzhang undecided. He asked Liu Ji to stay behind after the meeting and solicited his view.

Liu Ji said, "Those who advocated surrender or retreat deserve, in my view, to die."

"Then how do you propose to thwart the attack?" asked Zhu Yuanzhang.

"The enemy has traveled a great distance to attack us," replied

Liu Ji. "We have the advantage of a well-rested army against its exhausted troops. It is not difficult under these circumstances to defeat the enemy. By offering monetary incentives to your officers and men, and by laying ambushes to hit the vulnerable points of the Han troops, you have a very good chance of defeating Chen Youliang's force."

Zhu Yuanzhang was pleased by Liu Ji's analysis. The two went on to map out the battle plan.

Zhu Yuanzhang summoned his subaltern Kang Maocai, who was an old acquaintance of Chen Youliang, and told him, "Your help is indispensable for executing my plan to ensnare Chen Youliang. I need you to write a letter to him feigning surrender and offering your assistance as his sleeper agent. You are to feed him misinformation and advise him to attack Yingtian along three routes so that his army will be stretched thin."

"This won't be difficult," Kang Maocai replied, "I have an old servant in my household who once ran errands for Chen Youliang. If he delivers the letter, Chen Youliang will not find it suspicious."

Kang Maocai went home and immediately composed a letter as instructed by Zhu Yuanzhang. That very night, his old servant was dispatched with the letter to Caishi in order to seek a meeting with Chen Youliang. As predicted, the letter did not arouse any suspicion in Chen Youliang, who asked the servant, "Where is Mr. Kang now?"

The old servant replied, "He's now camped near Jiangdong Bridge with his army, waiting to join forces with you."

"What is Jiangdong Bridge like?" asked Chen Youliang eagerly.

"It's a wooden bridge," the old servant replied. "You can't miss it."

After talking with the old servant a while longer, Chen Youliang ordered food and wine for him. Before the servant set out for home after the plentiful meal, Chen Youliang said to him, "Tell Mr. Kang that I will soon go to Jiangdong Bridge to meet with him. When I approach the bridge I will call out his name, 'Lao Kang, Lao Kang,' a few times. That will be the signal for him to immediately join forces with me."

Upon his return, the old servant rendered a full report of his meeting with Chen to Zhu Yuanzhang.

"Bravo! Well done!" Zhu Yuanzhang gushed effusively. That very night, he ordered the wooden bridge at Jiangdong dismantled and replaced with a stone bridge.

With information obtained from Chen Youliang's deserters, Zhu Yuanzhang had advance knowledge of Chen's planned route of attack and deployed troops accordingly. Under the command of generals Xu Da and Chang Yuchun, troops laid ambushes at strategic points along the river. Zhu Yuanzhang camped with the bulk of his force at Lulong Hill, the modern-day Shizi, or Lion Hill, close to Nanjing. Two flags, one red and one yellow, were to be used as signals: when the red flag was raised, it would signal the approach of enemy troops; the yellow flag would be an order for troops to come out of their ambush and attack the enemy. They waited patiently for Chen Youliang to walk into the trap.

Shortly after the departure of the old servant, Chen Youliang ordered his entire naval force to set sail toward Jiangdong Bridge, with him in personal command. At the appointed location, there was no wooden bridge in sight. To their puzzlement, what greeted them instead was a stone bridge, causing Chen's troops to pause in confusion. Chen Youliang, however, thought it didn't matter whether the bridge was stone or wooden, as long as Kang Maocai was there to meet with him. As he approached the stone bridge, Chen repeatedly called out, "Lao Kang! Lao Kang!" Only when there was no reply did Chen realize he'd been double-crossed and ordered an immediate withdrawal.

On receiving confirmation that the enemy had walked into his trap, Zhu Yuanzhang ordered the yellow flag raised to signal an attack. At the signal, battle drums started rolling and the ambushers on the shore surged out of hiding, with naval troops joining the attack.

Caught by surprise, the tens of thousands of troops led by Chen Youliang were thrown into disarray. Many were slain or drowned; twenty thousand men and over a hundred battleships were captured by Zhu Yuanzhang's troops. Escorted by his subalterns, Chen Youliang managed to commandeer a small boat and flee to freedom.

Chen Youliang's fighting force suffered a major setback in this battle while Zhu Yuanzhang's emerged stronger. Not prepared to accept defeat, Chen put his troops through a period of rigorous training, determined to exact his revenge. Three years later, having built a large number of battleships, Chen Youliang again led 600,000 troops in an attack on Zhu Yuanzhang's territory, this time on Hongdu, or modern-day Nanchang in Jiangxi Province.

On hearing of the attack, Zhu Yuanzhang raced with 200,000 troops to defend Hongdu. On Zhu's arrival, Chen lifted the siege and moved his naval force to Lake Poyang. Zhu's forces responded by blocking all outlets of the lake to force Chen Youliang to a decisive duel in the lake.

Chen Youliang's armada of tall ships extending for miles confronted Zhu Yuanzhang's much inferior naval force consisting mainly of small crafts. In three days of dueling, Zhu's troops suffered setback after setback.

"We are seriously outnumbered," Zhu's general told him. "Conventional fighting is hopeless. We must resort to fire attacks."

Zhu Yuanzhang took his general's advice and readied seven small boats loaded with gunpowder, each with a fast, lightweight boat in tow. That evening, a helpful northeasterly wind rose and a death-defying team drove the seven boats, now ignited, into Chen's armada of tall ships. With the aid of the wind, the tall ships were soon engulfed in towering flames, coloring the lake red. The majority of Chen Youliang's troops were either captured or burned alive.

Chen Youliang led his remnant force on a dash toward one of the lake's outlets but found it blocked. Chen died in a hail of arrows in his attempt to run the blockade.

After quashing Chen Youliang, leader of the most powerful separatist regime in south China, Zhu Yuanzhang proclaimed himself King of Wu.

Following the death of Liu Futong, Zhu Yuanzhang had installed King Ming, Jr. in Chuzhou, pledging nominal allegiance to him. But now, Zhu's interest in the throne had grown to the extent that he began to find King Ming, Jr. a hindrance to his ambition. In 1366 he sent a ship to transport King Ming, Jr. to

Yingtian. At the Guabu crossing, southeast of modern-day Liuhe in Jiangsu Province, King Ming drowned when his boat, sabotaged under Zhu's orders, sank.

The following year, Zhu Yuanzhang succeeded in quashing the separatist regime of Zhang Shicheng. Zhu went on to launch a northern expedition with two hundred fifty thousand troops, led by Xu Da as Zhenglu General-in-chief and Chang Yuchun as deputy commander. Two months later, Zhu's troops took control of Shandong. So it followed, that in January 1368, Zhu Yuanzhang ascended the throne in Yingtian as Emperor Taizu with the dynasty name of "Ming."

The incumbent Yuan army retreated before the inexorable march of the victorious Ming troops. And in the following August, Xu Da's army marched into the Yuan capital of Dadu, forcing Emperor Shundi of Yuan to flee toward Shangdu. Thus ended the Yuan dynasty, which had ruled China for ninety seven years.

MING DYNASTY (1368–1644)

152. Liu Bowen Prays for Rain

IN HIS CAMPAIGNS to unify China, Emperor Taizu of Ming relied on brave and battle-savvy generals to capture towns for him and expand his territory. He also brought in advisers to help him formulate strategies and devise tactics. Liu Ji was one of the most prominent.

Liu Ji, also known as Liu Bowen, had previously served in the Yuan government. Yet, disaffection with the corruption rife in political circles had prompted him to write pieces lampooning current events, eventually leading to his dismissal and premature retirement to his home town of Qingtian (modern-day Qingtian County in Zhejiang Province). When Zhu Yuanzhang's army moved into the eastern part of Zhejiang, Liu Ji was recruited as an adviser to Zhu. Zhu relied heavily on Liu Ji's advice in the campaigns that led to the defeat of Chen Youliang and Zhang Shicheng. Liu earned the trust of Emperor Taizu of Ming by his resourcefulness and shrewdness.

Besides his expertise in strategic and tactical thinking, Liu Ji also possessed an excellent knowledge of astronomy. In ancient times, astronomical phenomena were often interpreted as omens of earthly events. Although Liu Ji's ability to make generally accurate predictions about current events was actually grounded in keen observation and thorough analysis, his ability was generally perceived to derive from his knowledge of astronomy. Liu Bowen was treated in popular legend as someone with the gift of prophecy.

During a severe drought in the lower reaches of the Yangtze River, during Zhu Yuanzhang's reign as King of Wu, Liu Ji, who was in charge of astronomical matters, was asked by Zhu Yuanzhang why the drought had happened and what it would take to invoke rain. Liu Ji told him the long dry spell had been caused by the incarceration of wrongfully convicted prisoners.

Zhu Yuanzhang believed in Liu Ji's wisdom and asked him to review the cases of those sentenced to prison terms. The review found a significant number of cases of wrongful imprisonment. After reporting his findings to Zhu Yuanzhang, Liu overturned the wrongful convictions and freed the prisoners in question. A few days later a soaking rain poured down from an overcast sky, fulfilling Liu's prophecy.

The rain, in fact, had nothing to do with the overturning of wrongful convictions and neither did Liu Ji possess any magical rain-making powers. It may well be that his knowledge of astronomy had enabled him to observe an imminent change of weather which he deftly exploited to persuade Zhu Yuanzhang to correct those miscarriages of justice. Taking advantage of Zhu Yuanzhang's high spirits after the rain, Liu Ji made a case for enacting and implementing laws to prevent future miscarriages of justice and loss of innocent lives.

Upon his accession, Emperor Taizu of Ming made Liu Ji Palace Aide to the Censor-in-Chief, in charge of the administration of justice. Liu Ji proved a strict law enforcer. Shortly after his appointment, an offense was committed by a trusted aide of grand councilor Li Shanchang. Li had contributed much to the founding of the Ming dynasty and was from the same village as Emperor Taizu of Ming. Despite Li's obstructions, Liu Ji had the aide executed after informing the emperor. This naturally incurred the ill will of Li Shanchang.

The imperial capital suffered another severe drought that year, causing high anxiety in Emperor Taizu of Ming. Liu Ji seized the opportunity to make another case for justice before Emperor Taizu.

"The wives of soldiers and officers who gave their lives on the battlefield await compensation," he pleaded. "And the bodies of craftsmen who died building the city walls are still exposed to the elements without a proper burial. If these problems could be taken care of, heaven might be moved to rain."

In his eagerness for rain, Emperor Taizu of Ming naturally approved the requests of Liu Ji with alacrity: the wives of fallen officers and soldiers received prompt financial compensation and the remains of the city wall builders killed in the line of duty were duly buried. Liu Ji had intervened in a worthy cause, but the method he relied on to persuade the emperor proved not consistently reliable. This time, his prediction proved false, and ten days later the sun still blazed down from a cloudless sky without a hint of rain.

The lack of rain invoked the wrath of Emperor Taizu, and with Li Shanchang fanning the imperial ire with derogatory remarks about him, Liu Ji could not help but feel afraid. It happened that Liu's wife had just died of illness in his home town and so he wasted no time in obtaining leave to go home.

Despite this failure, Emperor Taizu of Ming still highly valued Liu Ji's service and advice. In fact, he intended to make Liu Ji a grand councilor. Liu hastened to decline the offer.

"Choosing a grand councilor," he told the emperor, "is like choosing the main beam of a house. You need strong, bulky timber for it. Flimsy timber will likely cause the house to collapse."

When Emperor Taizu eventually dismissed Li Shanchang as grand councilor, he once again brought up the subject of having Liu Ji take over the post.

"I have a short, impatient temper," responded Liu Ji, "especially when it comes to dealing with unsavory characters. Besides, at my advanced age, I am no longer fit for undertaking such a weighty responsibility. There is no dearth of talent in the country. Your Majesty only needs to pick the man best qualified for the job."

Liu Ji retired to Qingtian to lead the life of a recluse. He never mentioned his past contributions to his family and neighbors. All requests made by the local county magistrate to pay a visit were courteously refused. Finally, the county magistrate dropped by, disguised as a peasant. Liu Ji was washing his feet when the stranger approached. He immediately put on his shoes and invited the peasant into his home and even asked him to stay for a meal.

When Liu Ji asked for the stranger's name, the county magistrate had to reveal his true identity.

"I am the county magistrate of Qingtian," he told Liu Ji. "I have come to pay you a visit."

Liu Ji, greatly surprised, rose from his chair to make a bow, describing himself as just a common person. That was the last meeting he allowed himself with the county magistrate.

Even in retirement, Liu Ji remained concerned about the political wellbeing of the Ming dynasty. One day, an envoy was sent by Emperor Taizu of Ming to Qingtian to consult Liu Ji on meteorological omens.

"After the severe, freezing winter" prophesized Liu Ji, "comes balmy spring. Now that the country is blessed with peace and stability, it is hoped that Your Majesty will rule with leniency."

153. The Hu Weiyong Affair

COMING FROM A peasant family himself, Emperor Taizu of Ming had some understanding of peasant life. After his accession to the throne, Emperor Taizu recognized the importance of allowing the people to rest and recuperate.

"The country has only recently emerged from civil strife," he admonished local officials. "The populace is financially strapped—it's like a fledgling whose feathers will not stand plucking, and a sapling whose root will not stand rigorous shaking."

The emperor exhorted officials to practice clean governance and abide by the law in order not to add to the people's burden through official corruption and lawbreaking. He organized displaced peasants in a land reclamation project, exempting them from obligatory duties and taxes for three years. He ordered troops to engage in agriculture and the cultivation of waste land for food growing so that they could be self-sufficient. Major irrigation and drainage projects were undertaken and the planting of cotton and hemp encouraged. As a result of these measures, agricultural production made remarkable strides in the early Ming period; this in turn solidified the rule of the newly founded Ming dynasty.

But Emperor Taizu of Ming had misgivings about those credited with major contributions to the founding of his dynasty. He established the Jin Yi Wei or "Guards of Embroidered Coats," a secret service tasked with spying on his ministers. With the Jin Yi Wei reporting to him directly, Emperor Taizu was able to have intimate knowledge of all the doings and sayings of his ministers, wherever they were, including in the privacy of their own homes.

Anyone coming under suspicion risked jail or execution.

Emperor Taizu of Ming was strict to the point of cruelty with his officials. If a minister incurred his wrath during the daily assembly, he would be forced to lie prostrate on the ground and then flogged in front of the entire court. Some officials were beaten to death in these "court canings." This practice put the ministers on tenterhooks. Every morning before they attended the imperial audience they would bid adieu to their families with a heavy heart and worried mien. If a minister came out of the audience unscathed, he would receive hearty congratulations from his family when he got home for having survived another grueling day.

In 1380, grand councilor Hu Weiyong was denounced for treason and seditious intentions. Emperor Taizu of Ming immediately had all the members of Hu's family beheaded and started a witch hunt for his partisans. Upwards of fifteen thousand civil and military officials were implicated. Emperor Taizu cold-bloodedly massacred all those suspected of being cohorts of Hu Weiyong.

Song Lian, an academic, was, like Liu Ji, a trusted aide of Emperor Taizu of Ming in the early years of the Ming dynasty and acted as the crown prince's tutor. Song Lian was a very cautious man but that didn't prevent Emperor Taizu from questioning his loyalty. One day, Song Lian had a few friends over to his home for drinks. The next day, Emperor Taizu of Ming asked him if he had drank the day before, who he'd invited over and what dishes were served. Song Lian answered all the emperor's questions truthfully.

"You did not lie to me," said Emperor Taizu with a satisfied smile.

Emperor Taizu had in fact ordered covert surveillance on Song Lian's party the night before. As a result of his honesty, the emperor was heard to praise Song Lian before the entire court.

"Song Lian has never once lied to me or uttered a single derogatory remark about others in his nineteen years of service to me," he proclaimed. "He is a true sage."

At the age of 68, Song Lian retired to his home town. Emperor Taizu of Ming gave him a parting gift of a piece of brocade.

"Save this for 32 years," the emperor told him. "When you turn

100 you can have a centennial dress made from it."

However, during the investigation into the Hu Weiyong affair, Song Lian was implicated through his grandson Song Shen, who had been branded a Hu partisan. Emperor Taizu sent his "Embroidered Coats" to Jinhua, Song Lian's home town, to bring him to Beijing to be executed.

When Empress Ma learned of the fate reserved for Song Lian, she tried to make Emperor Taizu change his mind.

"Even common folk know how to treat their children's teachers with respect," she chastised him. "Is this the respect an imperial tutor gets from you? Besides, Mr. Song has stayed all this time in his home town; you can't expect him to know about his grandson's doings in the capital."

In the heat of his anger, Emperor Taizu was in no mood to forgive Song Lian. That day at dinner, Empress Ma sat quietly at the table, touching neither drink nor meat. Emperor Taizu was puzzled by her unusual behavior and asked her if she felt unwell.

Empress Ma replied in sorrow, "I feel deeply saddened by Mr. Song being charged with a capital offense. I am praying for him."

Empress Ma had loyally supported Emperor Taizu since their youth, and he valued her opinions. Her words produced an effect on him, causing him to reduce Song Lian's death sentence to the more lenient sentence of garrison duty in exile. Song Lian was duly exiled to Maozhou, modern-day Mao County in Sichuan Province. However, the aged Song Lian died on the journey to Maozhou as a result of the harrowing experience and the rigors of travel.

Ten years later, Li Shanchang, Emperor Taizu's former grand councilor, was denounced for having had close contacts with Hu Weiyong and having certain knowledge of Hu's seditious intentions. Instead of denouncing Hu, Li Shanchang chose to do nothing and thus committed a cardinal sin. Li Shanchang was considered to have made the greatest individual contribution to the founding of the dynasty and was related to Emperor Taizu by marriage. When Emperor Taizu meted out rewards to those who had helped put him in the throne, he gave two imperial life-sparing certificates to Li Shanchang. Despite these guarantees given by the emperor, the 77-year-old Li Shanchang and the rest of his family—

more than seventy of them, were executed by Emperor Taizu, who showed no regard for past service, affection or promises.

In another roundup of Hu partisans, a further fifteen thousand people were executed.

Since the Hu Weiyong crisis, Emperor Taizu no longer felt comfortable entrusting ministers with military and executive powers. He abolished the post of grand councilor and ordered the heads of the Ministry of Personnel, the Ministry of Revenue, the Ministry of Rites, the Ministry of War, the Ministry of Justice and the Ministry of Works to report directly to him. He abolished the Chief Military Command, which was in charge of all military forces and established in its place five Chief Military Commissions (the Left, Right, Center, Forward and Rear Commissions), each in charge of its own military force, to be put under the emperor's command in times of war. Power was thus greatly centralized under the emperor of the Ming dynasty.

The crisis of Hu Weiyong was not the last, and three years later the Jin Yi Wei denounced General Lan Yu for seditious intent. Emperor Taizu had Lan Yu executed and ordered an investigation to ferret out his co-conspirators. As a result, fifteen thousand civil and military officials were found implicated and executed.

In the aftermath of these two high-profile cases, the imperial court was purged of nearly all those who had made a contribution to the founding of the Ming dynasty. Emperor Taizu of Ming thus gained notoriety in history as a ruthless dictator.

154. The Prince of Yan Marches into Nanjing

AS EMPEROR TAIZU of Ming busied himself with killing off his powerful ministers, he concurrently made each of his twenty-four sons Prince of a fiefdom. Some of the feudatory princes had their own armies. Emperor Taizu of Ming believed that this arrangement would solidify the rule of the Ming; little knowing that he had sown the seed of future anarchy.

When Emperor Taizu of Ming reached his sixties, his crown prince Zhu Biao died and Zhu Yunwen, Zhu Biao's son, was designated heir to the throne on account of his status as oldest grandson of the reigning emperor. Most of the feudatory princes were uncles of Zhu Yunwen and were upset by the likely succession of their nephew. One prince in particular found it difficult to accept the designation of Zhu Yunwen as heir apparent. He was Zhu Di, Prince of Yan, who was the fourth son of Emperor Taizu, stationed with his troops in Beiping (today's Beijing) and credited with many battle victories.

Zhu Di was among the more capable and intelligent of Emperor Taizu's sons. It is said that Emperor Taizu once asked Zhu Yunwen to complete a matching couplet. The emperor read out his line:

"The wind blows at the horse's tail, creating a thousand lines".

Zhu Yunwen came up with the matching line:

"The rain beats on the sheep's wool, raising a big bad stink".

Emperor Taizu's face fell in disapproval. Zhu Di, who happened to be present, said, "I have a matching line too." When prompted by Emperor Taizu, Zhu Di read out:

"The sun turns the dragon's scales into ten thousand glitters of gold."

Zhu Di's matching line clearly aimed to please the emperor as it referred to the dragon, a symbol of imperial power. Emperor Taizu had high praise for Zhu Di's matching verse and Zhu Di became even more dismissive of Zhu Yunwen.

Although relatively unsophisticated, Zhu Yunwen was not unaware of Zhu Di's low opinion of him. One day Huang Zicheng, an official in the Eastern Palace (reserved for imperial heirs) and Zhu Yunwen's teacher and reading companion, saw the latter sitting alone outside the eastern entrance of the palace, with his brow tightly knit and heaving deep, long sighs. Huang Zicheng asked the clearly troubled and pensive heir what was weighing on his mind.

"All my uncles have their armies," replied Zhu Yunwen. "How can I control them in the future?"

Huang Zicheng told Zhu Yunwen the story of how the Western Han had overcome the Rebellion of the Seven States.

"As powerful as the Wu and the Chu and the other five feudal states were," Huang Zicheng concluded, "the moment Emperor Jing of Han unleashed his army on them, their rebellion crumbled. In the same vein, as a direct descendant of the emperor, Your Highness need not worry about rebellion by your uncles."

His teacher's tale reassured Zhu Yunwen to an extent.

Upon the death of Emperor Taizu of Ming in 1398, Zhu Yunwen acceded to the throne as Emperor Hui of Ming, also known as Emperor Jianwen (Jianwen being one of his era names). The imperial capital was soon abuzz with rumor about contacts between the other princes in preparation for a coup. Taking fright at the reported coup preparations, Emperor Jianwen called in Huang Zicheng.

"Do you remember what you said to me near the eastern entrance of my palace?" he asked him.

"Don't worry, Your Majesty!" Huang Zicheng replied. "How could I have forgotten?"

As soon as Huang Zicheng left the imperial palace, he met

with Qi Tai, another of Emperor Jianwen's trusted aides. Qi Tai was of the view that of all the princes the Prince of Yan had the most powerful army and had big plans for his future. He should therefore be the first to have his wings clipped. Huang Zicheng disagreed. In his opinion the Prince of Yan had prepared himself for a confrontation and therefore it would be prudent to act first against princes on the periphery of the Prince of Yan's fiefdom. Zhu Xiao, Prince of Zhou, was the Prince of Yan's brother and had his fiefdom in Kaifeng. Neutralizing the Prince of Zhou would be tantamount to clipping the wings of the Prince of Yan and facilitating his elimination.

After reaching a consensus, the two trusted aides reported back to Emperor Jianwen, who liked what he heard and sent troops on some vague pretext to Henan to arrest Zhu Xiao and bring him back to Nanjing. He was stripped of his title and sent to Yunnan on garrison duty. Another three princes were soon found to have violated the law in some way and all similarly lost their title of prince.

The Prince of Yan had long been training his army for a rebellion. In order to lull Emperor Jianwen into a false sense of security, he feigned insanity, talking nonsense all day long and sometimes lying on the ground for days. When an envoy was sent by Emperor Jianwen to visit him, he found the Prince of Yan trying to keep warm by a brazier, all the while complaining of feeling cold, in the middle of summer! After hearing the envoy's report, Emperor Jianwen was convinced the Prince of Yan was really sick.

But Qi Tai and Huang Zicheng had their suspicions about the veracity of the Prince of Yan's illness. They sent a party to Beiping to detain members of the Prince of Yan' family while issuing a secret order to Zhang Xin, Regional Military Commissioner of Beiping, to send troops to arrest the Prince of Yan. Some officials in the prince's household had also been enlisted to provide support for the action. They had not counted on the possibility that Zhang Xin would side with the Prince of Yan and inform him of their plan—which he did.

Upon learning of the arrest plan, the Prince of Yan rounded up all those officials in his household who had agreed to collaborate with Emperor Jianwen and set the coup in motion. Shrewd as he was, the Prince knew that publicly rebelling against Emperor Jianwen, a legitimate ruler, would be to his own disadvantage, so he devised a pretext for his military action, claiming it was aimed at helping Emperor Jianwen to eliminate the evil ministers Huang Zicheng and Qi Tai. This civil war is known to history as Jing Nan Zhi Bian or the "Campaign to Clear Away Disorders."

The Prince of Yan was a seasoned military commander with real combat experience and had a well-trained army. He was therefore able to quickly secure a number of strategic positions during his march to the south and the officials of many regions and counties surrendered to him. In a fright, Emperor Jianwen sacked Qi Tai and Huang Zicheng in an attempt to induce the Prince of Yan to pull back his troops, but the Prince persisted.

This civil war lasted nearly three years. In 1402, a fierce battle erupted in Huaibei, north of the Huai River, between the Prince of Yan's army and the southern troops sent by the Ming court. While some commanders in his army urged a temporary retreat, the Prince of Yan told them, "In this campaign retreat is not an option!"

Soon, the army of the Prince of Yan cut off the government troops' supply route and launched a surprise attack that put them to rout.

From then on, the Yan army met little resistance and easily and quickly arrived at Yingtian. Realizing the dire straits he was in, Emperor Jianwen ordered his troops to defend the capital to the death, and at the same time sent peace envoys to the Prince of Yan, offering to cede territory in exchange for the Prince's agreement to withdraw his troops. The peace overture was again rebuffed by the Prince of Yan.

A few days later, Li Jinglong, the general in command of the capital garrison, opened the city gates in surrender and the capital fell to the Yan army.

The Prince of Yan entered the city at the head of his troops, only to find the imperial palace engulfed in a raging fire. The Prince of Yan immediately ordered his troops to put out the fire but many had perished in the inferno by the time they succeeded. When he demanded to know the whereabouts of Emperor Jianwen, he was told that before the Yan army had entered the city, Emperor Jianwen had given the order to torch the palace and the emperor and empress had committed suicide by throwing themselves into the flames.

Zhu Di, the Prince of Yan, ascended the throne as Emperor Chengzu of Ming. In 1421 Emperor Chengzu of Ming moved his capital to Beijing and it remained the imperial capital through the rest of the Ming period.

155. Sanbao the Eunuch Explores the "Western Oceans"

AFTER SEIZING THE throne by force from his nephew, Emperor Chengzu of Ming was troubled by a nagging doubt about the real fate of Emperor Jianwen: his remains were never found amid the rubble of the torched palace. Did he die in the fire or not?

Rumors abounded in the capital. According to some, Emperor Jianwen did not commit suicide but had taken advantage of the chaos created by the fire to escape with a number of attendants and eunuchs through an underground tunnel that led out of the city. More bizarre stories came back to the capital, alleging Emperor Jianwen had settled in this or that town and eventually became a monk. The specific details that accompanied the stories seemed so compelling that Emperor Chengzu's doubt was reinforced. He trembled at the thought that if Emperor Jianwen was still alive he might be regrouping somewhere in preparation for an attack against him in the name of legitimacy. In order to get to the bottom of the matter, Emperor Chengzu sent out trusted aides across the country on a secret mission to track down the missing emperor. Since the real purpose of the mission was best kept secret from the general public, the mission was officially described as one to scour the land for divinities. The search went on for nearly three decades.

It occurred to Emperor Chengzu that Emperor Jianwen might have fled overseas. China was then a nascent and rising naval power and Emperor Chengzu thought he would be killing two birds with one stone by sending a fleet abroad with the combined mission of projecting the empire's power, trading with foreign nations, procuring some precious stones and trying to locate Emperor Jianwen.

Thus the decision was made to dispatch such a fleet. The next question was who should lead this mission. Clearly it had to be someone that enjoyed his total trust. His thoughts turned to Zheng He, a eunuch who had served at his side for many years. He would be an ideal candidate for the job.

Zheng He's name at birth was Ma He, yet he was nicknamed "Sanbao". Zheng was born to a Muslim family in Yunnan. His grandfather and father believed in Islam and had completed the pilgrimage to Mecca. Zheng He garnered snippets of information about other countries from his father from a young age. When he was taken to the household of the Prince of Yan and made a eunuch, his knowledge and ability earned him the trust of the future Emperor Chengzu. The honorific surname of Zheng was awarded by the emperor, but the nickname Sanbao stuck and he continued to be known among the people as "Eunuch Sanbao" and the appellation even found its way into some books.

In June 1405, Emperor Chengzu of Ming formally designated Zheng He envoy at the head of a fleet of ships bound for "the Western Oceans" or "the West." The "West" of that time did not refer to the European continent but rather to the seas and the states bordering those waters to the west of the South China Sea. Zheng He's fleet consisted of more than 27,800 crew members, including soldiers and sailors as well as technicians, interpreters and physicians. They traveled in sixty-two large ships that were 145 meters long and 60 meters wide—a rare size in those times. The impressive fleet sailed from Liujiahe in Suzhou, present-day Liuhe in Taicang of Jiangsu Province, and hugging the coast of Fujian, headed south.

Zheng He's first voyage included visits to Champa (in the south of modern Vietnam), followed by Java, Palembang (on the southeastern coast of modern Sumatra, Indonesia), Sumatra, Malacca, Calicut and Ceylon. When his treasure-laden fleet arrived in a kingdom, he would deliver a letter by Emperor Chengzu to the local king and offer gifts as a token of China's good will. He was warmly received in many kingdoms, which realized that Zheng He did not intend his awe-inspiring fleet to be an instrument of intimidation, but was friendly towards them.

Zheng He returned to China in September of the third year of his voyage through the "Western Oceans." He was accompanied by gift-bearing envoys sent on a return visit by the kings of lands along his routes of exploration. The voyage had not been without incident, and many fierce storms and high waves had been encountered. But the ships were manned by seasoned sailors who ensured that they weathered the storms without incident. As the returning fleet approached Palenbang, however, it ran into trouble.

A man by the name of Chen Zuyi, who had installed himself on an island near Palenbang, was the head of a gang of pirates who robbed passing merchants. Chen salivated at the news that the treasure-laden fleet of Zheng He was approaching. After some discussion with his co-conspirators, it was decided to feign a warm reception for Zheng He and wait for the moment of his lowered guard to raid the treasures.

However, local resident, Shi Jinqing, got word of the pirates' plan and secretly sent word to Zheng He, whose fleet was anchored offshore.

With his twenty thousand soldiers, Zheng He was not unduly disturbed by the planned attack of the pirates. Rather, he decided to teach them a lesson. Zheng He ordered the large galleons to disperse and weigh anchor in the port of Palenbang. The soldiers were told to be on battle alert, with gun powder, swords and other weapons at the ready.

When night fell, Chen Zuyi and his gang of pirates, riding in dozens of small crafts, sailed directly toward the port on a calm sea to carry out a sneak attack. Yet before they knew it, the large galleons surrounded them at the signal of a single cannon shot, fired from Zheng He's flag ship, hemming in the pirates' boats. As a result of their overwhelming numbers and their readiness, the Ming troops decimated Chen Zuyi's party. The soldiers on the large galleons hurled torches into the pirates' boats. As his boat burned, Chen Zuyi, realizing escape was no longer possible, allowed himself to be taken captive without resistance. Zheng He bound Chen Zuyi, and took him to China. In the capital, Zheng He presented Emperor Chengzu with Chen Zuyi and his fellow prisoners.

In an audience with Emperor Chengzu, the envoys of numerous kingdoms presented him with rare and precious gifts and the emperor's face glowed with genuine pleasure at the brilliant success of Zheng He's mission.

Emperor Chengzu was eventually convinced that Emperor Jianwen had indeed died and there was no longer a need to continue the search for him. The voyages overseas, however, offered many other benefits, notably the gain in his empire's prestige and the promotion of trade with countries to the west of his empire. So the voyages through the "Western Oceans" led by Zheng He continued. In the nearly three decades between 1405 and 1433 , Zheng He led seven voyages that visited a total of more than thirty nations in the Indian Ocean, reaching as far as Mogadishu, in today's Somalia on the African coast.

In the year Zheng He returned from his sixth voyage, Emperor Chengzu died of illness. His son Zhu Gaochi, who succeeded him with the title of Emperor Renzong of Ming, died less than a year later. The next successor, Zhu Zhanji, who acceded to the throne as Emperor Xuanzong of Ming, was only eight or nine years old and real power was held by his grandmother Empress Dowager Xu and three senior, holdover ministers. The ministers believed that the seven voyages of Zheng He had proved too much of a financial burden to the state and China's maritime enterprise was stopped in its tracks.

Zheng He's seven voyages not only embodied the irrepressible exploratory spirit of China's ancient inhabitants, but also attested to the advanced state of China's ocean-going technology in the period of the Ming dynasty. Zheng He's expeditions promoted friendship and economic and cultural exchanges with many countries in Asia and Africa. To this day, stories about the Chinese explorer-eunuch "Sanbao" still circulate in these countries.

156. Yu Qian Defends Beijing

IN 1436 ZHU Qizhen, the nine-year-old crown prince, ascended the throne as Emperor Yingzong of Ming. The eunuch Wang Zhen, as Director of Ceremonies, helped Emperor Yingzong with the reading of memorandums and reports presented by ministers. In his wanton pursuit of pleasure Emperor Yingzong totally neglected the running of the state and Wang Zhen had a perfect opportunity to usurp civil and military power.

It was at this time the Oirats, a Mongol tribe, rose in strength. In 1449 the Oirat leader Esen Tayisi led a battalion to attack Datong. Emperor Yingzong, never known to have a mind of his own, was persuaded by Wang Zhen to take the rash decision to personally lead the counterattack over the objections of other ministers and advisers.

The result was the collapse of the 500,000 strong Ming army at Fort Tumu (east of modern-day Huailai in Hebei Province). In the battle, Wang Zhen lost his life and Emperor Yingzong was taken prisoner. When news of the defeat reached Beijing, the frightened empress dowager and the empress melted into tears. They secretly sent eunuchs with an impressive hoard of gold, silver, gems and silks picked from the private vaults of the imperial household to seek out the Oirat army and offer the treasures as ransom for the return of the emperor. It was all in vain.

Ming soldiers wounded in the battle of Fort Tumu began to appear in the streets of Beijing with their arms or legs missing—adding to popular unease and uncertainty about the fate of the emperor. Besides, the inhabitants wondered, with the sharply reduced strength of the troops defending the capital, how could we defend ourselves against an invasion by the Oirat army?

In order to calm the public's fears, the empress dowager announced that Zhu Qiyu, the Prince of Cheng, would henceforth act as regent. She called the top officials together to discuss ways to deal with the Oirats. There was much talk, but little result—good ideas were in short supply.

"There's no way we could withstand attack by the superior force of the Oirats," the minister Xu Youzhen said. "My astronomical observations tell me a major catastrophe is looming over the capital. It would be wise to retreat to the south to sit out the disaster before considering our future options."

Yu Qian, a vice-minister of the Ministry of War, said with a serious expression to the empress dowager and the Prince of Cheng, "Anyone advocating running away should be decapitated. The capital is a central symbol of the state. If the central government pulls out from the capital, it will spell the end of the state. Have we forgotten the lesson of the Song dynasty?"

Yu Qian's view had majority support among the ministers, thus the empress dowager put Yu Qian in charge of the defense of the capital.

Yu Qian had risen through the ranks of local bureaucracy to the position of "Grand Coordinator" (official sent by the central government to supervise provincial administration) of Henan. When the power of Wang Zhen was at its zenith, the integrity and independence of Yu Qian had caused him to conflict with Wang Zhen, who encouraged his partisans to denounce Yu Qian to the government on a trumped-up charge, leading to his incarceration and death sentence. When local officials and the common people of Henan and Shanxi learned of his being framed, tens of thousands of them joined forces to sign a petition to Emperor Yingzong asking for Yu Qian's release. Confronted by popular wrath and lacking any substantiating evidence against Yu Qian, Wang Zhen saw no alternative but to free Yu Qian and reinstate him. Yu Qian was eventually transferred to Beijing as vice-minister of war.

At this moment of crisis, Yu Qian bravely took on the onerous responsibility of defending the capital. He redeployed troops and commanders to strengthen the defense of the city and reinforce strategic positions. He simultaneously launched a cleanup operation, leading to the arrest of a number of traitors spying for the Oirat army.

One day, at an assembly presided over by Zhu Qiyu, the Prince of Cheng, in his capacity as Regent, the ministers clamored for a public airing of the crimes of Wang Zhen. Zhu Qiyu did not want to take responsibility for such a decision. Ma Shun, a eunuch who was a close associate of Wang Zhen, tried by bluff and bluster to disperse the ministers who showed little inclination of leaving without their request being satisfied. Yet, he had not reckoned on the angry reaction of the ministers, who, swarmed around Ma Shun and began to beat him with fists and feet. Ma Shun did not survive the "mob" attack.

When Zhu Qiyu tried to leave the riotous scene by ensconcing himself in the inner quarters of the palace, Yu Qian blocked his exit.

"Wang Zhen is the main culprit responsible for the recent defeat," he told Zhu Qiyu. "Public opinion will not be appeased unless he is held responsible and punishment administered accordingly. The ministers will be satisfied with a public acknowledgment by Your Majesty of the crime of Wang Zhen."

Acquiescing to this advice of Yu Qian, Zhu Qiyu ordered the confiscation of all the assets of the family of Wang Zhen and the prosecution and punishment of Wang Zhen's partisans. These measures had a calming effect on public opinion.

After capturing Emperor Yingzong, Esen Khan, the Oirat leader, did not kill him but rather used him as a hostage while continuing to attack the Ming borders. Realizing the awkwardness of governing without an emperor, Yu Qian and other ministers petitioned the empress dowager to formally announce the enthronement of Zhu Qiyu and to change the title of Emperor Yingzong in captivity to "Super-Emperor." Zhu Qiyu finally ascended to the throne with the title of Emperor Daizong of Ming (also known as Emperor Jingdi).

Realizing the determination of the Ming dynasty to resist the Oirats, Esen Khan launched a massive attack against Beijing on the pretext of restoring Emperor Yingzong to the throne.

In October of that year, the Oirat army easily fought its way to Beijing and camped outside Xizhi Gate. Yu Qian called a council of war. Shi Heng, an army general, believed that given the inferior strength of the Ming army it would be prudent to pull back the troops inside the city walls and close all of the city gates. The Oirat army just might decide to go away of its own accord when the siege dragged on for too long.

Yu Qian observed, "The enemy is already overconfident. Any show of weakness on our part would only fuel their arrogance. We must ride out to deliver a decisive blow."

Thereupon he deployed his commanders to lead their troops outside the nine gates and get into battle formation.

After making these deployments, Yu Qian personally led a contingent out of the city to guard Desheng Gate and ordered all gates closed—demonstrating he had committed himself to conquer or perish. Yu Qian gave orders that any commander found to abandon his troops and lead a retreat would be executed, and any soldier who deserted against orders would be executed by troops that followed.

The troops were inspired by the courage and determination of Yu Qian and vowed with heightened morale and will to battle the Oirat army to their last breath in order to defend Beijing.

Meanwhile, Ming troops stationed in other parts of the land had answered the government's call and arrived near Beijing to help allay the siege. The Ming troops outside the city now swelled to 220,000.

The now considerably enlarged Ming army offered a formidable resistance and courageously repelled repeated offensives by Esen Khan. The civilian inhabitants outside the city walls worked hand in hand with the Ming troops, climbing on roofs and enclosure walls to hurl bricks and tiles at the enemy soldiers. In five days of pitched battle, the Oirat army suffered heavy casualties.

Having incurred heavy losses and afraid that his route of retreat could be cut off by the Ming army, Esen Khan lost his resolve for continued fighting and pulled back with Emperor Yingzong of Ming and his remnant troops. When he was sure Emperor

Yingzong of Ming was out of range, Yu Qian ordered an attack by cannons, laying low yet more of the Oirat soldiers. The defense of Beijing was a brilliant success.

The bulk of the credit for this important victory went to Yu Qian, whose popularity among the military and the civilian population grew. Emperor Daizong of Ming had great respect for him and wanted to build a proper residence for him to replace his family's modest house, which merely served as a shelter against the elements and not much more. But Yu Qian declined, saying, "How can I think of living in comfort when the country is in great danger?"

After his latest defeat, Esen Khan knew that detaining Emperor Yingzong no longer served a useful purpose, so he freed him to return to Beijing.

While Yu Qian dedicated his life to the defense of the country, Xu Youzhen, who advocated fleeing the capital when Beijing was in danger of falling, and General Shi Heng, who was once berated by Yu Qian, nursed their resentment against him and quietly plotted their revenge.

In 1457, seven years after the return of Emperor Yingzong to Beijing, Emperor Daizong fell seriously ill. Xu Youzhen and Shi Heng saw their opportunity. In collusion with some eunuchs they forced their way into the palace and restored Emperor Yingzong (Zhu Qizhen) to the throne. This is known to history as the "Break-in Incident." Emperor Daizong died shortly afterwards.

Following his restoration to the throne, Emperor Yingzong, who had long harbored a grudge against Yu Qian for helping his younger brother accede to the throne during his own captivity, was further inflamed by Xu Youzhen and Shi Heng's constant slander of Yu Qian. Thus he cold-bloodedly had Yu Qian killed on a charge of "seditious intent."

157. Hai Rui, Man of Integrity and Independence

IN 1522 ZHU Houcong ascended the throne as Emperor Shizong of Ming. In the period immediately following his accession, Emperor Shizong introduced some political reforms, including the curbing of eunuch power and tax reforms. But he later became infatuated with Taoism and increasingly engrossed in the invocation of deities and spirits on altars installed in his palace. He began neglecting the running of state. Grand Secretary Yan Song was so adept at drafting the prayers used in these Taoist rituals that he was eventually elevated to Senior Grand Secretary of the Grand Secretariat (equivalent in rank to Grand Councilor). In this position of Senior Grand Secretary, he and his son Yan Shifan built a clique around themselves to obtain private gain through corruption, larceny, shady dealings and unscrupulous deeds.

At the height of Yan Song's power, even his followers rode roughshod over the general public on account of their connections in high places, not to mention with Yan Song and his son themselves. Everyone, from ministers at the imperial court to local officials, had to show deference to them.

But an obscure county magistrate in Chun'an County of Zhejiang was an impartial judge and showed no special consideration for Yan Song's partisans. His name was Hai Rui.

Hai Rui was a native of Qiongshan of Guangdong. His father died when he was a child and he was raised by his mother in poverty. After obtaining his *ju ren* degree in the provincial civil service recruitment examination in his twenties, he became a school instructor in his county. He was a conscientious and strict teacher. Soon he was promoted to the position of county magistrate of Chun'an of Zhejiang. Most of his predecessors decided cases based on the bribes they received. When Hai Rui took office in Chun'an, he carefully reviewed the outstanding cases. Regardless of the complexity of the case, once it was taken up by Hai Rui, it would invariably be solved and there was never an innocent man wrongfully convicted. The local inhabitants took to calling him Qing Tian or "blue sky," a term reserved in ancient China for incorruptible officials.

Hai Rui's boss, Hu Zongxian, Governor of Zhejiang, was Yan Song's follower and his connections in high places emboldened him to enrich himself by extorting money and exacting bribes. He who dared to ruffle Hu Zongxian's feathers did so at his own peril.

On one occasion, one of Hu Zongxian's sons passed through Chun'an with a large entourage and stayed at the government guesthouse. In any other county, officials would scramble to flatter and fawn on the son of a governor, but in Chun'an County Hai Rui had issued a directive that all high officials and their family members were to be treated like any other guests.

When Hu Zongxian's son, accustomed to a life of luxury and pleasure, saw the kind of food served to him at the guesthouse, he believed it was a deliberate slight. In anger he tipped the table over and told his bodyguards to hogtie the staff member who served the meal and hoist him up on a beam, upside down.

Other staff immediately reported the incident to Hai Rui. The county magistrate was already annoyed by the fanfare with which Master Hu arrived in the county; his brazenness in hoisting up a county employee was the final straw that compelled his intervention.

After hearing the report of the staff, Hai Rui said with apparent calm, "The governor is a squeaky clean high official and has instructed all the counties in his jurisdiction to eschew extravagance in receiving officials passing through town. That flamboyant playboy flaunting a high style and arrogant manners could not possibly be Governor Hu's son. This character must be a crook passing off as his son to con us."

Thereupon he took a large group of bailiffs with him to the guesthouse and had Hu Zongxian's son and his entire entourage rounded up and taken to the county house to be questioned. In the beginning, Master Hu was still jumping up and down with fury, his ego inflated by the high position of his father. But when Hai Rui insisted that he was a fake and threatened to mete out a severe penalty, he became crestfallen. Hai Rui confiscated the several thousand taels of silver found in his suitcase and ran him out of the county after haranguing him about proper behavior.

By the time Master Hu returned to Hangzhou to tearfully complain before his father, Hai Rui's report on the case had been delivered to the governor's office, detailing how a fake Master Hu hoisted up a county official and beat him up. Hu Zongxiang knew his son had received unfair treatment, but Hai Rui's report did not implicate the governor and if he made a fuss about the matter, it was he who would lose face. So he decided to "swallow the front tooth that was knocked loose" or to grin and bear it.

On another occasion Yan Maoqing, a censor dispatched by the central government, went on an official inspection tour of Zhejiang. He was Yan Song's adopted son and had an insatiable appetite for bribes. Wherever he went, local officials had to make large "donations" to him, or else. News of Yan Maoqing's coming inspection tour through Zhejiang understandably cast a shadow of gloom over the local officialdom. But Yan Maoqing had a perverse habit of keeping up the appearance of law-abiding propriety; he notified the counties on his itinerary that he was a stickler for simplicity and frugality and disliked sycophancy and flattery.

When he learned of Yan Maoqing's impending visit to Chun'an, Hai Rui wrote a letter to him.

"We have received your notification that you prefer simple and frugal receptions," he wrote. "But to our knowledge, wherever you go you are wined and dined at sumptuous banquets. We are in a quandary. If we act according to your notification, we worry that it might appear to be a slight to you; on the other hand if we do as other counties do and throw lavish parties in your honor, we fear going against your exhortation to frugality. Please advise as to proper behavior."

Yan Maoqing read the letter with gnashed teeth because it exposed him and put him on the spot. But he had heard about the strict impartiality of the tough judge Hai Rui, and he also knew how Hu Zongxian's son was given his comeuppance in Chun'an. Nervous about his encounter with Hai Rui, Yan Maoqing changed his plans and bypassed Chun'an.

Yan Maoqing bore a grudge against Hai Rui for this incident and later instigated his partisans to badmouth Hai Rui before Emperor Shizong of Ming, making serious accusations against him. As a result, Hai Rui was stripped of his functions as county magistrate of Chun'an.

Eventually, Yan Song fell into disgrace and Yan Maoqing was exiled to garrison duty. Hai Rui was duly reinstated and transferred to the capital.

In the capital, Hai Rui had the opportunity to see up close the absurdity of Emperor Shizong and the corruption endemic in the central government. By that time, Emperor Shizong had absented himself from imperial audiences for more than two decades. He whiled away the time with fellow Taoists in the confines of his palace. The high-ranking ministers were afraid to say anything to the emperor but the low-ranking Hai Rui had the nerve to write a candid memorandum to the emperor, making a scathing critique of the causes of official corruption.

"The people's misery is made worse by the corrupt officials and arrogant bureaucrats," he wrote. "Popular discontent directed at Your Majesty has simmered for a long time now."

After submitting the memo, Hai Rui believed it would incur the wrath of the emperor and his life was likely in the balance. On his way home he picked out a coffin. His wife and children were spooked by the sight of the coffin. Hai Rui explained the whole thing to his family and made meticulous arrangements in case of his death. He also dismissed all his servants in anticipation of his arrest and execution.

His memorandum, as foreseen by him, caused a big stir at the court. Emperor Shizong became furious when he read it and, throwing it on the floor said to his attendants, "Arrest this man immediately and don't let him slip away!"

A eunuch at his side, who had long heard of Hai Rui, told Emperor Shizong, "Everyone knows this man is a learned person. He knows he will not live because he has offended Your Majesty and has made all the arrangements in case of his death. I don't think he will run away."

Emperor Shizong had Hai Rui arrested and turned over to the "Embroidered Coats" (secret service), where he underwent questioning under torture. It was only after the death of Emperor Shizong of Ming that Hai Rui regained his freedom.

158. Qi Jiguang Gets Rid of the *Wo Kou*

THE REIGN OF Emperor Shizong of Ming was plagued by raids of Japanese pirates along China's southeastern coast. These Japanese pirates worked in cahoots with Chinese local tyrants and unscrupulous businessmen to plunder the coastal communities, wreaking havoc on life and property, and casting a pall of insecurity and fear along the coast. These Japanese pirates are known to Chinese history as *wo kou*.

In 1553, the Japanese pirates, supported by the Chinese collaborationists Wang Zhi and Xu Hai, assembled a fleet of several hundred sea-going boats and landed on the coast of Zhejiang and Jiangsu. They then fanned out in small bands to sack dozens of cities and towns. Government officials and troops did not dare to put up a resistance, fleeing at the sight of Japanese pirates.

As the problem of the wo kou incursions got worse, even Emperor Shizong of Ming, snugly ensconced in his palace, began to worry. He instructed Yan Song to think of a way to deal with it. Yan Song's supporter Zhao Wenhua offered an idea: the only way to stop the *wo kou* invasions, he believed, was to pray to the sea god in the East China Sea for protection. The credulous Emperor Shizong accepted this nonsensical strategy of Zhao Wenhua's and sent him to Zhejiang to pray to the sea god.

The central government later dispatched Yu Dayou, a veteran general who had had long experience with coastal defenses, to fight the *wo kou*. He had initial success, winning a series of battles.

But with Zhang Jing, the governor of Zhejiang, out of power as a result of being framed by the scheming Zhao Wenhua, Yu Dayou was implicated and thrown in jail. Taking advantage of the vacuum in coastal defenses, the *wo kou* came back with a vengeance. Only after deploying General Qi Jiguang from Shandong to Zhejiang, was the central government able to turn the critical situation around.

Qi Jiguang is a well-known national hero in Chinese history. Once taking up his post in Zhejiang, he discovered after a review of the local troops that they suffered from lax discipline and their battle-worthiness was next to naught. He concluded he must recruit fresh blood. As soon as the recruitment campaign was announced, a large number of peasants and miners fed up with the *wo kou*'s ravages, enlisted. Some militias organized by landowners inclined to resist the *wo kou* also joined up. Soon the new army of Qi Jiguang swelled to 4,000 men.

A commander well versed in the art of war, Qi Jiguang understood that troops could not be sent into battle without going through rigorous training. He carefully devised battle formations adapted to the marshlands characteristic of the southern geography and took a personal interest in training his troops in the use of all types of weaponry. This new army was forged into a strong force with impressive fighting capabilities and the fame of this "Qi Army" spread far and wide.

A number of years later when the *wo kou* raided the Taizhou area (modern Linhai of Zhejiang Province), Qi Jiguang marched his new army to Taizhou and hounded the marauding *wo kou* wherever they went. The ragtag hordes of pirates were naturally no match for the Qi Army, which engaged them in battle nine times and came out the victor in every single one. No longer able to survive on land, the *wo kou* were forced to flee to the safety of their ships, which were subjected to bombardments by the cannons of Qi Jiguang. As the ships caught fire, large numbers of *wo kou* were burned to death or fell into the sea and drowned. Those who had not made it to their ships surrendered without a fight.

The strengthened defenses of Zhejiang deterred the *wo kou* from further incursions. The following year they moved their looting operations south to the Fujian sea coast. One band of *wo kou* went south from Wenzhou to take control of Ningde; another horde moved north from Guangdong to operate in the Niutian area. The two strands of bandits in mutual support became a formidable force that threatened to overwhelm the generals defending Fuzhou. When the central government received their urgent calls for help, it sent Qi Jiguang to the rescue. Arriving in Ningde at the head of his new army, Qi Jiguang discovered the enemy's lair was on Hengyu Island, ten *li* from the city of Ningde. Protected by the water surrounding them and inaccessible terrain, the *wo kou* set up camp on the island, in the secure knowledge that the local Ming troops would not venture there.

Qi Jiguang personally surveyed the topography of Hengyu Island and its surrounding area and found that the waterway was not as wide or as deep as feared. That evening at low tide, Qi Jiguang ordered his troops to each carry a bundle of straw and throw it into the water. Thousands of sheaves of straw formed a pathway across the waterway, on which the Qi troops were able to sneak into the *wo kou* camp without being detected. After a fierce battle, the more than two thousand *wo kou* on the island were killed off.

After taking Hengyu Island, the Qi Army went on to march to Niutian. As it approached its destination, Qi Jiguang issued the order: "It has been a long march and both men and horses are fatigued. We will stop here to recuperate."

News of this order soon made its way to the enemy camp. The *wo kou* in Niutian, believing that the Qi Army was temporarily halting its advance, relaxed their vigilance. That night Qi Jiguang ordered an all-out attack against Niutian. The *wo kou*, caught totally off guard, put up a haphazard fight but were quickly beaten back by the strong offensive of the Qi Army. The leaders of the *wo kou* fled to Xinghua with their remnant troops. The Qi Army tracked them through the night and destroyed more than sixty enemy encampments, eliminating the enemy soldiers in flight. When day broke, the Qi Army entered the city of Xinghua. It was then that the city inhabitants learned for the first time the *wo kou* had been wiped out by the Qi Army. Buoyed by the good news, they feted the troops with freshly butchered steers and wine.

The following year, the *wo kou* again attacked Fujian and recaptured Xinghua. By that time Yu Dayou had been reinstated and the central government appointed him as Regional Commander of Fujian and Qi Jiguang as deputy Regional Commander. Working together, these two legendary figures in the fight against the *wo kou* successfully routed the *wo kou* and recovered Xinghua. In 1565 the two generals dealt another, fatal blow to the *wo kou* in a joint operation. The coastal communities were finally rid of the *wo kou* that had plagued them for decades.

159. Li Shizhen Scours Mountains for Medicinal Herbs

LIFE WAS FILLED with pleasures for Emperor Shizong in his more than forty years on the throne, but he began to worry that physical decline and his eventual death would cut short his happy days. He embarked therefore on a desperate search for a recipe for longevity and immortality.

In 1556, the central government instructed all local governments to recommend their best doctors of medicine. The Prince of Chu, who had his fiefdom in Wuchang, recommended Li Shizhen, his own resident doctor, to the Tai Yi Yuan or Imperial Medical Administration.

Li Shizhen was from Qizhou, present-day Qichun of Hubei Province. His grandfather and his father were both doctors. His father, Li Yanwen, who had an excellent knowledge of medicinal herbs, had a great influence over the young Li Shizhen, who would make frequent outings into the mountains with other children to collect a wide variety of herbs. With time, he knew not only the names of the herbs but their uses in treating various diseases. His medicinal knowledge grew prodigiously.

But, in those days, doctors commanded little respect among the social elite. Himself a doctor, Li Yanwen wanted his son Li Shizhen to study for the civil service recruitment examination instead of following in his footsteps. Under his father's encouragement, Li Shizhen was able at the age of 14 to qualify as *xiu cai*, or candidate for the Provincial Examination, which he then failed three times in a row. While this caused much hand-wringing among family and friends, Li Shizhen was not unduly disappointed. He was much more interested in becoming a good doctor to treat illnesses.

From then on, Li Shizhen started to study medicine in earnest under his father's tutelage. That same year, his home village was hit by a large flood, which brought in its wake an epidemic that disproportionately affected the poor. Although financially modest themselves, father and son had deep compassion for the poor and treated them with care, regardless of their ability to pay. The community was grateful to them for their medical expertise and devotion to patient care.

In his effort to hone his medical skills, Li Shizhen studied many ancient medical texts. The medical literature went back a long way in China. *The Shen Nong's Materia Medica* written in the Han dynasty was followed by fresh crops of new medical treatises throughout the more than a thousand years that preceded his time. Li Shizhen had an opportunity to borrow from the impressive collections of books found in the homes of the rich and powerful who were treated by him. His voracious reading made him a powerhouse of knowledge and sharpened his medical skills.

Li Shizhen's fame grew as patients successfully treated by him vocally praised his medical expertise. Patients from nearby regions and counties flocked to Li Shizhen's home for treatment.

When his son, the light of his life, was one day racked by convulsions, and even the resident doctors in his household could not cure the disease, the Prince of Chu was understandably worried. When someone suggested that only Li Shizhen could cure this disease, the Prince of Chu immediately sent for him. By examining the patient's facial complexion and feeling his pulse, Li Shizhen concluded the convulsions had a gastrointestinal origin. He prescribed a course of medicine to treat the patient's digestive system and sent the prescription to be filled by an apothecary. The convulsions stopped after the administration of the medicine.

The Prince of Chu was so pleased that he insisted on Li Shizhen's staying in his household as resident doctor. It was at this time that the central government launched a campaign to recruit medical talent. In order to ingratiate himself with Emperor

Shizong, the Prince of Chu recommended Li Shizhen for a position in the Imperial Medical Administration in Beijing.

The Imperial Medical Administration was supposed to be the highest medical institution in the country. But Emperor Shizong gave short shrift to real medical science, instead holding a blind faith in the coterie of alchemists who performed Taoist rites and attempted to produce an elixir of life to ensure his immortality. Li Shizhen was a doctor of conscience and felt disgusted by the insalubrious new environment of his workplace. He resigned from the Imperial Medical Administration and went home after only one year.

On his way home following his resignation, Li Shizhen visited many renowned mountains and places of interest, not for the scenery but for the purpose of collecting medicinal herbs and studying the medicinal attributes of plants. His travels took him to the Wudang Mountains in Junzhou, modern-day Jun County of Hubei Province, where, he had heard, a plum called the *langmei* plum could rejuvenate whoever ingested it, thus the nickname "immortality fruit." The nobility of the imperial court considered it a treasure and demanded an adequate supply of the plum by the local government in the form of annual tribute. Common folk were prohibited from picking the fruit for their own consumption. Li Shizhen had never been a believer in the so-called "immortality fruit." In order to get to the bottom of it, he climbed precipices at great peril to obtain a sample of the plum and took it home with him. After meticulous research, he came to the conclusion that the *langmei* plum was no different from the common plum in that it promoted the production of saliva and slaked one's thirst but had no "immortality" property whatsoever.

Li Shizhen amassed a wealth of scientific data in the course of his long years of medical practice and collection of medicinal herbs. He identified many errors in ancient medical texts. There was also the fact that new medicinal herbs, unrecorded in past medical books, had been, and were still being, discovered since the publication of the ancient texts. He decided therefore to compile a new, comprehensive pharmacopoeia. After returning to his home village from the capital he spent nearly thirty years completing the famous *Compendium of Materia Medica*, which recorded 1,892 medicines and collected more than ten thousand prescriptions. It was a great contribution to the development of China's medical science.

After the publication of the "Compendium," it spread abroad and was eventually translated into Japanese, German, English, French, Russian and Latin, earning an important place in world pharmacology.

Ironically, Emperor Shizong, in his enthusiasm for discovering an elixir of life to ensure his immortality, lost his life when he accidentally swallowed a toxic "golden pill."

At his death, Emperor Shizong was succeeded by his son Zhu Zaihou as Emperor Muzong of Ming.

160. The Tutelage of Zhang Juzheng

IN THE REIGN of Emperor Muzong, Zhang Juzheng, a Grand Secretary, won the trust of the emperor on account of his outstanding abilities. When Emperor Muzong died in 1572, he was succeeded by the crown prince Zhu Yijun as Emperor Shenzong of Ming. On his deathbed, Emperor Muzong designated Zhang Juzheng and two other ministers as Bulwarks of Government to help the next emperor run the country.

Shortly after the accession of Emperor Shenzong, Zhang Juzheng became Chief Bulwark and, as instructed by Emperor Muzong, began to tutor the ten-year-old emperor much like a conscientious teacher. He compiled a collection of illustrated historical tales entitled *Illustrated Lessons for Emperors*. His daily reading and explanation of these tales was eagerly awaited by Emperor Shenzong, who was delighted by the book. Once, after finishing the tale about Emperor Wen of Han visiting his troops at Camp Xiliu to boost their morale, Zhang Juzheng told the young Emperor, "Your Majesty should pay attention to war preparedness. When peace has been around for so long, people tend to take it for granted and lower their guard in the matter of arms. It is high time to give it urgent attention."

Emperor Shenzong vigorously nodded in agreement.

On another occasion, Zhang Juzheng had just finished a story about how Emperor Renzong of Song disliked the use of pearls and jade as ornament.

"He was right," Emperor Shenzong commented. "An emperor should treasure ministers who offer wise counsel instead. What's the use of pearls and jade?"

Zhang Juzheng was pleased to hear such wise words from the mouth of a ten-year-old child.

"A wise ruler values grain and despises gems and precious stones," he said. "For he knows people can live on food, while precious stones could neither assuage hunger nor offer protection against the cold."

Zhang Juzheng took Emperor Shenzong's education seriously. The emperor venerated Zhang as a strict teacher and was somewhat in awe of him. With the support of the empress dowager and the eunuch Feng Bao, Zhang Juzheng had final say on nearly all matters of state.

Zhang Juzheng was a capable statesman in the Ming dynasty. After assuming real power, he pushed through bold military, economic and political reforms.

Although the problem of the *wo kou* on the east coast had been solved, the frequent incursions led by Tartar noblemen in the north grew into a major threat to the Ming dynasty. Zhang Juzheng sent Qi Jiguang, the legendary nemesis of the *wo kou*, to the north to head the garrison of Jizhou, in the north of modern-day Hebei province. Qi Jiguang constructed three thousand defensive works along the Great Wall from Shanhai Pass to Juyong Pass. After the well-disciplined and well-armed Qi Army repelled numerous Tartar offensives, Anda Khan, a Tartar leader, expressed a wish for reconciliation and trade. The proposal was reported to the emperor by Zhang Juzheng and it was decreed that Anda Khan would be made Prince Shunyi. Zhang implemented a policy of trade with the Tartars coupled with strengthened border defenses, intensive military training and agricultural development in the border areas by the Ming troops. There ensued nearly thirty years of peace between the Ming and the Tartars and improved security for all the ethnic communities in northern China.

In those times the Yellow River, whose maintenance had long been neglected, frequently overflowed its banks, flooding farmland and wreaking havoc on agriculture and transportation. Zhang Juzheng appointed Pan Jixun, an irrigation expert, to oversee the repair of the system of dykes along the Yellow River. Pan Jixun rebuilt the dykes and repaired the breaches to contain the river. As a result, transportation flowed again and agricultural production resumed and grew.

Before the reforms, political corruption allowed large landowners to consolidate and enlarge land holdings and to evade taxes. As a result, powerful gentry and large landowners amassed increasing wealth while state coffers dwindled. Zhang Juzheng ordered a land survey, which uncovered previously undisclosed land holdings owned by members of the imperial clan, nobility, local gentry and landowners. This had a deterrent effect on the large landowners and brought in more revenue for the state.

After the land survey, Zhang Juzheng simplified and consolidated the complex system of taxes and compulsory services, all convertible to monetary levies. The new system was called the "integrated cash taxation scheme." The fiscal reform closed the loopholes that had enabled officials to obtain private gain through fraud; it increased government revenue and lightened to some extent the tax burden on peasants.

In ten years of bold reforms, Zhang Juzheng succeeded in breathing a breath of fresh air into the culture of corruption prevalent in Ming politics, filling state granaries with enough grain reserve to last ten years. But these reforms naturally conflicted with some of the interests of the rich and powerful. While publicly they had to bend to the new regulations, privately they had a visceral hatred for Zhang Juzheng.

In the fifth year of Zhang Juzheng's tenure, his elderly father died in his home town of Jiangling. The traditional etiquette of feudal times demanded that he leave his official duties to go home and observe mourning for a period of three years. But he was worried that his departure would cause the ongoing reforms to falter. Emperor Shenzong and some high officials also wanted him to stay in the capital, so he sent his son to attend the funeral on his behalf so that he could stay "on the job" in the capital. Some people took advantage of his failure to attend his father's funeral and used it to petition Emperor Shenzong for the impeachment of Zhang Juzheng. "Attack ads" sharply critical of him started springing up all over town. The attacks subsided only after

Emperor Shenzong felt compelled to issue an edict that threatened to execute anyone challenging Zhang Juzheng's continued service.

With the bulk of power concentrated in Zhang Juzheng, Emperor Shenzong, by now an adult, began to feel bored by having little business to attend to. The eunuchs tried various tacks to amuse him in the back palace. On one occasion, a drunken Emperor Shenzong beat two young eunuchs almost to death for no apparent reason. When the incident came to the empress dowager's attention, she sent for the emperor and gave him a severe tongue-lashing. She handed him a copy of the biography of Huo Guang in the *History of the Han Dynasty* to study. During Huo Guang's tutelage in the Western Han period, wasn't there a Prince of Changyi named Liu He who was overthrown by the empress dowager and Huo Guang shortly after his accession to the throne? Well, Zhang Juzheng now occupied the same territory as Huo Guang did in the Han dynasty. Emperor Shenzong shuddered at the thought and immediately went down on his knees to ask the empress dowager for forgiveness.

A decision was later made by Zhang Juzheng to turn out those eunuchs who lured Emperor Shenzong into unwholesome pastimes. The empress dowager asked Zhang Juzheng to draft a mea culpa edict on the emperor's behalf. Although the matter was thus taken care of, Emperor Shenzong's fear of Zhang Juzheng had now turned into hate.

In 1582 Zhang Juzheng died of illness and Emperor Shenzong took over the reins of state control. High officials who had long resented Zhang Juzheng, now came forward to denounce his arrogance and high-handedness. The following year Emperor Shenzong stripped Zhang Juzheng of his official titles and had all the assets of his family confiscated. A dozen of his offspring were put under house arrest and eventually starved to death. His oldest son committed suicide after being tortured. The reforms instituted by Zhang Juzheng were undone and the Ming government, which had begun to show signs of improvement, resumed its decline.

161. Nurhaci Founds the Later Jin

AS THE MING government became increasingly corrupt, its border security suffered from neglect and a tribal subgroup of the Jurchens, called the Jianzhou Jurchens, took advantage of the slack to expand and grow stronger. Its leader was Aisin Jioro Nurhaci.

Nurhaci was born to a noble family of the Jianzhou Jurchens. His grandfather Giocangga and his father Taksi were Jurchen noblemen appointed by the Ming as officials of the left Jianzhou garrison. Nurhaci, who started riding and shooting arrows at a young age, became an accomplished horseman and warrior. His mother died when he was ten and his stepmother was cruel to him. Nurhaci had to eke out a living away from home by hunting game, digging ginseng roots, picking pine seeds and collecting mushrooms deep in the forests with his friends and selling them in Fushun. At the bustling bazaars and fairs in Fushun, the Jurchens traded their mountain fare and ware for the iron implements, food, salt and fabrics of the Han people. In his long contact with the Han people in Fushun, Nurhaci learned to speak Mandarin. He enjoyed reading Chinese novels such as the *Romance of the Three Kingdoms* and *Heroes of the Water Margin*.

Several clans of the Jianzhou Jurchens were constantly fighting each other for domination. Li Chenliang, Regional Commander of the Ming, exploited this rivalry to maintain tight control. When Nurhaci was 25, Tulin's Nikan Wailan, a Jianzhou Jurchen, accompanied Ming troops to attack Atai's Fort Gure. Atai's wife was a granddaughter of Giocangga and when the latter heard of the attack, he took Taksi with him to visit his granddaughter at Fort Gure. They were in the fort when the Ming army began its assault and both Giocangga and Taksi were killed in the battle.

Nurhaci cried over their death and buried his grandfather and his father. Knowing he was not strong enough to take on the Ming army, he directed all his venom against Nikan Wailan.

"It was Nikan Wailan who killed my grandfather and my father," he told Ming officials. "I will be satisfied if you turn over Nikan to me." The Ming government refused.

The embittered Nurhaci returned home, got out the thirteen suits of armor his father left behind and distributed them to his followers. He led them on an attack on Tulin. Nikan Wailan, who was no match for the brave and battle-savvy warrior Nurhaci, fled in haste. After capturing Tulin, Nurhaci pressed on and conquered some other clans of the Jianzhou Jurchens.

Following a harried flight, Nikan Wailan finally arrived near what is modern-day Qiqihar and requested the protection of Ming troops. Nurhaci soon caught up with him there. Realizing that Nurhaci was not going to take no for an answer, the Ming army allowed him to slaughter Nikan Wailan in order to avoid an armed confrontation.

With Nikan Wailan eliminated, Nurhaci became more powerful than ever. A few years later he succeeded in unifying the Jianzhou Jurchens. This caused panic among other tribes of the Jurchens, which at the time comprised three large subgroups: the Jianzhou Jurchens, the Haixi Jurchens and the "Wild" Jurchens. In 1593 the Yehe tribe, the most powerful among the Haixi Jurchens, entered into an alliance composed of nine Jurchen and Mongol tribes and launched a 30,000-strong coalition force against Nurhaci in a three-pronged attack.

Nurhaci made all necessary preparations in anticipation of the attack by the nine-tribe coalition force, including the laying of ambushes by his best troops and the placing of heavy logs and rocks atop cliffs along the road. When he was satisfied that everything was ready, he went to sleep like a baby. His anxious wife woke him up.

"How can you sleep with the nine tribes marching on you?" she asked. "Have you been scared out of your wits?"

"If I were scared," Nurhaci answered with a laugh, "I wouldn't be able to fall asleep even if I wanted to."

The next day, when the scouts sent from Jianzhou came back with the report that the enemy force was massive, both leaders and the rank and file troups began to feel nervous.

"Don't worry!" Nurhaci reassured them. "We have formidable terrain on our side. They may have the numbers, but they are a ragtag force. They have disparate components who each expect the others to take the initiative. When they start the attack, we will kill a couple of their leaders. That will make them pull back."

When the nine-tribe coaliton force arrived at the foot of the Gure Mountains, the Jianzhou Jurchens, already waiting for them in battle formation, sent out one hundred cavalrymen to challenge the coalition to a fight. When a Yehe leader charged forth, his horse was tripped by a wooden pole and the Jianzhou troops swarmed around him and killed him; another Yehe leader fainted at the sight. The nine-tribe coalition force, lacking unified command, dispersed in a disorderly retreat. Nurhaci gave chase and defeated the Yehe. In another few years he largely completed the unification of all the Jurchen tribes.

In the course of the unification of the Jurchens, Nurhaci organized the Jurchens into eight "banners." A banner was at once an administrative unit and a military organziation; each banner comprised numerous niru of three hundred men each, who farmed and hunted in peace time and performed combat duty in times of war. The system effectively promoted production and increased combat readiness. In order to lull the Ming court into a false sense of security, he kept up his tribute relationship with the Ming, which awarded him the title of Dragon-Tiger General in recognition of his submission. He went to Beijing several times to assess first-hand the true state of the Ming government. In 1616, judging the time ripe, he proclaimed himself Khan of Hetu Ala, near modern-day Xinbin in Liaoning Province, founding the Great Jin dynasty. To distinguish it from the Jin dynasty in antiquity, historians have called it the Later Jin.

162. Battle at Sarhu

AFTER THE FOUNDING of the Later Jin, Nurhaci spent two years cleaning house, expanding production and building up the military. In 1618, Nurhaci summoned the commanders and troops of the Eight Banners to arms and announced his Seven Grievances (Manchurian: nadan koro) against the Ming, with the unprovoked slaughter of his father and grandfather topping the list. The announcement served as a declaration of war against the Ming to venge his elders' deaths.

The following day, Nurhaci led 20,000 men to attack Fushun. He wrote a letter to the city's commander urging him to surrender. The Ming commander Li Yongfang did so without a fight in the face of the overwhelming force of the Later Jin. The Jin troops captured 300,000 people and cattle. The troops sent by the Ming's Grand Coordinator in Liaodong were intercepted and defeated by the Jin army. Nurhaci ordered the city of Fushun destroyed and returned to Hetu Ala loaded with the spoils of war.

When news of the debacle reached Beijing, Emperor Shenzong of Ming was furious. He appointed Yang Hao as Military Commissioner of Liaodong to undertake a punitive expedition against the Later Jin. It was with much effort that Yang Hao was finally able to put together a 100,000-strong force. In 1619, Yang Hao's troops advanced on Hetu Ala along four different routes under four regional commanders. The left flank of the center army was led by Du Song, Regional Commander of Shanhai Pass; the right flank of the center army was led by Li Rubo, Regional Commander of Liaodong; the north army was under the command of Kaiyuan's Regional Commander, Ma Lin; the south army under Liu Ting, Regional Commander of Liaoyang. The force strength was announced at an inflated 470,000 for psychological effect. Yang Hao directed the campaign from Shenyang.

The total troop strength of the Eight Banners was little over 60,000. Some commanders of the Later Jin were nervous when they received intelligence about enemy troop movements. They went before Nurhaci for advice.

"Don't worry!" Nurhaci told them with self-assurance, "Their many routes will not hold up against my one route."

Through reconnaissance Nurhaci knew that the left flank of the enemy's center army led by Du Song was the Ming's main force; it had left Fushun and was marching toward them. He concentrated his force against Du Song.

Du Song was a renowned, battle-hardened general. When he led his troops out of Fushun, it was snowing heavily, but eager to be the first to score a victory, Du Song put his troops on a forced march despite the blizzard. He captured the mountain pass at Sarhu, east of present-day Fushun in Liaoning Province, before dividing his force into two, with half of them camped in Sarhu while he led his elite troops to attack Jiefan (northwest of modern-day Xinbin) controlled by the Later Jin.

Nurhaci restrained his as he discovered Du Song had stretched thin his force. He directed all the troops of the Eight Banners to the Ming camp at Sarhu and by overrunning it, succeeded in cutting off Du Song's retreat route. He then turned around and rushed to Jiefan's rescue on a forced march. The Ming troops attacking Jiefan became demoralized when they learned that they had been outflanked. In the meantime, the Jin troops defending Jiefan came down from high ground and attacked Du Song's army, decimating it. When Nurhaci arrived with his army, they encircled the Ming force in a tight noose. As Du Song dashed about to find a gap in the encirclement, he was shot in the head by an arrow. He fell from his horse and died on the spot. The bodies of his massacred troops strewed the battlefield. His elite force was wiped out in the bloodbath.

When the north army under the command of Ma Lin marched

within 40 *li* of Sarhu, not long after setting off from Kaiyuan in Liaoning Province, it received news of Du Song's failure. Ma Lin, shaken by the development, made the immediate decision to switch from the offensive to the defensive posture. He ordered his troops to pitch camp in order to take advantage of the mountainous terrain. Three rows of trenches were dug as the troops settled in for a long resistance. The eight-banner force under the command of Nurhaci raced from Jiefan and again overran the Ming camp. Ma Lin fled hastily back to Kaiyuan. Thus a second Ming army was defeated.

Yang Hao, directing the campaign from Shenyang and waiting for news of victories from the various fronts, was instead shocked by the news of two fiascos in two days. Recognizing a formidable foe in Nurhaci, he sent rapid orders for the remaining two armies to immediately halt their march.

Li Rubo, Liaodong's Regional Commander leading the right flank of the center army, was well known for his timorous nature and propensity for acting in a slow, deliberate manner. He was all too happy to pull back upon receiving the order from Yang Hao. When the twenty or so Jin sentinels on patrol in the hills saw the Ming withdrawal, they raised a loud clamor, which led the Ming troops to believe they were being pursued by a large Jin contingent. This triggered a stampede resulting in many Ming soldiers being trampled to death by their own comrades.

That left the south army led by Liu Ting. When Yang Hao issued the order to halt the troops' advance, Liu Ting's army had already penetrated deep into Jin territory and had no knowledge of the grievous defeats suffered by the other Ming armies. Liu Ting was a Ming commander famous for his prowess in battle; he wielded a broad sword weighing some one hundred twenty *jin* with such ease and deftness that it seemed to fly in the air, thus earning him the nickname of "Broad Sword Liu." Liu Ting ran a tight ship as commander and his army was well-armed and equipped. He had already overrun a string of enemy forts as his army went deep into enemy territory.

Nurhaci knew that he couldn't count on direct confrontation to defeat the valiant Liu Ting. He had a Ming defector, disguised as

Du Song's subordinate, carry a letter to Liu Ting, saying Du Song's army was now at the gates of Hetu Ala, waiting only for Liu Ting's army to join him for an assault on the city.

Liu Ting, who had not yet received the new orders of Yang Hao and did not know Du Song's army had been wiped out, did not doubt the veracity of the story. Not wanting Du Song to keep all the credit for himself, he ordered an immediate march on Hetu Ala. The road was too narrow even for men or horses to march two abreast, so they had to form a single file. A sudden, murderous clamor erupted around Liu Ting's troops. The hills and valleys now swarmed with Jin ambushers, who charged at them from all directions. In his consternation, Liu Ting saw a contingent of troops in Ming uniform flying Ming flags coming to his rescue. Without hesitation, Liu Ting brought his troops into the midst of this "Ming" contingent, which was actually composed of Jin troops in disguise, sent by Nurhaci to lure Liu Ting into a trap. Hemmed in on all sides by Jin troops, the Ming army fell into disarray. The valiant Liu Ting, wielding his broadsword, was able to kill a number of Jin soldiers, but was soon overwhelmed. With serious injuries to both arms, he finally fell.

The entire campaign lasted a mere five days from start to finish, with half of Yang Hao's force decimated, and more than three hundred high-ranking civil and military officers killed. This is known as the famous "Battle of Sarhu" in Chinese history.

The battle at Sarhu seriously drained the strength of the Ming. The Later Jin pressed its advantage in further attacks. Two years later Nurhaci, at the head of his eight-banner force, captured the important strategic towns of Shenyang and Liaoyang in Liaodong in quick succession.

In March 1625, Nurhaci moved the capital of the Later Jin to Shenyang, which he renamed Shengjing. Henceforth, the Later Jin became the greatest threat to the Ming.

163. Xu Guangqi Studies Western Sciences

THE ENTIRE MING court was in a state of shock after the near annihilation of all four armies under Yang Hao at Sarhu. The entire civil and military leadership assembled at the entrance of the palace to call on Emperor Shenzong to confront the Jin threat by building up the military and increasing military pay and spending. Xu Guangqi, an official of the imperial Hanlin Academy, fired off three petitions in quick succession arguing for the necessity of selecting the best talent and recruiting new blood into the army, for whose training he volunteered his own service. Having heard that Xu Guangqi was well versed in military matters, Emperor Shenzong agreed to send him to Tongzhou to train troops.

Xu Guangqi was from Shanghai. Before his birth, Shanghai shores were plagued by *wo kou* (Japanese pirates) incursions. Frequent accounts by his father of the heroic deeds of popular resistance against the *wo kou* instilled a patriotic passion in the young Xu Guangqi.

In his adulthood, as Xu Guangqi passed through Nanjing on his way to take the civil service recruitment examination he learned that a European missionary named Matteo Ricci gave frequent talks there about Western sciences and was befriended by many Chinese intellectuals. Through an intermediary, Xu Guangqi was able to meet Matteo Ricci. He found that the scientific knowledge disseminated by Matteo Ricci was nowhere to be found in the ancient Chinese texts he had studied. He developed an intense interest in Western sciences.

Matteo Ricci disseminated scientific knowledge mainly to facilitate his missionary work. He believed that in order to widen the appeal of his religion, he must obtain the blessing of the Chinese emperor. In that period, the Ming prohibited missionary work in Beijing. Matteo Ricci lobbied local high officials to intercede with the emperor on his behalf. He traveled to Beijing and with the help of the eunuch Ma Tang, offered a Christian bible, an icon of the Virgin Mary and a few newfangled chiming timepieces to Emperor Shenzong as gifts.

Emperor Shenzong didn't understand the bible, nor did he know who the Virgin Mary was. But the novel chiming clocks piqued his interest and he immediately had Matteo Ricci brought to his palace.

At the reception of Matteo Ricci, Emperor Shenzong asked him to describe Western customs and mores. Matteo Ricci, who was Italian, tried to inflate his importance by claiming to be from the country of Da Xi Yang, or "Great Western Ocean." When a check of the world atlas produced no country of such name, some began to doubt his provenance and urged Emperor Shenzong to run him out of the city. But Emperor Shenzong disregarded this advice and instead offered him money and gave him permission to do missionary work in Beijing. The support of the emperor greatly facilitated Matteo's contact and interaction with court officials.

A few years later, having won the title of Metropolitan Graduate after succeeding in the highest-level civil service recruitment examination, Xu Guangqi arrived in Beijing to serve at the Hanlin Academy. Believing that the study of Western sciences would contribute to increased national prosperity and strength, he decided to ask Matteo Ricci to be his teacher in scientific disciplines, including astronomy, mathematics, survey and weapon manufacture.

One day in class, Matteo Ricci mentioned to Xu Guangqi a major mathematical work by the Greek mathematician Euclid entitled *Elements*. He said it was a pity that the translation of such an important work into Chinese proved such a difficult undertaking.

"Since this book is so important and you express the willingness to offer advice and assistance," said Xu Guangqi, "I will translate it no matter how difficult it is."

From then on, Xu Guangqi would go to Matteo every afternoon after work to work on the translation of Euclid's *Elements*, with Matteo explaining the text and Xu Guangqi committing it to paper in Chinese. No one had ever attempted the translation of a foreign mathematical text before and an accurate rendering of the original into Chinese was no mean feat. After spending more than a year carefully weighing each word and sentence and repeatedly revising the draft, Xu Guangqi finally completed the translation of the first six parts of *Elements*.

In addition to Euclid's *Elements*, Xu Guangqi also collaborated with Matteo Ricci and another missionary, Sabatino de Ursis, on translations of scientific works on survey and irrigation and water conservancy. By combining his study of ancient Chinese calendric systems with the latest advances in astronomy in contemporary Europe, he raised astronomic and calendric research to a high level.

In his devotion to science, Xu Guangqi never stopped being deeply concerned about the harsh fate of the struggling masses. When his father died Xu Guangqi returned to Shanghai to observe mourning. That summer a large flood in southeast China submerged vast agricultural areas planted with rice or wheat. After the water receded, not a kernel was left on the farmland. Xu Guangqi was pained by the dire situation.

"If no other food crop is substituted, how will people survive the food shortage come next spring?" he fretted.

It so happened that a friend had brought some sweet potato seedlings from Fujian and Xu Guangqi began an experiment by planting them on some uncultivated land. Soon the seedlings thrived and formed an abundant mass. He eventually published a booklet dedicated to the popularization of sweet potato farming. The plant, which originated in coastal Fujian, was thus successfully transplanted to Jiangsu and Zhejiang.

Emperor Shenzong's approval of his ideas about training the military filled Xu Guangqi with hope and he couldn't wait to start training new recruits in order to make a contribution to national defense. But he had not expected to run into so much corruption in government bureaucracies. A month after the setting up of the military training office, Xu Guangqi had still not received recruits or troop salary and had no useful work to perform. When he finally received some funds to pay troop salary, he traveled to Tongzhou and reviewed the seven thousand new recruits. Most of them turned out to be mostly elderly, frail or suffering some form of disability. Only two thousand of them could serve, at a pinch, in some military capacity, but by no stretch of the imagination could be deemed good soldier material. In disappointment he submitted his resignation.

In 1620, Emperor Shenzong died and was succeeded by his son Zhu Changluo as Emperor Guangzong of Ming, who died of illness shortly after. When Emperor Shenzong's grandson, Zhu Youjiao, acceded to the throne as Emperor Xizong of Ming, Xu Guangqi returned to the imperial capital. He again made a strong pitch for the manufacture of Western-type cannons to confront the increasing threat posed by the Later Jin. This created tension between him and the Minister of War and led to Xu's expulsion from the Ming court.

When Xu Guangqi returned to Shanghai, he was in his sixties. His long interest in agronomy led him to carry out experiments in his own fields. His findings were the basis for his *Complete Treatise on Agricultural Administration*, which provided detailed descriptions of farming implements, soil, water conservancy, fertilization, seed selection and grafting. It was a veritable encyclopedia of agriculture in those times.

164. Zuo Guangdou Goes to Jail

IN THE LATE reign of Emperor Shenzong of Ming, Gu Xiancheng, an official known for his courage in speaking truth to the leadership, was sacked after incurring the displeasure of Emperor Shenzong. After returning to his home town of Wuxi in Jiangsu Province, he organized a group of kindred spirits to study under him at the Donglin Academy outside the East Gate. Intellectuals and scholars in surrounding cities and towns, drawn by Gu Xiancheng's renowned learnedness, flocked to Wuxi to attend his lectures, filling the far from spacious halls of the academy to capacity. Disgusted by the corrupt and shadowy practices at the Ming court, he would inevitably pepper his lectures with criticisms of the politics of the court and direct his fire at some incumbent high officials. Those who attended his lectures largely shared those criticisms, which also found support among some high officials in the capital.

As the fame of the Donglin Academy steadily spread, the hatred for Gu Xiancheng among bureaucrats and members of the rich and powerful who had been pilloried by him rose to a new pitch; they took to branding those who supported the Donglin Academy partisans of the "Donglin Clique."

In the period immediately following the accession of Emperor Xizong of Ming, some partisans of the "Donglin Clique" rose to power. The most renowned of them were Yang Lian and Zuo Guangdou. On one occasion Zuo Guangdou was sent by the central government on an inspection tour of the environs of the capital, where he was also charged with overseeing the civil service recruitment examination.

One day, Zuo Guangdou was drinking in his office while outside a bitter north wind blew and large flakes of snow steadily drifted down from the sky when suddenly, he was seized with an impulse to go out for a jaunt. Accompanied by a few aides, he rode to the outskirts of town through a snow-blanketed landscape. An ancient-looking temple in a quiet setting came into view; Zuo Guangdou decided to go in for a rest.

They dismounted. When they entered the temple through the door, which stood ajar, they found in a small room opening left off the corridor a scholar who had dozed off, slumped over a desk with a few scrolls of manuscripts lying on it. Zuo went up to the desk and picked up the scrolls, which he read with interest. He marveled at the elegance of the calligraphy and the verve and grace of the writing. As he put down the manuscripts and turned to leave, it suddenly occurred to him that with the heavy snow and freezing temperature outside, the young scholar, who was clearly not wearing enough warm clothing, would surely catch cold in his sleep. He undid the mink cape draped on himself and without hesitation put it gently on the scholar.

After withdrawing from the room and pulling the door closed, Zuo Guangdou sent an assistant to find out more from the monks of the temple. They learned that the scholar's name was Shi Kefa; he had come to the capital to present himself at the civil service recruitment examination. Zuo Guangdou made a mental note of the name.

On the day of the examination, Zuo Guangdou presided over the examination hall as the names of the candidates were read out one by one. When the name of Shi Kefa was called, Zuo Guangdou took a careful look at the candidate walking up with his dissertation and confirmed that it was the same scholar he had seen the previous day in the temple. Zuo Guangdou took the dissertation from the young man and marked it "Rank number 1" on the spot.

After the examination, Zuo Guangdou received Shi Kefa in his official residence, offering words of praise and encouragement. He then took him to the family quarters to meet Mrs. Zuo. He glowingly introduced Shi Kefa to his wife.

"Our own children are undistinguished," he told her, "so I count on this young fellow to take over my mantle."

From then on, Zuo Guangdou and Shi Kefa developed a close teacher-student rapport. In light of the difficult financial situation of Shi Kefa's family, Zuo Gaungdou had him move into his official residence so that he could give personal attention to his studies. Sometimes, when Zuo Guangdou worked deep into the night, he would walk over to Shi Kefa's room to have intellectual discussions with him. They would become so engrossed in the lively exchange that they sometimes forgot it was well past bed time.

Zuo Guangdou and Yang Lian were committed to government reform, but Emperor Xizong was hopelessly incompetent and fatuous. He gave Wei Zhongxian, an evil eunuch, free rein in running the infamous secret service "the Eastern Depot." The powers and privileges he enjoyed enabled Wei Zhongxian to build a power base doing a brisk business of reaping private gain by selling patronage, taking bribes, doing shady dealings and all manner of unscrupulous deeds. Some bureaucrats opposed to the "Donglin Clique" offered their allegiance to Wei Zhongxian the eunuch and formed a clique known to history as the "Castratists." Revolted by the excesses of the Castratists, Yang Lian fearlessly presented a petition to the emperor containing a 24-count indictment of Wei Zhongxian's crimes. Zuo Guangdou offered him his unreserved support.

This action brought grief on them. In 1625, Wei Zhongxian and his Castratists launched a coordinated attack against Yang Lian and Zuo Guangdou, accusing them of being partisans of the "Donglin Clique." They were thrown in jail and tortured.

After Zuo Guangdou's arrest, Shi Kefa became agitated and frustrated by his inability to help. He paced back and forth outside the prison gate, desperate for a chance to visit his mentor. But the Castratists kept a tight watch, holding Zuo Guangdou incommunicado.

Despite being tortured by the Castratists, Zuo Guangdou refused to buckle. When Shi Kefa heard that Zuo Guangdou was on the brink of dying from the torture, he offered fifty taels of silver to the prison guard, at great peril to himself, for a chance to see his mentor before his death.

The prison guard, moved by Shi Kefa's devotion to his mentor, agreed to find a way for Shi to visit the inmate. That night, Shi Kefa changed into a tattered tunic and put on straw sandals to pass for a collector of human waste. With a bamboo basket slung on his back and a shovel in his hand, he was led by the prison guard into the prison.

When Shi Kefa came to the cell of Zuo Guangdou, he found him sitting in a corner, with bruises and injuries all over his body, his face burned beyond recognition and his left leg rotted to the bone. Shi Kefa's heart contracted with pain at the sight; he walked up to Zuo Guangdou, fell down on his knees and started to sob uncontrollably, his arms holding Zuo's leg.

Zuo Guangdou was unable to open his eyes because of the bruises covering his face, but from the sobs he could tell it was the voice of Shi Kefa. Lifting up his hands, he pried his eyelids open with the last ounce of his strength; a pair of angry eyes bored into Shi Kefa, seemingly ready to breathe fire.

"Fool!" Zuo Guangdou scolded. "Do you realize what kind of place this is? Why have you come? The country is in such a sorry state and I am finished. Now you have risked your life to come here. If you are found out, who will be left to carry on our cause?"

When Shi Kefa couldn't stop his sobbing, Zuo Guangdou said harshly, "If you don't leave this moment, I will take care of you myself to save the crooks trouble." Thereupon he picked up the leg irons at his side and made as if to hurl them at Shi Kefa.

Afraid to say a word more, Shi Kefa, repressing his sorrow and pain, left the prison.

A few days later, Zuo Guangdou and Yang Lian were killed by Wei Zhongxian. By bribing the prison guard again, Shi Kefa was able to obtain the remains of Zuo Guangdou for burial. Whenever the last scene in the cell came back to him, Shi Kefa would say, with tears streaming down his face, "My mentor's heart must be made of iron and stone."

165. The Battle of Ningyuan

IN THE PERIOD when Wei Zhongxian was making a stinking mess of Ming politics, Nurhaci, the Great Khan of the Later Jin, stepped up his attacks against Ming troops in Liaodong. In the wake of the Battle of Sarhu, the Ming government appointed Xiong Tingbi, a veteran general, to the defense of Liaodong. Xiong was an outstanding commander but Wang Huazhen, the Grand Coordinator of Guangning in Liaoning Province, did his best to put a stick in the spokes of Xiong's command for fear that Xiong's posting would erode his own influence and position. During an offensive launched by Nurhaci against Guangning in 1622, Wang Huazhen fled south into China proper, leaving General Xiong too weak to counter the offensive. Xiong had no alternative but to retreat with some of the inhabitants to the safety inside Shanhai Pass.

With the fall of Guangning, the Ming government indiscriminately threw both Xiong Tingbi and Wang Huazhen into jail. Wei Zhongxian pounced on this opportunity to extort money from Xiong, threatening capital punishment unless he paid 40,000 taels of silver. Xiong Tingbi, who was a man of integrity with modest means, categorically refused. The Castratists had him executed on the trumped-up charge of having stolen from troop pay.

With the execution of General Xiong, who was going to lead the fight against the Jin army? While the War Ministry was fretting about a replacement, it suddenly realized an administrative aide, Yuan Chonghuan, was missing. His family told ministry officials that they were unaware of his whereabouts. Yuan Chonghuan reappeared a few days later. Worried by the critical situation of the Ming, he had ventured unaccompanied beyond Shanhai Pass on his horse to do some reconnaisance.

Yuan Chonghuan reported his assessment of the situation inside and outside the pass to Sun Chengzong, the Minister of War.

"If I am given the troops and their pay," he concluded, "I will assume the responsibility of defending Liaodong."

When ministers unnerved by the offensives of the Later Jin heard about Yuan Chonghuan's volunteering to assume the defense of Liaodong, they were all for supporting his attempt. Emperor Xizong approved 200,000 taels of silver in troop pay and gave him command of the Ming troops stationed in the northeast.

In the aftermath of several years of war, the areas beyond Shanhai Pass were largely laid to waste and strewn with the bodies of dead combatants. The freezing weather, the snow, and the feral beasts roaming the landscape added to the harshness of life. Yuan Chonghuan rode with a number of soldiers out of Shanhai Pass. After traveling all night across the vast, uninhabited northeastern land, they arrived before the first light of dawn at the forward outpost of Ningyuan, modern-day Xingcheng of Liaoning Province. There they began taking in refugees and fortifying defensive works. Yuan Chonghuan's courage, willpower and tenacity brought him the respect and admiration of his troops and superiors.

After surveying the situation in Liaodong, Yuan Chonghuan decided to station troops in Ningyuan and build fortifications there. He submitted his proposal to the central government and won immediate support from Sun Chengzong.

Yuan Chonghuan erected a wall ten meters high and six meters thick around Ningyuan, on which were mounted various kinds of weapons and cannons. Sun Chengzong deployed contingents to nearby towns, including Jinzhou and Songshan to serve as support for Ningyuan.

Yuan Chonghuan endeared himself to the populace and the military by enforcing a strict discipline over his troops. Traders across Liaodong, drawn by the security offered by the fortification of Ningyuan defenses, brought their business to the city. Soon Liaodong's critical security situation was turned around.

By making headway in Liaodong defenses, Sun Chengzong and Yuan Chonghuan earned the ill will of Wei Zhongxian, who succeeded in forcing Sun Chengzong out of his post of minister of war by mobilizing his partisans to mount a mudslinging campaign against him.

After getting rid of Sun Chengzong, Wei Zhongxian put his partisan Gao Di in command of Liaodong defenses. No sooner had the feckless, incompetent Gao Di arrived at Shanhai Pass to assume command, than he summoned his commanders and told them the Jin force was too strong for Ming troops to resist outside the pass and therefore all Ming forces were to pull back inside Shanhai Pass.

Yuan Chonghuan was dead set against the idea of withdrawal, arguing, "We have solidified our foothold in Liaodong at great pains. We can't sacrifice our hard-won gains so lightly."

Gao Di insisted that Yuan Chonghuan abandon Ningyuan.

"My duty is to defend Ningyuan," said Yuan indignantly. "I'd sooner die in Ningyuan than withdraw."

Unable to budge Yuan Chonghuan, Gao Di allowed him to remain in Ningyuan with some troops but set a deadline for Ming forces to withdraw from all other locations to south of Shanhai Pass. As the order was issued at short notice, the Ming troops made a hasty withdrawal, leaving behind five million kilos of military rations.

The disorganized withdrawal of the Ming troops convinced Nurhaci that it would be easy to deal with the Ming. In 1626, he led a 130,000-strong force across the Liao River to attack Ningyuan.

With Ming troops already pulled from surrounding positions, Ningyuan had to defend itself with a paltry ten thousand troops without any external support. But Yuan Chonghuan refused to lose heart. Drawing blood by biting on a finger, he wrote in blood a vow to fight the Jin to his last breath and showed it to his troops as he gave his pre-battle speech. The troops were roused to redoubled ardor and vowed to stand by General Yuan in the defense of the city.

Yuan Chonghuan instructed inhabitants outside the city walls to move into the city with all their food and implements and to torch their houses in order to deny Jin troops food and cover. He assigned duties to city officials, some charged with rations and supplies, some with ferreting out traitors. He wrote to the commanding officer at Shanhai Pass with instructions to summarily execute any deserter from Ningyuan. This had a calming effect on the city: people now entertained no other thought than that of the defense of their city against the enemy.

Twenty days later, Nurhaci arrived with his awesome force. The Jin troops, in massive numbers, stormed the city behind their shields, braving the hails of arrows, rocks and cannonballs unleashed by the Ming defenders. Although the Ming troops put up a valiant fight, the enemy onslaught was relentless, as fallen enemy soldiers were quickly replaced by more troops. At the critical moment, Yuan Chonghuan ordered the great cannons into action. Jin troops were blown to pieces in fiery explosions as the cannons were fired at them. The remaining Jin army beat a retreat.

The next day, Nurhaci led a massive assault upon the city. Yuan Chonghuan climbed up to the observatory tower atop the embattlements to watch calmly the movements of the Jin force. When the Jin troops came very close to the walls, he ordered his soldiers to fire their cannons at the dense concentrations of enemy soldiers, inflicting heavy casualties. Nurhaci was badly wounded in the battle and had to call off the attack.

Yuan Chonghuan seized the momentum of victory and gave chase with his troops, returning triumphantly to the city only after pursuing the enemy force over a distance of a dozen miles.

The badly wounded Nurhaci said to his subalterns upon their return to Shenyang, "I've been an invincible commander since the age of 25, never losing a battle. I can't accept that I wasn't able to conquer a small town like Ningyuan." A few days later, Nurhaci died from his festering wound and his anger and sorrow. His eighth son Hung Taiji (also known as Huang Taiji) succeeded him as Great Khan of the Later Jin.

166. Hung Taiji Sows Disinformation

AFTER NURHACI DIED of his wounds, Yuan Chonghuan sent an envoy to Shenyang to offer his condolences, with the unspoken intention of sizing up the situation in the Later Jin. While Hung Taiji nursed a bitter grudge against Yuan Chonghuan, the Later Jin needed time to recover from its recent military setback. Hung Taiji also wanted to probe Ming intentions. He therefore not only received the envoy of Yuan Chonghuan, but also dispatched his own emissary to Ningyuan to express his thanks. Behind the facade of reconciliation, both sides were actively preparing for the next confrontation.

The following year, Hung Taiji led a massive attack against the Ming. The Jin troops marched south along three routes and laid siege to Jinzhou. Yuan Chonghuan was certain that Hung Taiji's real target was Ningyuan, so he decided to stay to defend the city and sent his subalterns to relieve Jinzhou with four thousand cavalrymen. As predicted by Yuan, even before the departure of the Jinzhou relief force, Hung Taiji had launched a simultaneous attack against Ningyuan. Yuan Chonghuan directed the battle from the ramparts and ordered heavy artillery fire against the Jin troops; Ming reinforcements outside the city in coordination with the city defenders drove off the Jin attackers.

Hung Taiji pulled back his army to Jinzhou but the Ming defense of Jinzhou proved impregnable. The warming weather also depressed the Jin troops. Hung Taiji decided to withdraw his army.

Although Yuan Chonghuan won another major victory, the partisans of Wei Zhongxian took the credit for themselves and faulted Yuan for dereliction of duty by not having personally led the relief of Jinzhou. Realizing Wei Zhongxian was bent on making his life difficult, Yuan Chonghuan decided to resign.

In 1627, the weak and inept Emperor Xizong died and was succeeded by his brother Zhu Youjian as Emperor Sizong of Ming, also known as Emperor Chongzhen (Chongzhen being an era name of his).

Emperor Chongzhen had long been aware of the depth of popular anger at the evil Wei Zhongxian. Upon his accession he lost no time in announcing the crimes of Wei and exiled him to garrison duty in Fengyang. Knowing he was not going to survive, Wei Zhongxian committed suicide on the way to exile.

Emperor Chongzhen outlawed Wei Zhongxian's Castratist Clique and overturned the wrongful convictions leading to the imprisonment of Yang Lian and Zuo Guangdou. He was determined to thoroughly clean house. Many high officials petitioned him to call Yuan Chonghuan back to government service at the Ming court. Emperor Chongzhen followed this advice by promoting Yuan Chonghuan to Minister of War in charge of the defenses of Hebei and Liaodong. Emperor Chongzhen also received Yuan Chonghuan in person and asked him about his plans.

"If I am given the authority and assured of the support of other ministries and department of the government," said Yuan Chonghuan, "I will be able to recover Liaodong within five years."

Emperor Chongzhen exulted over the prospect and gave Yuan Chonghuan a *shang fang bao jian* (an imperial sword conferring supreme authority on the person carrying it), investing him with full power.

After returning to Ningyuan in his new capacity, Yuan Chonghuan promoted deserving commanders, streamlined troops and enforced discipline. Morale soared as a result. Mao Wenlong, the regional commander of Dongjiang, was killed by Yuan Chonghuan's *shang fang bao jian* because of poor performance in battle, inflated account of battle successes and insubordination to Yuan Chonghuan.

Hung Taiji was naturally determined not to passively accept defeat. Realizing Ningyuan and Jinzhou were well-defended, he decided to modify his route of attack. After meticulous preparations, he took his hundreds of thousands of troops in October 1629 on a circuitous route through Longjing Pass and Da'ankou (north of modern Zunhua of Hebei Province) to enter Hebei and head directly toward the Ming capital of Beijing.

This caught Yuan Chonghuan by surprise, and by the time he rushed his troops to block the advance of the invasion force it was already too late. The Jin troops cut through territory little defended by Ming troops, and soon entered the outskirts of Beijing. When news reached Yuan Chonghuan, he rushed with his troops toward Beijing. Arriving after two days of forced march, without pausing for rest, he engaged the Jin army in fierce combat. Ming troops coming from other locations later joined the battle.

The surprise Jin attack against Beijing sent a shock wave through the city. Emperor Chongzhen was flustered and at a loss as to what to do. He calmed down somewhat when he learned of the arrival of Yuan Chonghuan's reinforcements. He received Yuan Chonghuan to express gratitude to the troops. But some holdovers of Wei Zhongxian's clique started rumors that the Jin troops attacking Beijing by taking a roundabout route did so with Yuan Chonghuan's help. They insinuated there was some kind of intrigue involved.

Emperor Chongzhen, who was a paranoid person, began to be swayed by these rumors. At his time a eunuch captured by the Jin escaped from the Jin camp and reported to Emperor Chongzhen that Yuan Chonghuan had concluded a secret pact with Hung Taiji promising to surrender Beijing to him. This information hit Emperor Chongzhen like a bolt out of the sky. He was flabbergasted.

In fact, two eunuchs of the Ming court had been captured and detained in the Jin camp. A eunuch named Yang woke up one night and overheard their captors talking in hushed tones outside.

"Do you know that it was the emperor (meaning Hung Taiji) who decided to suspend the attack today?" one Jin soldier said.

Another soldier asked, "How do you know?"

Yet another soldier said, "I just saw our emperor ride alone toward the Ming camp and two persons rode out from the Ming barracks to meet him. They talked to him for quite a while before returning to their camp. I heard that those two had been sent by General Yuan, who had concluded a secret pact with our emperor. It seems the deal has been clinched..."

The eunuch who overheard the conversation escaped the Jin camp in a moment of distraction on the part of his captors and hurried to the palace to report it to the emperor. Emperor Chongzhen bought the story, little knowing that it was disinformation deliberately fed to the Ming through the guards' conversation staged by Hung Taiji.

Emperor Chongzhen summoned Yuan Chonghuan immediately. Completely unaware, Yuan Chonghuan hurried to the palace.

"Yuan Chonghuan!" The stern-faced Emperor Chongzhen asked reproachfully, "Why did you kill General Mao Wenlong without authorization? Why were your troops late in coming to the rescue of Beijing after the Jin launched an attack on the capital?"

Yuan Chonghuan gave a start, mystified by the accusations. Before he had time to reply to the charges, Emperor Chongzhen had already ordered the "Embroidered Coats" (secret service) to tie him up and throw him in jail.

A minister who knew Yuan Chonghuan had always been a devoted patriot, felt that something didn't add up.

"Your Majesty may want to proceed with prudence on this matter," he urged Emperor Chongzhen.

"Prudence my foot!" declared the emperor. "Prudence can only bring disaster."

Emperor Chongzhen refused to heed the advice of his ministers; some remnant partisans of Wei Zhongxian also jumped on the anti-Yuan Chonghuan bandwagon. The next year Emperor Chongzhen ordered Yuan Chonghuan executed.

After successfully eliminating his nemesis, Yuan Chonghuan, through a stratagem of sowing distrust and suspicion in the Ming court, Hung Taiji took his troops back to Shengjing. The Later Jin's strength grew steadily from that time. In 1635, Hung Taiji changed the name of Jurchen to Manchu. A year later, Hung Taiji proclaimed himself Emperor in Shengjing and changed the dynasty name to Qing. He became Emperor Taizong of Qing.

167. Li Zicheng, the Trailblazing King

IN 1628, THE second year of Emperor Chongzhen's reign, famine broke out in Shaanxi. After eating all the grass roots and tree bark, the hungry populace was reduced to eating earth in the hills. This did not prevent some local government officials from demanding land tax and other levies, and life became unbearable for the people. Soon, peasant rebellions erupted across Shaanxi.

In the winter of that year, the Ming court ordered a troop contingent to redeploy from Gansu to Beijing. When the contingent reached Jin County, modern Yulin of Shaanxi Province, the soldiers, who had not received their pay, took their complaint to the county government, where they raised a stink. When high officials tried to quash the unrest by force, a young soldier stepped forward and led his fellow soldiers in a mutiny, killing both their generals and the county magistrate. The young soldier's name was Li Zicheng.

Li Zicheng was born to a peasant family in Mizhi, Shaanxi. He had loved to ride and shoot arrows since childhood and had become an accomplished warrior. After the death of his father, Li Zicheng became a horse groom at a post house in Yinchuan to escape the poverty of his family. His friendly disposition endeared him to the runners at the post.

Li Zicheng's family used to collect rent for the government. After years of poor harvests, the peasants of Mizhi were no longer able to pay land rent. A large landowner named Ai, seeking to profit from this situation, lent money to the peasants at exorbitant rates. Li Zicheng knew the peasants could not come up with the money to pay their land tax, so he borrowed from Ai and paid the tax on the peasants' behalf. After some time, the landowner named Ai pressed Li Zicheng for repayment of the debt. Li did not have the money to pay back the loan. Ai sent bailiffs to take him into custody and beat him senseless. He was then shackled and left to bake under the sun without any food. When the local people and the runners of the post house entreated the county magistrate to move Li Zicheng to the shade and give Li something to eat, the county magistrate refused. This provoked the anger of the crowd, who surged forward and shattered the shackles on Li Zicheng. They took him from Mizhi to Gansu, where he became a soldier.

After Li Zicheng killed his superior officers in Jin County, he took dozens of soldiers with him to join the peasant militia led by Wang Zuogua and became a leader of the militia troops.

Yang He, the governor appointed by the Ming government, was frightened by the proliferation of insurgencies. He coupled armed repression with a policy of co-opting commanders of peasant militias with promises of high positions and money. Wang Zuogua could not resist these temptations and surrendered, forcing Li Zicheng to find another perch. He eventually decided to join the insurgency of Gao Yingxiang, who called himself "Chuang Wang" or "Trailblazing King."

Gao Yingxiang was pleased to have Li Zicheng and his men join his organization, and made him commanding general of a regiment. People took to calling Li Zicheng Chuang Jiang, "Trailblazing General."

Gao Yingxiang's insurgency, in alliance with other insurgencies operated in five provinces including Shanxi and Hebei, continued to expand. The government forces' pacification and encirclement attempts were thwarted. In frustration, Emperor Chongzhen gave orders to all the government forces in various provinces to encircle and wipe out the insurgents in one fell swoop.

To counter the government plan, Gao Yingxiang called a meeting of commanders from thirteen insurgencies at Xingyang to thrash out a response.

The discussion at Xingyang was lively. Some believed that the enemy was too powerful and they should fight their way back to their home villages in Shaanxi and lie low for a while; others disagreed but could offer no better alternatives. Li Zicheng rose to his feet.

"If a soldier is willing to risk his life, he has a fighting chance," he said. "We have a hundred thousand men. What can the enemy do to us?"

Gao Yingxiang said approvingly, "What do you propose then?"

Li Zicheng proposed that the insurgents should divide into several strands, each attacking in a different direction. This way they would have a better chance of breaching the encirclement. There was general agreement with the idea. After some consultation, the thirteen insurgencies were organized into six armies. Some were tasked with pinning enemy forces down and others were to fight a mobile war. The troops of Gao Yingxiang, Li Zicheng and Zhang Xianzhong would break through the enemy encirclement in the east and head to Fengyang near the confluence of the Huai River and the Yangtze.

Fengyang was the home town of Zhu Yuanzhang, Emperor Taizu of Ming. It became the "Middle Capital" of the Ming after Emperor Taizu's death. The peasant insurgents intended to humble the Ming court by attacking Fengyang.

The insurgents led by Gao Yingxiang and Zhang Xianzhong cut through Ming defense like a hot knife through butter. In less than ten days, they captured Fengyang and burned down the ancestral tombs of the Ming royal house as well as Huangjue Temple, where Zhu Yuanzhang was once a monk. This was a serious blow to the Ming court. When Emperor Chongzhen learned of the fall of Fengyang, he was so furious he had the Grand Coordinator of Fengyang executed.

Gao Yingxiang and Li Zicheng marched their troops back to Shaanxi. They continued their roving attacks on government troops, keeping them overstretched and on the defensive. Emperor Chongzhen and local government officials considered the insurgents a thorn in their side and vowed to wipe them out. Once, Gao Yingxiang marched his troops on Xi'an and walked into an ambush near Zhouzhi (modern-day Zhouzhi of Shaanxi Province) laid by Sun Chuanting, the Grand Coordinator of Shaanxi. Caught by surprise, Gao Yingxiang was captured and killed after a fierce battle.

Li Zicheng was able to break out with the remaining troops. The death of their supreme commander was a painful loss to the men. Since Li Zicheng, the Trailblazing General, was considered by all to be Gao Yingxiang's most trusted commander and an accomplished, brave warrior, he was acclaimed by the troops as the new Chuang Wang (Trailblazing King) to take Gao Yingxiang's place. From then on, the name "Li Chuang Wang" became a household name.

The fear and hate Li Chuang Wang inspired in the Ming court was proportional to the growth of his fame. Emperor Chongzhen ordered Governor Hong Chengchou and Grand Coordinator Sun Chuanting to devote themselves exclusively to the encirclement and destruction of Li Zicheng and Li increasingly felt the heat of their intentions. However, the valor of the insurgents and Li Zicheng's resourcefulness and astute use of tactics enabled them to breach government encirclement lines on numerous occasions and to challenge government forces in Sichuan, Gansu and Shaanxi.

During this difficult period, Zhang Xianzhong and Luo Rucai, the leaders of two other insurgencies, submitted to the Ming. Some commanders under Li Zicheng also defected. This only added to Li's growing difficulties.

In 1638, Li Zicheng moved his troops from Gansu to Shaanxi, with the intention of fighting his way out of Tongguan Pass. Tipped off about his troops' movements, Hong Chengchou and Sun Chuanting laid ambushes at three separate locations in the high mountains near Tongguan, deliberately leaving the main road leading to Tongguan free and clear for passage to lure Li Zicheng into the noose they'd prepared for him.

And Li Zicheng took the bait. When his massive insurgent force entered a valley near Tongguan, swarms of Ming troops materialized and charged down from the hills. With their advantages in numbers and terrain, the Ming army unleashed waves upon waves of assault on the insurgents. The close combat lasted several days and nights, ending in the death of tens of thousands of rebel combatants and the collapse of the insurgent army.

Only 17 insurgents, including Li Zicheng and his subaltern Liu Zongmin, succeeded in breaking out of the encirclement after beating back large numbers of Ming troops. They traveled across high mountains under extremely harsh conditions to reach the Shangluo hills in the southeastern part of Shaanxi, where they went into hiding.

After taking control of Tongguan, the Ming army sent out mounted scouts to track down Li Zicheng. The trail turned cold after months of searching. The intensive manhunt was relaxed only after the Ming army learned that Li Zicheng had reportedly died from the mortal wound he had received in the recent battle.

168. Zhang Xianzhong's Stealth Attack on Xiangyang

IN MAY 1639, Zhang Xianzhong launched a new rebellion in Gucheng of Hubei. His submission to the Ming had been a ruse to enable him to secretly regroup for a comeback. When Ming generals became aware of his intentions and were on the point of sending troops after him, he made a pre-emptive strike by killing the county magistrate of Gucheng and torching the county government house before relaunching his rebellion. Soon Luo Rucai raised arms in his support.

Zuo Liangyu, a regional commander of the Ming, sent his troops to confront Zhang Xianzhong. Zhang succeeded in defeating Zuo Liangyu's force and only a few hundred Ming troops survived and fled back. In a rage, Emperor Chongzhen sacked both the supreme commander Xiong Wencan and the regional commander Zuo Liangyu. He dispatched Yang Sichang, the Minister of War, to besiege Zhang Xianzhong's stronghold in the Huguang area.

With the *shang fang bao jian* (sword of imperial authority) given to him by the emperor and a hundred thousand troops under his command, Yang Sichang arrived in Xiangyang amid great fanfare. He ordered his commanders, including Zuo Liangyu, to hem in the insurgents from all sides. When Zhang Xianzhong moved his troops to Manao Hills, they were lured into an enemy trap by a hidden traitor who had infiltrated their ranks. The insurgents were defeated by Zuo Liangyu's troops and lost huge amounts of gold and silver as well as a large number of battle horses. Zhang

Xianzhong's wife and sons were taken prisoner in the clash.

With his one thousand cavalrymen, Zhang Xianzhong retreated to Sichuan. Yang Sichang followed closely and moved his field headquarters to Chongqing, with the intention of wiping out the insurgents in Sichuan.

Yang Sichang posted a reward across Sichuan, promising ten thousand taels of gold and the title of marquis for whoever was able to capture Zhang Xianzhong. The next day, the field headquarters of Yang Sichang was found to have been plastered with posters bearing the counter-reward: "Three *qian* (a miniscule unit of weight) of silver for the head of Yang Sichang."

Yang Sichang sent out large forces in pursuit of the insurgents. But Zhang Xianzhong's troops were a mobile lot, never giving the government troops the satisfaction of knowing where they would crop up. It was not until January of the following year that the government troops were able to catch up with the insurgents. When the exhausted troops led by the Ming generals Meng Ruhu and Liu Shijie came near, Zhang Xianzhong's force, outflanking the government troops, came charging down the hills behind them, amid loud battle cries. The government force crumbled, with Liu Shijie killed in battle and Meng Ruhu escaping by the skin of his teeth. Having beaten back the enemy, the insurgents sang, clapping their hands.

"First there was this Grand Coordinator of Sichuan named Shao, who often ran in circles about us; then there was this Adjutant Liao, who fell in line without a fight; good old Minister Yang is three feet away."

When the ditty reached the ears of the Ming troops, the embarrassed Yang Sichang didn't know whether to laugh or cry.

In 1641, Zhang Xianzhong discovered that with the bulk of Yang Sichang's troops concentrated in Sichuan, there was a vacuum in Xiangyang. He shook off the pursuing Ming army and abruptly took his troops out of Sichuan and raced east, covering three to four hundred *li* of territory in a day's forced march, leaving the army of Yang Sichang in the dust. Near Dangyang of Hubei, they encountered a Ming interception force. Leaving Luo Rucai behind to face the enemy in Dangyang, Zhang Xianzhong led an elite force to continue the advance on Xiangyang.

When Yang Sichang, who was in Chongqing, learned of the development, he immediately dispatched a messenger to Xiangyang, with the order that the city ready itself for the impending attack. The messenger was discovered and detained by the insurgents as he made his way toward Xiangyang. He carried with him the official token authenticating his status as conveyer of the order and papers bearing the seal of Yang Sichang's field headquarters. Zhang Xianzhong had his adoptive son, Li Dingguo, pass for Yang Sichang's messenger to gain entrance into Xiangyang with a few "aides" and his official token and documents.

It was nightfall when Li Dingguo arrived at Xiangyang with the official token and papers. He called out to the Ming troops inside the gate announcing himself as Minister Yang's messenger. After examining his official token and papers and finding them in order, the Ming guards let Li Dingguo and his accompanying soldiers into the city.

That night, the insurgents who had thus tricked their way into Xiangyang started several fires in the city. The city inhabitants were roused from their sleep by the ensuing commotion and found the city engulfed in flames and plunged into chaos. Amid the confusion, the imposters opened the city gate to let in the insurgent troops. It was by then too late for the Ming defenders to put up an effective resistance.

Once in the city, the insurgents threw open the prison gate and rescued their fellow insurgents and their family from captivity. A detachment raced to the residence of Zhu Yiming, the Prince of Xiang, and took him prisoner.

Zhang Xianzhong presided in the main hall of the Prince's residence as soldiers brought him in. Zhu Yiming, shaking like a leaf, begged for his life.

Zhang Xianzhong said, "All I want is to borrow your head for a purpose I have in mind."

Terrified by this announcement of his death sentence, Zhu Yiming repeatedly knocked his head on the floor and said, "Your Highness can have all the gold, silver and treasures in my palace! But please spare my life!"

Zhang Xianzhong burst into a peal of laughter and said, "I have already taken Xiangyang. All your treasures are mine for the taking anyway. But without your head, I will not be able to take Yang Sichang's life."

He barked an order and Zhu Yiming was taken outside and executed.

By taking control of Xiangyang, Zhang Xianzhong seized a huge amount of war spoils in the form of troop rations and weapons stored by Yang Sichang in the city. He distributed the more than one hundred thousand taels of silver found in the vaults of the Prince of Xiang to the local famine victims. To say that the populace rejoiced at the execution of the evil Prince of Xiang would be an understatement.

Zhang Xianzhong's capture of Xiangyang stunned Yang Sichang as news traveled to Sichuan. His meticulously devised counterinsurgency plan was now in tatters. How was he going to explain to Emperor Chongzhen that right before his eyes, and on his watch, a prince of the Ming was killed in a surprise attack by Zhang Xianzhong?

The distraught Yang Sichang made his way from Sichuan to Hubei. The moment he arrived in Shashi he learned that Li Zicheng's insurgents, now regrouped and reinvigorated, had left their haunts in the mountains of Shangluo to capture Luoyang by taking advantage of the relative weakness of Ming defense in Henan. Zhu Changxun, the Prince of Fu, was killed in the battle. Shocked and terrified, Yang Sichang committed suicide, having come to the painful conclusion that there was no future for him.

169. Li Yan and the Red Lady

WHEN LI ZICHENG arrived in Henan from Shangluo, Henan was in the middle of a severe drought. Tens of thousands of famine victims roamed the land in search of food. When they learned that Li Chuang Wang, the Trailblazing King, had come down the mountains, the famished and displaced people flocked to him to join forces, for better or worse.

One day, a group of famine victims brought a young man, who appeared to be a scholar, to Chuang Wang. Li Zicheng found out after a few questions that the young man, whose name was Li Yan (also known as Li Xin), had just been rescued from the county jail of Qi County, Henan.

Li Yan was the son of a wealthy man in Qi County. A few years ago, when famine was at its worst and many peasants were no longer able to put food on the table, Li Yan helped them out with his family's grain. It was rare for someone from a wealthy family to offer relief to the hungry poor. The needy found him to be a decent man and took to calling him "Li Gong Zi," or Master Li.

When the poor were starving from years of unrelenting famine, the county government continued to send out bailiffs demanding from them payment of the land tax and repayment of arrears. Worried that the government's persistence in its tax collection effort could provoke civil unrest, Li Yan went to see the county magistrate named Song and tried to persuade him to announce a tax moratorium and to allocate part of the holdings in government granaries to aid the famine victims in the form of food loans.

The county magistrate said to Li Yan, "Higher authorities have been pressing local governments to fulfill their quotas for troop rations. How am I going to accomplish that without collecting taxes and debt repayments? Besides, the county granaries have long been depleted. There's nothing left to lend to the famine victims. Unless the wealthy families are willing to offer their grain holdings."

Rebuffed by the county magistrate, Li Yan went home and distributed the two hundred or so hectoliters of grain in his family granary to famine victims.

The famine victims were delighted by Master Li's generosity, but the Li family's grain alone was insufficient given the large number of the needy. Someone came up with the idea of sending a few dozen representatives to the other wealthy families to petition them to follow the example of the Li family.

The other wealthy families not only rejected their request but claimed, shooting dirty looks at the representatives, that they had no grain left. Frustrated, the hungry people became unruly and forced their way into the granary of a wealthy family and helped themselves to the stored grain.

The panicked wealthy households brought their complaint tearfully to the county magistrate, who said angrily, "This is a rebellious lot!" He immediately sent bailiffs with his official token of authority to stop the rioting and promised to mete out harsh punishment to anyone continuing to engage in mob violence. The hungry crowd in the heat of anger was unimpressed by official intimidation. They tackled the bailiffs and threw the county magistrate's official token of authority on the ground, shattering it to pieces; the crowd then moved in front of the county government building and shouted, "Without food, we will die anyway. We might as well die fighting you!"

The county magistrate cowered in his office, frightened by the hungry mob. He remembered Li Yan was on good terms with the famine victims, so he sent for him to discuss a way out of the impasse.

"If you want to avoid a riot," said Li Yan, "you must stop pressing for repayment of arrears and persuade the wealthy to donate relief grain."

The county magistrate, seeing no other alternative, gave his reluctant consent. The famine victims in front of the county building were only placated when they learned that Li Yan had persuaded the county magistrate to undertake food relief.

"Let's all go back now," some said. "If we don't see any grain in a few days, we will come back to settle accounts with them."

No sooner had the angry crowd dispersed than the magistrate regretted his decision. By announcing a tax moratorium, he thought, he might have averted a riot in the making, but what was he going to do when he was pressed to fulfill the county's quota for troop rations? Would he be able to keep his job then? The more he thought, the more he hated Li Yan. He blamed all this trouble stirred up by the famine victims on Li Yan. He immediately instructed his secretary to draft a memorandum to his superior, falsely accusing Li Yan of planning a rebellion by ingratiating himself with the populace.

When news about this memo got out, there was general concern for Li Yan. There was a band of peasant insurgents in a forest nearby, under the leadership of a young woman, who used to make a living by giving street performances. She was popularly known as the "Red Lady." An admirer of Li Yan for his generosity in offering famine relief, the Red Lady went to Li Yan's home and took him into the forest under her protection after hearing about the danger he was in.

Li Yan was at first confused about the intention of the Red Lady, but when he realized she intended to make a rebel of him, he balked and soon sneaked back home. When Li Yan arrived home, the truculent bailiffs were waiting with handcuffs and leg irons, which they put on him the moment he walked in. He was taken to the county building for trial.

When the inhabitants of Qi County learned of Li Yan's arrest, they said to each other, "We cannot sit idly by while Master Li languishes in prison." The Red Lady also appeared with her troops. A large crowd of famine victims followed her with knives and sticks to advance on the county government.

The county magistrate and his bailiffs slipped away in the realization that they were hopelessly outnumbered by the attackers. The Red Lady and the famine victims stormed the jail and freed Li Yan. Under these circumstances Li Yan realized there was no future for him if he returned home, so he heeded the advice of the Red Lady and followed the insurgents to join Li Chuang Wang the Trailblazing King.

Li Zicheng understood that although Li Yan was a scholar born to a wealthy family, he was also a victim of persecution. Besides, he had been looking for an adviser. So he allowed Li Yan to stay. Li Yan, who had long heard that Li Zicheng was a man with a mission, decided to dedicate himself to helping Li Zicheng topple the Ming government.

As his insurgency gained in strength, Li Zicheng instituted troop reforms and tightened discipline. Following Li Yan's advice, he adopted the slogan of "Equitable distribution of farmland and tax moratorium." Insurgents disguised as traders were dispatched by Li Yan to towns occupied by government troops, where they would tell anyone who cared to listen, "Li Chuang Wang's troops are well-disciplined; they don't kill civilians and they don't loot." People were generally fed up with the killing and looting of the government troops and when they heard that Li Chuang Wang's troops were a disciplined lot, they naturally began to throw their support behind him. A ditty created by Li Yan circulated among the peasants:

"We look to Li Chuang Wang for food and clothing; we welcome him with open arms because under him we don't pay tax in the form of grain.

"Day and night the poor scrounge around for something to soothe their hunger. The sooner we swear fealty to Chuang Wang, the sooner the happy days will come."

Li Zicheng's insurgents enjoyed popular support. After killing Zhu Changxun, the Prince of Fu, they went on to win a string of major victories in Henan. In 1643, Tongguan fell to Li Zicheng. He killed the Ming supreme commander and Minister of War, Sun Chuanting. Shortly after, his troops took control of Xi'an.

QING DYNASTY (1644–1911)

170. Wu Sangui Borrows Qing Troops

IN 1644, LI Zicheng formally established his regime in Xi'an with the dynasty name of Great Shun. Soon after that, Li Zicheng led a million insurgents across the Yellow River to attack Beijing along two routes. Li's forces made rapid progress and converged outside Beijing in March of that year. Three of the Ming's best regiments defending the periphery of the capital surrendered.

The insurgents subjected Beijing to a relentless assault. The following night when Emperor Chongzhen climbed the Meishan Hills behind the palace (present-day Jingshan Hills) and looked around, all he saw was a landscape of towering flames. He realized the direness of the situation and ran back to his palace to ring furiously at a bell in the hope of summoning help. He waited for a long time, but no official answered his call for help. Realizing his day of reckoning had come, he returned to the Meishan Hills and hanged himself on a scholar tree close to the Shouhuang Pavilion. The Ming dynasty thus came to an end after ruling China for 277 years.

At the fall of Beijing, General Liu Zongmin was the first to enter the city at the head of his troops. He was followed by Li Zicheng, Emperor of the Great Shun, on his steed, wearing a straw hat and a black cloth tunic, making a leisurely entry into the Forbidden City. The inhabitants of Beijing gave the insurgents a festive welcome.

The Great Shun government issued a public statement to reassure the citizens that they would now be able to resume normal life. The new government prosecuted without mercy members of the Ming royal house and corrupt officials. At instructions from Li Zicheng, Lui Zongmin and Li Guo demanded the elite surrender the spoils they had exacted from the people to fund the insurgent troops' rations. Those who refused were given stiff sentences. Some members of the royalty and aristocracy most hated by the public had to be executed.

Liu Zongmin confiscated the family assets of a high official named Wu Xiang and had him detained in order to recover his ill-gotten gains. Li Zicheng was told by someone that Wu Xiang's son, Wu Sangui, was the Ming's regional commander at Shanhai Pass, with hundreds of thousands of troops at his disposal. If Wu Sangui could be persuaded to submit, then the Shun dynasty would be rid of a major threat.

Li Zicheng thought the idea made sense; he instructed Wu Xiang to write to his son to urge him to submit to the insurgents.

Wu Sangui had been dispatched by the Ming court to the north, outside Shanhai Pass, to block the advance of the Qing forces and was stationed in the Ningyuan area. When the insurgents pressed closer to Beijing, Emperor Chongzhen issued a succession of orders to Wu Sangui demanding that he lead his troops back into China proper to deal with the insurgents. By the time Wu Sangui reached Shanhai Pass, Beijing had fallen to the rebels. A few days later, when Wu Sangui received his father's letter urging him to surrender to the rebels, Wu Sangui couldn't make up his mind. He certainly was unwilling to surrender to the rebels. If he refused to surrender, however, he knew he was no match for the superior rebel force known for its valor and fighting abilities. He was also not yet ready to abandon his family and assets in Beijing. Since

Li Zicheng had made him an offer, he might as well go back to Beijing to assess the situation there.

When Wu Sangui reached Luanzhou, on the approach to Beijing, he met people who had fled the Ming capital. After questioning them, he learned with irrepressible anger that his father Wu Xiang had been arrested and their family assets confiscated. When he learned that his favorite singer—companion Chen Yuanyuan had also been detained by the insurgents, his blood boiled. He immediately marched his troops back to Shanhai Pass, where he demanded that his troops change into white helmets and white suits of armor to signify his determination to avenge Emperor Chongzhen.

After learning that Wu Sangui had refused to surrender, Li Zicheng decided to personally lead a 200,000-strong force to attack Shanhai Pass. Wu Sangui, who had always had a fear of peasant troops, was scared out of his wits by the imminent attack. Throwing national pride out of the window, he dispatched a letter by fast horse to the Qing court, asking for help in putting down the insurgents.

When Prince Dorgon, who was regent of the Qing court, received Wu Sangui's call for assistance, he saw opportunity beckon and instantly replied affirmatively to the letter. No sooner said than done, he raced a hundred thousand Qing troops toward Shanhai Pass.

When Dorgon and the Qing army arrived outside Shanhai Pass, Wu Sangui was already waiting expectantly with his five hundred bodyguards. He resignedly entreated Dorgon to help him with his revenge. Dorgon was happy to oblige, as this course of action perfectly corresponded with his own plans. Wu Sangui invited Dorgon inside Shanhai Pass, lavishly wined and dined him, and swore a pact of alliance in a sacrificial rite complete with the butchering of a white horse and a black ox.

In the meantime, the army of Li Zicheng approached Shanhai Pass from the south. He arrayed his two hundred thousand troops in an impresseive, single rank stretching from the hills to as far as the eye could see in the direction of the sea. The shrewd Dorgon, surveying the enemy formation from atop the battlements, knew they had before them a formidable foe. He let Wu Sangui have the honor of taking the leading position in the advance while his Qing troops lay in ambush. Dorgon and his generals observed the action from a hilltop a safe distance away.

As the battle commenced, Li Zicheng climbed the West Hills on his horse to direct operations. Soon after Wu Sangui sallied out of the gate, his troops were hemmed in from left and right by insurgents. The Ming troops dashed about, unable to find a way out of the encirclement. The insurgents fought a fearless battle, their war cries creating a deafening din.

As the battle raged, a strong gust blew from the sea, whipping up a sand storm that obscured the sky. In the sudden darkness, combatants were unable to make out the people around them. Taking advantage of the confusion, Dorgon ordered his tens of thousands of Qing troops that had lain low in the rear to launch a lightning attack against the insurgents, who were caught off guard and couldn't tell from which direction the enemy combatants were coming. They fell into disarray in a moment of panic and confusion. Only when the wind subsided and the dust settled did they realize that they had been attacked by Qing troops sporting pigtails.

On the West Hills, Li Zicheng came to the realization that Qing troops had been admitted inside Shanhai Pass. It was too late to regroup and fight back, so he ordered a retreat. Sandwiched between the attacking troops of Dorgon and Wu Sangui the insurgents suffered heavy casualties.

Li Zicheng retreated with his force, fighting to fend off the troops of Wu Sangui, who, emboldened by the presence of the Qing army, doggedly pursued the insurgents. The insurgents returned to Beijing a much weakened force.

Following Li Zicheng's return to Beijing, an enthronement ceremony was held in the great hall of the imperial palace, where he received the homage of the officialdom. First thing the following morning, he led his troops out of Beijing to move toward Xi'an.

The third day after Li Zicheng's departure from Beijing, Dorgon at the head of Qing troops entered Beijing triumphantly.

In October 1644, Dorgon brought Emperor Shunzhi to Beijing from Shenyang and made Beijing the capital of the Qing dynasty. Thus began the reign of the Qing dynasty in China.

The following year, the Qing sent a force to attack Xi'an along two routes. One route was taken by Ajige, Wu Sangui and Shang Kexi and the other by Dodo and Kong Youde. Li Zicheng resisted the Qing attack at the head of his peasant army at Tongguan; after a fierce battle, he was forced to abandon Xi'an and retreat toward Xiangyang. A few months later, his peasant army was attacked by the local landowners' militia in the Jiugong Mountains in Tongshan County, Hubei. Li Zicheng was defeated and killed.

At the time of Li Zicheng's departure from Beijing, Zhang Xianzhong proclaimed himself emperor in Sichuan, with the dynasty name of Great Xi, and continued fighting the Qing. In 1647, the Qing sent troops into Sichuan. In a battle in the Fenghuang Mountains near Xichong in northern Sichuan, Zhang Xianzhong was killed by an arrow. Thus, both of the two major insurgencies in the later period of the Ming ended in failure.

171. Shi Kefa's Valiant Defense of Yangzhou

WHEN NEWS OF Emperor Chongzhen's suicide in Meishan Hills reached the Ming auxiliary capital of Nanjing, the high officials there were thrown into extreme consternation. They proceeded to install as emperor a certain Zhu Yousong, the Prince of Fu, a member of the imperial house who had fled south. This regime founded in Nanjing is known to history as the Southern Ming, and Zhu Yousong is known as Emperor Hongguang.

Emperor Hongguang was a grotesque character who had a hopeless weakness for alcohol and sex. The fatuity of Emperor Hongguang enabled Ma Shiying, Governor of Fengyang, and holdovers from Wei Zhongxian's clique to usurp the power of the Southern Ming. Emperor Hongguang and Ma Shiying never intended to fight the Qing army; they both wallowed in carnal pleasures.

Shi Kefa, the Minister of War of the Southern Ming, was against the idea of installing Zhu Yousong in the throne, but in the interest of internal harmony he gave his reluctant consent. After the accession of Emperor Hongguang, Shi Kefa volunteered for military duty on the frontline.

In that period there were four Ming armies north of the Yangtze, called the Four Garrisons. The commanders of these four garrisons were without exception arrogant and overbearing. They carved out their turfs, jockeyed for power and condoned their troops' atrocities against the civilian population. Shi Kefa was a man of stature and high prestige among the military in the southern Ming. When he arrived in Yangzhou, the generals there deferred to his authority; whether they liked it or not. Shi Kefa personally went to see those generals to urge them to refrain from infighting. He then deployed them to the periphery of Yangzhou while he established his command inside Yangzhou. He was known as "Supreme Commander Shi."

As Supreme Commander, Shi Kefa won the respect and affection of his troops by his exemplary behavior and his common touch. On New Year's Eve that year, Shi Kefa gave orders for the troops to take a rest for the festive occasion and stayed in his office to read official communications and memos. Late at night, Shi Kefa felt tired of working and called the cook to ask him to prepare some food and wine.

"In accordance with your orders," the cook replied, "all the meat in the kitchen was distributed to the troops for the festive occasion. There's nothing left to go with your wine."

"Then bring me some salt and sauce to go with my wine," said Shi Kefa.

The cook brought his wine and Shi Kefa began drinking at his desk. He was a man with a large capacity for alcohol, but he had quit drinking after taking up his post in Yangzhou. That evening, however, he needed an alcoholic boost to stay awake. As his thoughts turned to the difficulties the country was going through and the rampant government corruption and incompetence, he was filled with frustration and worry. Tears streamed down his face as he refilled his cup without realizing it; soon he had drunk too much and fell asleep on his desk, intoxicated.

The next morning, when the civil and military officials of Yangzhou came as usual to the Supreme Commander's office to transact official business, they found the door still tightly shut. This was highly unusual because the Supreme Commander was normally an early riser. After a while a soldier came out to announce, "The Supreme Commander had a few drinks last night and has not yet woken up."

Ren Minyu, Governor of Yangzhou, said, "The Supreme

Commander is overworked. It is not often that he gets such rest. Let's not disturb his sleep. He needs it." He called in the night watchman and instructed him to keep signaling on his drum the one to two a.m. hours in order to make Shi Kefa believe it was still night.

When Shi Kefa woke up to find it was late morning and yet the night watchman was still beating the one to two a.m. hours on his drum, he flew into a rage.

He summoned a soldier and demanded, "Who is marking the wrong hours on his nightwatch drum in violation of my orders?"

The soldier explained the instructions given by Ren Yumin. Shi Kefa calmed down and summoned the officials to begin the day's business.

From that day on Shi Kefa decided never to drink another drop.

When Dodo marched a massive Qing army against the Southern Ming, Shi Kefa led the commanders of the Four Garrisons in resisting the Qing advance, with some success. But the Southern Ming government was racked by internal strife: General Zuo Liangyu, garrisoned in Wuchang, began marching his troops on Nanjing in a contest of power with Ma Shiying. Frightened to death, Ma Shiying immediately ordered the troops of the Four Garrisons north of the Yangtze to come back to the capital to confront Zuo Liangyu. He also ordered, in the name of Emperor Hongguang, Shi Kefa to return to Nanjing with his troops to protect him.

Shi Kefa knew he should not leave Yangzhou when the Qing army was threatening to attack. But in the interest of easing the internal tensions in the Ming court, he had no alternative but to return to Nanjing with his troops. When he crossed the Yangtze, he learned that Zuo Liangyu had been defeated; by the time he doubled back, the Qing army was already within striking distance of Yangzhou.

Shi Kefa issued an urgent appeal for the commanders of the garrisons to converge on Yangzhou to help with its defense. But days passed with no response. Shi Kefa realized that he had to fight the battle without counting on external help, relying only on the military and civilians inside Yangzhou.

When the Qing army arrived at the foot of the city walls, Dodo sent an emissary to Yangzhou to urge Shi Kefa to surrender. He sent four emissaries in succession and each was rebuffed by Shi Kefa. In a rage, Dodo ordered a siege.

Yangzhou was in dire danger and some commanders with less than steady nerves were frightened. The next day a regional commander and an Army Supervisor went out of the city with their respective troops and surrendered to the Qing army, without Shi Kefa's knowledge. The city defenses were further weakened as a result.

Shi Kefa assembled all the officials and leaders of the city and called on them to unite against the Qing attackers. He assigned them to various tasks. According to his assessment, the west gate was the most vital link in the line of defense, so he assumed personal command there. The troops were inspired by the calm determination of Shi Kefa and vowed to fight to their last breaths by the Supreme Commander's side.

Dodo mounted a continuous assault on the city by rotating his troops. As the valiant people and troops defending Yangzhou thwarted one wave of attack, another wave of Qing soldiers would take the place of the dead comrades before them. The situation was becoming more and more precarious for the defenders of the city.

Dodo soon escalated the attack by using cannons. His intelligence told him that the west gate was the most heavily defended spot and was under Shi Kefa's personal command. He ordered his gunners to shell the northwest corner of the city. Under the steady bombardment, the wall section near the west gate crumbled and a gap appeared.

As Shi Kefa was directing the inhabitants and troops to repair the breach, large numbers of Qing troops swarmed into the city. Realizing the city could no longer be defended, Shi Kefa pulled out his sword and swung it toward his neck, but he was quickly tackled by nearby commanders who wrested his sword from him. Shi Kefa refused to leave Yangzhou but his subalterns coaxed and dragged him to safety through the east gate. They ran into a group of Qing soldiers who, seeing Shi Kefa in an official gown of the Ming court, yelled at him to reveal his identity.

Shi Kefa, not wishing to implicate others, shouted, "I am Supreme Commander Shi. I'm ready to die!"

In April 1645 Yangzhou fell to the Qing and Shi Kefa was killed.

Dodo, angered by the heavy casualties suffered by the Qing army in the assault on the city, committed a crime against humanity by ordering the massacre of Yangzhou's inhabitants. The atrocity went on for ten days and is known to history as the "Ten Days in Yangzhou."

In the wake of the massacre, Shi Kefa's adoptive son Shi Dewei went into the city to look for the remains of Shi Kefa. But there were simply too many dead bodies; all decomposed beyond recognition in the hot weather. He had to content himself with burying an official gown and a tablet (held during imperial audiences) used by Shi Kefa in a tomb in Mount Meihualing outside Yangzhou. This tomb containing only articles of clothing belonging to Shi Kefa has been preserved to this day.

Several days after the fall of Yangzhou, the Qing army captured Nanjing. Officials of the Southern Ming either surrendered or fled and the regime of Emperor Hongguang was toppled.

The Qing continued its southward advance. It issued an order that gave the Chinese people ten days to adopt the Qing (Manchu) custom of shaving the front half of their head leaving a pigtail at the back. Violaters would be executed: "if you want to keep your head, lose your hair; if you want to keep your hair, lose your head." This further antagonized the people south of the Yangtze. Under the leadership of Yan Yingyuan, a minor official of Jiangyin, its inhabitants and troops held the town against two hundred thousand Qing troops for more than eighty days. Not one of its inhabitants surrendered and the Qing troops suffered heavy casualties in the battle. In Jiading, its people and military fought the Qing troops for three months and suffered three massacres costing twenty thousand lives. This atrocity is known to history as the "Three Massacres of Jiading."

172. Zheng Chenggong Recovers Taiwan

AFTER EMPEROR LONGWU established a regime in Fuzhou, Huang Daozhou, a committed anti-Qing minister of his, was eager to help Emperor Longwu to launch a northern expedition against the Qing. But Zheng Zhilong, who controlled the military, was more concerned about preserving his military strength than risking it in a military operation. A year later, when the Qing marched on Fuzhou and sent an emissary to persuade him to surrender, Zheng Zhilong could not resist the temptation of wealth and power and surrendered to the Qing, abandoning Emperor Longwu. That spelled the end of the Longwu regime.

Zheng Zhilong's son, Zheng Chenggong, was a young general of 22. Zheng Chenggong had tried to talk his father out of surrendering to the Qing. When he realized his father was not amenable to reason and persisted in his defection, he left home in annoyance and went to Nan'ao Island, where he recruited several thousand men to continue fighting the Qing. The Qing saw an outstanding general in Zheng Chenggong and tried several times to co-opt him but were rebuffed each time. The Qing army dispatched Zheng Chenggong's younger brother carrying a letter from their father, Zheng Zhilong, urging him to submit to the Qing.

"If you continue to refuse to surrender," warned his brother, "our father's life will be in danger."

Zheng Chenggong remained unswayed and disowned his father Zheng Zhilong in a written reply.

Zheng Chenggong's force grew and he built a navy in Xiamen. In alliance with the anti-Qing general Zhang Huangyan, he sailed a sea-going fleet of ships with 170,000 troops into the Yangtze in an attack on Nanjing by land and water. His fleet fought its way into Nanjing, but he was fooled by a fake surrender by the Qing army. He returned to Xiamen, defeated.

By the time of Zheng Chenggong's return to Xiamen, the Qing had taken control of most of Fujian. The Qing army imposed a blockade against Zheng by ordering all settlements along the coast of Fujian and Guangdong moved inland by forty *li* to deny Zheng Chenggong logistical support. With his source of manpower and funds drying up, he decided to move his operations to Taiwan.

Taiwan had been Chinese territory since time immemorial. However, having taken advantage of the corruption and incompetence of the Ming in its later years, the Dutch now occupied coastal areas of Taiwan and had built fortifications. The people of Taiwan rebelled against the harsh levies imposed by the Dutch, but their frequent uprisings were put down by the Dutch invaders.

Zheng Chenggong had visited Taiwan with his father when he was an adolescent. Witnessing the harsh life of the Taiwan inhabitants under alien rule, he became obsessed with the idea of recovering Taiwan from foreign occupation. Now more than ever determined to expel the invaders, he commissioned the building of ships and stored up rations in preparation for a crossing.

A man named He Tingbin, who had been an interpreter for the Dutch troops, came at this time to Xiamen to see Zheng Chenggong and urged him to recover Taiwan from the Dutch. He said that the people of Taiwan, suffering under the Dutch invaders, had long considered a revolt. With the arrival of Zheng's troops, they were sure to run the enemy off Taiwan. He Tingbin gave Zheng a map of Taiwan showing the details of the military deployment of the Dutch invaders. With this reliable information in hand, Zheng Chenggong felt greater confidence in his planned attack on Taiwan.

In March 1661, leaving his son Zheng Jing in charge of the defense of Xiamen with some troops, Zheng Chenggong and his fleet of hundreds of battle ships carrying twenty-five thousand troops set out from Jinmen (Quemoy). They braved the waves of the Taiwan Strait and arrived at the Penghu Islands (Portuguese name: the Pescadores), where they paused for a few days rest, preparing for the voyage to Taiwan. Some officers and troops were apprehensive about the cannons of the Europeans, which, they had heard, were lethal. Zheng Chenggong moved his own flagship to the front of the fleet in an attempt to boost troop morale.

"There's nothing to fear from the cannons of the redheaded Dutch," he declared. "Just follow my ship!"

The Dutch invaders were rattled by the news of Zheng Chenggong's attack on Taiwan. They concentrated their troops in the fortresses in Tayoan City (Dutch name: Fort Zeelandia, in present-day Dongping) and Chikan (Dutch name: Fort Providentia, in today's Tainan) and sank a number of old ships in the harbors to prevent Zheng's ships from berthing.

With He Tingbin as guide, Zheng Chenggong's fleet successfully took advantage of high tide to enter Lu'ermen and land their troops on the Taiwan shore.

Large crowds of Taiwan inhabitants welcomed the Zheng troops by bringing water and tea to them. When the flustered Dutch troop leader ensconced in the fort sent a hundred soldiers against them, Zheng Chenggong ordered his troops to surround the Dutch soldiers. One Dutch officer was killed and the rest dispersed in defeat.

The Dutch invaders called in their largest battleship. The colossus bore down on the Zheng fleet in an attempt to stop him from landing more troops. Without losing his cool, Zheng maneuvered his sixty battleships into a circle around the Dutch ship. Zheng's ships were smaller but also nimbler; when Zheng gave the order, the sixty ships fired their cannons at the Dutch ship, setting it alight. The flames turned the sea surface bright red. As the Dutch ship began to sink, three other Dutch ships became alarmed and they turned tail and steamed away.

Soundly beaten in the encounter, the Dutch invaders battened down in the two fortresses, not daring to venture out to engage the Zheng force. While quietly sending an emissary to Batavia (modern Java) for help, they dispatched an envoy to the Zheng headquarters to appeal for peace. They offered a hundred thousand taels of silver in return for the Zheng army's pulling out of Taiwan.

Zheng Chenggong, his eyebrows raised in indignation, replied, "Taiwan has always been Chinese territory. It is within our right to recover this land. If you insist on staying here, we will drive you out by force!"

After rebuffing the Dutch peace overture, Zheng Chenggong launched a strong offensive against Chikan (Fort Providentia). The Dutch force at the fort put up a stiff resistance and Zheng's attack stalled. A local man gave vital information to Zheng's army: Chikan received its freshwater from the hills outside the city; if the water was cut off, the Dutch defense would crumble without a fight. Zheng took the advice and within three days the Dutch at Chikan surrendered.

The Dutch invaders occupying Tayoan City (Fort Zeelandia) kept up their resistance while waiting for reinforcements. Zheng decided to force them to surrender by a long siege. After eight months of siege, Zheng launched an all-out assault on the fort. The Dutch defenders, sensing they had run out of options, hoisted the white flag. In early 1662, the leader of the Dutch invaders went to Zheng Chenggong's headquarters to sign the Dutch surrender that ended the Dutch presence on Taiwan.

Zheng Chenggong's recovery of Taiwan, an integral part of Chinese territory, from the Dutch invaders has earned him a place in Chinese history as a great patriot.

173. Li Dingguo Campaigns in Southwest China

AFTER THE FALL of the Southern Ming regimes of Longwu and the Prince of Lu, the Qing sent its army along three routes into southwest China. Qu Shisi, a Ming official in Liangguang, alongside other Ming officials, hailed Zhu Youlang (Prince of Gui) as emperor in Zhaoqing with the reign name of Yongli. He is known to history as Emperor Yongli.

In November 1647, remnant troops of the Great Shun under the command of the Ming general He Tengjiao won a major victory in Quanzhou against the Qing army. Qu Shisi also repelled a Qing attack in Guilin. The Southern Ming military was riding high; but soon Huguang and Guangxi were retaken by the Qing army as a result of internal disunity in the regime of the Prince of Gui. Two years later He Tengjiao was captured and killed in Xiangtan and Qu Shisi was also killed after Guilin fell to the Qing army. As the regime of the Prince of Gui teetered on the brink of collapse, the Daxi (Great West) peasant army led by Li Dingguo became a major player in the anti-Qing cause. It operated in the southwest for over a decade.

Li Dingguo was one of the four top commanders under Zhang Xianzhong. Both he and Sun Kewang, his senior, were Zhang's adoptive sons. After the death of Zhang, Sun and Li led the fifty to sixty thousand insurgents into Guizhou and Yunnan in the southwest. They proposed to Emperor Yongli that they form an alliance against the Qing. After several flip-flops, Emperor Yongli was finally forced by the critical situation he found himself in to enlist the help of the Daxi army and pronounced Sun Kewang Prince of Qin.

An ambitious man, Sun Kewang soon had Emperor Yongli under his thumb and became a local tyrant in Guiyang. The anti-Qing cause was far from his thoughts. Li Dingguo, on the other hand, remained committed to the fight against the Qing. In a year he had raised thirty thousand well-trained troops and actively pushed for the manufacture of weapons and armor. He hired elephant trainers to form an elephant brigade. When the conditions ripened, he marched his troops against the Qing army.

Li had a well-disciplined army with a high morale. His force battled its way from Yunnan and Guizhou to Hunan, winning an unbroken string of victories and recapturing a number of strategic towns. It then marched on Guilin along three routes. Kong Youde, the Qing commander defending Guilin sent his troops out to engage the enemy several times but each time his troops fled before battle was joined. Kong Youde decided to personally lead a force to Yanguan to confront the Ming troops. Li Dingguo's impressive army was preceded by the brigade of tall elephants, whose trumpets startled the battle horses of the Qing army and sent them running in all directions. As a heavy rain fell amid thunderclaps and flashes of lightning, the elephants charged ahead and the Qing troops were defeated. Many were killed by the pursuing Ming army.

Kong Youde beat a hasty retreat with his troops into the city of Guilin and closed the city gate. Li Dingguo surrounded the city with his troops and mounted round-the-clock assaults. When Kong Youde climbed the battlements to direct operations, he was hit by an arrow on the forehead. Following this near-fatal injury, he was told that the high ground north of the city had been taken by Li's troops. Distraught, he started a fire and threw himself into the flames.

Li Dingguo entered Guilin with his troops. As a clean-up operation went on, he appealed for public calm and invited back the Southern Ming officials who had fled into the hills.

At a banquet thrown by Li Dingguo at Qixingyan for the

officials, he told them, "Our situation is akin to that prevailing in the waning years of the Southern Song. You are admirers of Wen Tianxiang, Lu Xiufu and Zhang Shijie. They have earned a place in history as great patriots. We are patriots too but, we don't want our country to go the way of the Song in its last gasps."

The officials were deeply impressed by Li's vision and perspective.

When Emperor Yongli received news of the victory, he declared Li Dingguo Prince of Xining. Li went on to take Yongzhou, Hengyang and Changsha. As his army approached Yuezhou, the Qing court was greatly alarmed and immediately sent Prince Nikan with a hundred thousand troops to retake Changsha. Not wanting to directly confront a strong enemy, Li pulled out of Changsha by choice but laid an ambush along the way to Hengyang. Nikan led his troops in pursuit and walked into the trap. He was hacked to death in the battle.

Li's victories aroused the jealousy of Sun Kewang, the Prince of Qin. Sun invited Li Dingguo to meet with him on the pretext of discussing affairs of state, with the intention of eliminating Li. Discovering Sun's intentions, Li Dingguo left Hunan with his troops and returned to Yunnan. In a bid to raise his own stature and prestige, Sun Kewang led a force into Hunan to attack the Qing army but suffered a major defeat.

The ambitious Sun Kewang attempted to force Emperor Yongli to cede the throne to him. Knowing he must eliminate Li Dingguo in order to accomplish this, he led a 140,000-strong force into Yunnan to attack Li. But his troops were disgusted by his divisive tactics; when battle began, they switched their loyalty to Li Dingguo and Sun's army suffered a debacle. When Sun Kewang fled back to Guiyang, the troops of Guiyang wanted nothing to do with him. With nowhere to turn, he fled to Changsha, where he surrendered to the Qing army.

The Southern Ming was much weakened as a result of the betrayal by Sun Kewang. In 1658, a Qing army led by the defector Ming generals Wu Sangui and Hong Chengchou attacked Yunnan and Guizhou along three routes. Li Dingguo tried to check their advance on three fronts but failed and was compelled to return to

Kunming. The panicked Emperor Yongli accompanied by some trusted aides fled to Myanmar.

After Emperor Yongli's flight, Li Dingguo continued to recruit anti-Qing troops along the Yunnan border in preparation for recovery of lost territory. He sent thirteen missions to Myanmar to urge Emperor Yongli's return but the emperor did not have the nerve to come back.

In December 1661, Wu Sangui entered Myanmar with a hundred thousand Qing troops and forced Myanmar to surrender Emperor Yongli, whom he took back to Kunming and strangled to death. The last Southern Ming regime thus perished.

Unable to accomplish his goal after more than ten years of hard struggle against the Qing, Li Dingguo, stressed and frustrated, fell ill and died. On his deathbed, he said to his offspring and subalterns, "Better die in the wild than surrender!"

174. Emperor Kangxi Subdues the Three Feudatories

THE YEAR THE last regime of the Southern Ming fell, Emperor Shunzhi of Qing died and was succeeded by his son Xuanye as Emperor Shengzu of Qing, also known as Emperor Kangxi.

At his accession Kangxi was only eight. In accordance with Emperor Shundi's deathbed instructions, four Manchu ministers assisted him in the running of the state. Of the four minister-regents, Oboi dominated because of his control of the military and the young age of Emperor Kangxi. Ministers who crossed Oboi or did not share his views were sidelined or persecuted.

After the Qing's arrival in China proper, it appropriated vast farmland and distributed it among the nobility of the eight Manchu banners. At the height of his power, Oboi used the influence of his office to enlarge his land holdings and to exchange his poor holdings for better land owned by others. When local officials raised objections, Oboi had them executed on trumped-up charges of treason.

When Emperor Kangxi took over the reins of the state at the age of 14, another minister-regent Suksaha came into conflict with Oboi. Deeply offended, Oboi and his partisans falsely accused Suksaha of serious crimes and petitioned Emperor Kangxi for authorization to execute Suksaha. When the emperor balked, Oboi got into an argument with Emperor Kangxi in the audience hall, getting so worked up that he even rolled up his sleeves, bared his knuckles and started to throw a tantrum. Emperor Kangxi deeply resented Oboi's outburst but saw no profit just yet in antagonizing the powerful Oboi; he checked his anger and acquiesced in Suksaha's execution by Oboi.

This incident reinforced the determination of Emperor Kangxi to be rid of Oboi. He recruited from among the nobility a group of strong young men in their teens as his bodyguards. They were assigned to the close protection of the emporer and trained daily in wrestling.

These noisy youngsters wrestling in the imperial garden did not bother Oboi, who thought they were merely playing.

One day Oboi was summoned to a private audience to discuss important matters of state with the emperor. He headed to the palace with his usual swagger and strut. No sooner had he cleared the threshold of the private quarters of the emperor than a group of young men rushed forward and massed around him. Some held his arms and some his legs. Although Oboi was a military man with great physical strength, the young men had numerical advantage and were trained wrestlers. Oboi was wrestled to the ground and no one came to his help despite his loud protestations.

Oboi was thrown in jail and Emperor Kangxi immediately ordered his ministers to begin a probe into Oboi's crimes. The ministers believed that Oboi deserved to die because of his despotic ways, his arbitrary killings and numerous other offenses. Emperor Kangxi showed leniency by stripping Oboi only of his rank and title.

The entire Qing court was delighted by the clever ousting of Oboi by Emperor Kangxi. Ministers who used to be arrogant and disdainful now had a foretaste of the young emperor's astuteness and learned to climb down from their high horses in his presence.

After assuming personal rule, Emperor Kangxi instituted government reforms, introduced incentives to stimulate production and cracked down on corruption. The recently founded Qing dynasty grew in strength. While the Southern Ming regime had been quashed, the three feudatories in the south remained a thorn in Emperor Kangxi's side.

These feudatories were Ming generals who had sworn fealty

to the Qing; they were Wu Sangui, who was instrumental in letting the Qing army into China proper, Shang Kexi and Geng Zhongming. In recognition of their contribution in helping the Qing to topple the Southern Ming and quelling peasant revolts, the Qing court pronounced Wu Sangui Prince Pingxi (who pacified the west) and awarded him land in Yunnan and Guizhou, Shang Kexi as Prince Pingnan (who pacified the south) with land given in Guangdong and Geng Zhongming as Prince Jingnan (who cleaned up the south) with land in Fujian. Together they were called the "Three Feudatories."

Of the three, Wu Sangui was the strongest. After becoming a feudatory, Wu was more arrogant than ever. He now not only controlled the military but also oversaw finances. He had the authority to appoint his own officials and no longer toed the line of the Qing court.

Emperor Kangxi found the Three Feudatories a big obstacle to his effort to centralize command. He waited for the right moment to curtail their influence and power. By a happy coincidence Shang Kexi, who was getting on in years and desired to retire to his home town in Liaodong, petitioned Emperor Kangxi in this period for permission to allow his son Shang Zhixin to succeed him as prince in Guangdong. The emperor approved Shang Kexi's retirement but denied his son's succession as prince and his request to stay in Guangdong. The matter shocked Wu Sangui and Geng Jingzhong (Geng Zhongming's grandson). To test the reaction of Emperor Kangxi, they offered, without sincerity, to give up their title and rank of prince and return to the north.

When Emperor Kangxi received this information, he called a meeting of his ministers to discuss the matter. Many of them were of the opinion that the offer to give up feudatory status was disingenuous and if the request was approved, Wu Sangui was sure to mutiny.

Emperor Kangxi said with resolve, "Wu Sangui has long harbored ambitions. He will revolt if I strip him of his feudatory title. Yet he is sure to rebel sooner or later even if I don't. I think I should pre-empt him."

The emperor immediately issued an edict approving Wu

Sangui's proposal to have his feudatory title and rank revoked. Wu Sangui flew into a rage at the response. He considered himself one of the founding fathers of the Qing dynasty. He never expected the still very young emperor to dare to strip him of power. He was left with no choice but to rebel.

In 1673 Wu Sangui raised arms in Yunnan. In order to win the hearts and minds of the populace, he shed the official uniform of a Qing feudatory and donned the armor of a Ming general to weep with insincere tears before the tomb of Emperor Yongli of the Ming. He vowed to venge the Ming. But the people still had a vivid memory of Wu Sangui's direct responsibility in opening the door to the Qing's invasion of China and the murder of Emperor Yongli. He could fool nobody with his call for the restoration of the Ming.

Wu Sangui had a strong presence in the southwest, so his rebellion made good headway in the beginning and soon reached Hunan. He got in touch with Shang Zhixin in Guangdong and Geng Jingzhong in Fujian, calling on them to join the rebellion. With Wu Sangui as champion, the other two feudatories also took the plunge. This is known to history as the "Rebellion of the Three Feudatories."

With the three feudatories in revolt, all of south China was now in rebel hands. Undeterred, Emperor Kangxi concentrated his attack on Wu Sangui while putting a stop to the revocation of the feudatory title and rank of Shang Zhixin and Geng Jingzhong to appease the latter two. Realizing the situation was not in Wu Sangui's favor, Shang Zhixin and Geng Jingzhong surrendered to the Qing court a second time.

Wu Sangui enjoyed initial successes in his rebellion but as the Qing army grew in troop strength and prowess, Wu Sangui's force became weaker and more isolated. Eight years into the rebellion, he knew he could no longer keep up the struggle. In frustration and regret, he fell seriously ill and soon died.

In 1681, the Qing army marched on Kunming along three routes. Wu Sangui's grandson Wu Shifan committed suicide. The Qing succeeded in quelling the rebellion and in unifying southern China.

But the celebrations of the victory against the southern rebellion at the Qing court were spoiled by news of the invasion of Tsarist Russia along the northeastern border of China. Emperor Kangxi's attention was forcibly wrenched from the south to the northern frontier.

175. Victory at Yaksa (Albazin)

TO UNDERSTAND THE circumstances that allowed Tsarist incursions into China's northeast, one needs to go back to the the last years of the Ming, when the Qing was so engrossed in the southward march into China proper that it neglected its northern defense. This afforded Tsarist Russia an opening to make inroads into China in the Heilongjiang area, where it engaged in looting and killing, provoking the resistance of various local ethnic communities. After entering China proper, the Qing sent troops to attack the Tsarist invaders and succeeded in recovering Yaksa, which had fallen under Russian control, on the north bank of the Heilongjiang River (northwest of modern Huma and east of Mohe of Heilongjiang Province).

At the time when Emperor Kangxi deployed large numbers of troops to China's southeast to subdue the Three Feudatories, a Russian fugitive brought a gang of 84 desperados into China's Yaksa and started to build fortifications there, from which they made looting raids. The mink fur they grabbed from the local population was presented to the Tsar. In exchange, the Tsar not only pardoned the fugitive's offenses, but appointed him to the position of chief administrator of Yaksa, in an attempt to make Russian occupation permanent.

Emperor Kangxi, flush with the victory won against the Three Feudatories, was understandably very upset when he learned of the violation of the Qing's northeastern frontier. He traveled to Shengjing in order to assess first-hand the enemy inroads and he sent his generals Pengchun and Langtan on reconnaissance missions along the border under the guise of a hunting expedition. In the meantime he instructed local officials to build battleships and fortresses in preparation for a punitive campaign.

When all preparations were in place, Emperor Kangxi sent a letter to the Russian chief at Yaksa, ordering him to pull out of there as fast as he could. However, instead of pulling out, the Russian army sent reinforcements to Yaksa in a direct challenge to the Qing. Realizing the matter could not be resolved peacefully, Emperor Kangxi gave the order to march on Yaksa.

In 1685, a 15,000-strong force comprising land and naval troops under the command of Pengchun arrived at Yaksa and surrounded the settlement.

The fortress had been impressively fortified through years of work by Tsarist troops. After a survey of the terrain, Pengchun had an earthen platform built south of the town, from the top of which his soldiers rained arrows on the defenders. The Russian troops were led to believe the assault would come from the south side and concentrated the bulk of their force in the southern section of the town. Taking advantage of the momentary vacuum of defense in the northern section, Qing cannons previously hidden from view in the north began bombarding the town. Shells whizzed over the town, hitting its buildings and setting them on fire.

As the day progressed, the Qing troops placed piles of hay and firewood against the wall protecting the fort, getting ready to torch the town. This frightened the town leader into hoisting the white flag.

Acting on Emperor Kangxi's instructions, Pengchun freed all those Russian troops who had surrendered and ordered them to return to Russia. Tolbuzin, the dejected Russian commander, departed with his remaining troops.

After the departure of the Russian troops, Pengchun ordered his soldiers to dismantle the fortress at Yaksa and returned the land to farming by the local inhabitants. He then led his troops back to Aihui.

But the badly defeated Russian commander did not learn his lesson. As soon as he realized that the Qing troops had pulled out of Yaksa, he returned with his troops and rebuilt the fort, making it stronger.

When news of the retaking of Yaksa by the Russians reached Beijing, Emperor Kangxi set out to destroy the invading Russian troops. In the summer of the following year, a second campaign was launched against Yaksa under the command of General Sabsu of Heilongjiang. The Qing troops couldn't wait to destroy these enemy troops who had repaid the leniency previously shown them by reinvading. This time around the Qing troops redoubled their fire power and beat back repeated Russian sorties out of the fort. The Russian commander Tolbuzin was killed by a bullet and his remaining troops barricaded themselves in the cellars. After a few days many of them fell ill or died, leaving 150 who survived.

Only when the Tsarist government dispatched an envoy to Beijing with an urgent request for negotiations did Emperor Kangxi call a halt to the operation.

In 1689, negotiations were held at Nerchinsk with Songgotu representing the Chinese government and Golovin present on behalf of Tsarist Russia. The resulting Treaty of Nerchinsk delineated the boundary between the two countries and recognized vast areas of the Heilongjiang (Amur) River and Ussuri River basins as Chinese territory.

176. Three Expeditions against Galdan

THE TSARIST GOVERNMENT did not take their defeat at Yaksa with a good grace. The year following the signing of the Treaty of Nerchinsk, it prompted Galdan, chief of the Dzunghars (a Mongol tribe), to attack the Mobei Mongols north of the Gobi.

In that period, the Mongols were divided into the Mo Nan (south of the Gobi), the Mo Bei (north of the Gobi) and the Mo Xi (west of the Gobi) Mongols. Besides the Mo Nan Mongols, who had submitted to the Qing much earlier, the other two groups also recognized the authority of Qing. The Dzunghars were a branch of the Mo Xi (western) Mongols, who lead a nomadic life in the Ili area. When the ambitious Galdan became chief of the Dzunghars, he first forcibly integrated the other Mo Xi Mogol tribes before moving east to attack the Mo Bei (northern) Mongols. After their resistance crumbled, hundreds of thousands of Mo Bei Mongols fled south across the Gobi to seek the protection of the Qing. Emperor Kangxi sent an envoy to Galdan to demand the return of the land he had taken from the Mo Bei Mongols. Galdan, emboldened by Tsarist Russian support, not only refused to withdraw his troops but marched south across the Gobi with a large force purportedly to pursue the Mo Bei Mongols.

Emperor Kangxi summoned his ministers to announce his decision to personally lead a punitive expedition against Galdan, whose arrogance, ambition and cross-border action, he believed, must be firmly resisted. In 1690, Emperor Kangxi led a force split into two armies: the left army under the command of the Fuyuan General Fuquan was to march out of Gubeikou Pass; the right army under Anbei General Changning was to march out of Xifeng- kou Pass. The emperor directed the campaign from the rear.

The right army of the Qing was the first to engage Galdan's troops and was defeated. Galdan's force was able to drive unopposed into Ulan-Butung (modern Hexigten Banner in Chifeng of Inner Mongolia), which was only seven hundred *li* from Beijing. The smug Galdan sent an envoy to the Qing army to demand the surrender of his enemies.

Emperor Kangxi ordered a counteroffensive by Fuquan. Galdan gathered his tens of thousands of cavalrymen at the foot of Mount Dahong, taking advantage of the natural cover provided by the woods behind them and river in front of them. Ten thousand camels were made to lie on the ground with their legs bound together and boxes wrapped in wet felt blankets tied to their backs to form a long wall of camels. The rebels took cover behind these boxes in lieu of battlements and shot arrows through the gaps to stop the Qing assaults.

The Qing troops concentrated their cannon and gun fire on one section of the camel wall. Amid the thundering, earth-shaking attack, a breach was made in the camel barrier and the Qing infantrymen and calvalry charged toward the breach. Fuquan sent troops to outflank the rebel position and charge at the enemy from behind the mountain. With its front and rear under simultaneous attack, the rebel force was defeated and forced to flee and abandon their camp.

Sensing that the balance had tipped against him, Galdan was quick to send a lama to the Qing camp to appeal for peace. Calling a halt to his pursuit of the Galdan force, Fuquan sought instructions from Emperor Kangxi, who issued the order: "Resume the pursuit without delay! Don't fall for the rascal's ruse!" He was proved right: Galdan's peace overture was a ploy to buy time. By the time the Qing army resumed its pursuit, Galdan had made it north across the Gobi with his remaining troops.

After returning to his haunt north of the Gobi, Galdan

continued to rebuild his force quietly while outwardly submitting to the authority of the Qing. In 1694, Emperor Kangxi invited Galdan to meet with him with a view to signing a pact. Not only did Galdan refuse to attend the meeting but he also sent his people south across the Gobi to instigate a revolt. He claimed to have borrowed sixty thousand musketeers from the Tsarist government and was ready to launch a massive attack. Emperor Kangxi received numerous denunciations of Galdan from Mongol princes in Inner Mongolia.

In 1696, Emperor Kangxi undertook another campaign, the second upon which he embarked in person, with the Heilongjiang General Sabsu commanding the east army, the General-in-chief Fiyanggu commanding the west army composed of troops from Shaanxi and Gansu to cut off Galdan's retreat and the center army led by Emperor Kangxi setting out from Dushikou. The three armies were to launch a simultaneous attack at a predetermined time.

As the center army led by Emperor Kangxi reached Ketu, it ran into the vanguard of the enemy force. The east and the west armies had not yet arrived and there was talk of Tsarist Russia planning to send troops to help Galdan. Some ministers in the emperor's entourage became nervous and urged Emperor Kangxi to take the troops back to Beijing.

"How would I explain it to the nation if I withdrew my expeditionary force before laying eyes on the rebel leader?" the emperor retorted angrily. "Besides, if I withdrew the center army, the rebel army would concentrate its attack on the west army and the west army would be in danger."

So Emperor Kangxi decided to continue the march toward the Kerulen River and sent an emissary to tell Galdan that Emperor Kangxi had embarked on the expedition in person. When Galdan saw from a hilltop the yellow standards of Emperor Kangxi fluttering in the breeze and the disciplined arrays of Qing troops, he decamped that very night.

Emperor Kangxi kept in pursuit of Galdan and sent instructions to the east army general, Fiyanggu, to intercept Galdan's troops.

After marching for five days and nights with his troops, Galdan reached Jao Modo (southeast of present-day Ulan Bator of the People's Republic of Mongolia), where he encountered Fiyanggu's army. Jao Modo was, at that time, a massive forest with an adjascent large open space that was a scene of many battles north of the Gobi. Following the plans of Emperor Kangxi, Fiyanggu placed ambushers in densely forested areas in the hills and sent out a vanguard of four hundred men to draw the enemy out. As the vanguard drew back in battle towards the ambush, the rebel troops followed; the Qing troops then dismounted to fight as foot soldiers. At the sound of bugles, the Qing soldiers leapt onto their horses and galloped up the hill to take the hilltop. As the rebel troops began an assault in the direction of the hilltop, the Qing army fired guns and shot arrows from the top. A fierce battle unfolded. Fiyanggu sent a detachment to attack the supply vehicles of the rebels at the foot of the hills. The rebels, attacked from above and below, died or surrendered in large numbers. Galdan escaped with only dozens of cavalrymen.

After the two major battles, the Galdan insurgency collapsed. Emperor Kangxi called on Galdan to surrender but he kept up his stubborn resistance. A year later Emperor Kangxi mounted another punitive expedition across the Yellow River. By this time, Galdan's base of operations in Ili had been wrested from him by his nephew Tsewang Araptan. Many of his close associates surrendered and volunteered to be the Qing army's guides. Having nowhere to turn, Galdan committed suicide by ingesting poison.

From that time on, the Qing government regained control of the Mobei (northern) Mongols east of the Altai Mountains and began awarding official titles and ranks to members of the Mongol nobility. The Qing government also established a generalship in Uliastai to govern the Mobei Mongols.

Some time later Galdan's nephew, Tsewang Araptan, launched an attack into Tibet. In 1720, Emperor Kangxi dispatched an expeditionary force to Tibet to drive out Tsewang Araptan and escort the Sixth Dalai Lama back into Tibet. The Qing government later appointed a resident minister to Tibet to co-manage Tibet affairs with the Panchen and Dalai Lamas on behalf of the central government.

177. Literary Inquisition

THE QING RULING elite's carrot-and-stick policy toward the Ming literati consisted of co-option coupled with severe suppression of those who refused to submit to Manchu rule. In the second year of the reign of Emperor Kangxi, Zhuang Tinglong, a man of letters in Huzhou, Zhejiang was reported by some officials for organizing a group of scholars without authorization to write a history of the Ming containing anti-Qing wording and references to era names of the Ming. As Zhuang Tinglong had already died at the time of his denunciation, the Qing court ordered his body exhumed so that he could be "executed" posthumously. Zhuang Tinglong's sons, along with those who had written the preface to the book, those who had sold the book, those who had worked on the wooden blocks, and the printers of the book as well as local officials were all executed or exiled to garrison duty. More than seventy people were implicated and punished in the case.

In 1711, Dai Mingshi, an official at the Hanlin Academy, was accused of casting the Ming in a sympathetic light in his anthology and of referring to the era name of Emperor Yongli of the Southern Ming. He was thrown in jail and sentenced to death. This case implicated more than three hundred people, including family and friends as well as those taking part in the production of the anthology.

Since these cases of literary inquisition arose entirely from writing, they were called *wen zi yu* or "imprisonment caused by writing."

Emperor Kangxi died at a ripe old age, after sixty-one years of power. His fourth son, Yinzhen, succeeded him as Emperor Shizong of Qing, also known as Emperor Yongzheng. He turned out to be a cruel, paranoid ruler. Under his rule, cases of literary inquisition grew in number and severity of punishment. One of the most prominent cases involved Lü Liuliang.

Lü Liuliang was another renowned scholar, who had turned to teaching students at home after unsuccessful attempts to make a mark in the anti-Qing cause. He was recommended for the "special examination for broad learning and extensive words" but categorically refused. Officials tried the carrot and the big stick, but he remained unmoved. Lü finally shaved his head and became a monk; the government gave up on him.

After becoming a monk, Lü Liuliang spent his time writing in the temple. Anti-Qing sentiment found its way into his books. Fortunately, the books he wrote were not widely circulated and after his death they were forgotten.

Zeng Jing, a native of Hunan, one day stumbled upon a piece written by Lü Liuliang and was greatly impressed by his erudition. He asked a student named Zhang Xi to travel from Hunan to Lü's home town in Zhejiang to look for more of his manuscripts.

Zhang Xi not only found more of Lü's manuscripts in Zhejiang, but also met two of his students. They had an agreeable conversation. After being briefed on Zhang Xi's trip upon his return to Hunan, Zeng Jing arranged a meeting with the two students of Lü, where the four voiced their anger at Qing rule. They began to explore behind closed doors ways to overthrow the Qing.

They realized that not much could be accomplished by members of the educated class alone. Zeng Jing had heard about the governor of Shaanxi and Gansu named Yue Zhongqi, who was of Han extraction and had at his command a significant number of troops. His service was valued by Emperor Yongzheng because of his battle victories that had quashed rebellions along the frontier. Zeng Jing believed if Yue could be persuaded to champion the anti-Qing cause, the odds for success would be greatly increased.

Zeng Jing sent Zhang Xi with a letter to Yue Zhongqi. When

Yue read the letter and found it was an invitation to join the anti-Qing cause, he gave a start.

"Who sent you?" he demanded of Zhang Xi. "How dare you deliver such a monstrous letter?"

Without losing his self-possession, Zhang Xi replied, "You have a family feud with the Qing. Don't you want to avenge your family?"

"Explain yourself!" Yue Zhongqi again demanded.

"Your name is Yue," replied Zhang Xi. "You are a descendant of General Yue Fei of the Southern Song and the ancestors of the Qing royalty were Jin people. General Yue was killed as a result of collusion between the Jin (Jurchens) and Qin Hui. Everyone knows that he was framed. With the troops you command, you are in a perfect position to avenge General Yue Fei."

At this, Yue Zhongqi's face writhed in anger; he barked out an order and Zhang Xi was thrown in jail. Yue instructed the local officials to question Zhang Xi to find out who put him up to this.

Zhang Xi refused to confess despite being subjected to various forms of torture.

"You can kill me," he said, "but my answer will still be: no one put me up to this."

Yue Zhongqi concluded that the tough approach wouldn't work on a strong man like Zhang Xi, so he switched to a gentler tactic. The following day he had Zhang released from jail and received him in a private meeting. Yue said with duplicity that the questioning the day before had merely been a test and that he was moved by what was said by Zhang; thus he had decided to raise arms against the Qing but needed advice from him.

Zhang was initially unconvinced but, by putting on a serious air and invoking heaven and earth as witnesses of his sincerity, Yue finally removed his doubts. After several days of conversation, the two became closer. Zhang, his tongue loosened by the newfound friendship, disclosed details of the instructions given by his teacher Zeng Jing.

Acting on the information thus coaxed out of Zhang Xi, Yue sent his men to Hunan to arrest Zeng Jing and in the meantime wrote a report to Emperor Yongzheng giving a detailed account of the subversive plot being hatched by Zeng Jing and Zhang Xi.

On reading the report, Emperor Yongzheng was furious. He immediately ordered Zeng Jing and Zhang Xi brought to Beijing, where they were questioned under torture. Zhang Xi realized he had been royally duped by Yue Zhongqi and it was useless to recant now. Further probing by the court revealed that Zeng Jing had had contact with two students of Lü Liuliang.

The case now implicated Lü Liuliang's family. As Lü Liuliang was no longer alive, Emperor Yongzheng had his tomb razed and his coffin smashed. For good measure, he ordered the execution of Lü Liuliang's offspring and all members of the families of his two students. A large number of intellectuals who believed in Lü Liuliang were implicated and exiled to garrison duty in remote frontier regions.

This was a case involving proven anti-Qing activities. Many other cases were much more far-fetched, some based on strained, hair-splitting interpretations of purportedly seditious words and phrases. A single line of verse, even a single word, could invoke disastrous consequences. Once, an official of the Hanlin Academy named Xu Jun wrote " 狴 " (a legendary beast painted on prison doors) for " 陛 " (His Majesty) by a slip of pen in a memorandum to the emperor. He was immediately sacked by Emperor Yongzheng for this unintentional mistake. In a follow-up investigation, inspectors came upon two lines of verse in an anthology of Xu Jun's poems:

"The breeze (*qing feng*) does not read,
Why does it randomly turn the pages?"

The investigators insisted that the word *qing* in *qing feng* (breeze) was an allusion to the Qing court. The unintentional offense of defamation of the imperial court proved to be Xu Jun's death sentence.

178. Emperor Qianlong's Book Bans and Anthology Creation

AFTER THE QING unified China, it made great economic strides under Emperor Kangxi and Emperor Yongzheng. During the reign of Emperor Qianlong (also known as Hongli and Emperor Gaozong of Qing, son of Emperor Yongzheng), China's power and prosperity grew to an impressive level, and its cultural achievements and military prowess reached an all-time high in this early period of the Qing.

In 1757, Amursana, the Dzunghar aristocrat who had submitted to the Qing, started a revolt. A force sent by Emperor Qianlong to Ili succeeded in supressing this revolt. The Uigur brothers Burhan Al-Din and Khwaja-i Jahan held hostage by the Dzunghars escaped back to the Tianshan Mountains in Xinjiang and started a revolt there against the Qing. Emperor Qianlong sent a punitive expedition against them. The two brothers ruthlessly oppressed the people there and were hated by the Uigurs, who rose up in support of the Qing army. The revolt was soon inhibited. In 1762, the Qing government established the post of Ili General in Xinjiang for more effective control of the territory north and south of the Tianshan Mountain range.

Like his grandfather and father, Emperor Qianlong did not neglect cultural development even as he busied himself with military campaigns. He continued to hold "special examinations for broad learning and extensive words" to recruit literati and scholars in the compilation of a variety of books. At the same time, he relentlessly carried out literary inquisitions to persecute scholars suspected of anti-Qing sentiment. On his watch, the number of cases of literary inquisition far exceeded that in the reigns of Emperors Kangxi and Yongzheng.

But Emperor Qianlong was aware that literary inquisitions alone would not assure cultural control by the government. Tens of thousands of books remained in private collections. He sought a way for the government to purge them of content considered inimical to its rule.

He finally came up with an idea: he would try to pool all the books in private collections into a library to form the basis of a voluminous anthology on a scale never attempted before. This would at once endear the government to a large number of intellectuals by demonstrating that the emperor gave high priority to culture, and afford an opportunity to subject all the private holdings to review and censorship. He would be killing two birds with one stone.

In 1773, Emperor Qianlong ordered the establishment of the Complete Library of the Four Treasuries. Members of the royal house, princes and grand academics were appointed as directors. These royal and aristocratic officers largely played an honorary, supervisory role. The editors who did the nitty-gritty work were renowned contemporary scholars, including Dai Zhen, Yao Nai and Ji Yun among others.

Since ancient times, China's books were divided into four general categories: *jing*, or classics, which included Confucian classics (e.g. *The Book of Songs*, *The Analects of Confucius* and *The Book of Mencius*) and books on linguistics such as studies of rhymes and sounds; *shi*, or history, which included books about history, geography and biographies; *zi*, or miscellaneous philosophy, which included ancient schools of thought and books on science and technology, such as agriculture, medicine, astronomy, calendric systems, arithmetic and art; and *ji*, or literary compositions, which included literary anthologies and monographs. A library collecting works from all four categories was called the Si Ku, or Four Treasuries Encyclopedia.

In order to compile such a massive anthology, the first step was to assemble all the books. Emperor Qianlong ordered all provincial governments to search for and acquire all kinds of books, which they would send on to the central government. Incentives were offered for donations of books from private collections, with rewards proportional to the size of the donations. Soon books began to pour in from across the country, reaching twenty thousand volumes in two years. With the large existing imperial holdings they formed an impressive library.

Once the books were assembled in Beijing, Emperor Qianlong ordered the editors to go through them with a fine-toothed comb. Any book found to contain subversive writing was to be destroyed outright. The review found letters and reports presented by ministers in the late Ming period, containing references to the Qing royal house's preceding generations that were less than respectful. The documents mentioned, for example, the fact that members of the older generation of the Qing royal clan received Ming offices and titles. This, in Qianlong's eyes, did not exactly echo the glory of his lineage, so he ordered such publications burned too. The writings of avowed anti-Qing scholars like Lü Liuliang and Huang Daozhou suffered, needless to say, the same fate. As the review went on, it was found that even books by authors of the Song dynasty contained critical remarks about the Liao, the Jin and the Yuan dynasties, which could easily be construed as hostile to the Qing and therefore deserved to be destroyed either completely or partially. An alternative was to expunge or alter such references. Thus, some of these books would survive, but beyond recognition. Emperor Qianlong really struggled to accomplish the anthology compilation. According to some statistics, nearly three thousand works were banned or burned in the process of compiling the Four Treasuries.

Regardless of Emperor Qianlong's motivation in undertaking this cultural project, the massive "Four Treasuries" anthology was finally completed and has been preserved to this day. The anthology's editor-scholars spent ten years editing, proofreading and transcribing the texts. Upon its completion in 1782, the anthology comprised 3,503 works in 79,337 volumes. Seven copies were produced at that time and placed respectively in the imperial palace, the Yuanmingyuan (Summer Palace), the Traveling Palace in Jehol (modern Chengde of Hebei Province), Fengtian (modern Shenyang), Hangzhou, Zhenjiang and Yangzhou. (Three copies were eventually destroyed by fire during war time.) This was a significant contribution to future scholarship on China's rich cultural heritage, even though the books banned and burned in the process of the creation of this collection represented a loss to China's culture. The ban was, by its nature, not exhaustive; many culture aficionados hid books of great value from the inquisitors, risking prison and worse. These prohibited books resurfaced in the late period of the Qing.

179. Cao Xueqin Writes *A Dream of Red Mansions*

THE BALLOONING DEFENSE spending in the years of military campaigning under Emperor Qianlong, the lavish expenses incurred during his six tours through the provinces south of the Yangtze and a culture of corruption and extravagance among public officials all contributed to the Qing's decline.

It was in this period that a novel entitled *A Dream of Red Mansions* became popular reading in the imperial capital. Initially, the authorship was unclear but after some research it was determined that it was penned by a man named Cao Xueqin.

Cao Xueqin was born to an aristocratic family. His great grandfather Cao Xi was a confidant of Emperor Kangxi and was dispatched to Jiangning to serve as *zhi zao* or Superintendent of Imperial Silk Manufacturing. Jiangning was then a prosperous southern city and the office of *zhi zao*—overseeing silk manufacture for the imperial household, was a lucrative post. After Cao Xi's death, Cao Xueqin's grandfather Cao Yin, followed by his father Cao Fu, inherited the position. Needless to say, after occupying the post of *zhi zao* for three generations spanning six to seven decades, the family had amassed impressive wealth.

After the accession of Emperor Yongzheng, fallout from the infighting in the royal house hit the Cao family. Emperor Yongzheng held a grudge against the Cao family for not taking his side in the quarrel. He not only removed Cao Fu from his post but ordered all assets of the Cao family confiscated. The catastrophe descending on his family was a traumatic experience for the ten-year-old Cao Xueqin, already sensitive to what was going on around him.

After his father lost his job, the family could no longer afford to stay in Jiangning. They moved back to their native Beijing and to an increasingly impoverished life. The family seemed dogged by misfortunes. Life became more difficult for Cao Xueqin after his father's death. He had to move to the western outskirts of Beijing where he continued his studies in spartan quarters. When food ran low, he was reduced to surviving on thin gruel.

In his new environment in the outskirts of the city, Cao Xueqin came into contact with impoverished laypeople. The contrast between their lives and the highlife he had enjoyed in his childhood set him thinking a lot. He later decided to write a novel based on his experiences to mirror contemporary life. *A Dream of Red Mansions* was the result.

A Dream of Red Mansions chronicles the events revolving around the aristocratic Jia family as it moves from its heyday to its decline. There is no shortage of parasites inside that aristocratic household who feed their extravagant habits and carnal pleasures with money from charging usurious interest rates and collecting rent. Some hide a filthy mind and mean spirit behind a sanctimonious facade. The main protagonists, Jia Baoyu, the son of the Jia family, and his cousin Lin Daiyu, are two young people who are disgusted by the aristocratic way of life and resist the tyranny of feudal conventions. In the environment in which they find themselves, their attempt at breaking free from the conformist mold is doomed to failure. As a result, Lin Daiyu suffers social condemnation and falls mortally ill. Jia Baoyu runs away from home. A great aristocratic family with a glorious past thus collapses like a decayed mansion.

Cao Xueqin draws with a sympathetic pen a vivid portrait of this young pair and of oppressed and abused maid servants. The book is an angry indictment of the decadence and vices of the feudal ruling elite. In *A Dream of Red Mansions*, there is an episode which exposes how bureaucrats and rich and powerful families work hand in hand to fleece the common folk.

The Jia family and the Xue family are related. The young

master of the Xue family, Xue Pan, kills someone in a fight over a maid servant. The servant of the victim's family files a complaint with the governor of Yingtian. When the governor Jia Yucun is on the point of sending his men to the Xue residence to arrest the suspect, his attendant stops him with a wink. After the hearing is over, he asks the attendant to stay behind and queries why he has stopped him from going after the murder suspect. The attendant produces a piece of paper on which is transcribed a popular ballad, which runs as follows:

"Jia (the Jia family) is not jia (a myth); they have halls of white jade and horses of gold.

Epang Palace, three hundred *li* in extent, is not big enough to house the Shi of Jinling.

Even Longwang, the king of the Dragons, comes to the Wang of Jinling, when the eastern sea needs a white jade bed.

A bumper year is presaged by plentiful 'Xue' (snow); to them pearls and gems are like dirt, and gold is like iron."

The attendant explains to the mystified Jia Yucun that in Nanjing there are four prominent families: the Jia family is related to the royal house; the Shi and the Wang families are high officials in Jinling (modern Nanjing); "Xue" (homophone of *xue* or snow) refers to the Xue family—rich local merchants. The four families are intricately linked by marriage and together wield unparalleled power. Any official who is interested in keeping his job should be careful not to get on the wrong side of the big four. The attendant reminds Jia Yucun that the murder suspect is none other than the young master of the Xue family. If he antagonizes the Xue family, not only will he lose his job but likely will lose his head too.

Jia Yucun gives a start at the attendant's words and immediately abandons the idea of arresting the suspect. He takes the attendant's advice and announces that the murder victim has actually died of a sudden illness. A murder case is thus summarily disposed of.

Cao Xueqin spent ten years writing the novel in the western outskirts of Beijing and became very frail as a result of a hard life, hard work and failing health. When he finished the eightieth chapter, one of his favourite children died of illness. Shortly after this traumatic loss, Cao Xueqin himself left the world before finishing his novel.

After the death of Cao Xueqin, his manuscripts, copied by friends, gradually spread to a wider audience. People were delighted and moved by the novel but lamented the fact that such a masterpiece remained an unfinished work. It was not until later that a man of letters, named Gao E, completed *A Dream of Red Mansions* with his 40-chapter sequel.

The circulation of the novel *A Dream of Red Mansions* grew as manual reproductions proliferated. Its appeal has endured to this day and it has been acclaimed the most outstanding novel in ancient China, prized not only for its superb artistic achievement but for its revelations about the historical and social circumstances immediately preceding the decline of China's feudal order. To this day, many Chinese and international scholars are still studying and conducting evidential research on this great literary work. This discipline is known as "Red-ology."

180. He Shen, Corrupt Mandarin with an Insatiable Greed

EMPEROR QIANLONG'S 60-YEAR reign was marked by brilliant military and cultural achievements. He became smug and took to calling himself *shi quan lao ren* (literally, ten-perfect old person) or, to borrow from modern popular culture vernacular, a venerable elder with "a perfect ten." With an increasingly inflated ego, he grew fond of flattery. This gave an opening to people who ingratiated themselves with the emperor to gain control over the levers of power.

Before one of Emperor Qianlong's tours, he instructed his aides to ready the royal procession, but these harried officials were unable to quickly locate the yellow canopies required for the procession. Emperor Qianlong lost his temper and demanded to know who was responsible for this glitch.

The officials were scared speechless by the royal reproach. A young commandant was heard to say with calm self-assurance, "Those in charge should be held accountable."

Emperor Qianlong turned his glance in the direction of the speaker and found him to be handsome, with delicate features, and self-assured. Pleased by the young commandant's words, Emperor Qianlong asked for his name, the matter of the yellow canopies now completely forgotten. The young commandant gave the name of He Shen and answered with ease all subsequent questions about his family and the books he had studied.

Emperor Qianlong was so impressed by He Shen that he put

him in charge of royal processions and pageants on the spot. He later appointed him Palace Guardsman. He Shen had a nimble mind and was able to cater to Qianlong's every need; knowing the emperor's eagerness to hear praise, He Shen never said anything that would grate on the royal ears. In time, He Shen became a confidant to the emperor and enjoyed a meteoric rise to power. In less than ten years he rose from guardsman to Grand Academic. Later, Emperor Qianlong gave his daughter, Princess Hexiao, in marriage to He Shen's son. With this new alliance through marriage with royalty, He Shen's power grew to new heights. Given Emperor Qianlong's frail health and advanced years, the running of state naturally fell to He Shen.

He Shen used his enormous power chiefly to amass private wealth through crooked means and not to advance the interests of the nation and society. Not only did he accept bribes, he openly extorted money. Not only did he steal from the state covertly, he plundered overtly. All tributes by local government officials to the emperor passed through He Shen's hands. The finest and rarest treasures were kept by He Shen and the rest would be sent on to the imperial palace. Luckily for him, Emperor Qianlong never checked, and no one dared to report the irregularities. Thus, He Shen's greed grew.

Once, a minister named Sun Shiyi was on his way to see Emperor Qianlong after returning from a trip to the south when he ran into He Shen at the entrance to the palace. Gesturing toward a box held in Sun's hand, He Shen asked, "What have you got there?"

"It's just a snuff bottle," replied Sun Shiyi.

He Shen walked up and unceremoniously grabbed the box from Sun. When he opened the box, a snuff bottle carved out of a big precious stone greeted his eyes. He Shen took it out of the box and couldn't take his eyes off it as he clucked his tongue in wonder.

"What a fine specimen! Why don't you give it to me?" he asked with an ingratiating smile.

"Oh, that's impossible," Sun Shiyi said quickly. "I promised this to the emperor yesterday."

He Shen's face darkened as he shoved the bottle into Sun's

hands and said with a snort, "I was only kidding. You are such a cheapskate."

Sun Shiyi presented the precious snuff bottle to Emperor Qianlong. A few days later when he saw He Shen again, the latter said gloatingly, "I got hold of a rare gem yesterday. Take a look at it! How does it stack up against the one you gave to the emperor?"

When Sun Shiyi moved closer to have a look, he found it to be the very same snuff bottle he had presented to the emperor a few days before. Sun Shiyi mumbled some vague response, wondering how it ended up in He Shen's possession. Emperor Qianlong must have given it to him as some kind of reward, he speculated. After some discreet inquiries he learned that the snuff bottle had been smuggled out of the palace by a eunuch who had been bribed by He Shen.

He Shen used his office and power to the full to rake in personal wealth. Officials of the court and local governments, knowing his likes and dislikes, left no stone unturned to find rare treasures and jewelry to buy He Shen's good will. With high officials extorting from lower-ranking officials and low-ranking bureaucrats extorting from the laypeople, it became harder for the people to make ends meet.

After sixty years of reign, Emperor Qianlong ceded the throne to the crown prince Yongyan, who acceded to the throne as Emperor Renzong of Qing, also known as Emperor Jiaqing.

Emperor Jiaqing had long been aware of He Shen's bribe-taking and unlawful acts. When Emperor Qianlong died three years later, Emperor Jiaqing immediately had He Shen arrested and ordered him to commit suicide. All his assets were confiscated by the government.

He Shen's fabulous wealth was common knowledge, but when his assets were inventoried for confiscation, the public was still astonished by what was revealed. The long list recorded incredible amounts of gold, silver, jewelry, fine silks and brocade, rare curios and antiques. By rough estimates they were valued at eight hundred million taels of silver—equivalent to ten years of state revenue. Those confiscated assets were reportedly transported into the imperial palace. This prompted the cynical doggerel:

"He Shen has fallen, but Emperor Jiaqing gets to eat his fill."

Paraphrased: "He Shen's loss is Emperor Jiaqing's gain."

At his death, Emperor Jiaqing was succeeded by his son, Minning, as Emperor Xuanzong of Qing, also known as Emperor Daoguang. He presided over the decline of the Qing dynasty, as Western imperialist powers stepped up their invasion of China and the nation entered a period of deepening crisis. In 1840, the twentieth year of Emperor Daoguang's reign, the Opium War broke out. The event marked the beginning of a gradual transformation of China from a feudal into a semi-colonial, semi-feudal society. As its people fought valiantly and tenaciously against imperialist invasions and feudal rule, China entered its modern history.